UNDER SUSPICION
The Legend of D.B. Cooper

A book of fiction
by

James Olszewski

Proofread by: Megan A. Olszewski

Order copies at
www.JamesOlszewski.com
Or
www.createspace.com/3358112

Published and printed in the United States of America

ISBN: 978-1440450358

Chapters

There is nothing more deceptive than an obvious fact.
–Sherlock Holmes

Fool's Passage

Washington State
November 24, 1971

The young man was on his hands and knees as he finished stuffing the rest of the parachute into position, then closed it up. After a quick look at his watch he shook his head in disgust—he was behind schedule. Repacking the chute took longer than expected. It was, however, crucial that he examine it thoroughly. After all, the Feds had given him the chute and he couldn't allow them to determine the integrity of his only means of escape.

Standing up, he looked down the aisle way of the 727. It was empty and quiet. A short time earlier on the flight deck, he checked to make sure they were on course. He ordered the flight crew to remain in the cockpit while he finished preparing the next step in his plan. Laying his jacket on the seat next to him, he opened it up revealing four pouches sown into the lining. He checked the first three to make sure that the money was evenly distributed, then zipped them shut.

Taking one last look around to make sure he was alone, he turned towards the back of the plane. He would not turn around to face the front again. If curiosity got the best of the flight crew, one of them might come back to get a good look at him. Taking off his sun glasses and wig, he slid them into the fourth pouch. He gently peeled the fake nose from his face and put it with the other two items. The disguise didn't change him much, just enough so that nobody could positively identify him.

He pulled a pair of goggles from a pouch then closed it up. Putting them on, he adjusted the straps to fit properly. Next came the jacket. With full pouches, the normally comfortably fitting jacket felt tight. The zipper strained as the young man pulled it to the top.

7

Reaching across the first seat, he grabbed the handle of his small brown leather suitcase and pulled it towards him. He quickly opened it, took a long strap from inside, then closed it up again. Attaching the strap to either end of the case, he pulled it over his head and around one shoulder. The case was heavy and he had to rest it on the seat in order to adjust the strap properly.

There, he thought, *perfect.* He lifted the heavy case off the seat, and rested it in front of him against his legs, just above the knee and below the waist. The case felt much heavier than it really was. He had been carrying it all day, and the weight of the large battery pack and instrument package inside wore at his stamina.

It was now time for the parachute. He reached across to the opposite seat and grabbed the chute. Pulling it onto his back, he fastened the buckles in the front, securely attaching it. He made a few minor adjustments to make sure that the suitcase was held fast in place. He didn't want to make the mistake of losing it. If he did, this game would be over before it started. Caution forced him to check every attachment one more time to be sure.

Again, a quick check of his watch. *Damn!* he thought. There was less than five minutes to the drop zone— he had to hurry. Moving swiftly to the rear door, he started turning the manual hand crank. A tornado of air rushed past as the door's seal opened. They were not very high, but he allowed a few seconds for the pressure to equalize before continuing. Warning lights would be going off in the cockpit, he knew. A radio call was certainly being sent out to the Feds to let them know what was happening.

As he turned the hand crank, he watched the door slowly roll outward becoming a small staircase. The rear door of the 727 dropped straight down and back directly behind and below the engine in the tail. Only a few steps were visible, the rest disappeared into an eerie darkness.

The roar of the engines and howl of the wind grew louder as he nervously made his way to the staircase. An icy blast of air struck him in the face, biting into every square inch of his exposed flesh. At this altitude, the storm was more ice than rain and the wind chill factor plummeted well below zero. From head to toe, his body was flash frozen and frost bite was already affecting his hands as his body heat was sucked out of him.

The storm— that he knew would be there— raged angrily against the plane as it flew through the night. It was worse than he had expected. As the cold made his body tremble and his teeth chatter, he wondered if there was anything *else* he had underestimated. Within seconds, a sheet of ice had formed on the staircase. Icicles hung from the handrails, bent and twisted by the wind as if made by some sadistic spirit.

Grabbing the handrail with one hand and holding the handle of the suitcase with the other, he lowered his weight onto the first step. The hurricane of turbulence grabbed at him like a thousand hands trying to rip him off the staircase. His foot slipped on the wet ice causing him to fall. In a desperate panic, he dropped the case and lunged at the rail with both arms.

His heart pounded as his mind frantically raced through reasons why he should turn back, but he knew that was impossible. He had come too far to turn back. His future was in front of him, not behind. Blinded by the darkness, he felt for the case. The straps had held it fast where it was supposed to be, and he allowed a small sigh of relief.

In a sitting position, he slowly eased his way down the steps while hugging the rail with both arms. As the plane sped through the night, the violent turbulence rocked him in all directions. The shaking and bouncing was such that he thought the staircase would be ripped from the plane.

He found it hard to control the burning fear as his heart pounded in his throat. To make things worse, the fluid in his inner ear was sloshing around so much he grew dizzy. That, coupled with the fact that his eyes had nothing to focus on in the dimensionless darkness, created a powerful disorienting feeling.

To help fight this effect, he forced his mind to concentrate on the plan. By running each phase over in his head, he was able to calm himself. Not much, but just enough to help him reach the bottom step.

Still in a sitting position, he wrapped one leg and an arm around the last hand rail post. A layer of ice was already beginning to build up around him. He hoped that he would not be there too long or he'd risk being encased and cemented to the stair. With his free hand, he grabbed the case and perilously opened it up on his lap. Fumbling in the black for the power switch, he turned the device on. He scrapped the ice from his goggles with his frozen fingernails so that he could see more clearly. A small light lit up the inside of the case.

Dials and gauges hunted sporadically for a signal, but found none. When he'd tested the device weeks earlier, it hadn't work properly. He needed a larger antenna. After making the size conversion calculations, he believed it would work with the 727.

It's now time to see if you were right, he told himself nervously as he unwrapped the cable from the case. He held the large alligator clip in his free hand. *Well, here goes nothing,* he thought as he clamped it to the aircraft. Instantly the dials and gauges snapped to attention. *It works!* He allowed himself a quick smile of relief. At least one thing was going as planned. *But don't get cocky,* he warned himself. For the most dangerous part of the game was upon him.

Sure, the device appeared to be working, but there was no way to be certain of its accuracy. Precision was key, he knew. His destination was a small narrow valley, just a thousand feet below, that he would jump into. Towering rocky peaks surrounded the valley. These jagged ridges reached up towards him from a mere three hundred feet beneath the plane. Cloaked by the stormy darkness they were invisible, but he knew they were there ready to crush him if his calculations were the slightest bit off.

He focused on the two lights in the center of the device. The red one shown brightly, warning him not to jump. *When the green light comes on, you must jump without hesitation,* he reminded himself. If he jumped too soon or waited too long, he would perish on the rocks below.

The others said that he was crazy to pull a stunt like this. After all, it was only a thousand foot jump. Sure, maybe on a clear day at twenty thousand feet a jump like this might be completed safely. But at this altitude and in complete darkness? —*Never!*

They told him it was impossible. If he opened his chute too early, the plane's turbulence would collapse and tangle it sending him spiraling out of control. If he opened it too late, the chute wouldn't slow him down in time. Either way, he would be dead.

He had argued with them. Told them it could be done if the timing was precise enough. He even joked, *"It's not the fall that kills you. It's the sudden deceleration."* They didn't think it was funny, and suddenly neither did he. For, with his adrenaline pumping and heart pounding, human error would be disastrous.

He tried to wipe the questions from his mind as he concentrated on the lights. The moment of truth was at hand. He was about to find out if he was really as clever as he thought, or the stupid young fool the others had called him.

Suddenly, the red light went out and the green light flashed. Simultaneously he released his vice like grip on the staircase as he detached the cable. The turbulence instantly ripped him from the plane.   Hurtled   into   the   darkness,   he   disappeared...

1

Small Town Dust

Almost Thirty years later…

Headlights burned through the patchy morning fog as the forest green 4x4 drove into town. Soft rays of sun had barely begun to crest the sharp peaks of the distant Cascade Mountains. The light was dull, filtered by the scattered clouds and low lying fog, but the fluorescent gold star of the Sheriff's department seemed to glow on the door of the vehicle as it slowed to residential speeds. Sheriff Jim Harper turned off the surface street and into the Lewis County Sheriff's Department parking lot.

It was the first day of yet another year's spring. He smiled as he thought of it—*another year.* He had been Sheriff for almost three decades now. This coming November he expected to be re-elected, making him the longest running public servant in Lewis County history! He knew everyone, and everyone knew him. Almost his entire life had been spent trying to improve this community—*his* community. At least, that was the way he had come to think of it. This was *his* community and *his* people. He watched over and protected them, doing everything he could to make life better, whether it was his job or not.

Sheriff Harper slowed his Chevy Blazer to a stop in front of the station next to several identical vehicles. But then, what *wasn't* his job? Over the years he had taken on more work for himself and the Department, just so he could have the staff necessary to do a decent job.

The County Council was constantly frustrated with him, and this year was no different than any other. They wanted to cut his budget, and, as usual, he was fighting them over it. *Why couldn't those over paid, uncreative pucks be more useful,* he thought.

He loved irritating them, though. The solution he came up with for last year's budget shortfall still gave him a kick. The

Council's idea was for the Department to lay off two deputies, and sell three patrol vehicles. That was the standard solution Jim had come to expect from these over educated bookworms.

Harper had come up with a better solution. He arranged for both the high school and vo-tec automotive training courses to be combined. Then he scheduled all County vehicles to have their maintenance done at this new facility. By consolidating, the training center could now handle more students at a lower cost, and because the students weren't employees the County benefited from not paying wages or benefits. Jim was also able to arrange for the local parts dealer to supply the training facility at wholesale prices rather than retail. This program saved the County a bundle.

The Council was really frosted when it was proposed. Both the County Executive and Treasurer swore there had to be something illegal about the plan and tried to prove it, but in the end, it met the requirements of the law and they had to accept it. Every year the Council received criticism and jeers from the community for a budget that would "have to be fixed by the Sheriff".

That was the best part, Jim thought. The Executive and Treasurer had Masters Degrees from Ivy League schools, and the inflated egos to prove it. Jim loved the way they got all burned up when he proposed a solution to a problem then add, "Not bad for a guy with only a high school diploma from a back water school, Eh?"

He had spent the last two weeks pouring over every budget of every County program in order to come up with a solution to this year's problem. So far, he hadn't a clue what it would be. He was, however, optimistic. He knew there was a solution and that he would eventually find it.

Sheriff Harper slowly opened the Blazer's door then stepped out. He wore a tan long-sleeved shirt and matching pants— each neatly pressed. The black tie, black leather belt, and shiny black shoes complemented the otherwise bland attire. Standing out from the rest of the uniform, the well polished shiny gold star rested neatly upon his shirt just above the left pocket.

Although he'd been wearing the uniform for decades, it now felt somewhat new to him. When he had first started out, he wore the full uniform vigilantly. But over the years, he had changed it a little at a time. First, he stopped wearing the tie. Then, he put on a few pounds, and the belt went out a notch, then another. Later, the dress shoes were replaced with tennis shoes. He was the Sheriff of a sleepy town— he hadn't grown lazy, just comfortable.

As of a few months ago, it was back to the full uniform. That was Nikki's influence. She had once commented that men in uniform were irresistible. The next day every scuff was polished, every line pressed, and every detail perfect. It made him feel like he was in the Army again— a reference he didn't care to make— but if Nikki liked it, he was all too willing to please.

As he stood by his patrol vehicle, Sheriff Harper slowly looked around at the dark low lying clouds. *It is a bit cool this morning,* he thought to himself as a shiver crawled up his spine. *Of course it would be. After all, winter had just ended and the frequent rains were still common place. Well, at least the afternoon might be nice,* he hoped. The past few days it had gotten all the way up into the sixty's, just enough to start drying things out before the rain clouds rolled in by evening.

Turning around, Harper reached into the Blazer, pulled a forest green jacket out, and put it on. It also had the gold Sheriff's Department star on the left breast. He then stretched across to the passenger side and grabbed his off-white Stetson. Placing it on his head, he gently pulled it down over his slightly gray, but otherwise dark, hair. Again, reaching into the cab, he pulled out a large bundle of business sized envelopes. Tucking them under his arm, he closed the door.

Taking another look around, he glanced down at the black top under his feet. The pavement covered the ground in front of the building, to each side of it, and then to the street. It looked good.

It's about time the County paved this lot, he thought. *Well, at least part of it. Too bad they wouldn't do the whole thing. With the other vehicles in the way, I can barely get my Blazer turned around,* he thought as his eyes moved from the asphalt to the gravel.

The gravel stretched from the street along the left side of the building and around to the back. It also covered the walking path to their outdoor shooting range. *Well at least its new gravel,* he chuckled to himself. *It is truly a shame I can't tell anybody how we really got it.* Turning around, he stepped onto the sidewalk and made his way along the front of the red brick building towards the door.

Nearing the entrance, he stopped and looked at the sign carefully: *Lewis County Sheriff's Station, Centralia Washington.* It was a bit faded, he frowned. *Tomorrow, I'll pick up some paint and touch it up,* he decided continuing on through the glass double doors.

To his right, there was a stairway leading down below. Next came the restrooms, and then the conference room. Straight in front of him, at the end of the hallway, the back doors led to the shooting range. The left side of the hallway opened up into office space. Separating the hall from eight desks was a long counter. A half dozen or so Deputies milled around in their normal morning routine.

13

"Good morning, Conley," Sheriff Harper smiled as he walked past the dispatch table immediately behind the counter.

"Good morning, Sheriff," Deputy Conley nodded and returned the smile.

"Anything happening out there this morning?"

That brought a smile to the young deputy's face. "No sir, everything's quiet as usual. Just the way you like it."

"That's the problem with this place," Deputy Thomas Milhouse growled from the desk directly behind the dispatcher. "There is *never* anything going on. The most excitement we get is when there's a fight to break up at the bar on Saturday night."

"What more do you want, Milhouse?" Sheriff Harper wanted to know.

"I don't know, maybe a bank robbery or a car chase," the tall young deputy answered.

Deputy Rissley, the young woman at the desk next to Milhouse, responded with a short laugh. "You're not supposed to wish for crime, Tom."

"I don't wish for it," he countered. "It's just that there should be more to this job than paperwork."

"I have been saying that for years," Harper consoled, as he patted Milhouse on the back. "Unfortunately, it's gotten worse and not better."

He continued on to the back of the room to his office. The front of it was almost entirely made of glass. Letters printed on the glass door read: *Sheriff James Harper.* He reached for the handle and walked in. Pulling the mail from under his arm, Harper tossed it on the desk in the middle of the small room, then walked to the corner coat rack to hang up his jacket and hat.

Glancing out the window he sighed. It was 6 AM, Monday morning— the beginning of another week. *Five more days of...* Harper looked at the stack on his desk, *paperwork.* Slowly reaching for his chair, he sat down and stared at the pile. *I'll start with the mail,* he thought as he reached for it and began thumbing through.

What's this? Jim lifted a curious eyebrow. It was a letter from the Portland City Police Department. Jim removed it from the pile to examine the envelope more closely. It was addressed to Thomas Milhouse c/o The Lewis County Sheriff's Department. Wondering what it was all about, Jim stood up, grabbed his coffee cup, and walked out of the office with the letter in his hand.

Actually, he wasn't *too* surprised. *You should have seen this one coming,* he told himself. Since Thomas Milhouse was a kid, everyone knew him as a thrill seeker. He raced motor cross dirt bikes, stock cars, and went bungee jumping. Life as a small town deputy had only made him grumpy.

As Harper walked towards the coffee pot, he stopped at Milhouse's desk and handed the letter to him. "I believe this is for you."

Milhouse's eyes widened with excitement at the envelope, then became apologetic. "I'm sorry, Sheriff. This was supposed to come to my house."

"That's all right, Tom. Why didn't you tell me you were looking for a transfer?" Jim reached for the coffee pot.

"I don't know. I guess I didn't want you to think I was deserting you," Tom answered. The other deputies started to come over from their desks and encircle Milhouse.

"Well, aren't you going to open it?" Deputy Rissley pried.

"It's none of our business, Rissley," Jim remarked. "He probably wants to wait and open it at home with Peggy."

"That's alright, Sheriff. I don't think I can wait that long," Tom offered as he fumbled with the envelope like a child opening a present. Pulling the letter out, Milhouse's eyes scanned the page while the others waited in silence. It was all too obvious to everyone what it said as they watched him slowly lower the letter to the desk and stare at it in disappointment.

"I'm sorry, Tom," Deputy Rissley consoled as the other deputies went back to what they were doing. "I know how anxious you and Peg are to get out of here."

"Why do you want to go to the city anyway?" Harper questioned.

"Peg wants to be closer to the theater. She has always been good at acting and wants to give it a shot before we start a family," Tom frowned then tilted his head slightly as he thought of his own reasons. "As for myself, I can't help but feel my career is at a stand still. I *need* a change. Something with a little more excitement. If I don't kick this small town dust off my feet soon, I think I'll *bust!*"

"Have you tried the Seattle PD?" Harper suggested.

"Uh-huh, but I got the standard form letter from them as well. Thank you for your interest but we're just not hiring. Blah, blah, blah…"

"Tell you what. Later on this week, when we've got a few hours to spare, we can sit down and write you a letter of recommendation." Jim offered.

That brought a smile to Milhouse's face. "Thanks Sheriff. I sure appreciate the help."

Jim nodded and smiled. Grabbing his coffee cup, he headed back to his desk. He couldn't help but be disappointed. He had spent a lot of time with Milhouse and Jim hoped that someday Tom would take over as Sheriff when he retired.

He had tried to get Milhouse interested in the business of running the County, but although he always listened, Jim could tell Tom's mind and heart were somewhere else. *So much for wishful thinking,* he thought sadly as he sat down to the paper work on his desk. He shook his head. Like everyone else, Harper hated paperwork and sometimes wished things weren't so hum drum boring. He didn't realize how quickly that would change.

Milhouse sat in silence as he stared again at the rejection letter. He knew the Sheriff hoped his desire to leave was just a passing fancy, but time had the opposite affect. As every year went by, Tom's wish to be a part if something bigger burned hotter inside him until that was all he could think about. Every time he watched the TV show *"Cops"* or *"The Worlds Most Dangerous Car Chases,"* he ached all over.

Ever since he was a kid, he longed for excitement and intrigue. Each week, he would sit in front of the TV watching *"Wild, Wild West",* then he and his friends would act it out. Tom always insisted on being the hero, James West, who would single handedly save the Country from the evil villains bent on destroying it. *For now,* he signed heavily, *that dream would have to wait.*

Deputy Josephine Rissley sat at her desk next to Tom's. When Sheriff Harper had come in, she noticed he had lost a few pounds and thought he looked better than he had in years—younger too. Nikki has been a good influence, she knew. She was especially appreciative that her influence on him didn't get projected onto his deputies.

Although Harper chose to wear the official full uniform, she didn't care for it. She never wore the tie and on her feet, although black, were tennis shoes. The biggest change she had made was when she convinced Harper to adopt a different style of hat. The Stetson never looked good on her so Harper allowed an option. The deputies could either wear the Stetson or a black baseball style cap with the gold Sheriff's star emblem on the front. She liked to wear

16

the cap, as she did this morning, with her blond hair pulled into a pony tail through the back of it.

Leaning back in the chair with her feet up on the desk corner, she slowly sipped her morning coffee as she reviewed last week's traffic violation report. It was the usual boring stuff, but she didn't mind. She had spent the last seven years learning all the ins and outs of this department, and ninety percent of it fell into the boring category.

At only twenty-seven Joe, as everyone had come to know her, was the youngest deputy in the department— yet she practically ran everything. She knew how many tickets were issued, to whom, and for what. She knew which cases were open or closed, and who was working on them.

She didn't have a photographic memory, just a really good one. She liked to test it often and did that by concentrating on the details. Usually these details were so boring that nobody else bothered with them.

Everyone got use to asking her for information, but she didn't mind. Helping in anyway possible made her feel good, and she quickly became an indispensable part of the team. Sheriff Harper relied on her constantly.

What's happening with that vandalism case? What were the results of the accident investigation? Where's my coffee cup? These were questions she received daily from the Sheriff on down.

The other deputies nick-named her "Data" from the TV show *Star Trek The Next Generation,* because she could rattle off facts on demand. Although it was suppose to be a compliment, she didn't care for the name because it implied a cold, unemotional personality, and she was far from that.

Born into an athletic family, Joe was the youngest of three children, as well as the only girl. Growing up as a tom boy, she had to learn how to compete with her older, bigger brothers and all their friends. She found that by being observant of people and situations, she could gain an advantage over others who just relied on size and strength to win.

Baseball was the family passion. Her father had been a great pitcher, and at one time played semi-pro ball. His arm had long since been thrown out, but his knowledge of the game was as sharp as ever. For as long as Joe could remember, her father coached the Centralia Mustangs, a baseball team in the State amateur league. When Joe was young, he would let her sit in the dug out with the team. She paid close attention to how he sat on the bench quietly. Always watching. Always thinking. She noticed how he moved the players around. He would signal the infield to shift over, put in a pinch hitter, or call for the hit and run. Each time she would ask. "Why did you do that, Daddy? Why?"

He was always patient with her and loved to explain the game. "According to Sun Tzu's, *The Art of War*," he told her, "In order to win consistently and be the best you must know two things. First, you must know yourself, and, secondly, you must know your enemy."

She had never forgotten this. He helped her figure out what her strengths and weakness were. Then he helped her work on the weaknesses until they became strengths. He also taught her how to read team and player statistics. How to find their weaknesses and use it to her advantage. She learned what different batters liked to swing at and where they usually hit it. Who was likely to steal a base and who could make the big play.

Her father coached each of his children and determined which position they should play in. Billy was the oldest, big and tall, like his father, he naturally followed in Dad's footsteps and became a pitcher. Danny, the second oldest, took after his mother's side of the family and was short and stocky. Joe's father made him the catcher.

Although tall for a girl, Joe was smaller than most players. She was, however, quick, fast and had a strong throwing arm. Combined with her knowledge of the game, she made a perfect short stop. She constantly worked on every aspect of her game. At bat, she was no power house and never swung for the wall. She spent hours in the batting cage and developed herself into an exceptional contact switch hitter. Last season was her best yet, she hit .300 from both sides of the plate.

A couple of years ago, she got interested in pitching. She watched her father coach Billy and got as many pointers as she could. Throwing a few with Danny quickly became a habit. She was getting good and her father started letting her pitch at batting practice to her teammates. Last season, with more help from her father, her arm became stronger and she threw the ball with more power and action. She knew she was onto something good when not even her brothers could get a decent hit.

By the end of the season the bull pin was faltering and gave away several key games in the last innings. She knew she could do better and *begged* her father to put her in as a reliever.

Her father was understanding but refused. "We've developed the infield into a well oiled machine of which you play a key role," he had told her. "I can't afford to make any changes this late in the season. It could throw off synchronicity." Although very disappointed, she knew he was right.

They finished the regular season with the bull pin still weak. During the playoffs, her father had compensated by keeping the starters in for as long as he could. The pitchers were exhausted, but they managed to hold it together and get the team into the championship game.

It was a wonderful sight. It seemed to Joe the whole town had come out to see the game. The packed stands were a collage of color and excitement. People carried signs, made banners and the high school band was playing the fight song.

They were to play the Tri-City Eagles. The Eagles had the best record in the State and a reputation for punishing pitchers. Joe's team had played them in the regular season and had come away without success.

Most of the game was an exciting pitching duel. Billy was pitching and by mid-game had orchestrated a phenomenal series of strike outs. But the other team's pitcher had done equally well and the game was tied with zeros.

Situations changed in the sixth, however, with hits being earned by both teams as the pitchers got tired. The Eagles scored first then the Mustangs answered. The Eagles were starting to light Billy up, but exceptional defensive play by the infield kept the Mustangs in the game.

Miraculously, by the end of the eighth, the Mustangs were ahead by one. The Eagles started the ninth with a fresh pitcher and the Mustangs went down one, two and three. The whole team was surprised when Joe's father sent Billy back to the mound to finish the game.

The first batter connected with Billy's first pitch and put it out of the infield for a base hit. Joe could see Billy had nothing left and she looked to the dug out wondering why her father didn't pull him out. The second batter was the top of the line up. He too jumped on Billy's first pitch and put it in the gap for a double.

"Time!" Joe's father yelled as he stepped out of the dug out then strolled slowly to the mound. Danny ran over from the plate and Joe came in from short stop to listen in. The tying run was on third and the winning run was on second with no outs.

Joe's father took the ball from Billy. "You pitched a heck of a game, son. Thank you. The bull pin can take it from here."

"Daddy!" Joe exclaimed. "Do you want to win this game or not?" She glared at him. It was the last inning of the last game of

the year. She knew his previous reasons for not letting her pitch were no longer valid.

Her father looked at her for a moment and sized up the situation. "Strike 'em out." Was all he said as he handed her the ball then turned and walk back toward the dug out. Both Billy and Danny flashed their little sister a proud smile before turning and leaving the mound.

The crowd was dumbfounded. What was the coach doing? they all wondered. Eagle fans jeered her and even some of her home fans booed the decision. Joe was on the mound, exactly where she wanted to be, but suddenly she realized the game was different some how.

All eyes were on her as everyone looked for any sign of weakness or misstep. With all of the attention her hands began to shake. No, she told herself. This wasn't the time for a case of nerves.

Her father saw what was happening and understood. He stood up and motioned for the rest of the dug out to do the same. "Let's go!" he yelled. "One, two, three!" The rest of her team cheered her on as well, then slowly her home town fans started in.

The encouragement helped but she struggled to stay focused. *"Know yourself,"* she remembered. *"Then know your enemy."* She forced her mind to replay the batters statistics she memorized the night before. She was calmer now.

"Batter up!" the umpire yelled. The next batter was the second in the line up. She would be pitching to the heart of the order.

Someone in the stands yelled. "She probably throws like a girl! Hit a home run so we can all go home!" This brought laughter from the stands but this time it didn't shake Joe. She was going to use it to her advantage.

She looked at the batter as he stepped into the box. He was smiling. She remembered his stats. He was a power hitter with a .292 average. He always, always, *always* swung at the first pitch. She knew he would be swinging for the wall and that he was over confident. She decided to throw him garbage.

Drawing back for the wind up, she appeared to put everything she had into it but instead throw a very weak slider. The ball headed for the center of the plate. The batter swung hard but as Joe expected, the ball fell out of the air at the last second and landed just short of the plate. The batter missed it by a mile.

"Strike one!" the umpire yelled.

This brought laughter and jeers from the stands. Even the batter began to laugh. "She can't even get it across the plate!" someone yelled.

Nobody realized she meant to do that. She looked again at the batter. He took a couple of practice swings then rested the bat lazily on his shoulder and waited. Joe wound up and this time fired a missile down the heart of the plate. The batter reacted too late and again missed by a mile.

"*Strike two!*" the ump yelled. Again laughter from the stands, but this time it was directed at the batter. He didn't like it, even his own teammates were razzing him. Now he was mad and more determined than ever. Cocking back the bat, he stood ready as he glared back at Joe.

She decided to waste another one and see if he went for it. Drawing back for the wind up, she aimed for the outside corner and let the fast ball fly. The batter leaned inward and began to swing hard. Realizing too late that it was outside the strike zone, he couldn't pull back and almost fell over as his bat found air yet again.

"*Strike three! Batters out!*" yelled the ump.

Head down, the batter stomped off angrily to the tune of more laughter and jeers. Joe heard the next batter tease the first. "I'll show you how to hit off a girl," he chuckled.

She recalled his stats. Hitting .307 during the regular season, he was currently in a batting slump and was dangerously susceptible to high heat. Knowing what she had to do, she wound up and fired bullets. Inside, outside then center, she sent him packing with three high fast balls in a row.

The atmosphere in the stadium had suddenly changed. There was no more laughter from anyone. Her home town fans were cheering while the visitors fell silent. People in the stand were starting to believe. Could she possibly pull it off? they all wondered.

Joe watched the next batter walk slowly to the plate. He was watching her, trying to size her up. He was not going to underestimate her as his teammates had. The crowd fell silent.

Joe recalled the batters stats. He was the clean up hitter. Batting .324 for the season, he hit everything well. He was calm, patient and dangerous. With new pitchers, he liked to see what they had so he routinely let the first pitch sail past in order to study it.

Joe was counting on it so she was going to make it a good one. She wound up and fired a fast ball down the heart of the plate. The batter's muscle tightened when he realized it was a perfect pitch. He began to swing then held back at the last second.

"*Strike one!*" the ump yelled.

The batter didn't care. He had gotten a good look at Joe's best stuff and knew that he would be ready for it when it came by again. Joe analyzed the data in her brain hoping to find some chink in the batters armor. Maybe she could fool him with another slider. She wound up and let it fly. The batter watched it coming in fast. He leaned in on it and began to swing but at the last instant pulled back as it dropped short of the strike zone.

"Ball."

Continuing to think, Joe ran through the situation in her head. Other pitchers had been afraid of this guy and threw to the outside trying to keep it away from him. Less that twenty percent of everything he had seen all season was inside. She hoped that would be enough of an advantage. She wound up and let fly an inside fast ball.

He was expecting a pitch to the outside, but this was in his wheel house. He swung hard and was able to turn on it. Putting solid lumber on the ball, he launched it deep down the left field line. There was a loud gasp from the crowd as every eye watched it sail over the fence just foul of the pole.

"*Strike two!*" the ump yelled.

Joe could have sworn her heart had stopped. As the echo of the crack of the bat faded from her ears, she had to remind herself to breathe. She could feel every hair on her body standing on end as a new ball was thrown out to her. She was afraid yet exhilarated at the same time.

"*What was she going to do?*" she wondered intensely. She looked over at him. He was slowly and calmly digging in for the final volley. Everything he had seen before he has crushed. Desperately looking for a solution, Joe again went over the stats, then it hit her. Everything he had seen before... She had thrown nothing but straight balls the whole inning.

Her eyes narrowed as the ends of her mouth curled up into a thin devilish smile. "*Time to throw this bum a curve,*" she decided.

Drawing way back, she wound up and gave it all she had. The crowd held their breath as they watched the ball race toward the outside corner of the plate. It seemed like slow motion to Joe as she watched the batter lean forward and swing. Instantly, the spin on the ball overpowered its forward velocity. The ball rose up and in towards the batters hands. He tried to correct but it was too late. The bat caught nothing but air as the ball sailed past it and into the catcher's mitt.

"*Strike three! Batters out!*" the ump yelled.

The crowd erupted with cheer. Her teammates threw hats and gloves in the air in triumph then raced to the mound to congratulate her. Billy and Danny lifted their little sister up into the air and carried her around on their shoulders. She looked for her father and saw him standing outside the dugout with a huge smile on his face. He couldn't be more proud of her and he knew, as she did, that she would be addicted to pitching for the rest of her life.

2
The Edge

In a large indoor shooting range, a group of Federal Drug Enforcement Agents honed their skills. Special Agent Angela Rodriguez, a young Hispanic woman in her late twenties, squeezed slowly on the trigger of her .45 caliber revolver, sending another round racing towards its silhouette destination.

After firing several more shots, she returned the weapon to her shoulder holster. Pushing the recall button for the target slide, the black and white silhouette moved quickly towards her. When it stopped in front of her booth, she shook her head in disgust as she examined it. Taking it from the clip, she rolled it up.

Agent Rodriguez picked up her brown tweed sports coat from the hook beside her and put it on. She then grabbed her target and walk off the shooting range and into the sound insulated viewing booth. Though the thick glass separating the two rooms, she could hear the muffled sounds of gun fire as the other agents continued to practice. The young woman pulled her protective ear muffs from her head then untied the ribbon holding her hair back. Her thick black hair fell to her shoulders as she gently shook it out.

Rolling out the target again, she examined it closely. She had actually shot exceptionally well, but not good enough to satisfy her. Angela's eyes came up from the target. Looking out the large viewing window of the booth, they rested on the shooter closest to her on the range. He was a tall man in his mid-thirties wearing an expensive, impeccably tailored gray Italian suit. His dark hair was pulled tightly back into a small pony tail and a thin well groomed goatee covered his face.

Special Agent Alan Bradley fired rapidly as Angela watched. She would *not* be satisfied until she could shoot better then he did.

25

Last month she had lost first place in the Agency's Regional Championship to Bradley. She didn't like Bradley and it bothered her to feel anyway inferior to someone that she held no respect for.

In almost every way, they were exact opposites. He grew up in the safety of the best neighborhoods. As a child, she fell asleep to the sounds of gun fire and sirens. He was out spoken and wore flashy clothes. She was reserved and conservatively dressed. He had been given everything he desired, while she had worked for what little she had. He stood out in a crowd, while she blended.

To her, Bradley was nothing more than a loud mouth peacock, strutting around trying to get everyone's attention. She stood there looking at him with his gold Rolex, diamond earring and perfect teeth. Don't be mistaken, she wasn't jealous or envious in anyway. In fact, she felt she was superior to him in almost every way. Every way, that is, except shooting.

She was proud of her up bringing and wouldn't have changed a thing about it because that was what molded her into the person she was today. Born and raised in the worst part of East LA, everyday was a lesson in survival. Her single mother immigrated to the US from Mexico and had to work two jobs to make ends meet. Even with the small amount of time she had to spend with her daughter, she managed to raise her in the strict Roman-Catholic tradition of her ancestors.

Because her mother worked most of the time, Angela was initially raised by the street and the TV. Walking home from school everyday was a lesson in itself. She had to learn quickly which alleys not to go through, when to cross the street to avoid thugs and how to spot trouble before it happened. Of the few friends she had, many of them were getting involved in the destructive influences so prevalent on the street. It was only what her religion had taught her that kept her from getting into too much trouble. That is, until she got arrested.

One night as a young teenager, her best friend picked her up to go cruising in a new car. They hadn't gone two blocks before they were pulled over by a cop. It was then that she found out the car had been stolen and the two girls were hauled down to the station.

It ended up being a blessing in disguise, however, because the cop had checked up on her and found that she had no criminal background. He talked to the judge and he said the charges would be dropped if she agreed to visit the youth center everyday after school. She didn't have to volunteer- her mother quickly promised that Angela wouldn't let them down.

Everyday after that she showed up at the youth center and started to participate in fun activities and make new friends. The policeman who arrested her taught martial arts at the center, and encouraged her to learn. It was hard and challenging, but the rewards were priceless.

At the age of fifteen, five foot three inches tall and ninety-five pounds, she was already fully grown. The daily workouts strengthened her body, toned her muscles and disciplined her mind. Not only did it surprise her, but she was also exhilarated the day she was able to throw her instructor across the room.

This new found feeling of empowerment was intoxicating, and it spilled over into the rest of her day. She realized that she was fairly smart, and started getting better grades in school. Even though she still crossed the street to avoid trouble, she no longer felt weak or afraid. As long as she was disciplined and applied herself, there was nothing she could not accomplish.

Before she graduated from high school, she had her first black belt. With the help of a Naval ROTC scholarship, she continued her education and training at USC. She majored in history, minored in law and competed in martial arts tournaments. By graduation, she'd earned the title of Master of the Do Jo.

In order to pay back the Navy for their financial help in college, Angela entered the force as an officer. Assigned to Naval Intelligence, she developed and honed her investigative skills. The narcotics division, where she was placed, worked to stop Naval personnel from smuggling drugs into the US.

It wasn't a huge problem because most all of people in the military were respectable professional people. However, the rewards were high enough that a small number of people tried to smuggle cocaine or heroin on a regular basis. Working as mules, they picked up a package while on tour in Asia or South America then delivered it to a dealer when they returned to the United States. Because Navy ships didn't pass through Customs, the risk of getting caught was small.

Angela found that the lessons she had learned from the streets of LA were now very valuable. The same things that tipped her off to trouble in the old neighborhood were common to drug dealing, no matter where it occurred. If someone suddenly started throwing money around, it was worth looking into. Such as the seaman, who normally makes fifteen thousand a year, that drove a new BMW.

They were called "people of interest". No full scale investigation was started, they were just watched. Large payoffs could make a person greedy. They took chances and eventually got complacent. When the time was right, Angela would move in with an assault team, arrest everyone involved, and shut down the operation.

She was proud of her work and fiercely determined to do a good job. Personal satisfaction was her main reward. She wore the uniform of the Navy with honor, and it infuriated her that others would disgrace it by smuggling drugs.

Every time one of her arrests turned into a conviction, it made her feel good. She quickly realized that law enforcement was to be her chosen field. When it was time to sign up for another four years with the Navy, she declined. Instead, she accepted a job with the Drug Enforcement Agency and was assigned to the Seattle field office.

Despite the nearly constant rain, she fell in love with the Seattle community. She got an apartment in West Seattle and established a daily routine. Every morning, she would be well into her five mile run around Alki point by dawn, followed by an hour in the weight room. From there, she went to the office. Three nights a week, she taught martial arts at the youth center to inner-city kids.

She liked and respected everyone she worked with. Everyone, that is, except Bradley. She felt that he didn't fit in. He took too many chances, always rushed into things, and didn't work well in a team setting. That made him dangerous.

He was very intelligent, she knew, and seemed to have a sixth sense when it came to figuring out how a drug operation worked. Even so, she considered him to be lazy in his investigative technique and thought he relied too much on instinct.

He seemed only to do just enough to get by. To pass the physical to get into the Agency, Bradley completed only the basic requirements. Just the right number of sit ups, push ups, and such. Seeing him regularly in the gym, he looked like he was in good shape, but she never saw him sweat. He always appeared too busy trying to pick up women.

Investigations done by him were hurried and lacked detail. His reports contained more guess work than actual fact. Mostly, she hated the way he patronized her. All in all, she considered him to be a stain that tarnished the badge they both wore.

The only thing she admired about him was how he shot his gun. Bradley *excelled* at it. It annoyed her that he didn't spend countless hours at the range practicing as she did. Not to mention, she felt that he used it too much like a crutch. Almost always,

Bradley's answer to mediocre investigation work was to pull out his gun and start firing.

Angela avoided him whenever she could. So the idea of asking him for help was repulsive, but she was at the end of her rope. Even with all the practice she had put in lately, she hadn't gotten any better. She needed the advice of an expert. Both her religion and martial arts training had taught her that too much pride was a bad thing. Maybe someone was trying to tell her something or maybe it was a test, but whatever the case, she decided to swallow her pride and ask Bradley for help.

Agent Rodriguez was deep in thought, hardly noticing a younger agent walking through the door from the range. His hair was cut in a high military style crew cut and he wore a loose fitting off-the-rack suit.

"Hello, Agent Rodriguez," he said, approaching her. "What are you doing?"

"Huh, What?" she replied, shaken from deep concentration. "Oh. Hello, Anderson. I was just studying Agent Bradley's technique." They both looked towards the range. "I don't understand how he does it. I use the slow steady rhythm taught at the Academy when I shoot, but look at him."

Anderson and Rodriguez watched in silence as Agent Bradley stood with his hands at his sides. Then, like a flash, Bradley reached for the large nickel platted pistol in his shoulder holster. Pulling it quickly he aimed and fired several shots rapidly, then returned it to his holster.

"Who does he think he is, some sort of old west gun slinger?" Anderson laughed.

Rodriguez shook her head. "I don't know, but it seems to work for him. I was division champ three years in a row until he showed up. I don't know what irritates me more- the fact that he beat me, or that he makes it look so easy."

They continued to watch as Agent Bradley put his suit coat back on, pulled the target from the holder, and smiled. Strolling to the door, he entered the preparation room.

"How did you do, Bradley?" Rodriguez asked, as she and Anderson walked over to him.

"Well hello, Angela." Bradley greeted her with a smile. "You look lovely today."

"Thank you. How did you shoot?" she asked again.

"If you'd like, I could give you some pointers. Over dinner, maybe?" Bradley suggested.

"How many times do I have to tell you? All I'm interested in is your shooting skill."

"That's too bad, because I'd like the opportunity to show you how multi-talented I am," Bradley flashed a cheesy smile.

"No means no," Rodriguez finished, trying not to sound irritated. Changing the subject, she turned to Anderson. "I don't believe you two have met. Special Agent Alan Bradley, this is Special Agent Neil Anderson. Anderson is fresh meat from the Academy." As the two men exchanged handshakes she continued. "We were hoping you'd show us how you scored."

"Certainly," he replied, then unrolled his target out on the table next to him. Rodriguez and Anderson looked at the target in amazement. Two groups of four shots, each within a one inch spread, were placed in the center of the silhouette's chest and head.

"Man! That's good shooting," Anderson exclaimed.

"What's your secret, Bradley? You don't practice near as much as I do." Rodriguez crossed her arms. She was clearly frustrated, and it showed.

"It's not so much practice as it is preparation," he replied with another smile. "If you put more thought into what you need before you shoot, you won't have to spend as much time on the range."

Rodriguez shrugged her shoulders. "What do you mean?"

"Well, for instance, your choice of weapons." Bradley pointed to her shoulder holster.

Rodriguez pulled her gun from the holster. "I shoot a long barreled .45. It's the same as many other expert marksman use."

"Yes it is, but is it the right one for *you*?" Bradley let the question hang in the air giving her time to consider it.

"I guess so," she thought out loud. "I've got a special grip fitted to my hand, and a national match barrel for increased accuracy."

Bradley nodded in agreement to her modification, but then continued his analysis of her overall performance. "I've watched you shoot. After about five rounds, your wrist starts to sag. It may be too heavy for you." Again, he gave her a moment to consider his words before continuing. "Besides, it's a revolver. You need a lot more control because when you pull the trigger you have to turn the whole cylinder."

Rodriguez thought about it for a moment, and then conceded the point. "Maybe you're right."

"What do you shoot?" Anderson was curious as he pointed to the large silver gun in Agent Bradley's holster.

Bradley pulled out his weapon and handed it over. ".44 Magnum Desert Eagle."

"Impressive." Anderson was wide eyed with amazement. He whistled as he examined the huge shiny gun, turning it over and running his hands across it with envy as he did so. "Isn't the Desert Eagle an Israeli weapon?"

"Yes it is," Bradley confirmed with a nod. "I had it custom made to my own specifications."

Rodriguez cocked her head to the side with a question. "What about accuracy? I didn't think they made a national match barrel for a semiautomatic?"

"You'd be surprised what you can get with the right amount of money." Bradley smiled as he pointed to his target. "I think the accuracy speaks for itself."

"What about your speed?" Anderson continued the line of questions. "I've got a 9 mm semiautomatic and I can't pull the trigger nearly as fast as you."

"The firing mechanism of my Desert Eagle has been modified to fire with a fraction of the squeeze pressure required for stock pistols."

Anderson understood immediately. "A feather trigger."

"Exactly." Bradley gave him a confirming nod.

"But what about lift?" Rodriguez knew that there had to be more to it, and she was determined to find out the answer. "When I fire my .45, the front of the barrel wants to rise. Then it takes time to re-aim and fire again. Your pistol is as powerful as mine, yet your barrel barely moves. Why is that?"

"I've had mag-na-ports installed into the slide and barrel."

"Mag-na-*what?*" Anderson's eyebrows lifted. He had no clue what Bradley was talking about.

"Mag-na-ports." Rodriguez's eyes went wide with excitement as if a light had just turned on in her head. "They're small holes which are drilled into the top of the barrel. They allow exhaust gases from the shell to escape when you fire the gun. The force of the gases counter acts the force which causes the barrel to rise."

"Very good, Angela." Bradley was clearly surprised at how much she knew. "If you know so much about them why haven't you done the same thing?"

"I did. I had a hole drilled just behind my front site. It settled the gun movement down nicely, but the hot gases ejected right into my line of sight." Her tone turned somber and she looked discouraged. "It was distracting, so I stopped using it."

Bradley understood. Taking his weapon back from Anderson, he pointed at the top of the slide. "That is why I've got two elongated holes off set from top center. They not only give me up and down stability, but also reduce some side to side movement without interfering with my vision."

"Good idea!" Rodriguez was astonished. "I wish I would've thought of that."

Bradley decided that they'd talked enough about weapon configuration. It was time to examine the actual results of their shooting. "Why don't both of you show me your targets." Rodriguez and Anderson unrolled their targets and laid them next to Bradley's. "Now you see, Angela." He pointed to the target. "This is exactly what I mean. Your first shots are nicely placed. But then you get tired and they move around on you. You should try out some different weapons."

Bradley then moved to Anderson's target. "Now yours are a lot sloppier. A few are nice, but then there's a couple too high and too low. I bet you're still using off the shelf factory shells, aren't you?"

"Yeah, what else is there?" Anderson was again confused and the look on his face confirmed it. He had never considered using anything other than the cheap, generic brand he was use to.

"You should use hand loads." This was a key point, and Bradley wanted to make sure Anderson understood. "The amount of powder used in factory loads varies from shell to shell because they're loaded by a machine. That causes the bullets with less powder to drop short and the ones with more to fly high. When shells are loaded by hand, the grains of powder can be carefully controlled. They will help you shoot more consistently."

Bradley pulled the alligator skin wallet from his pocket, and then took a business card from it. "Here, this guy makes them special for me. He even weighs out the bullets so that they're almost exactly the same. He'll fix you up." He handed the card to Anderson.

"Let me see that when you're through with it, Anderson," ordered Rodriguez.

Anderson nodded.

"So, it's not all luck then, is it?" Rodriguez felt relieved that the advice she'd received could significantly help her.

"It all depends on your definition of luck," Bradley frowned thoughtfully. "To me, luck is when preparation meets opportunity. I believe in being prepared for any situation."

Anderson turned his attention back to the shiny Desert Eagle. "Nickel plated. With an impressive weapon like that, aren't you afraid the criminals will see you coming?" He chuckled at his own joke.

"Actually, I count on it. I want them to notice it." Bradley's chin seemed to rise a bit and there was no small amount of pride in his voice. "I've made many arrests where the suspects have laid down their weapons and given up after they've seen it."

"I'll bet you spent a fortune on it, though." Rodriguez shook her head wondering how she could afford such a weapon.

"That's true, but much do you value your life?" Bradley turned serious for a moment.

"What do you mean?"

"This baby acts as a deterrent to stop suspects that don't have the balls to face it. For those that do, well, my results speak for themselves." Bradley looked from Rodriguez to Anderson and back. "They don't stand a chance."

"Do you think I could modify my Beretta to do what your Eagle does?" Anderson was now excited about making changes of his own.

"Well, it would help somewhat, but I think you should look into something more powerful." Bradley tried to discourage Anderson's suggestion. "The standard issue 9 mm has plenty of killing power, but in my opinion, not enough impact power."

Anderson did a double take between his companions, looking for an answer. "I don't get it."

Bradley started to explain with more detail. "The standard issue 9 mm will kill just about anything you're aiming at, but it won't stop a large man charging at you. Rodriguez's .45 or my .44 Mag will not only kill him, it will knock him backwards. If I carried a Beretta, I wouldn't be alive today."

"Why is that?" Rodriguez asked curiously.

Bradley lowered his head somberly. "A few years ago, I was stationed in San Diego. My unit was about to take down a suspected crack house when we were spotted. The suspects were three large Samoan males who locked themselves in the house. Another agent and I were sent around the house in order to go in the back door. As we came through the bushes and got closer, our full attention was on the house.

Suddenly, we were surprised by loud screaming which erupted behind us. We turned quickly to see the three suspects, obviously high on drugs, charging down on us swinging machetes in some sort of suicide run. We immediately lifted our weapons and fired. I took out the first two men, each with a single shot in the center of the chest, at a range of ten feet. The Eagle not only killed them, it knocked them back and off their feet.

The other Agent wasn't so lucky. He carried a 9 mm and put two bullets into the third suspect's chest. Even though the man was virtually dead, he had enough adrenaline and momentum to carry him a few more feet.

Before either of us could fire again, the suspect fell forward swinging his machete and fell on top of my partner. The blade practically cut him in two. The Eagle saved my life that day, while the 9 mm buried my partner." Bradley's words trailed off and his expression turned distant.

"I'm sorry to hear that, Alan," Agent Rodriguez consoled him.

A moment later, Bradley lifted the Desert Eagle up for them both to see. "So I'd say this baby was worth the price."

Rodriguez and Anderson pondered that for a moment as they watched Bradley return his weapon to his shoulder holster.

"Bradley, would you mind if I took the Eagle for a test drive?" Anderson was anxious to try something new.

"Sorry, Anderson," Bradley shook his head. "Nothing personal, but this is my most prized possession. I wouldn't let my mother fire it."

"I thought your corvette was your most prized possession?" Rodriguez joked.

"They both are," Bradley admitted. "I prize anything that gives me an edge over the competition."

"Don't you mean an edge over the criminals?" Anderson corrected him.

"No." Bradley turned and looked Rodriguez directly in the eye. "I mean the competition."

Rodriguez's eyes narrowed as she realized *exactly* what he meant.

3
Bears

"Hello Jim!" Came a familiar jolly voice from the office doorway. Harper looked up from his paperwork and half eaten lunch to see Buck Henderson, an elderly man with silver hair wearing a flannel shirt, blue jeans, and work boots. His hard, traveled face looked more like a well worn pair of leather gloves than actual skin. The man's nose was bent and flattened from having been broken too many times for a doctor to fix. Not that this man would have gone to a doctor.

"Buck!" Harper exclaimed with a smile. He got up and walked around the desk to shake the old man's outstretched, calloused hand. "It's good to see you! What's it been- two months?"

"Closer to three," Buck corrected. His smile made the deeply cut groves around his mouth and eyes more pronounced. "You're going to have to come out and see us soon."

"*Us?*" Jim asked, studying his friend. He looked older, but the steel-gray flecked blue eyes were full of life and his grip was like a vice.

"Oh, I almost forgot." Buck stepped out of the way to reveal the teenage boy in a gray sweatshirt, blue jeans, and white high top tennis shoes standing behind him. "Jim, I want you to meet Clifford. He'll be staying with me for the summer."

Jim stepped forward and extended his hand. "Hello, Clifford."

"It's nice to meet you, Sheriff Harper. Uncle Buck's told me a lot about you."

"*Uncle* Buck?" Jim snapped a questioning look at his friend. "Well, what brings you and Uncle Buck all the way into town?"

"We came to get me a jacket?" Clifford answered.

"That's right, Jim," Buck spoke up. "Do you still have some of those green jackets with the Forest Service emblem on them? If Clifford's going to be my assistant this summer, I want him to look official."

"I think so," Jim replied, turning to scan the deputies. "Rissley, take Clifford down to the store room and pick him out a jacket."

"Yes, sir." She walked around her desk and smiled at Clifford. "Come on, I'm sure we can find one your size."

"Well, if it isn't Smok'n Joe Rissley," Buck said when he saw her. "How's that throwing arm?"

"Just fine, Buck," she said with a smile. Buck had coined that nick-name after last year's championship game. People around town and at the office were slowly starting to call her "Smok'n Joe". She wasn't sure if she liked it yet, but anything was better than "Data".

"It's good to see you again."

"Likewise," Buck said, watching the two walk down the hall towards the stairs. "You'd better get me one of those jackets, too! My last one got ruined." He called after them.

Buck then turned his attention back to Harper. "One more thing, Jim," he said seriously. "I've closed trail seventy-four until further notice. I've already put the signs up at the trail head, but if you could have one of your deputies post it at the information center, I would appreciate it."

Jim thought for a moment before answering. "Lets see, isn't that the one that goes up the west fork of the Nisqually to Duck and Goose lakes?"

"That's it," Buck confirmed. "The winter thaw and spring rains really did a number on the trail. I was up there last week working on it when I came across three bears. They're a female and two cubs."

Jim rubbed his chin thoughtfully. "Hmm, I suppose it's about time they came out of hibernation." That brought a worried look to his face. "They're probably pretty hungry."

"Who knows how many hikers' camps they would've wandered into looking for a quick meal," Buck said. "It's best they be left alone for a while."

"Did you actually see them this time, or is it that wild imagination of yours?" Milhouse questioned Buck in disbelief.

Harper turned his attention to Milhouse as the other deputies looked up from their paperwork. "What are you talking about, Tom? If Buck says they're up there, then they're up there."

"It just seems like Buck is in here every couple of months or so, closing one trail or another because of bears. I've hiked those mountains all my life and have yet to see one," Milhouse answered, putting aside the reports he was reading. The results of the letter he received earlier had put him in a bad mood. He was looking to take his frustrations out on something and Buck was a convenient target.

"Yeah, well if you'd open up your senses instead of just your mouth once in a while maybe you would!" Buck growled, taking the bait.

"The way you drink, I'm surprised you can see anything but the bottom of your last bottle!" Milhouse added loudly.

"Knock it off! Both of you!" Jim barked. "You're carrying on like a couple of old hens."

Tom wouldn't stop. "Well it's true, Sheriff. Buck wouldn't need a new jacket if he hadn't gotten so drunk the last time we went fishing that he tripped and fell into the fire,"

Jim cocked an eyebrow at Buck. "Is that true?"

"You should tell your deputies to have a little more respect." Buck evaded the question and looked towards the ground with a guilty expression on his face.

"Now Buck, we've talked about this before," Jim scolded. "You promised me you'd control your drinking. Especially now that Clifford is staying with you. You have to set a good example."

"I will, Jim," he nodded. "I guarantee it."

Just then, Deputy Rissley and Clifford came back up the steps and walked towards them.

"We'll talk more about this later," Jim said in a quiet, yet stern manner.

"Here you go, Uncle Buck." Clifford handed him a jacket.

Buck took it and tried it on. "Thank you, Clifford," he said with a smile. "It looks like a perfect fit." He turned his attention back to Harper. "Well Jim, we'd better get going. We've got some supplies to pick up from the Super Mart before we head back to the house. Clifford and I will be going back up the trail tomorrow to work on it some more, and finish picking up the garbage on the trail left behind by the hikers."

"Hold on Buck," Jim said with a concerned voice. "I'll walk you out." Then he turned back towards Milhouse. "Make up a sign to post at the Information Center."

"I'll post the information on our new website," Rissley volunteered. "That way folks from out of town will know in advance of the closure and can plan ahead."

"Oh yeah, and while you're at it, call Morton Field," Jim added. "As long as the trails empty, they might as well have the forest fire unit send their pilot up to do some practice water drops in the upper clearings."

With that Jim, Buck, and Clifford walked down the hall, through the front door, and out of the building.

"Buck, why don't you let Clifford run and get the supplies while you and I talk," Jim suggested.

Buck looked at his friend curiously. "Yeah, all right. It's not like he can get lost in this town." Buck pulled a list from his shirt pocket. "Now Clifford, you have Mrs. Duncan give you a hand with this. Tell her its for me, she knows the brands I like. Especially the cigars—she orders them special for me."

"Yes, sir," Clifford replied, taking the list.

Buck then reached into his back pocket and pulled out his wallet. "Lets see." He fumbled with a large bundle of bills and handed some to Clifford. "This ought to take care of it. Oh yeah, stop by the filling station on your way there and fill up both tanks." He pulled out some more money. "Give this to Larry. He rebuilt the front end of the suburban a while back and I haven't paid him for it yet. Do you get all that?"

"Yes, sir," Clifford repeated with a smile. "No problem." With the keys in hand Clifford turned and ran out towards an old, dark brown GMC parked at the corner of the building. Both men watched as the boy climbed in the three quarter ton Suburban and drove away.

Looking over at his friend, Jim saw the thick wallet stuffed with cash still in Buck's hands. "I see you still don't believe in banks."

"Not hardly," came the reply as Buck struggled to put the wallet away.

"Where did you get all that anyway?"

"A couple of weeks ago, one of those Hollywood types called me up and offered me a thousand dollars, plus expenses, to take him fishing for a week"

"What I wouldn't do for your job," Jim joked.

"An outfitter's life is more than just fish'n and hunt'n, you know. I earn every penny." Buck defended. "Especially *this* time, I'm telling you it was no picnic."

"What happened?"

38

Both men turned and began to walk.

"Well, to start with, when I picked him up at the airfield he had a woman with him! It seems that at the last minute he decided to bring his wife. Hum, I wonder whose idea that was," he said with a sour look on his face. "Of course I complained. I mean it wasn't in our deal."

"Oh, of course you *had* to," Jim replied with mock sympathy.

"'Fine', he says as he whipped out his bill fold and gives me three thousand cash! At first I thought it was too much, and tried to tell him so, but he wouldn't listen. But then, who could with a cellular phone in one ear and that woman clucking away in the other? I swear, I don't know how he kept everything straight!"

"I hear some people are good at that. Personally, I wouldn't like the stress," Jim remarked.

"Well, it looked like it had taken its toll on him. You should've seen him, all pale and skinny." Buck shook his head sadly.

"Really sick, eh?"

"Who wouldn't be with a woman like that? She never stopped talking. I know you disagree with me, but it's like I've always said. 'The mountains are no place for a woman'. Especially this one. Everything that came out of her mouth was a complaint. 'The saddle's too hard!' 'The grounds too rocky!' 'There are too many bugs!'" he exclaimed in imitation. Buck snorted with disgust.

That brought a hearty laugh from his friend.

"It's not funny! It didn't take long before I *knew* she had to go!"

Jim immediately grew concerned. "What did you do?"

"Well for starters, on the first night I made my famous trail stew a little extra spicy. Then after supper, when we were all sitting around the camp fire, I started in with a story about bigfoot."

"Not that old lie about bigfoot stealing your box of apples?"

"No, I made this one up special just for her. I told her that bigfoot was really a mutant created by space aliens," Buck replied proudly, then posed a question to his friend. "Jim, did you know that a whole clan of them live in the mountains looking for human females to mate with, in order to purify their genes?"

"You didn't!" Jim's jaw dropped open in disbelief.

"Damn *right* I did! You should've seen her," Buck put his arm around Jim assuredly. "She was so frazzled from the story and the upset stomach that she didn't sleep a wink. The next morning, her husband had to call in a float plane to fly her out of there."

"Ah, Buck that's terrible! You should be ashamed of yourself."

"Not in the least," Buck looked at him. After a moment he raised his index finger implying there was more. "Besides, that only took care of *half* of the problem."

"What do you mean?"

"Well the phone, of course. If the week stood a chance of becoming a success there couldn't be any contact with the outside world. Heck, you know that as well as I do."

"So what did you do?"

"I didn't do anything, it was Molly."

"How is Molly and the other mules?" Harper asked.

"Well Tiny, Chuck, Blacky and the others are fine. Molly, on the other hand, worries me."

"How so?"

"Well, she's almost totally blind now. She relies mainly on what she hears in order to get around. Actually, that's how it all happened. You see, this guy was riding Molly up the trail while talking on his cellular. Molly was having a hard time telling which way the rest of the horses were walking so she finely got fed up and bucked him off."

"Did he get hurt?"

"Na! Just shook up a bit, but his phone landed in the middle of the trail. Before he could stop her, Molly's hoof came down and smashed it into a million pieces! You should have seen this guy. At first, I thought he was going to break down and cry, but all of a sudden he broke out laughing instead. From that moment on everything went great. We talked, fished, and told jokes. All as if we were old friends who hadn't seen each other for a while."

That brought a smile to Harper's face. "Good, I'm glad he turned out to be an all right guy."

"Most men are basically the same, Jim. We are all made of the same stuff and have the same philosophy. Sure, some men forget for awhile and it takes someone like me to wipe the cobwebs away and wake them up. But when its all said and done, we're all the same. Take this guy for example. He came up here skinny, pale, stressed out and looking for something to fill the void inside him. When he left he was a whole different person—he was *alive* again. Heck, I'd be proud to share my coffee and fire with any man like that."

"You make it sound like you're some kind of healer," Jim remarked jokingly.

"I may not have a degree, but I'm a healer just the same. Sure a doctor can cure your body, but what good does it do you if you're dead inside. People come to me looking for something they didn't know they'd even lost. I take them up into the hills and the mountains breathe new life into them."

The man seemed to be glowing now. He jabbed himself in the chest with his thumb and continued, "I give them back they're souls, Jim. If that's not a healer, I don't know what is."

Buck always made it sound more dramatic than it was Jim knew as they both stared silently out at the distant mountains, but there was something to his words. Every time he felt the weight of the world on his shoulders, Harper would go up there and come back relaxed and more confident than ever. Buck was essentially right, but Jim didn't believe it was the same for all people.

Through his experiences, Jim believed that people could become sick and weakened from the stresses and distractions of life. If they hadn't killed their spirit completely, then there was a chance for someone like Buck to help them find their way again.

There were others, however, who couldn't be saved. A growing number of city people were becoming members of, as Jim referred to them, the walking dead. Uncaring, selfish parasites who would never become useful members of society. That's why he always paid close attention to the types of people who came into town. Occasionally, members of the walking dead would arrive trying to spread their disease, and each time Jim would run them out of the County.

No sir, Jim thought. *That disease originated in the city and in the city it would stay.*

After a few moments, Buck stopped their silent stroll and finally spoke up. "So what's on your mind, Jim?"

"What do you mean?"

"You didn't bring me out here to talk privately about my customers did you?"

"Well no," Jim admitted, looking over at his friend. "Buck, we've been friends along time, and I don't mean to pry, but I thought you didn't have any family…"

Buck smiled back as if knowing what the question was going to be. "You mean Clifford? No, Jim, he's not family. He is Cliff Webb's boy."

"Lieutenant Webb? The chopper jockey from Nam?"

"That's him."

"Man that guy can fly," Jim replied. "He pulled me out of a couple tight spots. I remember it as if it were yesterday. He came in low and fast, then landed his bird where I wouldn't think possible. As soon as I jumped in, he was off again and he did it all under heavy fire! I swear that guy has more balls than brains."

"Oh, he had plenty of smarts!" Buck assured him. "It was his heart that made him go into seemingly impossible situations. Back when I ran Covert Ops., some of my men were pinned down and didn't have much time. I couldn't order anyone in because my team was on the wrong side of a line on the map. Before I could ask for volunteers, Webb was already in the air." Buck thought of him fondly. "I owe him for that, Jim, but he didn't do it to be owed anything. He did it because he couldn't stand to watch people die if there was a chance he could help them. I guess that's why when he came home he took a job in Seattle flying a rescue helicopter for one of the hospitals. That's how he met his wife, you know, she was a nurse at the time. They got married and had little Clifford Junior."

"Well that's great news!" Jim replied. "So how's he doing? You know, you should really invite him out to do some fishing, I'd really like to see him again."

Buck's expression turned grim. "He's dead, Jim," he said softly.

"That's terrible," he said, shaking his head sadly. "How did it happen?" Jim suddenly felt bad for not keeping in touch. He always meant to, but any reminder of the war brought out feelings that he didn't want to deal with.

"He got off work late one night a couple of years ago, and was mugged in the parking lot. After handing over his wallet the jerk shot him anyway." Buck's voice turned angry. "Can you believe it? A hundred yards from a hospital, and there was nothing they could do for him."

Both men stood in silence for a few moments contemplating the tragedy.

Buck finally continued. "Anyway, young Clifford started doing poorly in school and hanging around the wrong people. His mother caught him smoking pot with some friends one night so she called me for help. It seems that Cliff used to talk to her about me and how I used discipline and hard work to turn raw recruits into men. She was hoping that I could help Clifford before it got any worse."

"Yeah, I hear that kids in the big city schools learn more about drugs and guns than they do about math and science," Jim remarked sadly.

"Things sure have changed since the sixties," Buck added. "Back then you used to be able to tell the good guys from the bad.

Hard drugs were being used by people who were old enough to know better. Now they're gangs of junior high school kids dealing it on street corners."

Jim could see his friend's face turn sad as he looked at the ground.

"So maybe you'll get a chance to save one of them?" Jim was trying to raise his friend's mood.

Buck's head popped up with a smile. "That's right! I'm going to teach Clifford the ropes. Teach him how to run a pack line. Have him work hard all day so that he can look back at what he accomplished and smile. I'll turn him into someone his father would be proud of."

"Then I would imagine that providing a good example would be important."

"Heck yes, it's crucial. Lead by example, that's what I've always said."

"Then I can expect you to stop drinking?" Jim said more sternly.

Buck gnawed at the unlit cigar between his teeth, knowing he'd walked into that one. "Well..."

"We've talked about this before, Buck," Jim argued. "You've been drinking way too much lately, even for you. This is a perfect opportunity to quit."

Buck scratched the side of his head as he thought about it. If there was one thing he truly enjoyed, it was a good drink. "Tell you what. I'll cut back to one drink a night, before going to bed. No more unless there's an emergency."

"Let me guess, in case of snakebite?" Jim said sarcastically. But he knew that asking Buck to stop completely was unrealistic. "I guess that's a start."

Buck decided to change the subject before his friend could suggest any more improvements. "So, when did you get the new black top?"

Jim looked down for the second time that day and smiled. "They just finished it last week. Looks pretty sharp, doesn't it."

"I'll say. It's sure an improvement from the mud hole it used to be," Buck remarked. "So how did you get the County Council to spring for it?"

"I didn't have anything to do with it. They did it all themselves."

That brought a disbelieving look to Bucks face. "You've been asking for this for years, and those tight wads wouldn't do anything to help you. So out with it. How many arms did you have to twist or how many favors did you call in?"

"Like I said, I didn't do anything. What happened was that awhile back I was called down to a Council meeting to explain the new tires I had to buy for patrol vehicles. It just so happened that it had been dumping buckets all week, and right when the meeting started the storm knocked the power out to the building.

"If that wasn't bad enough, the emergency generator wasn't working and the engineer said it would take hours for it to be fixed. So, I suggested that we continue the meeting here at the station. Well it just so happens that some careless person left the hose running all night and that, added to the rain, turned this parking lot into a huge mud puddle." Jim almost started to laugh as he thought of it. "When each Council member ruined a five hundred dollar pair of shoes getting into the building, they voted unanimously to pave it."

"So all those things happening at the same time were just coincidences?" Buck rubbed his chin questioningly, already knowing what the answer would be.

"That's correct," Jim confirmed with a straight face.

Buck continued to look around suspiciously, and then an eyebrow lifted. "Still, I can't believe the Council fixed your whole lot."

"Oh they didn't. They just did this small section of pavement here in front. The gravel was donated by Mr. Remick down at the quarry," Jim answered.

"Donated!" Buck exclaimed. "Now you and I both know that tightwad Remick has never done anything for free. Heck, he charged his own mother for potting soil for her garden last year."

"Now Buck, I think you're being a little rough on poor old Remick. He's a model citizen, the Judge said so," Jim replied.

"What does Judge Lundeberg have to do with this?" Buck turned to look Jim square in the eye.

"I'm surprised at you, Buck. You're not up on the local gossip since you've been back?" Jim needled. That brought an impatient glare from his friend. Normally Buck dominated conversations with tales of his latest adventure, so Jim enjoyed the few chances he got to have center stage.

"Well, it all started when I caught Remick fishing on Riffe Lake."

Buck folded his arms in front him, becoming more impatient. "What's so strange about that?"

"He wasn't using a pole."

Buck thought for a second before replying, "All right, I'll bite. What was he using?"

A smile grew on Harper's face until it stretched from ear to ear, and a twinkle lit up his eyes as he continued his story. "When I showed up, Remick was in the middle of the lake in his little boat drunker than ten sailors," Jim remembered laughing. "As he sang 'Home on the Range' he would throw sticks of dynamite into the water then scoop up the fish with a net when they floated to the surface!"

"Holy cow!" Buck exclaimed as he laughed thinking of the sight. "Damn fool's luck he didn't blow himself sky high."

Both men laughed for a moment before Jim continued. "Anyway, when he finally sobered up, he was worried that Lundeberg would have his blasting license revoked."

"That would've put him out of business," Buck confirmed.

"When Remick asked me for advice on how to get on the Judge's good side, I mentioned that Lundeberg was a big fan of people who do community service."

"So you told him that if he graveled your lot, the Judge would go easy on him!"

"Hey! You make it sound as if I used my position as Sheriff to influence the court." Jim defended himself. "That would be unethical."

"Isn't that what you did?" Buck cocked an accusing eyebrow.

The accusation kind of hurt Jim's feelings. "No, I didn't say anything about the parking lot. At least, not in so many words. He just asked me for advice, and I gave it to him."

"Yeah, well it sounds a lot like that stunt you pulled with that book publisher from Bellingham last year. You remember him- he shot one of old man Johnson's cows thinking it was an elk."

"I remember I wrote him up for poaching and for just plain being an idiot, but I didn't do anything else," Jim assured him.

"Oh come on, Jim, you made a visit to his jail cell with a sad story about how the local high school didn't have enough text books to go around and that those they did have were old and in bad shape. I got it straight from one of your deputies," Buck remarked in a matter-of-fact sort of manner.

"Which one?" Jim ordered looking noticeably irritated.

"My sources are completely confidential," Buck replied with a smirk. Knowing by the look on his friend's face, the information he had gotten was accurate.

45

Jim was a private person who didn't like people meddling too much into what he considered his affairs, Buck knew, which made it all that more enjoyable for Buck to needle him about it. It was a constant game between these two old comrades. A kind of friendly competition where each tried to show the other that he had the scoop on something the other didn't. When the information was about the other, it made it all that more sweet.

Buck continued to spill what he knew. "When crates of text books arrived on the steps of the school the next morning, Lundeberg practically did a flip. He let that publisher go after reimbursing Johnson for the cow and promising not to ever go hunting again. You would think Lundeberg would've caught on by now. After all, you pull one of these stunts at least once a year. Do you think maybe he knows what you're doing and just looks the other way?"

Jim looked at Buck out of the corner of his eye, wondering how much he really knew and how much was a guess. Sure, he had stretched the authority of his position a little at times, but it was for the good of the community and everybody got what they wanted. Most of his dealings were known to only himself and the persons involved. *No, there's no way he could know that much,* he decided.

"All I'm going to say is, at times, this bureaucracy we've created doesn't work the way it was intended to. At which point, it's time for common citizens to step forward and do a little extra."

"Is *that* what you do?" Buck laughed.

"No, *I* didn't do it," Jim replied with an irritated voice. "Remick and that book publisher did. That's what makes them such good citizens. You should try it sometime. The drill team needs new equipment for next year, maybe you should take some of that newly found wealth of yours and donate it."

The thought of it made Buck squirm. Jim had changed tactics and was now on the offensive. B *last him. It's just like him to ruin my fun,* he thought.

The hum of a familiar engine interrupted their exchange. "There's Clifford now," Buck replied as he looked down the road. "I'd better get going."

Jim looked down the street. The suburban had just turned the corner, but was still a long ways off. "There's something else I wanted to talk to you about." Jim said in a serious voice. "Are you sure you want to take Clifford on this trip? You've never taken anyone with you on these kinds of trips before."

"Don't worry. I won't work him too hard the first time out," he replied pleased that the subject had changed.

46

"What about the bears, Buck?" Harper asked as he turned towards him to look his friend straight in the eye. "You're not going to let him get close to the bears, are you?"

Buck looked at Jim and hesitated for a moment, then replied seriously. "I won't let him see the bears. He won't even know they're there. I guarantee it."

That made Jim feel better. Turning, he watched the suburban pull in and come to a stop in front of them.

"Well, I'd better be going. There're things to get done before we leave." Buck said, walking towards the suburban. He stopped and turned around. "By the way, I put a few trout in the smoker. I prepared them with a little extra brown sugar, just the way you like them. If you come out for dinner when we get back, you can have all you want."

Jim's mouth began to water as he thought of it. If there was one thing Buck was good at it was smoking fish. Actually, anything he put in the smoker came out delicious. "You can count on it. Give me a call when you get back."

With that, Buck got in the passenger side of the vehicle and it drove away. Waving as it left, Jim stood on the sidewalk and watched it disappear out of sight. He would make it out there this week, he knew, but not for the reason he thought. Jim turned and walked back into the station. Rounding the counter he stopped Milhouse as he passed. "Did you make the call to the field?"

"Yes, sir. Shaffer will be up in the air first thing tomorrow."

"What about the notice. Have you got one ready for the information center yet?"

"No not yet."

"Well get on it, I want that trail closed off," Jim ordered.

"Why do we have to do this anyway?" Milhouse complained. "We're *always* doing things for the Forest Service. We're too busy as it is to do their work for them."

"We've been over this before, Tom. It was decided a long time ago, both the Forest Service and the Sheriff's department were short staffed. I fought hard for an extra deputy so the County Council and I came up with this solution. I would get the extra deputy as long as we did a few things for the Forest Service," Jim was starting to get tired of explaining these issues, but told himself to be more patient.

"But the Forest Service is Federal, *not* County. It doesn't make sense," Milhouse replied.

"If you're asking me to explain how the bureaucratic bean counters figured it all out, I can't. All I know is I got the deputy I needed, and it takes a little more work now and then to keep him. Now is that too much to ask?" Jim asked.

Milhouse thought about it then shrugged. "No, I guess not."

"Good, now get to work on that notice."

"Yes sir," Milhouse replied. He then returned to his desk.

Jim stepped back over to the coffee pot where he'd left his cup. Filling it to the top, he walked into his office and sat at his desk. "Another exciting day at the station," he said to himself as he looked at the pile of paperwork in front of him. Jim took a big gulp of coffee, opened the first folder, and started reading.

4
Security

Forest Service Trail 74

The noon sun broke through the canopy of the trees, flooding the clearing with sunshine. Barely large enough for a small camp, the clearing was surrounded on all sides by tall, thick cedars making it hard for a low flying aircraft to spot. It was also far enough off the main trail as to go unnoticed by any passer bys, or so the man thought a few months ago while scouting out new locations.

The straps of the heavy pack cut deep into his shoulders as he pushed through the last of the brush and stepped into the clearing. Walking to the center of it he slowly took the pack off, gently lowered it to the ground, and went down on one knee breathing hard, trying to catch his breath.

As the sweat poured off his bald black head and down his face, it made his goatee itch. After scratching at it furiously, he carefully took a look around. As expected, the 8x10 green canvas tent that he and the others had set up earlier in the morning was undisturbed.

I'm too old *for this kind of work.* He lifted his head in an attempt to breath in as much air as possible. *But that would soon change.* Not yet thirty, he had done well for himself. Selling illegal drugs on the streets at a young age, he'd worked hard and learned from the fatal mistakes of others.

When he was young, he learned the value of making a good impression. During daily dealings with his superiors, he learned to talk and act like they did. He wanted them to see him as one of them, not just another street punk. Giving up the street slang, he started using words such as raw materials, product, and return on investment.

Soon after making these changes, he was noticed by one of the bosses in the Organization who moved him from sales into production. There he quickly learned that security was crucial— either you had it or you didn't. That's why the locations he used remained a secret known only by himself. This made some of the bosses nervous at first, but they couldn't argue with the results. Always producing a quality product on time, the man had never lost a shipment to their competition or been busted. This made him a prime candidate to move into the "business" side of the Organization.

A smile spread across his face as he thought about it. There's more money and less work to be had on the business side, which was a fitting reward for his years of faithful service. All he had to do now is find a replacement to take over production, and success would be his.

That's what this trip was all about, after all. This is the final weeding out process. It had taken a long time, but he had to make sure his successor was both worthy and capable of taking over. If he wasn't, it would reflect poorly on him and that he couldn't allow. So, he would invest all time and effort needed to be certain his successor was not only smart, but had large stones as well. Suddenly, from the direction in which he'd come, a noise in the brush caught his attention.

"Tommy? Tommy! Where are you?" A young woman's voice exclaimed. Speaking of investments, he had many and with each he expected a healthy profit.

Finally pushing her way through, the young woman stumbled into the clearing and collapsed onto a log close to Tommy. "Ouch! Tommy, I've got blisters on my feet," she complained.

He looked her over. Beads of sweat were rolling down her face as she pulled some of the long curly blond hair off her forehead. Panting to catch her breath, he couldn't help but notice the way her chest stretched out the clean white tank top under her open jacket.

She was young and fresh, just the way he liked them. But that, too, would soon change. His eyes walked down her body, past the short raggedy cutoffs, down her skinny white legs, and to her feet.

"Why aren't you wearing the hiking boots I bought you?"

"They made my feet look too big, so I didn't bring them," she replied.

"Well, don't worry," he said kindly, "you won't have to do anymore walking until we leave in a few days."

"Oh, good." Relief flooded her voice. She paused, before asking the question that had been haunting her since she'd left the car.

"Tommy?"

"Yeah."

"Do you have any more...*stuff?*"

He looked at her closely. He'd seen it so many times before, even studied it so he could use it to his advantage. Her hands were slightly shaky and the discomfort on her face was from much more than aching feet. *She is close*, he thought, *but not quite ready yet.* He'd make her wait a little longer.

"Be patient, baby. In a few hours you'll be up to your neck in it," he replied, turning to look toward the trees. "Where are the guys?"

"I don't know," she shrugged. Maybe they got lost."

Tommy struggled to his feet. His neck and back ached from the pack, but then again the numerous gold chains hanging around his neck weren't helping either, he knew. Normally he wouldn't be wearing them or the large rings and Rolex on a trip like this, but this time they were essential.

This time he had subordinates with him, and that meant he needed to portray an image of success for them to admire and respect. It also gave them a very important goal to shoot for. All of the sudden, the brush started moving, not from the direction he and the girl had come, but from somewhere to his right.

"That must be them now," the girl said without looking up.

It probably was, he thought, staring in the direction of the rustling brush. The chance of being followed was slim, but not impossible. He hadn't lasted this long by being careless. Bending down he opened the pack, and drew out a shiny black oozy.

Pulling the bolt back, he loaded a round into the chamber and walked towards the noise. Someone or something was definitely moving their way. He stepped behind a tree and peered cautiously around it. Abruptly two Asian teenage boys with packs on their shoulders stepped out of the trees.

"Damn! This packs heavy!" the first one exclaimed, walking into the center of the clearing. Taking the pack off, he gently rested it on the ground. The other teen was too winded to speak. He pulled the strap off of one shoulder and let the pack fall to the ground with a thud.

"*Hey!* The scale is in that one!" Tommy barked.

51

Surprised by the sudden appearance, the two teens wheeled around quickly. Tommy walked over to the pack, opened it up, and removed the delicate object.

"Without a scale, the operation is over," he hissed angrily. "You better pray it's all right." After first zeroing it out, he removed a series of metric weights from a box. Placing each on one at a time, he checked the reading carefully.

"It looks like you got lucky," Tommy sighed with relief. "But remember, always be gentle with the equipment. You didn't pack it all the way up here just to break it."

"So when do we start making toot?" one of the boys inquired.

Standing up, Tommy addressed them in a serious manner. "You're not on the street anymore. People in the Organization refer to it as *product.*"

The teenager shrugged. "So when do we start making *product?*" he asked again.

"Just as soon as you two are done hauling the rest of the gear up. We'll finish setting up camp, then start the first batch."

"Just us!? Hey, man, this stuff is heavy. How bout giving us a hand," the other youth complained.

"You're here to learn how a production site works. Part of that is packing in and setting up your equipment. I helped out this morning, but, from now on, I'm just here to school ya," Tommy answered.

"But you're gonna score a lot more green from this shipment than us. It's not fair that—"

"—*Shut up!*" Tommy barked, cutting him off. "I'm tired of all the complaints! Everyone in the Organization started out the same way you are. The first thing you'd better get through your thick skulls is that the people who work hard, keep their mouth shut, and do what they're told make it in and move their way up. Those that don't...*Don't!*"

The two teens stared at him in silence, understanding the threat.

"*Anymore* questions?" Tommy asked.

After a moment, one of them quietly spoke up. "What about the girl? Is she going to help?"

"She stays."

"Then what good is she? She's just been getting in the way."

Tommy turned to look at the girl, making sure she was out of earshot before replying.

"She's entertainment," he said, turning back to them. The teens gave him a confused look.

"Think of her as an incentive. If you work hard and put out a quality product on schedule, I'll let you have your fun."

The eyes of the two teens narrowed and wicked grins replaced their previous looks of bewilderment.

"Now, you've got two packs, fishing rods, and a cooler left to bring up." Tommy said. He checked his Rolex. "If you hurry, you can have it all up here with one trip in about an hour."

"What? How are we going to do all that in one hour?"

"Be creative, but gentle," he replied. "And remember, the quicker the work gets done, the more time there is for *recreation*. Now get moving."

Both teens exchanged looks, then turned and ran into the trees at a sprint.

Tommy chuckled. *All companies should work on the incentive program*, he thought. You get so much more from the work force. He really didn't expect them to be back in an hour, probably closer to two. But they'd try, and that's all that mattered. Besides, he needed the extra time to do what he'd planned next. Turning around, he looked over at the girl. She sat, eyes closed, with a painful look on her face rubbing her feet.

He had done this so many times that he had it down cold. After all, she was just one in a long line of girls he'd brought into circulation. Like a crisp brand new dollar bill, everyone wanted to hold it in their hands and use it. That's how the bill got past around from person to person. Each person received it, used it, then passed it on. So it would be with her.

He had a lot invested in her. It took *months* of fancy gifts and all the free party she could handle to get her to this point. Now, she was completely dependent on him, and it was time to get a return from his investment. After all, what was she expecting? Nothing comes without a price.

Afterwards she would drown herself in product until she could coup with it, but that was normal. They all did that. It also made them easier to manage, so he didn't mind. Then in a few weeks, after she develops the proper attitude for business, he'll have her out on the streets peddling both herself *and* the product making him rich.

Ha! The beauty of it, he thought as he examined her closely. Her hands were shaking so bad she couldn't rub her feet, and the look on her face was shear agony. *Oh yeah, she's ready.* Reaching into his shirt pocket, he pulled out a small plastic bag of white powder. "Hey, baby, look what I've got for ya!"

The girl's eyes lit up at the sight of the bag. "Oh Tommy! I just *knew* you wouldn't forget me!" she exclaimed as she ran over to him.

Tommy lifted the bag in the air out of her reach, which brought an alarmed look to her face. "*Please*, Tommy! I really need it *bad!*" she pleaded.

"Then I guess its time you show me how bad you need it," he replied coldly, putting the bag back in his pocket.

It took a moment, but when she realized what he meant the bewildered expression on her face changed to one of shock, then fear. Instantly, she tried stepping away, but his hand gripped her arm firmly. He held her tightly as he walked her to the tent. Lifting the canvas door flap out of the way, he stepped inside pulling her in with him. He released the flap. It closed silently behind them.

In the bush next to the tent, an unsuspecting butterfly landed in a web. The spider quickly pounced, trapping it in silk. Gripping it tightly, the spider carried the doomed butterfly back to its lair to be devoured.

That evening, Buck and Clifford sat on the bench of the covered porch at Buck's home. Clifford surveyed his surroundings. They sat silently enjoying the view. Fifty yards in front of the house, and just slightly to the right, were the gravel shores of Mineral Lake. The sapphire blue, kidney shaped water stretched out a quarter of a mile to the opposite beach. Encircling the lake, tall Douglas Firs cut sharply into the evening sky, almost rivaling the snow tipped mountains on either side. Bushy, fat cedars filled in spaces between them, the darker green color breaking up the humbling forest of giants nicely.

Clifford gazed down from the porch of Buck's single story cedar log home. He let his eyes slowly travel over the gravel landscape, which stretched the distance between him and the lake, and studied the small aluminum boat tied fast to the dock Buck had built some years ago. To his left, Clifford could see the large, old, gray cedar barn used as shelter for the animals. The front of it faced the lake, similar to the house, but at perpendicular angle so as to look down the shoreline on his right instead of the left.

Making up more than half of its front face, the barn's two large, heavy doors were a pain in the butt to open and close. He had found that out earlier when he'd fed the mules. A pair of identical doors were in the back leading to a corral behind the barn.

He let his gaze move slowly up the brushy hill, behind the corral, and then to the tree line not much higher than the barn. Looking farther left, he could barely make out the private dirt road cutting though the trees and down the hill, separating the two buildings. Both buildings had matching lofty green metal roofs angled sharply to let the deep winter snow slide easily off.

The courtyard was triangular in shape, with the lake shore being the longest side and the faces of both buildings at almost ninety degrees to each other. Clifford took a drink from his can of grape soda then closed his eyes, breathing deeply in mountain air.

"Ya know, Uncle Buck," he exhaled, still taking in the view. "This is the kind of place where a guy can really relax."

Buck didn't answer. He just looked around slowly and smiled, knowing Clifford's statement was accurate.

Ding!

A small bell rang to Clifford's right. He looked over towards the end of the porch where a circular wooden object about three feet in diameter was attached to the side railing. He examined it closely. Its front surface was smooth, except for a section missing near the top like a piece cut from a pie. Dividing the middle of this piece was a dark horizontal line.

Actually, they were two separate pieces, he noticed. The top half had a bright orange "8" painted on it, and the bottom piece had a "00". As Clifford watched it, the bottom pieces rotated to the right, disappearing behind the cover, and was replaced by a piece with "05" painted on it.

"Where did you get this weird clock?" he inquired.

Buck turned, looked at the clock, and smiled. "I built it a few months ago when I was snowed in," he replied proudly.

"No way!" Clifford remarked surprised. "You never mentioned you were an engineer."

Buck snapped to attention, seeing the opportunity to show off his latest creation. "I just like to tinker," he commented. "I got the plans from an old copy of *Popular Science* and most of the parts came from the dump." Buck stood up and walked over to the clock. "Let me show you." Clifford got up and followed him.

"Ya see, rain water comes off the roof into the gutter and flows into this trough. The water is stored there and drains through this small copper tube into the top of the clock."

Reaching around the clock, Buck pulled out a pin on either side of the front cover then removed it. As the inner workings were revealed, a huge smile came over Buck's face. He observed it with pride. Inside were two old bicycle wheels set one behind the other, and each without a rim.

They were just gear hubs with an axle running though both and spokes sticking out from the center. Both spokes had a thin wooden shingle attached to the end. The wheel closest to them had twenty short spokes with minutes of the hour painted on the shingles in five-minute increments. The second wheel had twelve longer spokes with the number of the hour on each shingle.

"How does it work?" Clifford asked.

"The copper tube runs from the trough to the small turbine in the back." Buck pointed to a small black box in the back of the compartment. Clifford looked at it closely and noticed it emitting a slight hum. "The water turns the turbine which spin this gear in front of it," Buck continued. "It's attached to this set of reduction gears. They then turn the bicycle wheels that tell you what time it is."

The pair watched fascinated as the minute wheel rotated from the "05" shingle to the "10" shingle. "The hour wheel rings this bell each time it turns." Buck indicated a small brass bell hanging from the top of the inside housing.

"Then the water comes out of the bottom of the turbine, though another copper tube." Clifford said as he followed the tube with his finger. "And comes out the back of the clock and onto the ground."

"Very good," Buck remarked. "You'll make a good engineer yet."

Clifford looked at the clock, then to his watch curiously. "Your clock is almost an hour slow."

"Oh yeah, I've been having some trouble with the timing. I think the turbine's regulating orifice is too small," Buck frowned. "It loses about an hour per week."

"Maybe when we get back from our trip, I can help you fix it," Clifford offered.

"Hey! Great idea! I could use a good assistant," Buck replied enthusiastically. "Your first job is to help me get this cover back on."

Helping Buck lift the cover back in place, Clifford took one pin and slipped it into its hole while Buck did the same on the other end. Clifford then turned, leaned over the rail, and looked out at the lake. Buck returned to his chair. He picked up his glass and took a drink.

After a few moments, Clifford spoke up, "Uncle Buck?"

"Yeah?"

"How is it that you've never gotten married?"

Buck nearly choked on his beverage in surprise. "*What! You mean like to a woman?*"

Laughing, Clifford confirmed. "Yeah, to a woman."

Buck calmed himself then rested a foot on the chair next to him before answering. "A woman would make me give up all this," he spread his arms out to encompass their surroundings. "Oh sure, when I was younger I entertained the idea of falling in love and having a few rug rats, but I couldn't find a woman who'd put up with me. I know they look nice and smell good, but that doesn't last long and by that time you're stuck with em.

"Women!" Buck said with disgust. "Take it from me kid, I've seen it all my life. Why does a woman fall in love with a man do ya suppose? I'll tell ya. A woman becomes attracted to a man's independence. They see a man who is in control of his life, someone who's adventurous and exciting. They'd like to be that way too, but can't. So, a woman feeds off a man's life like a leach! I've seen it happen too many times, and to some of my closest friends. A man and a woman fall in love, get married, she moves in, and what do you think she does first?" He looked at Clifford questioningly.

Clifford just shrugged, unknowingly.

"She throws away all his stuff!" Bucked continued his rant, not missing a beat. "Everything he's collected over the years. The very things that define his entire existence as a man—*gone!*"

Buck shook a bony finger at Clifford. "And that's just the first step and it doesn't all happen over night either. It takes years. She makes him play house till his head falls off. She twists and bends his mind till she's made him into what she *thinks* she wants him to be. Sure, it takes ten to twenty years to do it, but she'll succeed. Then one day she'll look at him and wonder why she fell in love with him in the first place. Wonder why he isn't a man anymore. Then she'll leave him for another man and the process starts all over again. And *why?* Because there hasn't been a woman created that really knows what she wants! They just think they do."

Clifford listened intently as Buck rambled on. "A woman is like a lumberjack who goes into the forest and finds a tall wonderful tree. Instead of leaving it alone and admiring it she has got to chop it down and take it home with her. When the needles turn brown and fall off she'll wonder why it died, and she'll go out looking for another one to chop down. I've never gotten married because there has never been a woman created who can fit into a man's life without taking control. No, sir, there's no such animal!"

A moment later, Buck laughed at himself. "Look at me. You shouldn't let me get on my soap box, kid, I may never stop."

Ding!

They both looked to see that the water clock said nine o'clock, which really meant ten. Reddish light from the burning cigar lit up Buck's face as he puffed it. "You'd better hit the hay, son. We have to be on the trail early tomorrow."

"Okay." Clifford yawned, taking one more look around. "I'll see you in the morning." He walked past Buck, through the front door and disappeared.

Buck stood up slowly, pulled his arms up and stretched. Then he took a deep breath of fresh air and smiled. Putting the cigar back in his mouth, he walked into the house and closed the door behind him.

He walked through the living room and turned left into the kitchen. At the sink, he dumped the ice from his finished drink into the drain. Slowly lifting a stack of dirty dishes out of the full sink and carefully placed them on the already cluttered counter.

Women, Buck thought to himself, filling his glass with water. *A woman would nag me to do these dishes.* Buck took a drink, then put the glass down. He took one last puff from the stub of his cigar, before stuffing it out in the full ash tray beside him. *She'd tell me I couldn't smoke in the house,* he thought as he took the ash tray over to a twenty gallon garbage bag laying on the floor in the corner and emptied it. *She'd tell me to throw out this trash too, and the bags not even half full!*

Women are such wasteful creatures. In fact, it was a woman who threw out that couch, he looked into the living room at the lime green couch against the wall. *She'd said it was out of style.* Sure, it had a broken leg, but he propped it up on a piece of fire wood and it worked just fine.

It was the some story for the brown and gold chair in the corner. In fact almost half of what he owned he'd *rescued* from a trash heap at the local dump. His friend Tony Marcellous, the proprietor of the county landfill, had always let him hunt around for little treasures. Like the coffee table he had made from an old door and four spent mortar casings he found laying around. Or the lamp he'd made from a chipped bowling pin.

Heck! He thought, *a woman would destroy my creative nature.* Buck was known far and wide as being somewhat of a pack rat, but he considered himself to be a serious collector—admittedly, with unrefined tastes.

The rest of the stuff was his, however. His whole life was in this room. There were pictures on the wall of his platoon in Korea in the fifties, and then some more from Vietnam in the sixties. He'd been a career soldier most of his life and had collected a wall full of metals and memorabilia from the other side of the world. *That seems so long ago and so far away now,* he thought sadly.

Then there was his trophy bull elk and mule deer buck heads he'd mounted on each wall facing each other. Looking at them proudly, he almost laughed out loud. He rebuilt the entire roof just so the elk antlers would fit.

Besides the black and white TV in the corner, the most technologically advanced item he owned was the lava lamp. Green and gold globs slowly moved within the goo inside. It sat on the mantle next to his whiskey bottle collection and stuffed steelhead trout.

The whiskey bottles he had were from all over the world. He didn't care much for wine or beer but he sure loved his whiskey. He'd heard that so called sophisticated men collected wine in bottles as an investment. He wrinkled up his nose in disgust at the thought of it.

His bottles were empty, of course, and he wondered how anyone could collect something all their lives without sampling its contents. He'd also heard of beer-of-the-month clubs where you received a different beer each month from around the world. *It's too bad they didn't have a whiskey-of-the-month club,* he thought. *Now that would be something.*

In the far corner was his gun collection. He had a number of rifles, depending on what game he was after as well as a few shot guns. He also had the machine gun he used in Korea and the M-16 from Vietnam. Those he didn't fire them anymore. Unlike the other firearms, these were used to kill men and he prayed he'd never have to do that again.

Next to the gun cabinet was his fishing gear. He owned an assortment of poles from heavy lake rods to light fly and spinning rods. Over the years, he'd turned this part of the business into a science.

Next was a book shelf and in it was his collection of *Popular Science* magazines. He started collecting them when he first built this place over thirty years ago, and still had every issue. Most of the old ones were boxed in the attic. He couldn't bring himself to throw any of them away because each contained plans for something he knew he'd get around to building someday.

The shelves also contained a few favorite books as well as his scrapbook where he kept newspaper clippings pertaining to this area. His journal was also there. He didn't know why he wrote in it or kept it. He only seemed to write during the winter months when there was nothing else to do besides drink, and he'd done a *lot* of that.

Buck walked over to the light switch and turned it off. A soft glow came from the fire place. Bending down, he picked up a log and threw it on the fire.

Buck then turned and walked toward his room. Coming to the door he stopped, looking over his shoulder and observing the living room as flames quickly engulfed the new log sending streams of orange light dancing against the opposite wall. He frowned as he thought of what a woman might do to this room, glad that he wasn't a slave to such ideas as style, fashion or color coordination. Women just didn't understand. *Yes*, he smiled to himself. *This was his man cave. And only a man could love it.*

Buck opened the bedroom door and walked into the darkness. Kicking off his shoes, he stepped over the pile of dirty clothes he knew would be there. Without bothering to take off his clothes, Buck lay on his bed and belched loudly. He reached over and pulled the covers on top of him as he farted loudly. Buck then smiled to himself. A woman would probably tell him he couldn't do *that* anymore either. He rolled over, and a moment later began to snore.

5

The Kennedy Solution

Seattle. Monday Evening.

The private G3 jumped off the SeaTac Airport runway and raced for the sky. Punching a hole in the clouds, it banked left around Mt. Rainier then reached its cruising altitude before leveling off. Alan Bradley Sr. sipped the drink the stewardess had given him, as the flight crew of his private plane settled in for its five hour flight.

From the window beside him, he could see the orange-yellow brilliance of sunset fade behind the plane as they sped off into the darkness ahead. They were headed east, back to DC, where Senior could continue to labor on his son's behalf.

Alan was a man driven by ambition. Struggling most of his young life, he worked sixteen hour days as a salesman in the plastics industry. Reinvesting everything he made, he quickly put together a small fortune and started his own company.

Now, it took more than just hard work and dedication to make it. When you started playing with the big boys, you had to learn the new rules to the game of success. Connections needed to be made and loyalties had to be declared. Golf games and fancy parties with other CEOs and big investors became weekly events.

Politics also became a fruitful field of influence that he cultivated. The right contribution to the right election campaign got you the right government contracts and Alan Bradley Sr. played this game better than anyone. It didn't take him long before he completely dominated his competitors. He soon had more money than he thought he could possibly spend, and wealth suddenly lost meaning to him.

It was then that he realized *power* was the only useful yard stick to measure true success. He decided to make a change and set his sights on the most powerful position in the world. Someday, he vowed, he would be President of the United States of America.

Suddenly, political ties became more important. He became the election fund raising chairman for several Senators and Representatives. Working for Richard Nixon, he not only made a sizable contribution of his own, but called in every IOU and favor ever made to him to help in the election. For his help, Alan was given the title of Personal Advisor on Economics to the President of the United States.

His loyalties were clearly established. There was nothing he hadn't done to help this administration and he fully intended to reap the rewards. He had one hand on a rung of the ladder to power and the other was on Nixon's coat tails. Using both, he was determined to eventually reach the Oval Office.

Alan Sr. worked on his public image. He donated large sums of money to good causes and married into a politically powerful family. He only spent enough time with his new bride to have a son, Alan Bradley Jr. After which, he only came in contact with his wife and son for special events and holiday parties.

This completed the picture he wanted to show the public. Here was a man who was generous, good at business, and a loving husband and father. Who wouldn't want him as the next leader of the Free World? The facts didn't matter, it was how the public *perceived* those facts that did.

Along with the rewards, political ties have their costs. Alan Sr. soon found himself caught up in the Watergate scandal. Not just a little bit, but neck deep in it. While trying to keep Watergate out of the press, he was caught red handed attempting to destroy evidence and committing perjury to a Grand Jury.

It took every political favor and bribe he could come up with to keep himself out of prison. He was now politically in ruins. Deciding to cut his loses, Alan Sr. left Washington DC with the hope that one day he could rekindle his political career. Like a football team who no longer has a use for certain players, he put the wife and child that he never loved on permanent waivers.

He entered the computer software business and quickly accelerated his wealth. Several times he tried to use that wealth to push his way back into politics. Every campaign and administration was very happy to take his money, but he himself was just too hot of a potato. Some things you just can't bounce back from and he resigned himself to the realization that he would never hold the highest office in the land.

However, he still was determined his thirst for power was not to go unsatisfied. If he couldn't get there himself, then he must resort to plan B- *The Kennedy solution.*

Alan Sr. considered himself to be very similar to Joseph Kennedy. They were both among the mega-rich of their time. They both had a desire for power and both wanted to be President. They had both used their money to secure influential political positions. And both had been cast out of political favor.

He recalled that Joe Kennedy had been appointed Ambassador to England, under the Roosevelt administration. While there he was of the opinion that the United States should not enter the war against Hitler. Instead, he preached that Europe should take care of their own problems. This isolationist view was unpopular with the people and proved to be his downfall. His unyielding stance and outspoken manner sealed his political tomb—he would *never* be accepted as a leader by the American people.

Joe Kennedy's lust for power found new life in his son John. John F. Kennedy had just returned from the Pacific as a war hero. Joe arranged for John to marry into a politically influential family. Every advantage Joe could get was used to accelerate John's political career. What resulted was the creation of one of the most popular presidents in history. Also, the Kennedys became one of the most powerful and influential families in the world. Alan Bradley Sr. intended to do the same thing for his son, and share in the powerful dynasty that resulted.

Alan Sr. restarted a relationship with his son immediately. When Alan Jr. was only ten, Alan Sr. began to mold him into his own image. They were very much alike, so it wasn't hard to do. When the time was right, Senior told Junior of his secret plan. Alan Jr. loved the idea and couldn't wait to get started.

Started? Alan Sr.'s plan was suddenly dead in its tracks. He had planned for everything else except how to launch his son into the limelight. John Kennedy had been in the military, fought in a war and came back a hero. Everyone loves a hero.

Should Alan Jr. join the military? That idea wasn't popular with Junior. There were just too many rules and too much discipline and Alan Jr. was not one who took orders well. Besides, in order to become a hero, there had to be a war first and wars were just too unpredictable to be reliable. While Senior pondered the different ways that he could start one, Junior came up with the solution.

Why not law enforcement? Wasn't there already a war against drugs? You had an enemy to fight, battles to wage and it all could be done without digging a ditch or eating sea rations. Besides, it was politically popular because you didn't have to win. All you had to do was show that you put a serious dent in the situation and everyone will love you for it.

Senior thought it ironic that his connection to Richard Nixon had been his political undoing. However, it was President Nixon that declared a global war on drugs, and by executive order, created the Drug Enforcement Agency, or DEA. Without knowing it, Nixon created the means by which Junior would continue on Senior's ambitious path to power.

It was *brilliant.* His son was a chip off the old block. For every potential problem, they'd come up with an answer. Senior would continue to make connections in both the political and social arenas, greasing the political skids, so that Junior could quickly and easily slide from the west coast into the DC beltway.

When Junior finished college, Senior's connections would ensure a position in the Drug Enforcement Agency. He'd be assigned to a branch on the west coast, preferably in Seattle, so that his progress could be closely monitored by his father.

For his part, Junior had to work hard as well. He had to finish college with high marks, make influential contacts of his own, and nurture the relationships that Senior had established for him. But most of all, he had to make a name for himself. Junior needed to solve high profile cases to establish a record of distinguished service.

Senior had just started the process of interviewing politically influential families who had daughters old enough for marriage. Arranged marriages were nothing new, and he was determined to find the absolute best match for his son's career. Once the initial inquiries were made, he knew, the other families would start the process of investigating Alan Jr. They'd want to know what they were getting, so Senior decided that he had to know what they would find. He launched an investigation of his own, and the results had surprised and disturbed him.

At first, everything looked fairly normal. Junior's grades were exceptional and he graduated at the top of his class with honors. After checking into a few inconsistencies, however, a small group of people had been uncovered who had information that was unsettling.

It seems that Alan Jr.'s record wasn't entirely clear of blemishes. A few campus security guards, one police officer and even the dean of students had dirt on Junior. During Alan's college days, he had received a large number of parking tickets and one DUI, all of which mysteriously disappeared. Junior had bribed the guards and the cop to have it all just go away.

Unfortunately, the dean of students caught wind of what was going on and eventually found out the truth and wanted to expel Alan Jr. The dean believed that a person as unethical as Junior had no business being in the criminal justice field. However, Junior was able to find the dean's price tag as well. It was expensive, but not unreasonable and the whole matter was swept under the rug.

Even though the paper trail was destroyed, the word of mouth evidence was still out there. Alan Sr. had his investigators secretly video tape the people involved confessing to the bribes. He also checked into their pasts to find other incriminating facts. Using both, Senior was able to use the information to silence them forever. If they ever spoke of the situation again, then the incriminating information now in Senior's safe would be released and their lives would be destroyed.

Although Senior was shocked to find out what Junior had done, he couldn't help but be proud of him. Junior had learned to take care of his own problems without running to daddy for help. Still, he was very surprised at Junior's actions. Senior had used bribery and blackmail like an art form, but he never tried to teach these tactics to Junior. Was he so blind and foolish to think that his own son wasn't watching his father and learning? Junior was a very smart person, with an exceptional IQ, and he always got strait A's without bringing home a single book.

For all their similarities, there were a few areas in which father and son were complete opposites. Senior knew what it was like to be poor, working hard long hours struggling to get to the top. Junior had not experienced these things, and Senior believed that the life of privilege had made Junior somewhat lazy and sloppy.

A few hours ago they had argued about the situation. Senior wanted Junior to stay out of trouble, and avoid situations that could come back to haunt them. Junior had always resisted any attempts by his father to control him but this time yielded to his wishes. Senior didn't want to smother Junior's young instinctive energy, just temper it a little.

Senior had a business to run. A few years ago, he had started Titan Industries, a telecommunications company, which he'd since driven to the top of the industry. This month they would be launching the first of hundreds of communications satellites into orbit, and Senior was needed at the helm of the company. He didn't have time to be mopping up after his son.

Senior looked out the window. It was completely dark now. The only thing he saw was a twisted ghostly reflection of himself staring back at him from the glass. Senior pondered that in sad frustration. Knowing his son well, he wondered if Junior could ever be counted on to control himself.

But he couldn't worry about that now, he decided. A bride had to be found, and the sooner the better. Alan Sr. put down his drink and opened the file in front of him. It was a list of prospective candidates. Each young woman was listed and ranked according to family wealth and political influence. Senior had a team of investigators looking into the pasts of all of them. Sadly, he had already been forced to cross off two of the most promising candidates for various reasons.

"Kids, these days," he said in frustration. "They just don't know how to be discrete." He flipped open the file of the next candidate in line and began to study it.

Alan Bradley Jr. opened the refrigerator and pulled a bottle of Red Hook from the door. Taking a frosty mug from the freezer, he poured the contents of the bottle into it, then walked towards the deck of his high rise condo near the Seattle water front. He'd just finished meeting with his father, and their conversation deeply troubled him. Alan walked out onto the deck and peered up at the sky. It had stopped raining more than an hour ago and the clouds were starting to break up. A few faint stars appeared between the clouds, as the last rays of the yellow-orange brilliance of sunset faded over the Olympics. He could see the tower of billowing clouds just past the mountains and he knew *that* storm would be hitting Seattle sometime in the middle of the night.

Too bad, he thought. He had hoped for good weather, but it didn't look like he would be getting any. That wasn't the storm he should worry about, though. He and his father had argued and he had learned that disagreements with him were almost always lost. His father was also usually right, so Alan had come to trust his judgment.

During this particular disagreement they found very little middle ground. His father had checked up on Alan's college life, a prudent decision. He only wished that he had thought of it first. Alan had been too confident that his bribes would silence any future skeletons that could come back to haunt him.

Junior was wrong, however, and this was a point his father drove home all too well. For his part, Alan had learned another valuable lesson. Next time he'd check up on himself first.

He had also discovered two new tools to add to his arsenal—blackmail and discreditation. If the initial bribe didn't work to cover his tracks, the other two weapons could be used effectively. His father's words still rang annoyingly in his ears.

"Why can't you be more like your friends?" he had lectured him. Alan had grown up back east and spent most of his time there with a particular group of guys. Alan never really considered them his friends, just guys he associated with because they were from powerfully influential families.

More like his friends, *indeed.* Alan scoffed at the idea as he took a long drink of his micro-brew. How could his father have suggested such a thing?

Growing up back east, his friends were always long on talk, but little in action. Alan liked to take chances. When he drove, he liked to speed. While skiing, he would try to break the downhill records. He was the only one of their group to brave the huge pipeline waves of Hawaii. While the others watched from the safety of the beach, Alan rode the largest and most dangerous of waves into shore.

He remembered the criticism he had received when they found out he was moving west for college to study criminal justice. They thought he was throwing his life away. To them, if it wasn't an ivy league school, it was worthless. And if you didn't work and reside within one of the original thirteen states you were *nothing.*

The plans Alan and his father had devised, required that he move west. From his mother's side of the family, Alan already had contacts and influence in the east. Now he needed to establish a power base in the west. With his father's help, he planned on molding a successful career and powerful backing into a huge wave that he could ride across the country and into the Oval Office.

Alan wasn't like his friends and didn't want to be. They were stuffed shirts that sat in board meetings and went to power lunches, while he craved the danger and excitement of the calculated risk. He liked the heightened senses and the adrenaline rush that came from putting your life on the edge.

You had to be mentally prepared, for anything could happen during a drug bust. Alan had played countless scenarios in his head, training himself for all the possibilities so that he would never hesitate. A fraction of a second hesitation could get you killed. This he had learned just a few months ago.

They had a crack dealer pinned down in a house outside of town. The dealer barricaded himself inside, and the team of agents couldn't get close enough to the front door without being fired upon. Alan went around the side of the house and dove through a window. He rolled and came up staring directly into the eyes of the enemy just a few feet away.

Alan had prepared himself well enough that he could let his instinct react quickly without the thought process interfering. It seemed like slow motion as he pulled his gun around towards the dealer. Alan saw a moment of fear and doubt in his enemy's eyes.

The dealer quickly brought his gun around, but that half second of hesitation allowed Alan to reach a firing position first and pull the trigger. The dealer fired too, but he was late and off line. The slug sizzled harmlessly past Alan's head.

Could his friends do that? Would they be confident enough, sure enough, or quick enough? Did they have the *balls?*

Alan cocked an eyebrow at his own questions and grinned. *Not hardly.* It was for these same reasons that none of his friends could succeed on the path that Alan and his father had planned. It was Alan's sharp unwavering instinct that would see him through on this journey. The same instinct that told him to press on quickly.

His father was concerned about Alan's excessive partying and womanizing. He had put his butt on the line many times and after which he had an uncontrollable desire to taste the best of the fruits of life. So *what* if he satisfied those desires.

He would not be judged by others who didn't take the same risks that he did, and he had no intentions of living by the same rules and standards either. Still, his father had a point about image. How would it look to the public if a group of bimbos surfaced during his election campaign? By no means did he plan on cutting back these pleasures, but he would definitely be more discrete.

The plan was all mapped out. By summer, Junior would force his boss, Deputy Director Cranston, out of his job and fill in the position. Before this time next year, he'd start his campaign to unseat Adam Demsey for Mayor of Seattle. After one term in Seattle, he and his father would "encourage" the Governor to retire as well as endorse Alan for the office. From there, he would be able to launch himself into presidential contention.

Alan Bradley Jr. loved the danger of his current job and lifestyle, and was not in anyway looking forward to spending all his time in committees and meetings. However, he thirsted for the power that came with political office, and he couldn't wait to get a taste of it. If everything went according to plan, he'd soon be switching gears. Before that happened, however, he planned on squeezing every ounce of excitement out of his current position.

Alan felt drops of rain upon his face as he took another drink of his beer. Perhaps the storm was closer than he had anticipated. Alan stepped back into the living room of his condominium, securely closing the French doors behind him.

6
Demons to Exorcise

Morton Field. Tuesday Morning.

Forest Service pilot, Rick Schaffer, sat in the cockpit of his
PBY at the end of the tarmac, waiting for clearance to takeoff. His
aircraft was known as the Catalina Flying Boat, because of its wing
tip pontoons and contoured reinforced underbelly. Because of these
features, Rick's aircraft was as adept at takeoffs and landings on
water as it was on any airport runway.

It was just barely dawn, just light enough to see into the
shadows. Despite the low light, the white aircraft, with its red stripe
down either side, seemed to glow compared to its surroundings.

Rick had rushed through his preflight checks. Everything
would be perfect, as it always was. Not a moment after the engine
temperature gauges had came off low, Rick pushed the throttle
forward easing his plane close to the runway.

"Come on, come on. Hurry up would ya," he mumbled
urgently under his breath. He was anxious to get in the air. The
dream had come back again and he hadn't slept well. It was a cool
morning, forty-three degrees and mostly cloudy, yet he felt
uncomfortably warm and confined. His breathing became deeper
and more rapid as small beads of perspiration appeared on his
forehead. Reaching over to the air circulation fan, he adjusted it to
high and pointed it straight towards him.

"Forest Service One, you're clear for take off," squawked
the radio.

Finally! Rick picked up the mike. "Roger that tower."

Throttling up, he pulled onto the runway and straightened
out the plane. Looking down the runway, he checked the sky to

ensure that nothing was there. Small beads of sweat collected on his brow then ran down his face as he made one final check of the instruments.

Got to get into the air, he thought. With his eyes fixed at the end of the runway, he pushed the throttles forward. The engines roared to life, the plane beginning to roll down the runway. As the plane picked up speed, Rick kept checking his velocity as he gently adjusted the yoke to keep it straight. The plane traveled further down the runway, gaining more and more speed.

Rick gently pulled back on the yoke, lifting the plane off the ground. With full throttle, Rick pulled the yoke closer, bringing the planes nose to its maximum angle of attack. The engines strained as the plane clawed its way into the sky. Rick knew he was pushing it, but he just *had* to get in the air. With every foot of altitude, Rick felt like the weight of the world was being lifted from his shoulders. With a deep breath of relief, Rick eased the yoke forward and leveled it off.

Ah, there... finally, I'm free! he thought. Rick banked the plane sharply until his compass read due west, then straightened it out again. He decided to set the alarm before he forgot. On the seat next to him was a small wind up clock, which he set for one hour. To complete his monthly flight requirement, he had four hours of air-time to burn up. That made for one hour out over the ocean, another back, and two hours of practice runs.

Flying out over the ocean was soothing. There were no other planes to contend with, no mountains, and the winds were predictable. He liked that. It was just the kind of place where he could fly, not bothered by distractions, and completely relax in his thoughts.

He remembered the first time he flew over the ocean to escape the dream. He had lost track of the time and flew too far out, almost running out of fuel getting back. Since then he carried the alarm clock.

It wasn't even a dream anymore. He'd been able to come to grips with everything that's happened to him. Everything, that is, except for those eyes and that laughter. They were so evil and terrifying...

Time heals all wounds, his father told him as a boy when his mother died. He was right, of course, except from time to time those eyes and that laughter would still visit him in his sleep. He could still remember what a foolish young kid he was, anxious to leave the logging town where he grew up.

72

Desperate to put that small town in his rear view mirror, he enlisted in the Army Air Corps on his eighteenth birthday to become a pilot. The only thing he ever wanted to do was fly. His father wanted him to stay and work in the saw mill so they could be together. After all, they only had each other. There was no other family to speak of.

Rick tried to console his father and convince him that he wouldn't be gone long. Sure he'd have to go to Vietnam, but he wouldn't be doing any fighting. He'd just be flying cargo from base to base. He told his father his tour of duty would be over in no time, then they'd see each other on weekends.

Forcing a smile to his face, Rick's father waved as he watched his only son board a plane to pilot training school. After graduating, it was directly off to war in some small country on the other side of the world he'd never heard of. Pilot training was easy for him, so it seemed to go by quickly. Ground school, however, was difficult. He didn't realize there would be so much math. By no means did he graduate near the top of his class, but no one could out fly him.

He wrote to his father when he got his final orders. Like most young men, he felt invincible and was anxious to go. He tried to reassure his father that it wouldn't take long and that he wouldn't be in danger. After all, how long could a few rice growers last against the most powerful nation on earth. That's what everyone was saying. It was 1962, and most Americans didn't know what was going on or could care less—but that would soon change.

He was assigned a McDonnell Douglas C-130 Hercules cargo plane, with four powerful gas turbine turbo prop engines. It was beautiful, and a dream to fly. As the fighting escalated his duties shifted from flying in food and supplies, to flying out the wounded. He didn't see any fighting, just the results. His duties started to include flying empty body bags in and full ones out.

This weighed heavy on him. Like most people, he wasn't sure what it was all about. All he knew was that America was paying a high price for this war. But then, it really wasn't a war, was it? The politicians called it a police action. He wondered if any of them could explain the difference.

It was near the end of his tour when the call came in. Their northern most base was in danger of being overrun, and he had to help in the evacuation of troops and equipment. The spirits in the cockpit were unusually high, however. He and his long time friend and copilot, Bob Walters, had similar release dates, and they made plans to see each other state side when it was all over.

73

But the situation quickly changed. When they reached the base, they landed in heavy gunfire on a mortar damaged runway. The scene was chaotic. Buildings and equipment were burning. The frantic coronel quickly changed his orders. Pilot Rick would no longer be taking equipment, he was to stuff as many Army personnel as he could into his plane and get out fast.

That was all right by him, he didn't want to stay where he wasn't wanted. Within minutes they were loaded up and moving down the runway. As they lifted off, he looked down and saw what seemed to be hundreds of North Vietnamese Army troops just outside the base perimeter. He couldn't help but stare at an enemy he'd never seen before. His plane was hit by a borage of small arms fire as it passed over top. Then, as he looked at his altimeter, a streak of bright tracer fire lit up the cockpit.

"Where did that come from!" Bob yelled. Another streak and the starboard engine burst into flames. The cockpit filled with smoke, sparks flying from the instrument panel as he struggled to keep the plane under control. Terror filled his body. Rick yanked the yoke back with all his might, trying level it off. It was working, but they weren't high enough. They continued downward. Rick blacked out on impact.

When he awoke he was upside-down, held in the seat by his straps. In a pain filled daze, he tried to look around the cabin. He could hear gunfire and the sound of movement around the plane. As Rick moved his head, a sharp pain surged through him and he lost conciseness again.

The next thing he knew, he was laying in a throbbing blur on the dirt floor of a small bamboo and grass reed hut. It was hot, humid, and flies flew around him, crawling on his face. He tried to move, his aching head causing him to groan. Rick moved a hand over his face and was surprised to find he had a beard. He must have been unconscious for several days.

Reaching his hand up he felt the side of his head. There just inside his hairline was a swollen, four inch long gash. Dry, bloody clods of dirt caked his face from the wound, down the side of his head, past his ear, and to his chin. He hated bugs and tried to shoo the flies away, but there were too many. After awhile he gave up. He was just too tired and sore to care.

It was dark except for slivers of sunlight that bled through the openings in the reed walls. Staring at the light made him nauseous, so he shielded his eyes. He wondered where he was, and where the others might be. Finally curiosity got the best of him. He crawled to the door and tried to open it, but it wouldn't budge.

Moving over to one of the slivers of light, Rick tried widening it out with his fingers. As he did so there was a noise at the door, and it flew open flooding the room with light.

He crumpled to the floor, holding up his hands to shield his eyes. A voice came from the door. It spoke quickly yet calmly but the words were unknown to him. Rick slowly moved his hands away from his face, blinking his eyes and straining to see what was in front of him, but all he could see was a bright light with a silhouette of a man in the middle of it.

The man spoke again in a language he did not understand, but this time louder. Rick tried to talk. All he could muster was a cough. The shadow walked over and grabbed Rick by the hair. Rick could see a face now. It was a young North Vietnamese Army soldier. The NVA soldier spoke again, this time slower and even more emphatic as if trying to make Rick understand.

The soldier, now frustrated, pulled Rick up to a standing position by his hair and pushed him towards the door. Rick moved towards the light slowly. Reaching the entrance, Rick stopped and held his hands up to protect his eyes from the light. He strained to see what was out there. The soldier behind him pushed him in the small of this back. Rick stumbled out of the opening. As Rick blinked his eyes the things around him started to come into focus. *Where am I?* He wondered again.

As his vision began to clear, he saw several huts similar to the one he had been in. They bordered a crescent shaped court yard about thirty yards in diameter with rice paddies directly in front. A thick jungle encircled the prison camp. There were no fences or barbed wire, and the only person he was aware of was the one behind him. He could see the soldier clearly now. He was about Rick's age, wearing a dirty and torn military uniform, and carrying a rifle.

Trying to clear his throat, Rick muttered, "Do you speak English?" The soldier looked at Rick with a confused look on his face. "What is this place?" Rick asked. "I want to speak to your commanding officer."

Just then the guard yelled toward one of the huts. Rick turned to see three other soldiers coming out of it. One of them was an officer, older than the others, with graying hair. The other two were like the one next to him- young teenage boys carrying rifles. All of them wore similarly dirty, heavy, sweat stained, and tattered uniforms.

Rick noticed that the younger ones had emotionless, almost lifeless, expressions. The officer, on the other hand, was much different. He looked like a man possessed. As he came closer and stopped in front of him, Rick could see that the officer's face was heavily scared and the look in his eye was so hateful it made Rick's hair stand on end. The officer muttered something to the others and Rick was instantly surrounded.

"Are you the commanding officer?" Rick asked. They ignored him. The officer took one last drag off his cigarette, then pushed the smoldering butt towards Rick's face. Rick stepped away, but was stopped by the others who held him in place. Rick struggled as the cigarette came closer.

"No!" Rick yelled, fighting to get away. The officer stepped forward and kicked Rick in the groin with all his might. Rick collapsed to his knees. He couldn't breath. Someone pulled his head back and he looked up at the officer. With an evil smile, the officer extinguished the hot coals on Rick's forehead. Rick screamed in agony as he was held in place.

In angered pain, Rick broke free and tried to strike the officer. His effort was futile. The soldiers immediately started beating him with the butts of their rifles. Rick fell to the ground and curled up as they continued to strike him. Rick could hear the officer's hideous laughter in the background as the pain rocked through him. Slowly the blackness started to return. Pain was replaced by numbness as the impact of the soldiers rifles became dull thuds. As his consciousness slipped away, the officer's laughter echoed through the deepest recesses of his mind.

Rick was drawn back to consciousness by a tug on his arms and shoulders. They'd tied his hands and were pulling him up a bamboo pole to a standing position. If there was a place on his body that felt no pain, he didn't know where it was.

Opening his eyes, Rick saw a line of young Vietnamese boys in their early to mid-teens. The three soldiers and officer were there as well. Rick watched the officer. He was speaking to the line of boys and pointed to Rick with a long stick. It reminded him of a biology teacher instructing students as they all stared at a dissected specimen. The officer stepped closer to Rick as he continued to lecture.

"Does anyone speak English?" Rick asked. They all ignored his question as the officer continued to speak. The officer appeared to be describing Rick as he walked around pointing at him. The officer's opinion was apparently not a good one, Rick noted.

As the officer spoke, his facial expressions echoed a view of hatred and disgust. When the officer was finished, he ordered a recruit to step forward. Rick looked at him and the boy stared back without emotion. He then slapped Rick across the face and moved away. The officer laughed heartily, which brought smiles to the recruits' faces and they laughed as well.

A moment later, the officer exchanged the stick for a four foot long split bamboo cane. He stepped towards Rick and swung.

Rick tried to protect himself, but his bonds prevented him from doing so. The cane whistled through the air and, upon impact, tore cloth and sliced into flesh. The searing pain was tremendous and Rick let out a blood curdling scream.

The officer seemed to feed off Rick's pain, and he continued beating him enthusiastically. With every scream, the officer's laughter became more villainous. Rick managed to look up into his tormentors face, and saw the most evil expression he'd ever seen. He peered into the officer's eyes and found himself staring into the bowels of hell.

Rick collapsed, hanging from his bonds in a daze. When the beating was over, Rick was dragged to a pit with a bamboo cage door over top. He was thrown in, and the cage door crashed down above him and was locked.

Rick was tortured like this almost every day. In a sobbing broken mess, he begged the officer to stop, but was granted no relief. He lost so much weight, all of his bones were visible. His wounds became infected, and a terrible fever left him in convulsions. He no longer had the energy to brush away the millions of bugs that fell into his hole.

In the scorching jungle heat, Rick started to hallucinate. Day after day under the unforgiving sun, Rick' reality became the fire of hell. The Vietnamese officer starred as Satan himself, tormenting Rick with his evil stare and hideous laughter. He was trapped, and escape was impossible.

The encampment was a training facility for new soldiers. After a period of time, trained soldiers would leave and raw recruits came in. This meant the usual introductory beatings.

Other people, farmers and villagers from around the area, would come as well. Like an animal in a zoo, the officer put Rick on display. Usually these visitors would spit on him and call him names. The officer appeared to be somewhat of a celebrity now that he had his own personal, American whipping boy.

It didn't take long before Rick could no longer distinguish between reality and hallucination. All he knew for certain was that the haunting eyes and laughter never left him. He no longer had the strength or will to live. His constant prayer was to die, but each time he was beaten within an inch of death, they allowed him to heal just enough to continue to exist.

He asked himself why he hadn't died in the crash and why didn't they kill him. For whatever cruel reason, he was alive, but hadn't the will to be so. He finally decided to end the nightmare by starving himself. Without some form of nutrition in conditions like this, it would all be over in a few days. The cease of his will to live was replaced with an unyielding determination to die.

No long after this resolution, they drug him from his pit and fastened him to the pole. Rick was indomitable. He would not let the officer receive any more pleasure from his suffering. He didn't cower, flinch, or tremble as the bamboo cane whistled through the air.

There were no agonizing screams to answer each swing. There was not a single sound or tear from the officer's victim. Only defiant silence.

This infuriated the officer, who demanded the results he'd come to expect. As the blows came faster and harder, Rick's pain turned to numbness. This time he heard no horrible laughter and saw no hateful eyes as the numbness faded to darkness. Rick's last thought before he lost consciousness was that he had won—he had silenced the demon. But fate fancied the opposite.

A few hours later he awoke in his hole. Everyone was asleep, but his torment continued. He lay in the bottom of his pit weeping as the laughter in his mind continued.

What happened next, he remembered vividly. Explosions rocked the ground and flares burned through the night above the encampment. There was chaotic yelling and running around. Rifles where firing in all directions. Dirt and rocks fell down on him as grenades exploded near his cage. He could see flames dance in the sky from where he lay in his hole. The smell of smoke filled the night. Huts burned.

Even in all this confusion, Rick couldn't find the strength to pull himself off the dirt. He just continued to stare into the night past the bamboo bars. Pounding footsteps announced the racing approach of someone toward his place of keep. A face of a recruit appeared. He lifted his rifle to shoot Rick, but wasn't quick enough. The soldier fell flat on the top of the cage and didn't move. Someone had shot him first.

The recruit's almond shaped eyes remained open as blood poured from his chest into the hole, covering Rick. Rick just stared back in shock at the face that was as emotionless dead as it was alive.

When the gun fire stopped, the dark shadow of an American soldier walked over to the hole.

"Holy cow!" the American said with a surprised look on his face. Then turning he yelled, "Lieutenant! You'd better come see this!"

"What is it Johnson?" said a man with officers' bars as he walked up to the hole and peered in. "Oh my gawd!" the Lieutenant exclaimed in surprise, crouching on one knee in order to get a better look. "He's one of ours! Peterson! O'Malley! Get this door open and get that man out of there!"

"Yes sir," came the reply. Moments later, the door was busted open. Too weak to stand on his own, two soldiers grabbed Rick under his arms and lifted him out.

"Take him down to the rice paddy and wash him up," ordered the Lieutenant. The two soldiers continued to help Rick walk to the water. He looked around. There were dead Vietnamese everywhere, illuminated in the night by burning huts.

"Wallace!" shouted the Lieutenant. "Get on the radio, I want an immediate e-vac! The rest of you finish your sweep, then set up a perimeter. Now *move!*"

Before getting into the chopper, Rick paused. He looked at his hell for the last time. The air was heavy with the smell of death, and the smoke from the fires had turned the watching moon blood red.

That was about all Rick could remember. For all he knew it could be a dream. But as the helicopter gained altitude, all the pains he had suffered seemed to fall away. Ache was replaced by peace, and for the first time since he could remember, he fell asleep.

He awoke in an Army hospital with tubes in his arms. Surrounded by doctors and officers, he was debriefed while being poked and prodded for countless medical tests. For Rick, the war was over, but the terror remained. For many nights in a row he would wake up screaming, visited by his demons, and would have to be sedated in order to rest. He continually felt enclosed and trapped, no matter the size of the room.

His doctors decided to send him to San Diego where there was a military hospital better equipped to help him. The next day he boarded a plane for Hawaii, then to the mainland. As before, he felt relief being in the air. He thought it strange that in a large room he would feel uncomfortable, but in any size plane he would be at ease.

By the time he arrived in San Diego, he felt refreshed. He was gaining weight back now, and his wounds were almost healed.

Rick tried to contact his father, but received no reply. When he checked into the hospital, he was met by an officer who explained with regrets that Rick's father had passed away.

When Rick's plane crashed, the Army had assumed he died and reported it to his father as such. His father collapsed upon hearing the news and had lasted only a couple of days in the hospital before passing on. This hit Rick hard. He was now totally alone in the world and couldn't help but feel responsible for what happened to his father.

Rick was able to find a job at an air field as a mechanic and visited the hospital on an out patient basis. He didn't have much money, so his boss let him sleep in the hanger. Every penny he earned was saved. At the end of the week, Rick found he could afford a couple of hours of flight time in a rented plane. His boss took a liking to him because he worked hard and did a good job. He was even kind enough to ignore complaints from people who'd heard rumors of a psycho who would run out onto the runway in the middle of the night screaming, not knowing where he was.

The hospital was a different story. They had more doctors there than he could keep straight. Every week it was the same thing-some doctor wanted blood or urine samples and some wanted to check his eyes or have him turn his head and cough. Others asked him to look at ink blotches and tell them what he saw. Still others had him lie on couches and tell them about his childhood, asking if he had repressed feelings toward his father. Rick didn't understand what was going on, but these men were trying to help and, because of that, he'd do his part, even if it did seem ridiculous.

Then one day Rick picked up the phone and found he was talking to the head of the Psychiatric department who wanted to see him as soon as possible. The physician told him that the team of doctors had diagnosed his problem and could treat it. When he arrived at the hospital, he was taken into a room and was greeted by smiling faces. They asked him to sit down. Rick grew impatient as the doctor went on and on explaining about the delicate nature of the mind, and about how they came up with their conclusion. Finally, they gave him their answer.

After six months of studying his case, the doctors determined that Rick had a severe case of delusional claustrophobia. With an assortment of various prescription drugs, they could control his anxiety and help him return to a normal life. The moment Rick heard this, his heart fell to the floor.

That's it? he thought. *That's all they could come up with?* Rick couldn't listen any longer. The doctor continued to talk about

80

his treatment. Rick stood up, and walked out. He felt so depressed, he didn't even notice the shocked and surprised looks on the doctor's faces as he left the room.

What a waste of time. There was no way he could take drugs and be allowed to fly. Besides, an hour in the air did more for him than a month on a doctor's couch.

That evening Rick's boss took him to a small hanger at the end of the field away from anything else. Inside was a small twin prop cargo plane. The boss explained that in Mexico was a shipment of airplane parts that needed to be picked up, and he would let Rick do the job if he promised not to tell anyone.

Rick was too excited to care. All he wanted was to get into the sky, so he agreed. Before Rick could think twice, he was in the air with a map to a small remote runway on the other side of the boarder. He flew all night, and as the sun broke the horizon the next morning, he touched down on a dirt runway in the middle of nowhere.

Rolling to a stop, Rick was met by two trucks. One carried fuel, and the other delivered crates marked "airplane parts". A group of men quickly loaded and fueled the plane while Rick stepped out to stretch and answer the call of nature. When the plane was fully loaded, Rick walked around it checking the engines and flaps.

A cloud of dust suddenly enclosed him and the plane, taking him by surprise. Squinting his eyes, he could hear the sounds of vehicles moving swiftly around him. Men were running and yelling in Spanish. Rick was tackled and held to the ground.

Through the clearing dust he could see Mexican Army personnel all around him. Most were holding other men down while the others surrounded the area holding rifles. Two soldiers emerged from the plane carrying one of the crates. They dropped it on the ground and busted it open with the butts of their rifles. As the crate fell apart, plastic bags of hashish fell onto the ground next to him.

Damn, Rick thought, as the realization of what was happening swept over him. Rick was handcuffed and loaded into an Army truck with the others, and driven to a small prison out in the middle of nowhere. He was taken to a concrete bunker with a metal door across the front.

As he got closer, Rick's mind flashed back to the Vietnamese camp and he panicked and fought back. The guards beat him then threw him into the cage. Gasping in pain, Rick heard the slow eerie squeak of the door as it swung closed then slammed shut. It was dark except for small fingers of light which reached in through the air holes in the door and walls. Rick shook the door violently as he screamed to be let out, but it was no use. The soldiers walked away.

Rick lay on the floor weeping in his hot stuffy coffin. As the mid-day sun beat down on the bunker, the temperature rose steadily. Rick's mind started to wander. The heat made him dizzy. Terror filled his body as memories of his jungle nightmare overcame him. The eyes and laughter of the Vietnamese officer filled his head. His demons had returned.

Whether he was conscious or not, he was never free of them. Day after day he remained huddled in the corner of his cell trembling, mad with fear. He wanted to die, so he stopped taking any nourishment and quickly grew weak.

Then one day, Rick was shook back to consciousness as the sound of American voices filled his ears. Still in a daze, he was helped to his feet and carried out of the bunker. He was too exhausted to raise his head and see what was happening. All he could do was listen as American voices reprimanded the prison guards.

Rick was helped into a truck, and given food and water as they traveled down a dusty road to a town whose name he couldn't pronounce. He was met there by members of the American Consulate. While American doctors checked him out another man explained to Rick that they'd been trying to locate him for weeks. It seems that, because of the severe nature of his punishment and the fact that he was not given a trial, the American Consulate was able to have Rick released with time served.

Rick was flown back to the VA hospital in San Diego. Upon release he attempted to get a job, but like the song on the radio said, "The winds of change were blowing", and people looked at him differently. Labeled a psychotic Vietnam vet with a record, he drifted up the coast looking for work. Rick found that he couldn't keep a job. It wouldn't take long for word to spread about his nightmares, and he'd soon be thumbing his way to the next town. After months of this nomadic lifestyle, the Forest Service finally needed pilots. Forest fires in the northwest were consuming valuable timber, and the Forest Service wasn't very picky about who they hired.

Fighting fires by plane was something he picked up quickly, and his skill as a pilot was immediately noticed. Admired by the grateful community he served, Rick was adopted by an understanding town which had sent many a son off to war.

"But I wasn't the only one who'd been there, isn't that right girl?" Rick rhetorically asked, patting the armrest of his pilot's seat.

He could still remember the shape this plane was in when he first saw her. Saved by the Forest Service from the scrap heap after being shot up rescuing downed pilots in the waters off the Vietnam coast, Rick put his whole heart and soul into getting her back into the air. Because the plane was designed to takeoff and land on water, it was ideally suited for conversion to aerial fire fighting.

"I guess I'm not the only one who has demons to exorcise," he remarked as the alarm clock rang him back to reality. It was time to get to work. Rick reached over, turned it off, and checked his position with the GPS on the control panel. Like so many other times before, he had drifted off course and had gone too far out. Rick banked the plane to starboard, dropping in altitude as he headed back towards the coast.

7

Pack Train

A gust of wind hit Buck and his mule head on as they emerged from the trees and into the clearing. A small rain shower swept through the area during the night, just recently breaking up. Examining the low clouds, he pulled his collar up, then tugged his Stetson tighter on his head. *The wind will blow the rest of the storm away this morning*, he thought as he looked around. *Noon at the latest*, he nodded confidently. A red-tail hawk floated almost motionless on the air currents above the clearing, watching it like a silent sentry.

Wrapped loosely in Buck's leather-gloved hand, a rope led back down the trail to a string of three pack mules. Moving slowly behind him, each mule's back carried an aluminum frame. Attached to each frame were gray canvas packs. Some were filled with camping gear, while several others were empty, rolled and tied up neatly. An assortment of tools, necessary for trail repair, was also attached securely to the frames.

Clifford's mule was the last of the train. They'd only been riding for a couple of hours, but his butt and his back were already sore. With every lazy step the old mule took, Clifford shifted his weight from side to side. He couldn't wait to get off. *Why couldn't we use dirt bikes or ATVs?* he thought. Now *that* would be more fun. Instead, he was riding at a snails pace up a trail with nothing better to look at than a line of mule butts.

"I can crawl faster than this," he spat in frustration to his mule. "When we get back to the cabin, I'm going to call the processing plant and have you turned into dog food." They were falling behind, or so it seemed to Clifford, who was growing more impatient by the minute. He gave the mule a kick in the ribs and tried to drive it with the bridle.

"Let's go, dog food, pick up the pace." He received an angry whinny in reply.

"Let Molly have her head, Clifford. She knows this trail by heart," Buck said without turning around.

That only added to Clifford's frustration. Trying not to draw anymore attention to his inexperience, Clifford changed the subject.

"Hey, Uncle Buck."

"Yeah."

"What are all of the empty packs for?"

"They're for the garbage the hikers left behind, like I explained before."

"Yeah, but there are so many of them. Do you really expect that much trash?"

"No." Buck chuckled. "But its nice to have a few extras on hand just in case you run into a real slob."

They continued with the small talk for awhile, but it was just too difficult from so far away. Clifford wished he hadn't listened to Buck when he told him to leave his Gameboy at the cabin. He could be getting some serious Mario Brothers marathon action right now.

He looked at the sky and begged for some excitement. A moment later, he noticed Buck stop the pack train and look at the trail. Molly came to an abrupt halt behind the pack mules. Clifford watched Buck look slowly up and down the trail, then toward the brush on the side hill.

"What's wrong?" Clifford asked. Buck didn't answer. He just got off his mule, and looked at the ground. Clifford did the same, walking over to him.

"Someone's been through here recently, these tracks weren't here a few days ago," Buck told Clifford in a concerned voice as he pointed to a path stomped out in the grass leading away from the trail.

"Could it be deer?" Clifford asked.

"Not unless deer started wearing boots." Buck pointed to a waffle imprint in the dirt just off the trail. Buck closed his eyes, and lifting his head in the air, he took a deep breath. After a moment he nodded decisively. "Yeah, they're still back there."

"How can you tell?"

"There's a slight smell of smoke. They've got a campfire burning."

Clifford sniffed the air, but couldn't smell anything. "Maybe they didn't see the closure sign at the trail head," he said. "It was only put up yesterday."

"Maybe," Buck replied, doubtfully. "I guess we'll have to go in and let them know what's going on." Buck pulled the train off the trail, and tied them up to a tree. He and Clifford then got back on their mules to follow the path. A couple of hundred yards later, they could see the camp.

"Hello in camp!" Buck yelled as they rode slowly in. Instantly, a black man with an oozy emerged from the tent followed by two Asian teenagers with pistols. Buck stopped his mule, and Clifford rode up next to him. Clifford's eyes widened in surprise at seeing the weapons, but said nothing.

"What do you want, old man?" Tommy asked, rudely.

"First of all this isn't an established Forest Services camp site. If you want to camp up here you'll have to use one of the sites along the main trail," Buck replied as he watched the two teenagers slowly move to flanking positions on either side of him and Clifford. Buck kept his cool as he looked around wondering what he had ridden into.

"Is that all?" Tommy asked, impatiently.

Buck's attention was drawn back to the man in front of the tent. "No, that's not all," Buck replied, trying to sound more professional than mad. "This trail's been closed due to bear activity in the area. I'm going to have to ask you to leave."

"Yeah, well last I checked this is still a free country, and this is public land so we can be here if we want," Tommy said, nastily. "Besides, we're not afraid of bears. We've got protection." Lifting his hand, he showed off the shiny black mini-machine gun.

Buck calmly leaned back in his saddle, pulled a cigar from his shirt pocket, and lit it up. "Listen son." His eyes narrowed slightly as he leaned forward again looking into the man's eyes. "Have you ever seen what happens to a man when he comes between a mad mother grizzly and her cubs?"

Tommy didn't answer, he just starred back confidently.

"Well I have," Buck continued. "Can you imagine a paw the size of a garbage can lid with six-inch, knife blade like claws taking a swat at you? Rip your head clean off. Heck, those little pea shooters of yours will only make her angry."

Out of the corner of his eye, Buck could see Clifford and the two teenagers looking around nervously, but the man in front of him stayed cool.

"Look at all this food and garbage you've left laying around." Buck went on as he pointed to the half empty cans of food next to the fire. "With this breeze, you're advertising. I bet those grizzlies are on their way here right now, reading the menu as they go."

Lifting his head in the air as if imitating the bears, he took a deep breath and smiled. "Mmm, spaghettios, with three city boys for desert." Buck laughed heartily, but didn't take his eyes off the man with the oozy.

Instantly, the tent door flew open. A gust of wind pulled the canvas flap over the top of the tent as a frightened young teenage girl ran out to the black man.

"*Tommy!* You promised you'd protect me!" she yelled hysterically, grabbing his arm. "Let's get out of here! Do what he says! Please! Tommy, *please!*"

Clifford looked at her closely in her dirty tight shorts and tank top. She was so skinny and pale, and wasn't wearing a bra, he noticed immediately. Still, she was kind of cute even with messed up hair. Clifford looked at her blood shot eyes, and could tell she'd been crying. Without knowing why, he felt sorry for her.

The two Asian boys rushed in to close up the tent. Buck looked inside as they reached up to grab the canvas door. There was a long table with sleeping bags around it. On one end of the table were several packages, the size and shape of baseballs, wrapped in aluminum foil and cellophane. A couple of them were unwrapped and looked like cream colored play dough.

In the middle of the table was a large mixing bowl with wooden spoons and a pastry cutter. On the far end sat a small scale and a large number of small plastic bags filled with white powder. Under the table were two backpacks loaded with these same bags of powder. Lines of the powder were on a small mirror next to the scale. Buck's eyes narrowed, putting two and two together. Just then, Tommy was able to peel the frightened girl off him.

"Shut up and stay in the tent like I told you!" He yelled as he grabbed her by the arm and pushed her back down onto the floor of the tent. Her body hit the table knocking plastic bags on top of her. She looked up at Tommy, frightened and crying, as the door flap came down in front of her. Tommy turned his attention back to Buck.

"What are you looking at?!" he scowled. As his two companions joined him, he returned to the subject at hand. "If the bears are so dangerous, what are you doing up here?"

Buck again returned his attention to the man in front of him. "We're here to fix the trail. Parts of it have been washed out by the rains."

"What type of gun are you carrying?" Tommy asked, trying to determine what he was up against.

Buck was getting tired of the interrogation, but tried not to let it show. "I don't need a gun. You see, I know what they smell like so I can avoid 'em," he said as he sat high in the saddle and smelled the air, again. "Yes sir, they're close by. If you guys want to stay here, suit yourselves, but I think its time we leave." Buck gently turned his mule around, and Clifford did the same. "You boys have a good day," he said without looking back.

Tommy watched them ride out of camp. His two companions quickly turned to him with questioning looks.

"What about the bears, Tommy? Maybe we should move the camp," one of them said.

"Forget about the bears," Tommy ordered confidently. "Stupid animals don't concern me, but those two guys *do*."

"They're leaving, they won't bother us," the other teenager spoke up.

"They know we're up here, you fool," Tommy snapped angrily. "What if they tell someone? Our location's been compromised, it's time for us to get out of here. Pack up everything you can carry in one trip. We're going back to the city."

The two quickly turned and entered the tent. Tommy watched the riders disappear into the brush. It was only then that he allowed himself to look around at the garbage on the ground, then to the surrounding trees. Lifting his nose into the air, he took a deep breath, but smelt nothing. With another scowl he shook his head then turned and entered the tent.

Clifford quickly rode up beside Buck. "You didn't tell me there were *grizzlies*," he said excitedly.

"There haven't been any grizzlies up here in years. I just wanted to scare the little jerk," Buck replied with satisfaction. "Did you see that girl? She's high on drugs. I've seen hundreds like her in Korea and Vietnam." His expression suddenly turned sad.

"What were they doing back there?" Clifford wanted to know.

"Processing drugs to be sold on the street. I've run into a few camps like that while on patrol in the Army. Each with the same kind of jerks as those back there. They prey on the weak," Buck replied with disgust. "Like swatting flies, we'd torch the camps and wouldn't even feel bad...people like that are trash. Mind what I tell you Clifford, those who hang around people like that are losers and are bound to get hurt."

Clifford thought about the guys he knew at school that sold pot, and how he admired them. After all, they were very popular, always had money and cool parties. Then he thought of the girl at the camp. *Maybe Buck is right*, he thought. *Maybe that's not where it's at after all.*

"What can we do about those guys back there?" Clifford asked.

"Not much right now, I'm afraid," Buck answered, worriedly. "When we get back to town we'll tell the Sheriff. Jim's a smart man, he'll know what to do."

Clifford nodded in agreement, then followed Buck back to the main trail where they picked up the pack train and continued on. A short time later, Buck stopped the mules in front of a washout.

"You can probably do this one yourself while I go to the upper camp and pick up garbage," he told Clifford. "Just do exactly what I showed you at the last one and everything will go smoothly."

Clifford tied up his mule then removed a shovel, sledgehammer and some stakes from the pack mules. "That's everything," he said, walking over to Buck.

"All right, I'll see you in a few hours," Buck replied, then gave his mule a gentle kick and started up the trail. Clifford watched the pack train ride around the bend and out of sight before looking down at the washout. Rolling up his sleeves, he picked up the shovel, and got to work.

At that same time, in the DEA office in Seattle, Special Agent in Charge, Michael O'Leary, sat at his desk with a file folder open in front of him. He'd just finished his sandwich lunch and was sipping from his Coke-a-Cola, as he wondered what his family was doing. O'Leary, a forty-five year old red-haired, green-eyed man of Irish decent, was born and raised in Boston, Massachusetts. He had the accent and stubborn Irish pride in his heritage to prove it. Though his childish freckles had long since faded and been replaced by streaks of silver in his receding hairline, his face lit up with boyish animation whenever he talked about his family.

Born to Patrick and Mary O'Leary he was the youngest of three boys. His father, known by family and friends as Paddy, was third generation Boston PD. Michael's two older brothers were the fourth. He also had two uncles and several cousins on the force as well. This fact was the single most source of pride his family had ever known.

That's why from a young age, he told no one that his plans didn't include following in his father's footsteps. When he was a young teenager, he remembered one of his cousins moved to New York and became a police officer there. It was a huge scandal. Everyone speculated on where the parents had gone wrong in raising such a rebellious child.

Michael gave into the unspoken family pressure to continue the family heritage and he went through the Police Academy, graduating with honors. He then married his high school sweet heart and tried the life the O'Leary's had know for decades. But after a while, he finally admitted to his wife he wasn't cut out to be a beat cop.

She was very supportive, but didn't like the alternative idea he suggested. It just seemed too dangerous. He still remembered the looks on his parents faces when he announced at dinner that he wanted to become a Federal Agent. His mother almost fainted, and his father just about swallowed his fork.

Michael saw the eruption starting. His father's shocked, pale face started to turn red in anger. From his collar on up, a blood red wave moved upward until his face was completely engulfed, then *Boom!* Out of his chair he rose rattling on about family and tradition. His mother could only muster the words, "What will the neighbors think?" before shuffling off to church to pray for her lost son.

After a few days of not speaking to him, his father finally came and apologized. He told his son he loved him very much, and if he wanted to be a Federal Agent, then he'd be supportive. He and Mamma would just have to learn to live with the stigmatism of having a black sheep in the family.

Michael was able to get in the DEA training program, and soon he and Genna were uprooted and moved to the Northwest. It took some getting use to, but they grew to love the Seattle area. Genna, however, never got used to the long hours of an undercover agent. He was never home, and she was constantly worried.

She was amazed they were together long enough to have their twin girls. This type of work is hard on relationships, Michael knew. Divorce was an occupational hazard more prevalent than anything life threatening. Genna wanted him to change jobs, to get off the streets into a desk job so he'd be home more often.

He didn't like that idea. Being a desk jockey just wasn't his forte. He did, however, promise to look into the possibility but continually put it off. The accident that happened just a little more than a year ago changed all that. He called it an accident because no matter how hard you try, you can't plan for everything that could go wrong. Throughout his entire career he had planned countless raids where no one under his command had ever gotten shot or injured in anyway. He'd always been proud of that fact, but knew someday the odds might catch up to him.

Last year his luck finally ran out during a raid on a methamphetamine lab. O'Leary led the assault through the front door, and the suspect was waiting for them. The instant O'Leary kicked in the door a shot gun blast hit him square in the chest. His body was thrown backwards and he collapsed into a motionless mass.

He thought he was dead. Just before he passed out, a vision of his family came to him along with the horrible feeling he had wasted too much time away from them. He didn't want it to end that way, and prayed for a second chance.

The next thing he knew he woke up in the hospital feeling like he'd been hit by a Mack truck. Genna was there holding his hand, and looking as if she had been up all night crying. His body armor had stopped the shot gun blast, but the force of it managed to break most of his ribs and cause massive internal injuries.

After he'd recovered enough to go home, Genna informed him she was leaving. This lifestyle had taken its toll, and the accident was the last straw. She told him if he got a transfer to a desk job in Boston, they could be together again. With that, she packed up the kids and moved back to Massachusetts.

He was *devastated.* From that moment on, his goal was to get promoted off the streets and transferred back east. He had a distinguished career, but promotions and transfers were hard to come by. He desperately needed a large high profile bust to bring him to the attention of his superiors.

The Kingpin case was just what the doctor had ordered. Kingpin was the west coast arm of the Chicago mob—drugs, prostitution, gambling. You name it, if it was illegal, they were into it. It was the single largest crime organization on the west coast.

As Special Agent in Charge, O'Leary had worked the case for more than a year. They finally got a break when O'Leary was able to identify Kingpin's largest drug supplier. After countless hours and stakeouts, they'd been able to put an air tight case together against the supplier. Unfortunately, they couldn't prove a connection to Kingpin.

O'Leary decided to try a different tactic. The supplier was just a small fish in a large school of criminals. If they could get the supplier to cooperate and turn State's evidence against Kingpin, then they would reduce the charges.

He confronted the supplier, showed him the evidence against him and offered a deal, but the supplier refused. He said he would rather go to jail then double cross Kingpin. If he was caught making deals with the Feds, Kingpin would have him hunted down and killed.

That's when O'Leary came up with the plan. Kingpin wouldn't hunt him down if he thought the supplier was already dead. After listening to the plan, the supplier finally agreed to the deal. The supplier would feed O'Leary information and set Kingpin up to take a fall.

O'Leary thought he had the perfect plan, one that couldn't go wrong, but he found out otherwise, however, when months of preparation went up in smoke because of the blundering of a complete *idiot*. While O'Leary's team hid, waiting for Kingpin to arrive on the scene, Alan Bradley had rushed in and apprehended the supplier with his shipment of illegal drugs. The commotion spooked Kingpin, just moments prior to his arrival, allowing him to escape. The thought of it continued to burn him up, and his Irish temper made his blood boil as he sat at his desk.

But that would all soon change, he knew, as the thought of his plan calmed him. Tonight he had another stakeout. After which he hoped to have enough information to put the final touches on his master plan. Then he could sit back and watch the Kingpin Empire come crashing down.

Rick pushed the yoke forward and to port descending into the valley. When the plane came around, he cut back on the power and extended the flaps, leveling off just feet above the center of the emerald green mountain lake. Like the most fragile of porcelain, he held the yoke gently, feeling every vibration. His feet massaged the rudder pedals, almost without effort, as if he were just another cog in the machine acting flawlessly. Rick adjusted flap and throttle until he felt the belly of his plane cut into the water. With the flip of a switch, a large scoop was lowered. Water rushed into the plane filling tanks in the fuselage.

Rick pushed the throttle forward slowly to compensate for the added weight. Then, with the flip of a switch, the scoop closed and Rick eased the yoke back, lifting the plane into the air. He gained altitude slowly as he turned the plane and headed for the upper valleys of the north ridge above trail seventy-four.

Rick knew these mountains intimately. He knew every valley and ridge, and the different cross winds and down drafts associated with them. He held a high respect for these invisible dangers that lay in wait to tear a plane with an inexperienced pilot from the sky.

Rick loved his job. The Forest Service didn't have much money for pilots, but that was all right with him. After a few modifications, Rick was able to fly this plane without a copilot, and flying alone was a true joy. He'd been saving his money, hoping someday to open his own charter service, but he could never seem to make himself quit. His father had spent his whole life working with the timber of these mountains and it seemed to Rick a fitting tribute that he work to protect the trees that provided that timber.

Clifford stood up, wiped the sweat from his forehead and looked outward. He was gazing through the tops of the trees on the slope below when he heard the airplane. The terrain was steep here, and although he was surrounded by tall trees, the ones below him were low enough to look straight outward and see the Forest Service plane flying past and up the valley. *That must be the plane Uncle Buck warned me to stay away from,* he shook his head as he thought of it. *Grown-ups! Always trying to protect you from one thing or another.*

Buck had just come out of the trees and was about a third of the way through a large clearing when he heard the airplane. Looking back, he saw the PBY coming up the valley. *Right on time,* he thought. Buck stood up in the saddle and waved to the plane. As planned, Rick was on his way to the upper clearing.

Seeing the gesture, Rick waved the planes wings in reply as he flew past. Then an eyebrow lifted slightly and a mischievous grin appeared on Rick's face. Maybe a slight change of plans. He could hit *this* clearing instead. *No, I shouldn't.* He thought about it for second more... then with a hearty laugh, changed his mind.

"Ah! Why not!" he said out loud. Rick banked the plane slowly, in a wide circle, to line up on the clearing. He was still pretty far out and the large clearing appeared small, but he could make out the ant-sized shapes in the middle he knew to be his friend and his pack train.

There was his target. His approach was low, but not too low. He reminded himself that this was only a practice run. He wanted to stay high. That way his cargo would have a chance to break up in the air and land in the clearing like a heavy rain, doing no harm to the pack train below.

What's he doing? Buck thought as he watched the plane line up on the clearing. *I'm* sure *he saw me.* Standing up in the saddle, he waved both arms frantically and yelled. "This is the wrong clearing! It's the next one up!!!" As if expecting Rick to hear him. It was no use. The plane didn't waver from its path. In desperation, Buck looked quickly behind him, then in front for a way to escape. Kicking his mule hard, he started moving forward, but not fast enough.

"There's no escape," Rick laughed, watching Buck's feeble attempted at evading the inevitable. "Ah, what the heck! I'll probably never get this chance again. Let's see if I can knock him off his mule."

"You're doing this on *purpose?!*" Buck yelled angrily when he realized he wasn't going to make it. Stopping his mule, he again stood in the saddle, and lifting his fist towards the plane, he shook it angrily. "You big JERK!" he shouted as it was almost upon him.

Rick fought the cross wind, crabbing his plane, and skidding though the air slightly sideways towards his target. "Almost...just about there...NOW!" Rick flipped a switch on the control pad. Then, like a thousand times before, he heard the back end of the plane open up as he lifted the nose, spilling water into the clearing.

In one last defiant gesture, Buck yelled at the wave of water coming at him. "YOU SON-OF-A—"

SWOOSH!

"Bull's-eye!" Rick banked hard and looked back. As the mist cleared, he saw Buck rolling around on the ground covered with mud. The mules were running and kicking in all directions. Rick laughed uncontrollably with satisfaction.

"I'll get you fly boy!" Buck swore angrily and struggled to his feet to wipe the mud from his eyes, just in time to see the plane disappear down the valley. "I'm going to kick your *butt!*"

Clifford looked at his watch again as he sat next to the newly repaired trail. *Where is Buck?* he wondered. He had expected him to be back hours ago. It'd be dark in a few hours, and they didn't have a camp setup yet. A moment later, a mule's whinny drew his attention up the trail.

Getting up, Clifford walked over to Buck as he rode towards him. "What happened to you?" Clifford asked, looking him over. Buck's clothes were still wet and mud caked, and his skin was pale with the tips of his fingers and nose turning blue.

"That *damn* flyboy nearly broke my neck!" he replied with a shiver. "It took me nearly two hours to get the mules back together before I could make my pick up."

Clifford looked back at the mules. The bags that were previously empty were now all half full and hung neatly from each mule's pack. "You must be freezing," Clifford remarked.

"I'm not so bad anymore. I've had some help from an old friend," Buck answered, as he lifted a near empty bottle of Jim Beam and drained the last of it into his mouth.

Clifford saw Buck's body shivering. Buck returned the empty bottle to the saddlebag and remove a new full one.

"Just the same, we'd better start a fire and get you into some dry clothes."

"Let's head down to that camp we saw earlier. Those jerks should be long gone by now, and they had plenty of fire wood collected." Buck's words slurred out of his mouth in reply. Nodding in agreement, Clifford mounted his mule and followed Buck down the trail.

They were moving awfully slow, or so it seemed to Clifford, as he watched Bucks body slump in the saddle as if asleep. He was glad that at least the *mules* knew where they were going. Buck started to hum a tune as he rode, and Clifford rolled his eyes in amusement, hoping Buck wouldn't start singing.

It didn't take long to get to the camp, and, as expected, it was deserted. It looked like a tornado had hit it. Things were thrown everywhere. Full and empty food containers, clothes, and some equipment lay all around them. A pile of wood sat next to the still smoldering embers of the fire pit.

Clifford dismounted, then helped Buck off his mule. Without help, Clifford was able to get the fire going again while Buck changed into dry cloths. After only a few minutes in front of the fire, Buck felt better. He still shivered a little, but the color was coming back to his skin and he wasn't nursing quite so much from his bottle.

"We'd better get this place cleaned up, and set up camp before it gets dark," Buck remarked with a renewed vigor. Stumbling drunkenly around to the other side of one of the mules, Buck began removing a pack. As he stepped back, he tripped falling backwards onto the ground and into a pile of trash. The loud clanking of tin cans drew Clifford's attention. He turned to see half the contents of the bag spill out on top of Buck, then mix with the surrounding garbage. Rushing over to him, Clifford helped Buck to his feet.

"I'll do this, why don't you sit by the fire and get dinner ready," he suggested. Buck nodded. Clifford watched as Buck made his way back to the fire and sat down before he turned his attention to the garbage. Grabbing the bag, he began picking items up one at a time and putting them in.

What's this? He wondered, kneeling down to get a closer look. A shiny object the size and shape of a brick covered with aluminum foil and cellophane lay next to him. Clifford picked it up and examined it more closely. Opening one corner, he looked at the dark brown contents, and then smelled it.

His eyes opened wide as he recognized the smell. He wasn't sure what it was, but it reminded him of a drug one of his friends had showed him at a party once. Clifford smelled it again. It was much darker in color and the odor was stronger than the stuff he'd seen before, but he was sure it was drugs.

Clifford remembered that just a small amount of the substance at the party was much too expensive for him to try. His jaw dropped open as he looked at its size and felt its weight. He was *sure* it was worth a fortune! Instantly, visions of a hot sports car and the popularity that came with it filled his mind.

"Hey Clifford! Look what I found!" An excited voice called from behind him. Clifford looked over his shoulder to see Buck with a big smile holding up a couple of fishing poles and a tackle box. "Those guys must've been so scared. They'd left their heads if they weren't attached!"

Making sure to keep the package out of Bucks view, he slipped it into his jacket. "Boy, I'll say," he replied in agreement. He watched Buck turn around and head back to the fire where he stirred something in a pot. Clifford couldn't believe his luck. He quickly stuffed the rest of the garbage into the bag, then set out to unpack the mules and set up the tent.

8
Stakeout

Tuesday Evening.

King County Executive Russell Mossier stood in line at the bar in the Seattle Opera House, where he and his wife Mary had season tickets. It was one of the few things they both enjoyed which fit into both of their busy schedules. It was intermission, a time to get a drink and discuss what happened in the first act. He looked back toward where he'd left her. She was with a small group of their friends, talking and laughing.

Mossier watched as a man in an impeccably tailored tuxedo walked up to the group. It was Agent Alan Bradley. Mossier frowned at this turn of events. The evenings at the Opera he and Mary enjoyed were usually free of politics, and he hoped he wouldn't have to tolerate Bradley for long.

Russell considered Mary to be one of the really good people of the world. She spent all her time working for charity-organizing fundraisers for children's hospitals, abused women and the homeless. She had a big, pure heart that went out to everyone in need, and he loved her for it. Mary, and people like her, were the reasons he put up with political life in the first place. When he got frustrated with all the compromises and deal making that made him sick, he thought of her. What he did allowed her to have the freedom to accomplish all the good that she had.

He had struggled to keep his political life separate from his life with Mary—he didn't want her tarnished. That was why he was particularly concerned with Mary talking to Bradley. She had no knowledge about the deal he had to make with the Bradley's to get elected.

Mossier watched as their friends moved away and left Bradley and Mary standing alone talking. He finally reached the front of the line and ordered two glasses of white wine, paid for them, then walked back toward Mary.

"Here you go, Honey," he said, handing her a glass.

"You remember Agent Bradley, don't you dear?" she asked. "He was at your election fund raising dinner."

"Of course I remember," Russell replied and shook Alan's hand. "The Bradley's were big supporters of my campaign. How are you?"

"Very well, thank you," Alan replied, then taking a sip from his martini. "I was just discussing the first act with your charming wife. She let me in on some important points that I found very insightful."

Mary smiled and somewhat blushed at the comment. Russell knew Bradley's words were insincere and was annoyed, but didn't show it. As they continued to exchange small talk, he wondered how long he'd have to put up with Alan's bull. Russell wanted to have a good time with Mary, and didn't want to share her with anyone. He especially didn't want to be reminded of the deal he had made with the Bradley's during his campaign.

In order to get elected, Mossier needed Alan Bradley Sr.'s support, and to get that he needed to play ball. It was a fairly small matter, but it still left a bad taste in his mouth. Alan Bradley Sr. let Mossier in on the plan he had to make his son the next Mayor of Seattle. For Bradley's support of Mossier's campaign, Russell had to agree to support Alan's.

Once Alan was elected, Mossier was to show him the ropes, help him out so he would be a success. Actually, Russell knew *he* was the lucky one. The Bradley's could have just as easily supported someone else, or Alan could have wanted to run for King County Executive himself instead of Mayor. This political back scratching was fairly common place, but Mossier didn't care to be reminded of it.

"Shouldn't you be on stakeout or something, Agent Bradley?" Mossier asked, hoping for an excuse for Alan to leave.

"Actually, I *am* on stakeout," Alan lied. Alan found stakeouts to be boring and inconvenient to his personal schedule, so he avoided them as much as possible. They were, however, interesting subjects in conversations, and he often made up stories to tell in situations like this one.

"*Really!* Who are you watching?" Mrs. Mossier asked as she looked around.

"Don't look around!" he warned her. "They're probably watching us right now."

Mary's eyes got big as she put her fingers to her lips. "Sorry," she whispered. "What kind of case is it?"

"I'm not at liberty to say," Alan told her in a serious tone. "I will, however, tell you that I got a tip from an informant. There will be a drug exchange taking place on stage in the final act."

"Right on stage?" she asked while trying to keep her voice down.

"That's correct," Bradley confirmed. "That's how clever these people are. They make an exchange in broad day light in front of everyone. No one would ever suspect something illegal was happening."

"But you know otherwise, don't you, Agent Bradley," she gasped. "How *exciting*!"

"After the exchange is made, I'll be waiting back stage to cuff the perps," he added.

"Perps?" She looked at him questioningly.

"Perpetrators, Ma'am," he replied. "That's what we call them."

Russell couldn't help but roll his eyes at the line of bull. He especially didn't like the way Alan was taking advantage of his wife's naiveté.

"In that case, Agent Bradley, we should let you get back to work. Besides, it's time we found our seats for the second act." Russell put down his drink, and gently took his wife's hand in order to lead her away.

"That's a good idea," Alan replied. "You wouldn't want to be around when the bullets start flying."

That brought another gasp from Mary. "Please be careful, Agent Bradley," she said with complete sincerity.

"I will," he assured her as he watched her take her husbands arm then walk away. He couldn't help but laugh after they had disappeared into the auditorium. He'd seen this show before, and knew that in the last scene a bright red birthday present would be exchanged. She'd definitely be watching the people involved and wondering about what he had said.

He took a sip from his drink and cringed, *What was I thinking?* He hated martinis. It was just a prop he used when wearing a tuxedo. He liked to act smooth like James Bond and order them shaken not stirred. What was the difference, anyway?

Alan put the drink down, and walked toward the front door. He wasn't going to see the second act, and, in fact, never saw the first. This was a press the flesh mission—nothing more. He showed up only for intermission to be seen in public. Now he could have fun. He'd go home and change into something more casual. Then, it would be down to Jazz Alley for some music and a few micro-brews. *With any luck*, he thought as he walked out the door and down the street. *there would be a woman or two to pick up and take home at closing time.* Alan untied his bow, loosened his collar then disappeared into the crowd.

A few blocks away, under the Space Needle in Key Arena, Special Agent in Charge O'Leary and his team were on a *real* stakeout. Only this was like no other stakeout he'd ever conducted. Ninety-nine out of a hundred stakeouts occurred in dark alleys in the freezing rain. You'd spend days and nights wet, cold, and miserable with only cold coffee and a stale sandwich to put in your stomach.

Here, he sat in the stands watching his favorite hockey team, the Seattle Thunderbirds, slap the puck around. In one hand he balanced a foot long hot dog with the works, and in the other a piping hot cup of Starbucks. *Man, I could get used to this kind of work,* he thought as he looked down at his target. Below him, just ten rows down wearing a white coat, was the drug supplier turned informant. He was to meet another man, from the Kingpin organization, to decide a date and location for their next drug delivery.

There were a half dozen agents in the Arena covering the exits. When the man with the connections showed up to meet the informant, an agent would notify O'Leary by radio. The 900 MHz receiver in his ear could pick up a signal from half a mile away, a far cry from the old days when you had to put a water glass on a wall to hear what was going on.

In the rafters, behind the lights, another agent pointed a laser microphone at the Informant. O'Leary would hear every word of the entire conversation between the Informant and the Connection. Once they knew the date and location of the drug delivery, he could start planning the bust.

"The Connection has arrived." O'Leary heard in his ear piece. A few moments later, a man in a black trench coat walked up and sat down next to the Informant. O'Leary watched the game and stuffed his face with the dog as he listened to the conversation.

"Targets are on the move," his receiver announced. O'Leary looked down in surprise when he heard the report. The Connection in the black trench coat had gotten up, and the Informant in the white coat followed. This wasn't supposed to happen, but O'Leary was prepared for it nonetheless. The man in the rafters could record the conversation until they left the building. At this instant, the agents at the exits were heading to their hiding spots. They had laser microphones as well, and from their various vantage points could follow the conversation wherever it went.

O'Leary followed from a long distance away continuing to listen in. He stuffed the rest of the dog in his mouth as he watched the targets walk out of the Arena. He smiled, pleased with the reception while he followed them toward the Space Needle.

They walked past the Needle and to the street just beyond, where a limousine stopped at the corner. The back door opened. The Connection stopped, looked at the Informant, and told him the date, time, and location of the drug exchange. O'Leary then watched the Connection get into the limo and speed away.

Perfect, O'Leary thought. Now all he needed to do was iron out the details of the bust. Everything was going like clock work. With any luck, they could pull this off without a hitch.

"Everyone disband and regroup back at HQ," O'Leary ordered into the microphone on his throat. O'Leary turned and walked quickly towards the parking lot.

Deputy Joe Rissley sat in her patrol vehicle just off Interstate 5. It was a good location- lots of trees, and a curve in the road that hid her vehicle from view until it was too late. Her radar gun was set to alarm at 85 mph. She didn't waste her time with the small fries, but instead waited for the big money tickets to come along—three this evening already.

There was a Porsche at 97, a Jaguar at 106, and, surprisingly enough, a Geo Metro at 92. The first two she'd given straight speeding tickets, while the Geo received both speeding and reckless driving citations. Although illegal to do so, the Porch and Jag were designed for high speed. She didn't blame the owners for wanting to stretch their legs. The Geo, on the other hand, was just too dangerous at those speeds, and if she could have given the guy a ticket for being stupid she would have.

She didn't particularly enjoy being on speed trap patrol, but it did have it's benefits. In front of her, leaning against the steering wheel, was her psychology book. Being alone on patrol for long hours at a time allowed her to think, write term papers, and get her studying done.

This was her last year in the Masters of Psychology program. It had taken her seven years, while working full time, to get her undergraduate degree, then the Masters took another three. Next, she planned on getting her Doctorate, for which she had already started working on her thesis.

She didn't plan on being a psychologist, per say. She chose this line of study because of her intense interest in people. For as long as she could remember, she had always noticed both the differences and similarities in people. She constantly wanted to know what made someone tick, why they felt a certain way, or why they acted in a particular manner. Although she admitted occasionally trying to psychoanalyze people, it wasn't because she wanted to pry. It was instead because she cared about them. She had an intense desire to want to get to know people on a more intimate level. Not the day to day how's the weather babble, but really get to know them.

She also used her studies to help her with her career in law enforcement. She studied criminal behavior and wrote countless term papers on the psyche of the criminal mind. For research, she visited many prisons, interviewed inmates, and wrote profiles on each one. The vast majority of the criminals she came in contact with were nothing more than common uninteresting thugs. Small time murderers, thieves, and the like that had nothing more to offer society other than a tax bill for rent and board at the local pen. They were a dime a dozen, one profile could be written to describe most all of them.

There were however, a small number of intriguing cases. These cases were of people with a high level of intelligence, who planned their crimes with methodical precision and detail. These were people who otherwise would and could be productive and successful in the community, but instead, chose to be criminals. Doctors, lawyers, business professionals, engineers, stock brokers, you name it and there are criminals in those fields that haven't been caught yet.

What were the differences and similarities between these people and normal everyday law abiding citizens? The answers that she came up with had surprised her. Whether they were law abiding or criminal, successful people were intelligent, clever, focused and patient. The main difference was that these criminals either were unable to, or in her opinion, chose not to distinguish between what was moral and immoral, ethical and unethical.

Of course, each particular crime and criminal was different, but these types of people were basically just variations on the same theme. Such as the housewife in Houston who robbed convenient stores. She was a stay at home mom whose husband made six figures a year. She had plenty of money with not a want or care in the world, yet she planned and carried out her crime flawlessly.

She would shop in a convenience store for months before deciding on the right time for a robbery, and for seven years she got away with it. Wearing a wig, she would walk into a store, pick up a few things that she needed for dinner that evening, then go to the clerk and say, *"I'll have these items and everything in the till and safe please."* With her groceries and loot in hand, she'd calmly walk out of the store, get into her minivan and drive off to pick up the kids from school.

She wasn't caught until her husband started looking in old storage boxes in the attic and found the money. She never spent a dime of it, or told anyone what she was doing. When interviewed by Joe, she had said that the money was just a way of keeping score. She never considered spending it.

Although the housewife knew that it was illegal, she didn't consider it to be particularly wrong. When Joe had asked her why she chose a certain store the housewife replied, "Well, because they raised the price of Huggies seventy-five cents a pack," fully expecting people to consider that a justifiable answer.

Easily and without emotion, the housewife would describe her day. "I washed some cloths, did the dishes, paid some bills, had the oil changed in the minivan, robbed a convenience store, picked up the kids, and got dinner on the table by the time my husband got home," with absolutely no distinction between right and wrong.

Conversely, a rich banker in LA that considered people who stole money to be the lowest scum of the earth had no problem at all with stealing jewelry. He was a good husband and father, gave lots of money to charity, never cheated on his taxes, and always treated his employees fairly. Not particularly caring much for jewelry himself, he had however given plenty of it to his wife. Birthdays, anniversaries, Christmas, you name it, jewelry was always a convenient gift.

For years while shopping for his wife, he would plan his crimes. Then one night he would break into a jewelry store and walk out with everything he could carry. He never sold any of stolen property or gave it as presents. Instead, he kept a fortune of jewels in old paint cans in the shed behind the house. When Joe had asked him why he did it, his only reply, without remorse or guilt, was to say, "With all the jewelry I've purchased in my life, I've never felt that I had gotten my moneys worth." In addition to their main reasons, Joe was able to get both the banker and housewife to admit that they also enjoyed the added excitement of their secret lives hidden within their ordinarily humdrum existence.

With practice, Joe had become very good at profiling criminals. For extra credit she profiled such people as Ted Bundy, Al Capone, and Bonny and Clyde. Her professors considered her work so insightful that they made it available to the FBI. The FBI was so impressed that they offered her a profiler job upon graduation, but she turned it down. A fact she had told no one. Her reason was that she wanted to finish her studies, but she also wanted to stay local. It was her secret plan and dream to take over as Sheriff when Harper retired.

The Doctorate thesis, which she'd already started working on, was to be a comparison between the psyches of criminals verses that of the just. What were their differences? What were their similarities? Was a person born with a criminal mind, was it created as a defense mechanism to outside influences, or were they just bad people? Could just people be turned to crime given the right circumstances, or was that inherently impossible?

Conversely, could the criminal mind be changed so that the person could return to a normal productive life? She knew that these questions had been asked before without resolution, yet she felt that they must be continually asked until a successful solution was discovered. It was something she was determined to find out.

She wanted to profile and compare some of the worst criminals with some of the greatest leaders in history. This would be difficult because most of them were either dead, or it was just too impracticable to write about them. All of the most dynamic people in history have already had tons of material written about them, and she didn't want to have to borrow from others work in order to complete her own.

She decided instead to compare two of her own case studies. For the just leader she had decided to use Sheriff Jim Harper. She didn't yet know who she would use for the devious criminal mind, but she knew that eventually someone would turn up, in some prison somewhere, that would be worthy of her project.

A file with Jim's name on it had been sitting in a drawer at home for quite a while, but it was still very thin. Joe had known Harper all her life, but had just barely scratched the surface into learning more about him. She had plenty of material on who he was on the outside, but nothing about who the man was underneath. As

Sheriff and public leader for almost three decades, he was a pillar of the community. Harper was this County's protector, shepherd, and guardian angle.

No matter what problem big or small, Jim would be there to help. When the lumber mill went bankrupt, Jim found a way to save peoples jobs and keep it open. Somehow he got both a software firm and a computer chip company to locate facilities in the county and hire mostly local workers. Even if it was something like getting snowed in, Jim was the first to grab a shovel.

Although she'd asked him many times, Harper had never told her how he was able to accomplish these things. He was just too shy that way, never bragging or tooting his own horn. But then he didn't need to, everyone else in the community did it for him. She had interviewed everyone she could. They all had a story about how Jim had done this or that, and many had expressed a belief that he must have done some illegal arm-twisting along the way.

She had checked into each case and found that, although Jim had walked a fine line, he had always conducted himself within the letter of the law. The *intent* of the law, on the other hand, was occasionally bent or bruised, but she knew that it was what Jim described as small town justice. That's where many of the disagreements had started between her and Harper.

She would ask him about a method he'd used to accomplish this or that, then tried to analyze it. When she pried too hard, he would get defensive and clam up, which usually started the argument. Joe believed that the line between what was right and wrong was clear and rigid, and that the *intent* of the law must be strictly adhered to. She felt that, although creative, many of his methods had twisted, bent, and blurred the line between black and white until there was mostly gray.

Harper, however, disagreed with her. He told Joe that his interpretation of the law had been molded by years of experience that came from living in the real world. Harper believed that Joe was young and naïve, and that she was trying to live life too much through a text book to be realistic.

No matter what their differences, Joe admired Harper because he was so unselfish. Everything he did was for everyone else. Jim reminded her of the character Jimmy Stewart played in the movie *It's a Wonderful Life*. He lived and worked a thankless, selfless life, and for what? So that he could protect the people and way of life he cared so much about. Did these same people know about everything Harper did for them? And if so, did they really care? Did they even deserve it? Probably not. But Jim would have done it anyway, regardless.

Harper especially cared for the children, and did everything he could to be a positive influence. He taught drivers education, and lectured at the high school about the dangers of under aged drinking and smoking. He spoke to grade school children about not playing with matches, handed out Mr. Yuck stickers, and played an active role in every youth sporting event around.

She smiled as she thought of him. That was *her* Sheriff. Always watching, always helping, always vigilant. No matter what the situation, Jim Harper found a way. That was what she admired most about him.

Although she considered Jim to be a close personal friend, getting to know him better had been hard. Jim was the strong silent type, who spoke with actions not words. If she wanted to know something personal about him, she had to practically pry it out with a crow bar.

In frustration she would complain, "Why don't you talk more?"

He would jokingly reply back with something like. "You do enough talking for the both of us," or, "I didn't want to interrupt you."

He was too much like…well…a *man*! That was it, after all, wasn't it? Men didn't talk to each other like women do. They don't talk about feelings, hopes, or dreams the way women do. Sure, they care about each other, but it's usually unspoken.

"Do you want to go fish'n?" one would ask.

"Yup," the other would answer.

"Do you want another beer?"

"Yup."

Men! How they got a conversation out of that she didn't know. If it wasn't for women, human kind probably wouldn't have developed speech at all. Most of men's communication skills were lacking in some way or another, and she attributed that to how much female influence there was in their lives.

Joe believed that the more female contact a man had, especially at a young age, contributed greatly to a man's ability to communicate. Her father and brothers did pretty well most of the time, because they had both herself and her mother to practice with everyday. Even then, conversation would be centered on baseball, or when the next monster truck rally was coming to town. When that so called conversation was over, there would be dead silence for quite a long time until one of her brothers would say…

"Do you want to go Fish'n?"

It made her want to just scream! *Men!*

Jim was the worst of them all. His whole life he hadn't had much female influence to speak of, until Nikki came along. Since then, Joe had noticed a considerable improvement in Jim and was glad to see a change for the better. With any luck, Jim would open up more and make Joe's thesis easier to complete.

But that was something she had to keep secret. If Harper found out she was studying and writing about him, he wouldn't approve. Jim had never thought much of psychologists, and believed she was wasting her time pursuing such an obscure line of study.

She remembered the day that Jim had found out about her choice of majors. He came to her and tried to talk her out of it, and then when he couldn't, he decided to approach her father. She recalled the way her father had described the situation. Jim had pulled him over in the middle of town to have a discussion. Harper tried to talk her father into influencing her to studying something more useful, and added that he was surprised that he had allowed his daughter to become such a misguided youth.

This was a story that she and her father laugh about to this day. That was one of the reasons Joe never really talked about her studies to anyone other than her parents. When people found out you were studying psychology, they all begin to believe you were psychoanalyzing everything. People were just weird that way.

Beep!...beep!...beep!

Rissley's radar gun alarmed as a red flash sped by. Looking at the display, she saw that it read 93. Tossing her textbook on the passenger seat, Joe started the vehicle, flipped on her lights and siren, and hit the gas. The Blazer jumped onto the highway, tires squealing and smoking as it raced after its prey.

By the time their late dinner was over, it was completely dark, except for the light of the fire. Clifford looked over at Buck and watched while his companion took a long drink from the second near empty bottle of whiskey. Buck belched loudly, then patted himself on the stomach with a satisfied smile on his face.

Clifford rolled his eyes and shook his head disapprovingly at his drunken friend, but said nothing. Instead, he turned his attention upward to the millions of stars in the sky. He had never seen so many stars. The lights of Seattle washed out the sky so much you were lucky to see only a few.

"Ha!" Buck laughs.

"What is it?" Clifford asked.

"That Rick sure knows how to pull a practical joke," came the reply.

"I thought you were mad at him?"

"No, I can't stay mad at Rick. He's too good a buddy. Besides, I would've done the same to him if I got the chance," Buck said, then took another drink from his bottle. He watched Clifford stab at the fire with a stick while looking into the flames as if bored. It was time for a story, he decided.

"Did you know these are the very mountains D.B. Cooper jumped into from that airplane he hijacked?" Buck asked.

"D.B. *who?*" Clifford replied.

Buck squinted across the fire at Clifford. "Do you mean to tell me you've never heard of the great plane robber D.B. Cooper?"

Clifford shook his head. "I've heard of the great train robbers like Jesse James, Butch Cassidy, and the Sundance Kid, but I didn't think someone could rob a *plane.*"

"That's because no ones ever been able to do it except D.B. Copper," Buck said. "If you think about it, Copper's a lot like Jesse James or some of the other so called heroes of the West, only better. Cooper never shot people or blew things up like you see in the movies. He was smarter, had more style, more finesse."

"Really? What happened?" Clifford asked, leaning towards the fire.

Bucks eyes narrowed when he saw he had a captive audience. He hesitated, for affect, before continuing. "Let me tell you the story of D.B. Copper," he said softly as he reached down next to him and picked up a fresh log. Throwing it into the center of the fire, a barrage of red embers shot out of the coals, racing into the dark night. Clifford's eyes followed them as they danced their way towards the stars, then burned themselves out.

When he looked back at Buck, he saw the flames had risen such that all that could be seen of his companion was his face. Clifford watched Buck lean forward, towards the fire. Buck's face was lit up by the flame that danced between them, sharply contrasting the deep blackness in the background. Clifford could see the heat from the fire eerily bend the image of Buck's face, making it appear almost ghost-like.

"The year was nineteen seventy-one," Buck said in a soft, practiced, monotone voice. "It was Thanksgiving, and people were busy traveling to be with their families. High in the air, a single passenger on a crowded plane stands up and yells, *I've got a bomb!*"

110

"D.B. Cooper!" Clifford exclaimed.

Buck continued to weave his tale now in a louder voice. "Instantly, the plane erupted in chaos. Babes cried and women fainted, but the lone man reassured them. *No one will get hurt as long as I get what I want.*"

"Did he steal all of their money and jewelry?" Clifford asked, his eyes widening with excitement.

"No, he wouldn't steal a penny from common folk." Buck shook his head in reply. "Cooper ordered the plane to land. Once on the ground he told the authorities he would exchange the hostages for a suitcase full of money. The Feds came through with the cash, and Cooper let everyone go except for the flight crew. All alone, Copper ordered the plane to take off knowing full well, no matter where the plane landed, a swarm of Federal Agents would be waiting. In fact, a number of helicopters and airplanes followed Cooper's plane through the air towards its unknown destination. On that cold, dark stormy, night the clouds hung low in this very valley and spewed great quantities of rain so thick you couldn't see ten feet in front of you."

Buck threw a small log into the fire. As if conjuring up magic, red hot embers leaped into the sky. Buck lifted his arms above his head and looked upward.

"Suddenly, the rumble of a low flying jet plane cut though the silence of the night, then disappeared as quickly as it came. Moments later, the dark silhouette of a man ripped through the clouds accelerating perilously towards the earth." Buck lowered his hands slowly as if tracing a path in the sky.

"What happened? Did he hit the ground?" Clifford asked impatiently.

"A parachute shot open and stopped the man's fall just feet from the ground!" Buck exclaimed. "The dark figure rolled as he hit the earth, then squatted, looking around." Buck looked around as if imitating Cooper's actions. "Then, as silently as he had come, D.B. Cooper collected the parachute and money, and disappeared into the darkness."

Buck continued, not missing a beat. "Like a hungry pack of wolves, scores of Federal Agents and hundreds of the Army's finest scoured these mountains looking for clues, but Cooper was too smart to be caught."

Clifford looked at Buck in disbelief. "Are you saying that D.B. Cooper got away from the FBI *and* the Army?"

"That's exactly what happened." Buck assured him then took another drink from the bottle.

111

"How do you know?" Clifford questioned.

"Because he told me so," Buck replied.

"*What?*" Clifford laughed. "You know D.B. Cooper?"

"That's right. He is a good friend of mine," Buck said, before letting out a huge belch.

"If he's such a good friend of yours, why didn't he give you some of his money?" Clifford asked.

"Oh, he's given me a lot more than that!" Buck laughed heartily. "Actually, every time I come up here I take a little more of Cooper's treasure home with me."

Clifford gave Buck a strange look, wondering if he was nuts or just plain drunk. "What are you talking about?"

"Tell me, Clifford, what would you do with all that money anyway?"

Clifford's eyes lit up, and he smiled. "I'd spend it!"

Buck again let out a huge laugh. "You remind me of myself when I was younger. My whole life I worked, saved, and invested… and for what? I didn't know. Just for the sake of having money I guess. Then finally, just before I retired, I met these bankers in Saigon who had a get rich quick scheme they let me in on. They told me if I invested my life's savings, they could make me a millionaire." Buck took a long drink from the bottle.

"Well did you give it to them?" Clifford asked.

"Every penny," Buck laughed as he replied. "I was such a fool!"

"What's so funny about that?" Clifford asked, curiously.

"Nothing," came the reply. "At least I didn't think so then. After I gave them the money, they pretended not to know me anymore—I lost it all! I was so mad I drove a tank right through the front door of the bank! The Military Police drug me out kicking and screaming and I almost got court-martialed. Broke and humiliated, I spent the last of my tour in the lock up." Buck looked at the ground, sighing heavily. Then after a moment raised his head and smiled. "After that I moved here, and D.B. Cooper showed me what true wealth was."

"What wealth are you talking about?" Clifford asked.

"In the seventy's, I made a lot of money giving guided tours to would be Cooper hunters. I was making it hand over fist, and not only from my customers. The Forest Service paid me to keep the trails repaired and the trash picked up. So I was getting paid twice just for being up here," Buck explained. "Even now, I get a few nostalgia lovers who want to dig up the past. I bring them up here, tell them stories and let them poke around a little."

"But it hasn't made you rich," Clifford observed.

"Oh, I'm rich all right. In more ways than one," Buck assured him. "But as I got older I realized money wasn't as important as I originally thought. What is important is protecting the way of life I've come to know."

Clifford flashed him a confused look, so Buck continued to explain.

"Look around you, boy," Buck said as he stretched his arms out in both directions. "Don't you know where you are? This is God's country and I live right in the middle of it. I'm a *bizillionare!*" Buck smiled from ear to ear.

Clifford again gave Buck a strange look. "And you have to protect it from whom?"

"Big money, big business, big government." Buck counted them out on his fingers. "You name it, they want it. They'll cut all the trees, mine all the ore, and leave this place a waste land."

"And you stop that from happening?" Clifford asked, skeptically.

"I do what I can," Buck replied. "Even the simplest of gestures make a difference. I bring people up here and they go back to the city with a greater appreciation for the value of leaving nature alone and come Election Day they vote to keep it that way."

Now Clifford was really starting to think Buck was very drunk or off his rocker or maybe both, so he changed the subject. "So if Cooper wasn't interested in the money, why did he hijack the plane?"

"It wasn't so much for the money as it was to prove a point," Buck replied. "To show the Feds there was someone out here smarter than they were. Someone they could never catch. Cooper struck a blow for all us little guys."

Clifford thought about that for a moment then spoke up again. "If he's a friend of yours, then where is he?"

Taking another slug of whiskey, Buck replied. "Oh, he's around. Sometimes when I'm up here alone he walks out of the darkness to visit me. I share my coffee, food, and the fire with him and then we go fishing. Then as quickly as he appeared, poof! He's gone."

Buck wobbled as he sat on the log. Lifting the bottle high into the air, he lost his balance taking another drink, and fell over. Clifford saw the bottle fly backward and Buck's legs flew into the air. Buck landed flat on his back.

"Uncle Buck!" he yelled, jumping up and running over to see if he was all right. Clifford knelt next to the motionless man and felt Buck's wrist for a pulse.   Suddenly, Buck began to snore. Clifford slowly stood up and looked down at his drunken companion.   "Crazy old man," he said, then turning he walked to the tent. Clifford returned with a blanket which he placed over Buck's legs and chest.   Then yawning, he went back to the tent and disappeared inside it.

9
Cowboy

Wednesday. Noon.

DEA Deputy Director Ted Cranston, a tall, conservatively dressed black man with salt and pepper hair, walked into his Seattle office carrying an armful of paperwork, and was noticeably drained after meeting with the Mayor. He and Mayor Demsey had strongly disagreed on the matter of Special Agent Alan Bradley. Demsey wanted to give Bradley a Commendation for his role in a major drug bust, which occurred a month earlier. News footage had shown a drug delivery in which Agent Bradley came out of nowhere to foil and arrest those involved. On TV, Bradley looked like John Wayne coming in to save the day.

Cranston explained to Demsey that Bradley's actions were less than heroic. In fact, Bradley's actions destroyed months of work that a crack team of DEA agents had put together. Bradley had allowed Kingpin, the true target of the bust, to get away. Cranston didn't feel that these actions deserved an award.

Cranston went to a cabinet and retrieved Agent Bradley's personnel file, then returned to his desk and sat down. The Mayor then made some phone calls to the governor, then back east to Washington DC, and spoke to Cranston's Superiors. To Cranston's dismay, Bradley was issued the Commendation. The paperwork he had with him was the copy for Bradley's folder.

Cranston threw a couple of Tums in his mouth and sighed heavily before opening the file. Inside were several other awards from Bradley's service in San Diego, as well as a list of arrests longer that Cranston's arm. It appeared that in his relatively short time with the Agency, Bradley had put together a remarkable record. In fact, Cranston had never seen one more impressive, but he also knew it was all bull. What should've been in Bradley's folder were the dozen or so reprimands Cranston had written, but was later forced to remove.

The acids in Cranston's stomach burned as he looked at the file. Reaching down, he removed a bottle of Pepto from his bottom drawer and took a big gulp. When Bradley first transferred to the Seattle office, Cranston thought he had a lot of promise. Agent Bradley seemed to have an uncanny ability to look at cases and see connections that nobody else had even thought of. He made it look easy as case file after case file was solved due to his instinctive ability.

Unfortunately for Cranston, Bradley didn't work well with the rest of the team. He refused to do his part when it came to the investigative work, constantly disobeyed orders, and didn't share information, preferring instead to work solo without proper backup. The whole situation was seriously hurting moral among the rest of the team.

He and Bradley argued constantly about it, and Cranston started to put him on report. When the reprimands were put in Bradley's personnel file, Cranston received phone calls from his Superiors to remove them. His hands were tied. Any attempt at punishing Bradley was swiftly suppressed.

The only thing Cranston could do was remove him from important cases. Bradley's official duties were reduced to being in charge of the investigation on marijuana use by minors and control of the Agency's evidence locker. That only made things worse. Bradley started interfering with cases he had been removed from, and conducting solo investigations without proper clearance. As far as Cranston was concerned, Bradley had gone too far. His constant insubordination and disrespect for the chain of command were inexcusable, yet he was about to be rewarded for it.

Bradley had had life too easy, Cranston thought. There were some things you just could not learn while working solo. Like the respect for your teammates and the dedication to your collective work, while also keeping an eye on the true goal, that final objective of crushing the enemy—nobody could do it alone. Cranston tried to teach Bradley that and get him involved in the team environment but was fought every step of the way.

Cranston sadly glanced over to the wall, where the picture of his Marine troop and Purple Heart hung in their frame. Such conduct wouldn't be tolerated back then, he knew. Back then, he, and hundreds of others like him, took orders and did their job without question.

He recalled being ordered up countless hills under heavy fire. They would never be able to take the summit if anyone conducted themselves like Bradley did. Not once did he question or disobey orders.

Cranston smiled proudly as he thought of his years of faithful service to his country. In the military, he had fought to protect the principles of democracy and now, in the DEA, fought to uphold the laws of the land. He had always tried to be a good Marine and be ever faithful—*Sempher Fi!* But at times like these, it was hard.

Cranston thought about his military career and how he had learned some of his most valuable lessons while in the Marines. He also thought about the time he had spent in Vietnam. That was an experience that affected everyone differently—yet all the same. Going through that tore at ever fiber of a person's soul, and without the support of his other team members, he wasn't sure if he would have been able to endure it.

It wasn't just the bugs, leaches, snakes or heat. It was that constant, lingering *stench* of death that penetrated your nostrils, skin and clothing. You were never away from it. How could you explain that to someone who had never been there? It was a time when the world was upside down. For those who had never been there, no description is possible. For those who had, none was necessary.

Cranston remembered his last mission, the one where he had earned his Purple Heart. Day and night, guns were working all around him, and the ghostly whistle of the bombs dropped by air support screamed past overhead before punishing the earth with unnerving indiscrimination. Explosions, like giant pear shaped flashes, lit up the smoky hill.

Then the bombing stopped and it was time to move. He gave the signal, then led the assault forward, up the hill through the smoke and fire. They had been ordered to this hill, one they had taken before and for some unknown reason given back to the enemy.

Like an angry child threw a rag doll, leaving it a crumpled heap in a corner, a mortar shell lifted him up and threw him down the hill. He didn't know what hit him, just that he ended up in the hospital without half a lung. The scars on his chest looked like a road map that told the story of a field surgeon too busy to take his time or be careful. His hand subconsciously came up to his chest and felt the jagged marks under his shirt at the thought of it.

He was one of the lucky ones, he knew, but not just because he had lived. He was lucky because throughout the countless months of rehab and counseling, he had the strong support of a loving family. Without their help, he didn't know where he would be today. The months, even years, it took to heal and fit back into normal society were the hardest he had ever known—even for a Marine. There were others who weren't so lucky, who didn't have the family support that he had. Many came back without enough direction or focus and wound up in soup kitchens, or worse, prison.

He looked back at the paperwork on his desk and frowned. Tonight, the mayor would be giving an award to Special Agent Alan Bradley of the DEA. *At least his Agency deserved it,* he thought. Cranston put the commendation in Bradley's folder, then put it away.

Five hours later, at the Mayor's office in Seattle, a crowd of officials and reporters gathered in a large conference room. One of the reporters looked at his watch, it was 6:55 p.m., just five minutes before the ceremony was scheduled to begin. He checked his video camera, once again, to make sure it was working properly.

Chester "Chet" Green had never been a member of the *"in"* crowd. He wasn't particularly cool, hip or trendy. He never made headlines, scored the winning touchdown, got straight A's or was elected valedictorian. It was for this reason that he was known as a *"fringe"* player. He wasn't a part of the popular crowd, but he was always around it.

For as long as he could remember, he always wanted to be the center of attention, and he loved to hear himself talk. Not really developing an extraordinary life of his own, he borrowed from those that did, and reported it to others who would listen. As a child he was often heard saying things like, "Mommy! Mommy! Guess what Billy did!" Later it was things like, "Hey Jane, guess who Mary was seen with this weekend."

In high school, and then in college, he knew all the right people and went to all the right functions. He wasn't particularly liked or disliked, but he was seen as a necessity to those who wanted to be or stay popular. The members of the "in" crowd needed their entourage, especially Chet, who was known as a *key* fringe player. If you were cool, hip, and with it, you didn't do your own advertising or self-promotion. That was just too un-cool, un-hip and un-with it to do so. You needed someone like Chet.

If a cheerleader was going to have a party, she need only make a few key phone calls, the first being to Chet. After she invited him, she knew he would spend the next several hours calling people to tell them about it.

"Everyone that's someone will be there," he would say. It wouldn't take long for the person having the party to start receiving phone calls asking about it. Semi-popular people could become more popular or vise versa depending on whether they made or received such a phone call and when.

Chet would mingle from small group to small group at the party sharing the latest scoop, gossip, or dirt. The next day he could be counted on to make phone calls explaining to people how successful or unsuccessful the party was. This was more often than not directly proportional to how well he liked the host.

It was no surprise to anyone that Chet would choose journalism as a major in college. As editor of the college paper, he was often writing about the evils of the latest Administration, the freedom of speech, or the latest sorority scandal. He often quoted the First Amendment, although he had never read it all the way through. Some people called him an ambulance chaser because he considered a police scanner to be an important tool of the trade.

Chet disliked the title of reporter and insisted on being referred to as an investigative journalist. His idol was Ted Koppel and he dreamed of hosting a hard hitting program like *Night Line*, even though he rarely watched it. It was, however, rare that he missed an airing of *Hard Copy* or *American Journal.*

It was in college where Chet and Alan met. Chet believed he had discovered Alan, when in fact it was Alan who chose to seek Chet out. From the first day on campus, Alan made it a point to find out who was who. When he found out Chet was not only a key fringe player, but also a journalist, he thought he'd scored double bonus points. Alan "accidentally" bump into Chet on the street and changed a question about directions into a six hour dissertation about himself over lunch, beer. and a pool table. That was all right with Chet, he had nothing better to do. Besides, Alan was buying.

They became good friends, and within a few weeks decided to be roommates. Alan spent quality time learning about his new friend's strengths and weaknesses. He found out what he liked and didn't like, and what he wanted and didn't want from life. Alan found that with practice, he could manipulate Chet's stories and editorials—a skill that would prove useful.

Chet's decision to room with Alan wasn't a difficult one. After all, Alan was popular, rich, had an influential family, lots of

119

women, and a cool car. He also took advantage of the usual roommate benefits.

Having the use of Alan's car and the apartment for dates, not to mention, borrowing money he never got around to paying back were perks he could get used to. Besides, Alan turned out to be the best writing material Chet had ever had. Being a criminal justice major, Alan was constantly quoting laws governing such things as illegal search and seizures, the right to privacy, and probable cause.

With Alan's influence, Chet's writing style became better. He started writing informative pieces, useful to the reader's everyday life, not just the old, dry soap-box junk he was used to. Some of his articles were good enough to be carried by real papers in the real world, not just the campus rag. After graduation, Alan talked Chet into coming with him to San Diego. While there, Chet always got the exclusive on Alan's drug busts and, in exchange, Chet was always happy to put a pro-Alan spin on things.

Chet's career as a freelance investigative reporter for the most part floundered. He attempted to write a series on inner-city life. His few articles on *Teenage Street Kids* and the *Back Alley Urban Mental Wards* were not big hits. His college soap-box style just wasn't received well by the mainstream press.

He started to rely more and more on Alan, because crime scenes were always big attention getters. Even when Alan had nothing to do with an investigation, he could be conveniently found at the scene for an expert evaluation of the situation. The two quickly built up a series of canned questions and answers to different situations, eventually working it to a polished perfection.

Alan acted like a color commentator at a baseball game, filling in the slow periods with interesting facts about things like how to find fingerprints and other evidence gathering techniques. He didn't mind doing it either. Any opportunity to get his face and name on a prime time news cast was worth going out of his way for.

Chet considered the two of them to be a team. He believed that with Alan, they would rise to future fame and fortune. Alan, on the other hand, thought otherwise. Although he encouraged that train of thought, Alan really saw Chet as nothing more than a useful tool. Because of Chet's lack of acceptance by the main steam press, Alan thought that someday he might become a liability. He knew that one day he would have to trade up, so to speak, to a reporter who had more national coverage potential.

Seattle Mayor Adam Demsey didn't show his irritation. He'd been a politician for too long to make that mistake, but he couldn't help feeling it. Being in a city with Alan Bradley had been like wearing sandpaper underwear in a salt factory. For the past two years, Bradley was constantly under foot. You couldn't go to any major events without running into him. He was the most opportunistic little jerk Demsey had ever met.

Demsey knew that was no accident—he knew this kid's father. Alan Bradley Sr. had been a road block to social change for decades. One of the richest men in the northwest and a strong Republican, Alan's father seemed to mold or destroy political careers at a whim.

Demsey knew that Bradley's father was behind the many attempts to unseat him. From being labeled a "tax and spend" Democrat to an enemy of the business community, the most recent attacks were against his low-income housing project. Demsey knew that many politicians slipped into obscurity after retirement, and he had no intention on letting that happen to him. He intended for these housing projects to be his legacy. He wanted to leave office with a successful contribution to the community.

After being plagued with schedule delays and cost overruns, for which he knew Bradley's father had played a role, his future legacy was now weakened by a new disease—drugs. Low-income housing was suppose to bring hope to a portion of the community that was lacking. However, it had also been a magnet for drug dealers who wanted to take that hope away again. Special Agent Alan Bradley had made a few drug busts in these housing projects. Although relatively minor arrests, Bradley managed to make them front page headlines. Ignoring the fact that drug use and the crime rate was at its lowest in a decade, the press ate this kid up!

Demsey had let himself be caught off guard, a fact that kept him up at night. The election was practically around the corner, and the poles were showing that people believed he was soft on crime all because he didn't share the Governor's exuberance for building prisons.

No matter what the reason, nonetheless, his administration was scrambling. His advisors suggested that he should go with the flow and start giving out more awards to law enforcement agents. If drug busts were what the public wanted, then Demsey needed to be on the front page leading the way.

It was necessary for Mayor Demsey to get this publicity in a bad way. He needed one more term to make his legacy work, and if he had to sleep with the devil to make it happen, he would. The polls showed that as many people who knew Agent Bradley, knew the Mayor. With every interview, Bradley painted the picture of a city rampant with crime with an administration unwilling or unable to deal with the problem.

Tonight would be the start to changing that image. It would be all smiles and hand shakes as Demsey presented the award to Bradley in front of the press corp. He would continue having award ceremonies until everyone finally gave up on the rhetoric and realized that crime had actually decreased since he became Mayor— a point he would make again tonight.

"Well, it looks like everything is about ready," he said to himself as he saw that most everyone had taken their seats. "Time to get this show on the road." With that, he straightened his tie and walked towards the front of the room.

Special Agent in Charge O'Leary stood against the back wall in his wrinkled suit, watching all the people muddle about. Agent Anderson walked over to him.

"Hey, Agent O'Leary, do you have any idea what this is about?" he asked.

Looking slightly annoyed, O'Leary replied, "That jerk Bradley is getting a commendation."

Just then, Deputy Director Cranston, in his best suit, walked in, surveyed the room, and then walked over to them. Putting a hand on O'Leary's shoulder he said in a low tone of voice, "Is everything on for tonight?"

"Yes sir, everything is going as planned," O'Leary replied in a serious tone. "Are you coming along?"

"No," the Director told him, "I have to meet with the Mayor, then finish some paperwork. Besides, you've run a top-notch investigation up to now, I don't want to steal any of your glory. I'm only sorry you have to stand here and see someone else get your commendation."

"That's okay, sir," O'Leary replied. "If everything works out tonight, it will more than make up for it."

Pointing at the younger man, Cranston commented, "Take care of Anderson. This will be his first bust and I don't want him getting hurt. And whatever you do, don't let *Cowboy* find out what's going on."

"No problem, sir," O'Leary replied.

Then the Director turned his attention to Anderson. "Stay close to O'Leary tonight, kid. He's my best Agent and you can learn a lot from him."

"Yes sir," Anderson assured him. He waited until Cranston turned and walked away before asking the question. "Who's Cowboy, and what did he mean by all that?"

"Well kid, since you're fresh out of the Academy, I guess someone should fill you in on what's been going on here lately." O'Leary hesitated a moment and looked around before continuing.

"A couple of years ago, Agent Bradley transferred into our department from somewhere in California. He had a few commendations in his folder, and his former CO gave him a sparkling recommendation. Director Cranston assigned him to my team and, at first, he seemed to fit in all right. I was impressed by his results, but not by his methods. He's just too unpredictable and unreliable to be safe. Patient and careful planning is the key to safety, but Bradley prefers to rush in quickly on hunches."

"So why didn't you report him to Cranston?" Anderson asked.

"I did," O'Leary nodded. "Cranston backed me all the way and jumped his butt in front of the whole squad. I thought that would settle things, but it didn't. Bradley's actions never changed, so he was removed from my team and all major cases.

"Then, about six months ago, I got a tip from my informant that a large shipment of cocaine was coming into Pier 79. It was a special shipment, and Kingpin himself was supposed to be there to inspect it. I had thirty agents in position to seal off the area once Kingpin arrived, but we had no such luck. As the shipment hit the dock, Bradley came flying out of nowhere with guns blazing. The damn fool would've gotten himself killed if I hadn't called in the troops to save his butt. Needless to say, Kingpin got away, and months of investigative work went down the drain."

"That's against departmental procedure!" Anderson said, remembering how strict they were at the Academy about going by the book. "He should've gotten canned for it!"

"He did—well almost. Cranston suspended him and took his badge, but a couple of hours later Cranston got a phone call from the Governor's office asking him to reconsider."

"What does the Governor have to do with it? We're Federal, we don't answer to him," Anderson stated.

"That's what Cranston thought when he told Governor Wilson to go fly a kite. However, when the Regional Chief of Internal Affairs walked into his office to investigate him for harassment of one of his Agents, Cranston had to back down. Bradley got his badge back and credit for the bust. Cranston's been walking on egg shells ever since. We nicknamed Bradley "Cowboy" and nobody tells him anything about their cases anymore.

"If Bradley screwed up so bad, why is he getting a commendation?" Anderson asked.

"I'm not sure, kid." O'Leary shrugged. "All I know is that Governor Wilson won re-election last fall due to his hard on crime platform. It was so successful that Mayor Demsey must be trying to do the same thing. Look around, I've never seen this much press for an award before. This will get Demsey on the front page tomorrow for sure."

"I'm sorry to hear that, sir," Anderson said, sympathetically. "That could have been you on the front page with him."

"That's all right, kid. If everything goes well tonight, things will be different. There's another shipment coming in, and, according to my informant, Kingpin is taking the deliver in person." O'Leary could see that almost everyone had taken their seats. "It looks like this party's stating to get underway. I'll fill you in on the rest back at HQ, when this is all over." As he said this, Mayor Demsey stepped up to the podium.

"Good evening ladies and gentlemen, and thank you for coming," Mayor Demsey said with a smile. "Tonight we're here to recognize one of Seattle's finest. A bright young agent of the Drug Enforcement Agency who epitomizes everything I stand for in law enforcement. Special Agent Alan Bradley is a tough, aggressive, no non-sense cop who wants to make a difference. With the help of people like Agent Bradley, the steps this Administration has taken to reduce crime and drugs are working. We are cleaning up this city, and making it a better place to live."

"Oh, *brother*," O'Leary rolled his eyes, whispering to Anderson. "I'm going out to have a smoke." O'Leary walked out the door, and then lit up a cigarette. He stood outside and looked through the window as he watched the Mayor give his speech. He couldn't listen to that garbage without getting mad, and that wouldn't be productive for tonight's venture.

He couldn't help but worry. *Have I prepared for everything?* he wondered. *Could anything go wrong?* No, he had done this too many times before. If everything goes as planned, he would have the suspects cuffed and stuffed before they know what hit them. All this without firing a shot.

That's more than that little jerk knows, he thought as he watched Bradley, in his well-tailored Italian suit, step to the podium and shake the Mayor's hand. The Mayor and Bradley held the pose so that the reporters could get pictures from all angles. *Bradley has probably practiced that pose for hours in front of the mirror,* O'Leary thought, as the camera's lights reflected off Bradley's slicked back hair and sparkling teeth.

"Hello, Alan, and congratulations," a voice said from behind Bradley.

As Bradley turned he saw an elderly statesman. "Governor Wilson, it's good to see you. What are you doing in town?"

The two shook hands while the cameras clicked off picture after picture. "I'm here to give a talk at the Annual Washington State Mayor's Convention, and I thought I'd come see you and take advantage of a free photo opportunity," Wilson replied, changing positions for more photos. "How's your father, Alan? I haven't seen him since my re-election fund raiser last summer. By the way, I didn't get a chance to thank him for his generous contribution to my campaign. Will you do that for me?"

"He's doing great, and of course I will. I'll be having brunch with him at the club this Sunday, why don't you join us?" Bradley replied.

"I wish I could, but I have to be in Olympia by Friday. Besides, once your father and I start talking about the old days, you'll never shut us up," Wilson chuckled. "I've got to get going. I'm late for a meeting."

"Thank you for coming, sir," Bradley said as Wilson walked away.

After a few minutes, O'Leary could see that things were starting to break up, so he walked back into the room and over to Anderson. "Kid, get the team together and meet me at HQ ASAP, for a final briefing."

"Yes sir," came the reply, as O'Leary turned and exited the room.

10
Bust

"What time do you have, Chet?" Bradley asked, as he stood up and drank the last of his beer.

"Eleven o'clock," came the answer as Bradley pulled another beer from the cooler and tossed the empty off the pier and into the bay.

"Why did you get this stuff? You know how I hate domestic lager," Bradley said, then sat down next to his friend.

"You know I can't afford those fancy micro-brews. Besides, when did you start complaining about free beer?" chuckled Chet.

They both sat silently as they took in their surroundings. They were in the shadow of a large crate at the end of the pier, overlooking the mouth of the Duwamish Waterway. In front of them lay Elliott Bay which filled the crisp air with the smell of salt. Directly across from them was the Seattle skyline, softly lighting up the bay.

"Did you see Cranston's face tonight?" Bradley laughed. "I thought his head was going to explode!"

"You shouldn't push him so much, you know. He is your superior officer."

"That jerk can't tell his head from his butt," Bradley said. "It won't take me long to get his job."

"Look at you. You're in an awful hurry to climb the ladder. You sure have changed since we were back in college," Chet observed. "Back then all you cared about was having fun and chasing women."

"What's changed?" Bradley joked. There was no change. Alan had never told Chet about the plans he and his father had. "If anyone's changed it's you. You were so idealistic, trying to change the world by writing about all the injustice."

"I still want to do that, but it doesn't always pay the bills, ya know," Chet replied. "At least I'm not stepping on people to get to the top."

"Don't give me a lecture on ethics, pal," Bradley argued. "You've been known to put your own little twist on stories before."

"Only to serve a greater purpose," Chet defended. "People won't listen until you liven things up a little."

"Exactly my point," replied Bradley. "If I waited my turn, like those other bozos, I'd be ready to retire before I could change things. Look at us-we're young, empowered, and filled with energy and ideas. Isn't that what we were taught in college? That our generation has to take charge and fix everything that's been screwed up for so long. If so, who cares if I push a few old dinosaurs out of the way as I go?"

"I guess you're right," Chet said, timidly.

"Of course I'm right!" Bradley assured him. "It's like I've been telling you for years. You and I can be useful to each other. You can give me the press coverage I need to become known throughout the city, and I make sure you get the exclusive interviews and coverage of all my arrests. Just like tonight. Your story will be on the front page tomorrow."

"Yeah, we're like Ali and Cosell," Chet joked.

"Look at Governor Wilson and my father," Bradley continued. "There's a prime example of what two college roommates can do for each other. They stuck together and got to the top of their fields. You just stick with me and you'll have your own news staff working for you in no time."

They both were silent, for several minutes. They thought of the possibilities while sitting and listening to the waves breaking on the pier, gazing at the city that was laid out in front of them. From somewhere off in the distance, a soft drone broke through the otherwise tranquil atmosphere.

"What's that noise?" Bradley asked. Chet strained to listen as the low hum of a small boat came over the water.

"Fishing boat, I suppose," he said as he leaned back against the crate.

"Maybe," Bradley said. "But what is there to catch at this time of night and where are they? I don't see any running lights."

"Big deal, so his running lights are out. Is that a Federal crime?" Chet joked. "Why don't you just sit back and have another beer, Sherlock."

"Yeah, you're probably right." Bradley laughed, then leaned back against the crate. He tried to relax, but something about the lack of running lights nagged strongly at the back of his consciousness as the hum came closer. Bradley slowly leaned forward, squinted his eyes then lifted his hand and pointed. "There."

Chet leaned forward as he watched Bradley's finger trace the path of a dark shadow moving slowly among the waves.

"I wonder why he has no lights on." Bradley commented.

"If his running lights are burnt out, maybe the rest of his lights are too. Also any light on deck could trash his night vision, making it tougher to see where he's going," Chet guessed.

"Yeah, maybe," Bradley said. "I wonder where he came from?"

"It's not uncommon for boats to ferry seamen to and from those freighters anchored in the bay, you know," Chet informed Alan.

"That's true, but something rubs me the wrong way about it," Alan replied, as the shadow moved past them and up the river. "Stay here." Bradley stood and walked behind the crates where his black corvette and Chet's red Chief Grand Cherokee were parked. Bradley opened the corvettes trunk, and pulled out a pair of binoculars.

"What are you going to see with those?" Chet asked, when Bradley returned.

"When the boat moves under the West Seattle Bridge it'll pass under the bridge lights. Maybe I can see something then. Come with me," Bradley said, walking up the pier in the dark after the boat. Bradley trained the binoculars on the shadow as it slowly moved into the light.

"It's a dark blue twenty footer, with a single outboard and forward cabin. The drivers the only one on deck," Bradley reported softly. "Wait a minute." As he spoke another man emerged from the cabin carrying a coat. The man looked around slowly and he started putting on his coat.

"What's *that?*" Bradley asked himself out loud, focusing the field glasses on the man's shoulder. The man had an oozie strapped under his arm that he quickly covered up with the coat. As the man traded places with the driver, Bradley watched the driver pick up a pistol from off the dash and stick it in his coat. At that instant, the boat passed out of the light and back into the darkness.

"If those are fishermen, why do they need guns?" Bradley asked Chet when he lowered the binoculars.

"*Guns?*"replied Chet, surprisingly.

"Do you have your gear with you?" Bradley asked.

"Of course, I'm never without it. Why?"

"Something's going on and we're going to find out what. Come on! We've got to hurry." Bradley and Chet ran back to their vehicles. Bradley pulled out a map and a flashlight, then opened the map on the hood of the Cherokee.

"Let's see, there are four boat moorage clubs on this river, they'll have to go to one of them," Bradley said. "*Quickly!* Follow me to this first one. And keep your lights off."

Alan stuffed the map hastily in his car and started it up. Chet jumped into his Chief and followed as Bradley raced down the pier and onto the street. When they approached the first boat club, Bradley parked a half a block away and ran to the fence with his binoculars with Chet close behind. They scanned the water.

"There!" Chet pointed. The shadow had already passed the club and was moving up stream.

"Let's go! The next one is a mile away," Bradley said. They ran to their vehicles then sped off. They were gaining on the boat now, but when they arrived at the next two clubs the result was the same. They crouched in the shadows and watched as the boat slowly moved up river.

"One left. That's *got* to be it. It's two miles upstream, we should get there well ahead of them," Bradley said as they again jumped into their vehicles and raced off.

It was just past one in the morning when they approached the last club. They parked further away then before in an alley and ran quickly to the fence, crouching in the darkness. Bradley scanned the club below him slowly with his binoculars. There were four separate docks filled with boats. Each dock had a sign labeling them "A" through "D". There were a few empty slips scattered among the moored boats.

While they crouched in the darkness, Alan scanned the docks. "Nothing," he whispered. Then he had an idea. This was the perfect opportunity to try out his new toy. "Wait here," he told Chet, handing over the binoculars. Chet continued to scan the docks, but saw nothing. Alan raced back to his car and pulled something from the trunk. Running back to Chet, he crouched down and powered the unit up.

"What's that?" Chet asked.

"A night vision scope," Alan replied. "I ordered it from a catalog and it just got here the other day." He put it to his eye and started to scan the shadows. The darkness opened up as if lit by a green moon. He was careful not to focus on the marina. The lights from the marina were blinding to anyone using night vision, as if looking into the sun.

"It could dock in any of those," Chet whispered as he counted up the empty slips.

Bradley continued to scan the darkness slowly. "Wait a minute," he whispered. He caught some movement above dock D, the farthest one up stream. A figure moved slightly, but just enough for Bradley to notice. Behind a crate, he could barely make out three figures. They were well camouflaged, and he would've missed them all together if it weren't for that slight movement. Alan smirked slightly at the rookie-type mistake and guessed accurately that the figure was Agent Anderson. That meant O'Leary had to be one of the others.

"There are lookouts above dock D," Bradley reported. He then stood up slowly, being careful to stay in the shadows. Alan watched closely.

The three figures sat motionless behind the crate, using it to shield themselves from the light emitted from the direction of the marina as they patiently waited and watched for something on the river down stream. They were waiting for the boat, he guessed. There was something definitely going on tonight, he was sure of it. Alan and Chet were out of the lookout's field of vision, and weren't likely to go unnoticed.

"There has to be drug agents down on the docks," Bradley whispered. He took the binoculars and examined the dock carefully, but saw nothing.

Special Agent in Charge O'Leary crouched low behind a crate in the blackness of the night. To his right was Agent Case and to the left was the rookie- Anderson. They were decked out in the latest military assault attire and weaponry. Their black clothing blended them perfectly into the night. Boots, pants, jackets, gloves, body armor, and helmets- the only thing not covered with black material was their eyes. Covering those was the latest in American night vision technology.

Even their weapons were camouflaged. Case carried his sniper rifle in a loose relaxed fashion. He had been on countless raids, and knew that an Agent could get worn out simply waiting for something to happen. This was, however, the Rookie's first drug bust and he was fidgety. He held his M-16 assault rifle tightly, ready for action.

"Relax," O'Leary whispered to him. "It's going to be a while yet."

Anderson nodded and tried to do as he was told but, found it difficult.

O'Leary looked out over the target area. Although there was no moon and the clouds blocked the stars, the night vision goggles gave him a good view of his surroundings. It was an eerie green, but other than that the technology was excellent. He keyed the button on his belt for the radio. The microphone attached to his throat picked up his whisper.

"This is Lookout One," he said softly. "Lookout Two report."

"We are in position and the target zone is clear," came the reply in O'Leary's earpiece. He took the binoculars and examined the brushy bank on the shore across the river where Lookout Two was posted. Even with the night vision goggles, he couldn't see them. The one spotter and one sniper were well camouflaged.

"Assault Teams One and Two report."

"We are ready and holding position," came the reply. Both teams were on separate police boats, one up stream and the other down stream of the target zone. Tucked away in coves along the shore, they lay hidden from view.

"Backup Team report."

"Ready and holding position," came the reply. The backup team was hiding in several large crates next to the entrance of dock D.

"Air One report."

High above Seattle, a DEA helicopter shadowed its target using a telescopic night vision scope and infra-red detection equipment.

"We have target Kingpin in sight. We have one limousine escorted by two Lincolns, one leading and one trailing. In the limousine are Kingpin and his personal bodyguard. The two Lincoln's have three security guards plus a driver in each. They just turned onto the West Seattle Bridge. ETA to Zone, ten minutes," came the reply.

Excellent, O'Leary thought. Everything was going as planned. He reviewed the sequence of events again in his mind. Target One, the boat carrying the drugs and his informant, will come up the river soon. It will turn into deck D, come to a stop, and tie up in slip 5- the only empty slip on the dock.

By then, Target Kingpin will have arrived and made their way down to dock D with the pay off money. Kingpin is expected to be accompanied by his personal bodyguard, plus no fewer than six other security guards. At that time, the drugs will be unloaded from the boat, and put on the dock next to the money.

The drugs will be examined by Kingpin while the money will be counted by the supplier-informant. All of this will be recorded by the four video cameras and microphones hidden in different locations on dock D. From every angle, Kingpin will be recorded buying the drugs, securing an air tight case against him for court.

O'Leary will then give the signal to move in. Team Backup will come out of hiding and secure the only exit from the dock. O'Leary will identify themselves as Federal Agents and order them to put their hands in the air and not move. If any security guard pulled out a gun, the two snipers have been ordered to take them out.

Kingpin's personal guard may be a different story. He'll be right next to Kingpin and it will be too dangerous to shoot at him from a long distance. O'Leary wanted Kingpin alive. They cannot afford a bad shot.

Therefore the personal body guard would be the responsibility of Assault Team One, lead by Agent Rodriguez. Each police boat carried a team of four agents on its bow. Within seconds of the signal, they would reach dock D from opposite directions.

Agent Rodriguez will lead the assault, and is ordered to neutralize the body guard with any force necessary. He knew that Angela won't let him down. The only people left standing will be Kingpin and the supplier-informant.

Then the acting would begin. O'Leary would come down dock D with his pistol drawn. Only it was no ordinary weapon. It was instead a radio transmitter that looked like a gun and fired only blanks. When he was in position, in clear view of Kingpin, the informant would start the show.

The informant will pull out his own gun filled with blanks and pretend to fire at O'Leary. O'Leary will then aim and fire at the informant. The instant he fired, the gun would send a radio signal to the fake blood package under the informant's shirt. The pack would explode and the informant, covered with fake blood, will fall backwards into the water. Just under the surface, a diver was waiting to take the informant to safety. In front of Kingpin, they would pretend to look for a body, but none would be found.

Since the Kingpin will believe that his supplier was now dead, he won't suspect him as an informant. The informant would then rat out Kingpin's entire operation while safe in the Federal Witness Protection Program. This could be the bust that would make O'Leary's career. The information received from the informant could lead to hundreds more arrests and convictions. It could shut down the largest organized crime ring on the west coast.

O'Leary couldn't help but smile. After tonight, he should get the recognition, promotion, and transfer he wanted. Just as long as everything went according to plan.

He had worked it out a hundred times. The assault would consist of overwhelming numbers and fire power. The Agents were well trained, and had the latest in military weaponry and protective attire. Anything that could go wrong, he had planned for... or so he thought.

"Well it looks like you were right, Alan. It's like falling off a log for you isn't it?" Chet had always been impressed with his friend's ability. "Maybe I can get some pictures when those Agents hit the boat."

"Bull!" exclaimed Bradley. "Those jerks have a bust tonight and they didn't let me in on it! They're going to pay for that."

"What are you talking about?"

Bradley didn't answer. Instead, he trained his binoculars on the docks. There was only one open slip on dock D, while there were several in the other docks. It *had* to be dock D, he was sure of it. He knew that O'Leary would control the target zone environment as much as possible. Knowing O'Leary, Alan guessed that all the agents would be on Dock D and none would be on A, B or C.

"Here comes the boat," Chet informed Alan.

Bradley looked down stream and saw the shadow come around the bend in the river. "We have to move fast," he whispered.

"For what?"

"No time to explain. Just get your video camera and follow me. Whatever you do, don't let that lookout see you. Now hurry." Chet turned, then ran back to the Chief. Bradley crouched low and moved down the fence to the gate.

He took lock-picking utensils from his coat pocket, and inserted the metal sticks into the lock. As he turned them, the lock clicked and the gate opened. By that time Chet was back and crouching behind him. Staying low and looking around, they quickly made their way to the docks.

At the ends of docks A and B, respectively, there were two large boats tied up. One eighty foot sailboat, and the other a one hundred foot yacht. Too large for normal moorage, both were tied up at the end of each dock.

"Lookout One to Lookout Two, over," O'Leary said into the radio.

"Go ahead," squawked the ear piece.

"Remember, when Target One passes behind that sailboat and yacht, we will loose contact with them from this side. You'll have to keep us informed of anything out of the ordinary, over," O'Leary ordered.

"Roger that."

O'Leary took off his night vision goggles, then picked up his binoculars and trained them on the shadow in the water. He couldn't see the two figures moving down dock A.

"Target Kingpin has arrived." O'Leary heard Air One report. He could see the lights from the cars as they came down the street and began slowing down as they got closer. *Perfect timing*, he thought.

Bradley could hear the drone of the boat engine as he reached the eighty foot sailboat at the end of dock A. Chet stayed on the dock, behind a boat, while Bradley slowly eased his way onto the sailboat and into the shadow of its mast. As the motorboat came closer, Bradley pulled the shiny nickel plated .44 Magnum Desert Eagle from the shoulder holster under his jacket and loaded a round into the chamber.

Bradley could see the silhouette of the driver. He timed his jump. Bradley dove onto the deck tackling the driver. They both hit the deck with a loud thud, then Alan hit the stunned driver on the head with the Desert Eagle. Instantly the boat changed directions and lost power. Bradley spun around as the shadow of a man holding an oozy emerged from the cabin. Bradley kicked his arm as the machine gun fired into the air.

Rattitattat!

Boom! Boom!

Bradley immediately fired two rounds into the man's chest. As the shadowy figure fell backwards, Bradley saw another obscure gunman move towards him.

Boom! Boom!

Alan fired without hesitation.

The commotion on deck took the supplier-informant completely by surprise. He had been sitting in the dark cabin reviewing the plan in his head when he heard the struggle. The second guard instantly hurried to check on the first. When the thunder of shots rang out, the informant instinctively pulled out his fake gun. The last thing he saw was a shadow at the top of the stairs, a flash, and it was over.

"*Damn!* What was that!" screamed O'Leary.

"It looks like there's a fight on deck," the radio squawked.

O'Leary heard the sound of tires squealing.

"Target Kingpin is bugging out!" Air One reported as O'Leary caught a fleeting glance of the cars changing directions and speeding away.

"Assault Teams One and Two move in now! *Move! Move! Move!*" O'Leary yelled into the microphone. Instantly the pair of fifteen-foot police boats darted into the river from their hiding places one hundred yards up and down stream of the marina. Powerful spot lights on the boats lit up the entire river as they raced from both directions toward Target One.

"*Damn!*" Bradley said, as the boat was instantly lit up. Bradley slapped cuffs on the unconscious man on deck. He had to hurry, they were almost upon him. He flipped a switch for the cabin lights, and looked inside to see two men lying on the floor in pools of blood surrounded by bags of white powder stacked to the ceiling. It was like taking candy from a baby, he smirked, grabbing the wheel and slamming down the throttle. He spun the boat around and maneuvered it into an empty slip in dock A, then jumped out to tie it off.

"All agents to dock A! *Move it!*" yelled O'Leary into the radio as he and Anderson sprinted for the docks. They both instantly tore away the black cloth velcroed to their chest and back that covered the florescent yellow letters DEA, identifying them as Federal Agents.

Chet ran to the boat, his video camera recording the seen. As Bradley tied up the boat, Chet leaped aboard panning left to right with the camera.

The large flood lights from the police boat lit up the night. It raced towards its target with siren blaring. Assault Team One was hanging onto the front of the boat rail with their legs so that they could keep their weapons ready. The light from the boat cast long shadows through the marina.

One body was motionless lying on the deck of the target boat, while, in the shadows, Agent Rodriguez could see another person moving. Just yards away, the boat pilot announced into the load speaker. "Federal Agents! Put your chest on the deck and your hands out!"

Before a collision could occur, the pilot slammed the throttle in reverse, expertly coming to stop just feet from the dock.

With her revolver ready, Rodriguez yelled. "Cover me! I'm going in!" Using the boats forward momentum, she jumped, launching herself towards the target boat's deck. Her team members swept back and forth with their M-16s looking for targets. Landing in the center of the deck, she rolled and came up in a half kneeling firing position. When she saw that the shadowy target hadn't complied with the pilot's orders, Angela instantly spun driving her out stretched leg through the back of the knees of her target. The karate leg sweep had the desired affect she was looking for.

Chet hadn't a clue what hit him. He never suspected that the Agent's orders were directed at him so he continued to video tape

137

what he saw in the cabin. He was quite surprised when his legs went flying forward and up from his body.

"Ahhhhhhhh!" he yelled, as the camera flew off his shoulder and into the air. A half second later he landed squarely on his back, on the deck knocking the wind out of him. The camera hit the deck several feet away and shattered into several pieces.

Instantly, Agent Rodriguez came down hard directly on Chet's chest with one knee further choking off his breath. With her gun in his face, Angela quickly frisked him. Finding nothing, she threw him over like a rag doll and cuffed him. At that instant, two of her team landed on the deck on either side of her. In knee-firing position, they trained their M-16s on the cabin entrance while the fourth Agent covered from the high ground of the police boat.

At that moment, Assault Team Two landed on the opposite side of the dock. Alan had just finished tying off the boat as two agents rolled onto the dock on either side of him. They both came up and trained their M-16s on him. Alan had his ID out and lifted it up into the air.

"Federal Agent!" he yelled, as he tried to shield his eyes from the blinding floodlights. The two agents were dark silhouettes against the light and didn't budge from position, ready to fire.

"Put your chest on the deck and your hands out!" came an order from behind the light.

Alan immediately complied. He knew that these people were deadly serious.

Agent Dickson had recognized Bradley the second they had landed. He had orders to neutralize all targets, and that was exactly what he was going to do. Besides, Bradley had it coming. When Dickson jumped off the boat and rushed towards him, he was looking forward to roughing him up a little.

Dickson came down hard on Bradley's back with one knee and heard Alan gasp painfully on impact. Pulling his arms around his back, he cuffed him.

"I'm a Federal Agent!" Bradley yelled angrily, gasping for air. He never expected them to cuff him.

Dickson signaled the two agents with M-16s. They each jumped up onto the target boat and slowly worked their way down either side, towards the back of it, as Dickson covered them.

Back on her feet and in firing position, Angela worked her way to the cabin. Seeing no immediate threat, she stepped toward the doorway and went in.

Reaching the entrance to Dock A, O'Leary ran past the Backup Team as they held position. He heard the call in his ear piece as he ran towards the boat. "Target One neutralized and secure," he heard Angela report. The entire assault was over in seconds.

O'Leary saw the cuffed man face down on the dock and knew instantly it was Bradley. *Oh no,* he thought as he realized things had gone seriously wrong. He ran past him to the boat and climbed aboard. Looking in the cabin, his heart sank. He walked slowly down the steps and to the body of his informant.

O'Leary looked at him. With two holes in the center of his chest and real blood all over him, the informant's dead eyes looked up asking the question, "Why?" O'Leary, sadly, didn't have an answer as he bent down on one knee next to him. Then slowly moving his hand over the informant's face, he closed his eyes.

Bradley had finally convinced Dickson to uncuff him, and he quickly moved to the back of the boat and climbed aboard.

"I'm a reporter!" Chet was finally able to gasp.

"That's true. Let him go," Bradley ordered. As another agent moved in to uncuff Chet, Alan entered the cabin.

O'Leary sighed heavily in frustration. "What do we have, Rodriguez," he was finally able to say.

"A lot of coke, sir." She'd been counting the bags when O'Leary came in. "At least five million dollars street value," came the reply.

"Ten million, I'd say," Bradley corrected her as he stepped inside.

"Damn it! Bradley!" O'Leary yelled angrily as he turned around. Then grabbing Alan by the coat, he shoved him against the cabin wall. "You've screwed things up for the last time. I'll have your badge for this."

"I was only doing my job," Bradley scowled back. "I saw men with guns on a suspicious boat and I investigated. How was I supposed to know you had a bust going?"

Rodriguez pulled O'Leary off Bradley. "Stop it, sir. He's not worth it."

With his face as red as his hair, O'Leary glared at Bradley angrily then turned around slowly. "Get him out of here," he ordered with noticeable frustration.

Just then, Chet was able to retrieve the remains of his video recorder. "My Camera! You idiots broke my camera!"

"And get that reporter out of here too!" O'Leary ordered. Rodriguez took Alan's arm and spun him around.

"All right! I'm going!" Alan assured her. Another agent forced Chet off the boat as Rodriguez escorted Alan onto the dock.

"You can't treat me like this! The public has a right to know what's going on around them!" Chet said as he stopped to brush himself off. Two agents moved towards him. "I'm going!" he exclaimed, then walked hurriedly down the dock with the parts of his camera in hand.

"Get set up on the street for an interview," Bradley whispered to him as he past by. Chet nodded and kept walking.

"I think you had better go now." Rodriguez burned a deadly glare into Bradley.

"Maybe you're right. Its all over, but the clean up anyway." Bradley shrugged, then turned and walked away.

O'Leary came out of the cabin. "Pierce! Seal off the area and keep all unauthorized personnel out!" he ordered.

"Yes sir," came a reply as an agent jumped from the police boat with a roll of yellow barricade tape.

On the street above the dock, a crowd had gathered at the marina's fence. Bradley walked out of the gate and over to where Chet was setting up a new video camera on a tripod.

"Where did *they* come from?" Bradley asked.

"All the shooting must've cleared out that bar down the street," Chet replied. "Did you see what they did to me? They can't do that to the *press!* Haven't they heard of the first amendment?" He was red faced as he continued to set up the equipment.

The words fell on deaf ears as Bradley's attention was drawn to a girl leaning against the fence looking at him. She was tall and tan, with curly blonde hair, and too much makeup. A tight red dress revealed a body that obviously saw the inside of a gym on a daily basis. From her head to her stilettos she was prime, Bradley thought. He smiled at her and she smiled back.

"Are you ready for the interview?" Chet asked as he brushed the last of the dirt from his suit and straightened his tie.

"What? Oh yeah, just a second," Bradley said, as if shook from a trance. He took off his jacket revealing the shiny pistol in his shoulder holster. He then took his badge from his pocket, clipped it to his belt, and flung the jacket over the opposite shoulder and held it with two fingers. "What do you think?" Bradley asked.

"Nice touch." Chet nodded. "Now put the other hand in your pocket and turn slightly so the camera can get a full view of your gun and badge. That's good. Okay, let's roll."

He pushed a button on his remote microphone, and the camera and lights came on. Then he began to speak.

"Early this morning gunfire shattered the silence of this peaceful little community as a federal agent, with surgical precision, removed a drug supply line operating here. With me now is Special Agent Alan Bradley of the Drug Enforcement Agency. Agent Bradley, can you tell us what happened?"

"Yes I can, Chet. After months of painstaking investigative work, I was able to uncover a drug supply line which used a boat from this yacht club. The boat traveled in the darkness of night out to a freighter anchored in Elliot Bay. Cocaine was then transferred to the boat and brought here," Bradley reported.

"What's the street value of the drugs recovered?"

"Approximately ten million dollars," replied Bradley.

"*Really!* Well that's amazing, congratulations on stopping that much cocaine from hitting the streets of Seattle."

"I was only doing my job," replied Bradley, flashing a cheesy smile towards the camera.

"Agent Bradley, didn't you just receive a commendation last night for your excellent work in law enforcement?"

"Yes, I did."

"Then how is it that you were able to make so big of a bust within hours of your award ceremony?"

"Well, Chet, a drug enforcement agent's job is never finished. I must remain always vigilant," replied Bradley.

"Well, we all feel safer knowing that, and on behalf of the community, I thank you for your dedication. You heard it here first," he reported into the camera. "For Special Agent Alan Bradley, I'm Chester Green reporting from the Duwamish Yacht Club."

A moment later the camera lights went out. "That's it," Chet said hastily, as he rushed to the camera to dismantle it. "I've got to get home and put this together fast if I'm going to make the morning news." He placed the equipment in the jeep. "A little creative editing, and I'll make you look like Rambo taking on the drug lords single handed. Do you want to come along?"

"No, I've got other plans," Bradley said. Then he watched his friend climb into the jeep and drive off. Bradley turned to see the girl still standing at the fence. "To the victors go the spoils," he said to himself. He walked over to her and said hello.

11

Phantom

Thursday morning.

In a large office area, at the DEA building in Seattle, there were people moving about while others were talking on phones. In the back office with glass doors, Deputy Director Cranston sat behind his desk while O'Leary finished describing the previous night's events in detail.

"Damn it!" Cranston yelled, slamming his fist down on his desk. "Not only does he screw up the bust, but he kills the only man on board who can inform on Kingpin. This time he's gone too far. Rodriguez!"

From the desk just outside the door she turned around. "Yes, sir?"

"The minute Bradley comes in tell him to see me, escort him if you have to," Cranston barked as he got up and walked towards the door.

"Sorry sir, but Bradley called in sick this morning."

"Then get him on the phone. I want to talk to him, pronto!" he ordered.

"Yes sir," she replied before he closed the door.

"O'Leary, I want you and Anderson to get all the paperwork together that I need to can his butt! Now get moving."

"Yes sir," Anderson replied. The two agents walked out of the office and towards their desks.

Cranston opened the bottom drawer of his desk and pulled out a bottle of Pepto Bismol. With a shaky hand he took a long drink. *It's too early in the morning for this*, he thought to himself. But he knew there was no way he would get through the report without it. As he paged through countless photos and pieces of paper on his desk, he couldn't believe his eyes. Twenty years with the force and not once had he broken a rule, yet in what seemed like a blink of an eye, this boy had thrown the whole book out the window.

Not far away in the bedroom of his condo, Bradley sat up in bed. It was dark except for the light of the TV.

"That's it for the news, stay tuned for the morning traffic report," the television newscaster said.

Ring!

He glanced at the phone on the other side of the room. *Chet was right,* Alan thought with a smile as he clicked off the TV with the remote and reached for his robe. With this kind of press the Agency will be begging me to take Cranston's job. He walked to the window and opened the drapes, filling the room with dull gray light from a typical Seattle overcast day.

Ring!

Alan reached for it.

"Hello," he said, and he gazed out the window at Elliott Bay then across to West Seattle.

"Bradley, this is Rodriguez. Cranston wants to talk to you. You will have to hold while I transfer you."

Great, my biggest fan, he thought sarcastically. Alan had hoped to avoid a confrontation with Cranston until his boss had a chance to calm down.

"Bradley!" Cranston barked from the other end.

"Yes sir?"

"As of right now consider yourself suspended until a full investigation determines whether you should remain with the Agency or not."

"But sir, you haven't heard my side of it," Alan complained.

"Save the bull for the investigation. Now get your butt in here now!" Cranston ordered.

"Alan?" a soft voice said, as a blond head emerged from under the covers. "When are you coming back to bed, sweetheart?"

Alan looked over at her and smiled. "I can't come in today, sir. I've got some…under the covers work to do." He smiled at his little joke then hung up the phone. "I'll be right there, just let me make one more phone call." Alan thumbed through his private phone book, and dialed a number.

144

"Huh, what?...Bradley!" Cranston yelled, realizing that he was just hung up on. Cranston reached for the bottle of Pepto as he slammed down the phone. After taking a large gulp, he started to study the photos in front of him.

Fifteen minutes later, Governor Ted Wilson hung up the phone after talking to Agent Bradley. Standing up from behind the huge antique mahogany desk in his office, he stepped to the window and stared off into space. He had seen the morning news report and was extremely impressed. The report also opened a nagging question in the back of his mind that disturbed him. No law enforcement officer had ever enjoyed as much limelight as Agent Bradley. *Could it all be part of a bid for political power?* he wondered.

Wilson had been in politics his whole life and recognized a power play when he saw it. Months ago he had confronted his long time friend and former college roommate, Alan Bradley Sr., and asked him that very same question. To Wilson's dismay, Alan Sr. denied any plan what so ever.

That was bad news for Wilson. In politics there was always a plan. The denial of one meant certain doom to anyone not knowing about it. Not knowing was the worst thing possible because it didn't give you time to make plans of your own.

Of course there had to be a plan. Wilson had known Alan Sr. for too long, and knew all too well about his lust for political power. Alan Sr.'s fall from political grace had been a blessing to Wilson. After Alan Sr. lost his chance for the White House, he put his support and influence behind Wilson lifting him from the State Legislature to the Governor's mansion in what seemed like no time at all.

Alan Sr. was the best spin doctor Wilson had ever seen. His attention to detail on Wilson's campaign was impeccable, and he was sure Alan Sr. was now doing the same for his son. Wilson was now convinced that Alan Sr.'s efforts in helping him were really just a practice run for something bigger. Alan Sr. was going to try and launch Alan Jr. into the White House. He was *sure* of it.

Would that road take Alan Jr. through the Governor's office? Wilson analyzed the possibility, and concluded that the threat was real. But not right away. Bradley wouldn't throw his only son into a major political ring without some practice. That meant, most likely, the Seattle Mayor's office would be first. That was all right with Wilson. Demsey had been a pain in the butt for years, and Wilson was looking forward to having an ally governing the largest city in the State.

The Bradley's had two options for the next step, either the Governor's office or Congress. Wilson compared the records of previous Presidents and one fact stood out. All recent Presidents had once been the Governor of a State. Knowing Alan Sr.'s love of statistics favored only one conclusion. Wilson would soon be out of a job. The thought of it burned him up! How could Bradley, his best friend, betray him like this? How *dare* he!

Wilson quickly shook off those feelings as unconstructive. What did he expect? After all, blood was thicker than friendship. He was given no guarantee of future support, and it was foolish to expect it. This was just the normal shuffling of political power that happened everyday in every country throughout the world. One day you were in, and the next you were out.

But Wilson wasn't ready to be out. He had gained power by being useful to Alan Sr. and, by god, he was going to remain that way! He may not be a part of Bradley's plans now, but that could change if he was flexible enough—if he sailed with the tide instead of against it.

He decided to give Agent Bradley his unconditional support, and when it came time to step aside, he would do so gracefully. When that time came, he would remind his old friends of his faithful service, and perhaps they would throw him a bone. Maybe even make him a Senator or future Cabinet Member. Wilson smiled at the thought approvingly. After all, the young prince would need supporters in DC, wouldn't he?

A moment later he stepped back to his desk and pushed the intercom button for his assistant.

"Yes sir?" the assistant asked.

"Get me the DEA office in Seattle."

"Yes sir."

A few minutes later, there was a knock on the door and Rodriguez stuck her head in. "Um, sir, Governor Wilson is on the phone, do you want me to transfer it in?"

There was a long pause, then Cranston said in a calm voice, "Yes, I'll take it." When the phone rang he picked it up immediately. "Governor Wilson, what a pleasant surprise, what can I do for you?" he said cheerfully.

"Director Cranston, I think you should reconsider the action you're taking with regards to Agent Bradley," Wilson said calmly.

"Agent Bradley has broken departmental procedures and interfered with an investigation being conducted by other agents. He endangered himself and other agents by pulling off a dare devil stunt."

"Don't tell me about procedure, Cranston. From what I've been told, your entire department was involved in that bust last night. All except Bradley, that is," Wilson said with increased emotion. "Besides, that boy gets *results!*"

"I can't allow him to endanger the lives of other agents with his hotshot attitude," Cranston insisted.

"Did you see the news this morning, Director? Bradley looks like some sort of super cop. Heck! Mayor Demsey and I are on the front page of the paper with him today! Do you know what voters will do to me if they find out he was suspended because of *procedure?* It will look like Pontius Pilot crucifying the Savior."

"I'm not concerned with your problems, Mr. Governor, I've got plenty of my own." Cranston was starting to get hot under the collar.

There was a long pause before Wilson continued. "I'm playing golf with some of my friends in Internal Affairs this morning," he said calmly. "Don't force me to suggest changes that you can't live with." Cranston's heart fell to the floor when he heard this. "I hope we understand each other," Wilson said before he hung up the phone.

Cranston slumped in his seat, deflated by his situation. He sat silently listening to the dial tone for a moment before slowly hanging up the receiver. He then took a long drink from his Pepto bottle and walked slowly out of the office. Bradley's luck would eventually run out, he thought, and he hoped he would be around when it did. He walked up to Rodriguez and said in a quiet voice, "Call Bradley. Tell him that he is to report back to his marijuana case immediately."

"Yes sir," she said as she looked over at O'Leary. Cranston walked slowly past O'Leary without saying a word.

He looked old and defeated, O'Leary thought. He stared at the man's sunken eyes and lifeless face as Cranston continued down the hall.

Just then Anderson walked up hurriedly with an armful of papers. "I think I've got everything we need," he said almost out of breath.

"Good, now put it all back where you found it," O'Leary ordered. "It looks like we lost another one."

With a surprised look on his face, Anderson did a double take between O'Leary and Rodriguez, then back to O'Leary. As the realization of it set in, Anderson set the papers on his desk and slowly sat down.

Clifford helped Buck off his horse. *Lousy drunk*, he thought to himself. He was beginning to believe that coming here wasn't such a good idea after all. They should have gone home yesterday, but Buck refused to leave the mountains until the repairs on the trails were finished. Of course, drunk as he was, Buck was no help and Clifford finished the work himself.

The other night after the D.B. Cooper story, Clifford thought Buck was a little out there. But after last night's story, he was convinced that his drunken companion was certifiable. The previous night Buck had weaved a tale about Bigfoot being a Native American Spirit sent to protect a secret ancient temple on top of the mountain. Lucky for Clifford, the booze ran out just slightly before midnight.

They awoke at dawn. Clifford wanted to sleep in, but Buck had a disturbing vision. That, along with his hangover, induced migraine wouldn't let them. Buck explained that in his dream he had seen Native American symbols warning of future doom. Clifford thought he was delusional, but they quickly loaded the mules and got out of there, anyway.

With one of Buck's arms over his shoulder, Clifford helped him to the porch, up the stairs, and into the house. Guiding him to the couch, Clifford laid Buck on his back. Buck immediately started to snore. Deciding to attend to the mules, he shook his head, then walked out the door. Taking the packs off, he placed them in the corner of the barn, and put the mules in the corral. He would brush them down later, after having something to eat.

He was starving. They had skipped breakfast in order to get Buck and his hangover back home. As he walked back to the house, he heard a loud crash of pots and pans. *Well, guess who's up*, he thought. He walked into the kitchen and saw Buck leaning against the counter holding his head with an extremely painful look on his face.

"Why don't you take some aspirin and go lay down," Clifford suggested, as he picked the clutter off the floor. "I'll make lunch."

"Aspirin can't help a headache like this. What I need is the venom from the snake that bit me," Buck replied, then walked from the kitchen to his bedroom.

"The snake that *what?*" Clifford asked, putting the pans down. His question was soon answered when Buck emerged from the bedroom carrying a new bottle of whiskey. "Are you *crazy?* You're going to end up killing yourself," Clifford started to loose his temper. "You and mom ganged up on me because I smoked a little pot, and you're the one that has the problem!"

"Don't talk so loud." Buck cringed from the throbbing in is head. "There's a big difference between alcohol and drugs. Whiskey is legal and only losers use drugs," he replied as he took a drink.

"The only reason pot isn't legal is because the government is ran by old farts like you!" Clifford protested.

"Shhh!" Buck pleaded. "Let's talk about this later. Would you get me an ice pack for my head?"

Clifford turned grabbed a towel, then walked to the freezer and emptied an ice tray. When he returned, Buck was again snoring on the couch. After placing the pack on Buck's head, he returned to the kitchen. *He will probably sleep the whole day away*, he thought to himself.

Clifford was getting angry. He hadn't come down here to take care of a crazy old drunk. Then he thought about it for a moment. This might work to his advantage. If Buck slept all day, Clifford could drive to Seattle, make some phone calls, sell the brick, then be back here in time for dinner.

Again, Clifford looked over at Buck. He wouldn't even know Clifford had gone. Back in the kitchen, Clifford made a couple quick sandwiches and put them in a bag. He then found the aluminum covered brick in his pack.

"Time to get rich," he said with a smile. With his jacket and sandwiches in hand, he grabbed the keys to the Suburban and walked out the front door closing it quietly behind him.

What a waste of time and talent, Alan thought as he stood in line at the Dick's burger drive-in on Capital Hill. He'd spent most of the afternoon cruising the high schools, looking for kids buying and selling pot.

"May I take your order?" came the voice from behind the glass.

"Yes, I'll have a Dick's Deluxe, large fry, and a large coke— no wait, make that two large fries," Alan said as he pulled out his wallet. He knew they weren't healthy, but Dick's fries were the best in town and he just couldn't resist. He planned on working out that evening, which he hoped would make up for it.

I deserve better than this two bit marijuana case, he thought as he picked up his order and walked to the corvette. If it wasn't for that old road block, Cranston, he'd be running a higher profile case. He would have to step up his efforts to push the old fart out the door, he decided with a smile. Alan got into his vette and opened the bag.

"Mmm," he said, taking in the aroma of his lunch. He then started up the car and drove onto the street. "Where to now?" he wondered aloud, continuing down the street and stuffing his face with fries. School would be out soon and he decided to go down to Rainier Park and watch for anything unusual.

Twenty minutes later, Alan pulled to a stop on the street next to the park, shut off the engine, and looked around. It was fairly quiet, just a couple of joggers and a man playing frisbee with his dog. Opening the bag, he looked inside and saw that the fries were already gone. Next time he would have to get three orders.

Alan took a long drink from his coke then slouched down low in the leather seat. *Maybe I'll take a nap*, he thought as he took a bite of his Dick's Deluxe. The girl, whatever her name was and he didn't recall even asking, had kept him up all night. Besides there was nothing going on here anyway.

A few minutes later, Alan finished his lunch and began drifting off. Through half open tired eyes, he barely noticed the Suburban approaching. His consciousness followed it, not for any particular reason at first, but just because it was the only movement around. His keen powers of observation, though sluggish at first, started registering information in his head. A few questions started popping up, but Alan wasn't really listening and wished he could turn them off.

The Chevy 4x4 was covered in mud. Where did he get so dirty? It parked across from him, and the driver stepped out and looked around slowly. He was a teenage boy wearing jeans, tennis shoes, and a green Forest Service jacket. His pants and sneakers had dried mud still caked on them.

Alan's eyes followed the kid walking past the vette and into the park. A bulge in the kid's jacket was held securely—securely enough to lift an eyebrow. A Forest Service worker didn't exactly fit the profile of the area, and an alarm went off in Alan's brain. An old case file tugged Alan away from his slumber. He recalled a case where some nature loving pot smokers grew their stash out in the boonies where it couldn't be found. They would then bring it into the city to sell to the locals.

Alan decided to tag along for a while and stepped out of his car carrying his drink. He followed Clifford through the park, making sure he was far enough behind not to be noticed. Clifford made his way towards a stand of trees and bushes then stopped and looked around cautiously. A moment later, he disappeared into them.

Alan moved quickly around to one side of the trees and quietly worked his way inward. He peered through a bush and saw Clifford surrounded by five other kids wearing gang colors. Alan watched as they talked. A few of the boys appeared to be keeping a lookout. Clifford pulled out a silver brick and showed it to the other guys. "It's a drug deal alright," Alan smiled to himself as he put down his drink and pulled out his gun.

"Federal officer! Stay where you are and put your hands up!" Alan yelled from behind the bush. The boys frantically looked around then all ran in different directions. Stay with the drugs, Alan reminded himself, running after the kid in the green jacket.

Clifford looked behind him as he sprinted through the park carrying the package like a football. *Oh no!* he thought when he saw Alan chasing after him. He knew he couldn't get caught with the package.

Alan was catching up, but not very fast. He cursed Italian shoe makers for not making a model with a tread. *I've got you now*, he thought. Just then, he saw the kid throw the silver brick into a stand of bushes and disappear behind them.

A moment of hesitation was all the kid needed to escape as Alan decided to look for the brick. Alan stopped, worked his way

151

into the bushes, found the brick, and scooped it up. He could still catch the kid if he could beat him to his vehicle. Alan sprinted through the park toward the street carrying the package. When he reached the street, he couldn't believe his luck! The Suburban was still there! Alan stepped into the street and looked around, but saw nothing.

Clifford emerged from the bushes up the street, then stopped and crouched down when he saw movement next to the Suburban. He slowly pushed his way into the bushes, and laid down peering out from behind the leaves. He watched as Alan wiped the dried mud from the license plate, and then walked to the corvette carrying the package.

Damn it! Clifford thought as he lay there waiting, trying to think. There was no way he could use the truck again, the cops would nail him for sure. He cringed at the thought of how mad Buck would be when he found out. He would have to lay low and decided to hang with some friends in the U-district until the whole thing blew over. Yeah, that's what he should do, he nodded. Clifford pushed his way back through the bushes and disappeared.

When Alan got in his car, he crouched down low in the seat and checked the road behind him with his mirrors. He picked up the car phone then dialed a number.

"Drug Enforcement Agency. This is Agent Rodriguez, how can I help you?"

"Angela, this is Bradley, can you run a plate for me?"

"Let me have it."

"55201-R, Washington plate. Call me on my car phone when you get it," Alan said then hung up. After checking the street again, he turned his attention to the package. He opened the end of it and knew instantly it wasn't pot. He enlarged the opening to examine it closer.

He took some out and rubbed it between his fingers, then put it up to his nose. His eyes widened with surprise as his mind raced back to a thin dust covered file folder he had seen months ago. The case file described what was in his hand exactly, and he had seen a similar package in the Agency's evidence locker. He said the name of the case file out loud as he recalled it.

"Phantom!"

A few minutes later, the call came in and Alan picked up the phone. "Yes?"

"Alan, the vehicle is registered to one Eugene Buckston Henderson. No priors, wants, or warrants," the voice said over the line.

"Run a full profile on him through the computer, and get back to me when you're finished."

"Will do," came the reply. The receiver clicked dead.

How was a kid like that involved with a case like this? Alan asked himself, and he knew there had to be something more going on than it appeared. Alan checked the streets again and waited. An hour later the phone rang and he picked it up.

"Hello."

"Bradley, I've got the skinny on your man," Angela said.

"Let's have it." As the information came over the line Alan's mind digested it trying to determine a possible link to the case.

Six hours later, Alan turned the key to his condo and swung the door open. With a brown grocery bag under one arm and a white paper bag in the other, he walked in and kicked the door shut with his foot. He felt a lot more awake and alive than he did that morning due to all the excitement. Walking through his postmodern living room to the dinning room, he set the bags on the table before grabbing the phone and dialing.

"Chester Green, investigative journalist. If you've got the poop, I'll get the scoop. How can I help you?"

"Ha! Nice slogan. What are you- a reporter or a kennel cleaner?" Alan joked.

"Hi, Alan. What's up?" Chet replied, ignoring his friends slam.

"Get your butt over to my place for dinner," Alan said, taking some packages out of a Pikes Place Market bag. "We've got some celebrating to do."

"Do you mean about last night?"

"No, I'll explain later. When can you be here?"

"Well I'm only a couple of blocks away, and I'm just finishing up. Do you need me to bring anything?" Chet asked politely.

"I've got everything we need," came the reply.

153

"Okay then, I'll be there shortly. What are we having?"

"Steamed clams and baked salmon," Alan said as he looked into his dirty kitchen then changed his mind. "Make that barbecued."

"Sounds good, I'm on my way," Chet said.

Alan reached into the grocery bag, pulled out a micro-brew, and opened it. He took a drink as he walked to the French doors. Opening them up, he stepped onto the small deck. *What a beautiful day*, he thought, and it wasn't just because of the weather. He took another drink and gazed out at Elliott Bay. He could practically see the whole city. To the north one could see the Space Needle. Turning slowly southward, he looked down on Elliott Bay across to West Seattle and the Olympic mountains. Then came Safeco Field and finally Mount Rainier.

Alan smiled. He then turned, fired up the gas grill before walking back inside. As Alan prepared the fish the doorbell rang.

"It's open!" he yelled. The door opened and in walked Chet wearing brand new clothes. "Hey, nice suit," Alan complimented, reaching into the grocery bag for a beer, which he handed to his friend.

"Thanks, I made some pretty good money from that last report. I was able to sell the story to both networks, as well as the Times and PI."

"Good for you. It's about time you got a new wardrobe," joked Alan as he walked onto the deck with an armful of bowls.

Chet followed him. "I only got one suit. The rest I spent on electronic equipment for work. Some real state-of-the-art stuff."

Alan frowned disapprovingly. "You shouldn't spend all your money on work, Chet. Try to have a little fun with it, too."

"I will, someday. We can't all have rich fathers, you know," Chet replied as he looked around. "Wow! What a view!" He'd been to Alan's condo countless times, but the view always took his breath away. "Someday I hope to have a place like this."

"Someday might be closer than you think," Alan said as he tossed a handful of clams on the grill.

"What do you mean?"

"Tomorrow, my good friend, you and I are going on a little adventure," Alan said with a grin.

"Where to?"

"A little town in Lewis County called Morton."

"What's down there?" Chet asked, curiously.

"Nothing. Absolutely nothing," Alan chuckled. "That's why we're going."

"What?" Chet was puzzled.

"Just a minute," Alan said, then he walked back inside. A moment later he returned and handed Chet the package.

"What's this?"

"What's it look like?"

"It looks like a brick covered with foil and plastic."

"No, you butthead! Open it up." Alan removed some clams from the grill too put some more on.

Chet sat down and opened it up. "So, what is it?" he asked again.

"Opium." Alan put the bowl of barbecued clams on the small table between them and sat down.

"Opium!" exclaimed Chet. "Where did you get it?"

"Off a teenager in the park this afternoon." Alan removed a clam from its shell, dipped it in melted butter, and ate it.

"Where did *he* get it?" Chet asked as he too grabbed a clam from the bowl.

"I didn't get a chance to ask him, he got away."

"So… you find a package of drugs and all of a sudden we're off to Morton? Sounds like a brilliant piece of detective work, Sherlock," Chet laughed.

"No, no, let me explain."

"I wish you would," Chet replied, then scarfed down a clam.

"I ran a make on the truck the kid was driving." Alan stood up and walked to the grill for more clams. "It belongs to a seventy-three year old retired Army Colonel named Henderson. I waited around for two hours for the kid to return, but he didn't show, so I figured he saw me."

"So do you have someone watching the truck?"

"No, I didn't bother. I don't think the kid can tell me very much anyway," Alan said when he returned with a full bowl of clams.

"How do you figure?"

"Well, I don't think the package was his. I think he stole it and the truck from this Henderson fellow."

"I don't follow you." Chet wolfed down another clam.

"Look at this package. This is the purest uncut opium I've ever seen! What would a teenager be doing with it unless he stole it from someone else?" Alan held the brick in his hand.

"This package reminds me of a case file I saw when I first came to Seattle. It's called the Phantom file. It's an old case that's never been solved. The Agency's has arrested only a small number of dealers who had bricks of opium like this one. According to them, this supplier shows up on their doorstep unannounced. The dealer buys the bricks on the spot because he knows it's the finest stuff around and he can sell it for a premium. Before anyone can follow him, the supplier disappears into thin air."

"Like a Phantom," Chet recalled.

"Exactly."

As Chet ate clams and listened, Alan regurgitated everything he knew about the Phantom file. Phantom was no ordinary mob operation. A mob operation was a large established group of people who worked to dominate the entire drug market. They sold large amounts of drugs on the streets to anyone able to buy. Once established, it was always there. The Agency targeted mob organizations, like Kingpin, because there were always new leads and tips to go on. One arrest or seizure of drugs usually lead to more. It was a good use of Agency resources to target such an organization, because every victory had a major impact.

Phantom, on the other hand, didn't fit this stereotype. It was small, supplying less than ten percent of the market. They didn't try to sell to all types of users, but instead focused on the high end only. Because of the superior quality of the opium, they targeted rich users who could afford to pay a premium. Once the drugs were delivered, Phantom disappeared without a trace.

There were never any leads or tips to go on so stakeouts quickly became a waste of time. The case became a low priority for the Agency, who hoped Phantom would someday slip up on his own and be caught. Even with the low volume, the money made from this operation was enough to make anyone filthy rich.

After analyzing these differences, Cranston believed Phantom was not mob related at all. Instead, he felt that Phantom was a small, well organized, and disciplined group of individuals who worked as a freelance supplier. The setup worked so well that he compared it to a covert military operation.

Cranston started an investigation of every branch of the military, but instantly hit road blocks. It seemed that if there was one thing the military didn't like, it was being investigated by another branch of the government. Each branch listened to his theory and told him they would look into the possibility.

Cranston never got an answer back so the case again got filed away to collect dust. It wasn't until Agent Rodriguez came to the group that he got any answers. Because of her Naval Intelligence background, she had contacts in each branch of the service that would talk to her discretely. After a few phones calls, and meetings, she had gotten all the information available. Unfortunately, it wasn't what they had hoped for. Each branch did an in depth investigation based of Cranston's theory, but came up with nothing. There were absolutely no similarities between Phantom and any military drug case. Again, the file was shelved.

"So where does Henderson fit in?" Chet finally broke in. "Do you think he's Phantom?"

"I won't know for sure until we go down there," Alan answered. "However, there are some interesting similarities between Phantom and this case that make me lean in that direction. Like I said, this is high quality stuff. The only thing I've seen anywhere close to it came from Asia. Henderson spent most of his military career in Korea and Vietnam."

"So you think he made some connections over seas then set up shop here in the States."

"Exactly," Alan confirmed. "Cranston was on the right track when he suspected a military connection. However, I don't believe Phantom is on active duty. Instead, I suspect he's *retired* military."

"Okay, I follow you. Phantom got his training and made contacts over seas while on active duty, but didn't start the operation until he retired. That way, he couldn't be tracked by any military intelligence organization."

"That's what I'm thinking." Alan nodded. "There is one inconsistency though. The street dealers describe Phantom as a large Sicilian looking man with a European accent wearing an expensive Italian suit, diamond ring, and tie tack, and white fedora. Because of this, the first agents to investigate the case looked for a European supply line, but found none."

"But I thought you said this stuff was Asian?" Chet was starting to get confused.

"That's what *I* think." Alan nodded. "If there was a European connection, the DEA would've found packages identical to this back east and in the mid-west, but we haven't. They've only shown up on the west coast."

By now, Chet was completely lost and his face said it all.

"Don't you see?" Alan hesitated, hoping Chet would fill in the blanks, but it just wasn't going to happen. "It's a disguise, a costume to throw us off track."

Chet started to get it. "A subliminal trick to make you look in another direction."

"Right." Alan saw the light go off in Chet's head. "I mean, when was the last time someone wore a fedora, for Christ's sake."

"He dresses up like a mobster so that you would think he was one."

157

"Everyone's looking for a European connection when it's been Asian all a long."

"Very clever." Chet smiled, admiring its simplicity and the ease at which Alan had put it together. They sat in silence for a few minutes, getting their fill of clams, before Chet arrived at another question. "So why Morton? Wouldn't he operate from Seattle?"

"He probably just sells the finished product here after it's been cut. Heck, Morton is between Seattle and Portland, maybe he supplies both? Besides, as sophisticated of an operation I think this is, it would require a secret cutting location in order to make it work."

"What do you mean by cutting?" Chet's face looked confused.

"When drugs like opium are smuggled into the country it's usually done in as pure a form as possible. That way it can be shipped in small packages and concealed easier. When it gets to where it's to be sold, it's mixed with four to five times its weight in inert material. This brings its quality down to what you see on the street. Then it's divided up, weighed, and put in small bags. It's then ready to be delivered to the pushers on the street and sold."

Chet was baffled. "But I thought you said Phantom delivers the bricks whole."

"So far, that's all we know for sure that he does. But most all drug organizations have some sort of cutting operation, so we can't rule it out." Alan informed him. "But then again, Morton may just be a delivery site. An entry point where the drugs come into the country."

Chet nodded, accepting the explanation. "So where does the kid fit in?"

"Cutting and packaging drugs is a boring and monotonous job. It's usually done by the newest members of the organization. That way they can learn about the process and street value of the product without finding out too many details of the organization," Alan explained.

"So he was one of the grunts."

"That's the only way a kid could get close to this much opium," Alan confirmed.

"So how did he end up in Seattle?"

"He probably figured out how much the drugs were worth on the street, got greedy, then stole the brick and truck when everyone else was asleep. He then high-tailed it to Seattle to try to make a quick fortune and disappear." Alan went to the grill for more clams.

"How much do you think its worth?" Chet asked as he felt the package's weight.

"I'd say about a two hundred grand after it has been cut and packaged." Alan stuffed another clam in his mouth.

"Two hundred thousand dollars! I'll say that would make someone greedy!" Chet exclaimed.

"Well he wouldn't get that much selling it like it is, but any fraction of that is a small fortune to a dumb kid."

"So what happens if this kid tells Henderson the Feds have the drugs and the truck? Won't they close up shop?" Chet asked.

"That's why we have to move fast. This kid is probably out of the state by now, but Henderson is sure to have people looking for him." Alan walked into the condo for more beer, when he returned he handed one to Chet.

"I sure would hate to be in his shoes if he gets caught." Chet's tone was grim. "I've heard they like to make examples of people who betray the operation."

"Yeah, they would probably torture him in front of everyone so that nobody gets the same idea," Alan replied without emotion. "If you're ready, I'll put on the salmon."

"Yeah, go ahead." Chet stared out into space as Alan got up and disappeared through the glass doors. "Morton..., Mooortooon..., Morton, hum?" Chet said out loud to himself.

Alan emerged holding the salmon like a trophy. "Check this out. Isn't she a beaut?!"

"I'll say. We'll be eating good tonight."

Alan put the salmon fillet on the grill then placed lemon, butter, and onion slices on top. As the feast sizzled, Alan looked over and saw Chet starring out at the Olympics in deep concentration. "What's that you're mumbling about?"

As if awoke from a deep sleep, Chet's head turned towards Alan. "What? ...Oh, just Morton."

"What about it?" Alan walked over and handed Chet another bowl of clams.

Chet took the bowl then started prying a clam out of its shell as he replied. "Where have I heard that name before? It's sitting on the tip of my tongue, but I just can't get it."

"I've never heard of it. What do you think it could be?" Alan asked, then shoveled a clam into his mouth.

"I don't know, probably nothing, but I can't help thinking that something big happened there." A moment later, Chet shook the thought off. "Oh well, lets forget about that for now. What did Cranston think when you showed him the brick?"

159

"I didn't tell anyone. I just called in and took the next couple days off on vacation."

"*What?*" Chet exclaimed as he almost choked on a clam. "You're going down there without backup! Isn't that a little stupid?" Alan was known for doing things like this, but Chet had never gotten used to it.

"No, not really. The way I figure it, in order for this place to remain secret, Phantom can't allow too many people there. Probably two or three tops... so it shouldn't be too bad." Alan spoke confidently, but knew there was no way to be sure.

"I don't know, Alan." Chet fidgeted uneasily in his chair. "Won't Cranston be chapped when he finds out?"

"Who cares? That old crony's on his way out the door anyway," Alan replied. "Besides, if I would've told him he would've given the case to that jerk O'Leary and I'd be left in the cold. I need to solve this case alone. Even though it's a low priority case, it still holds a lot of weight with the Agency's upper brass."

"Phantom is the oldest open case the DEA has ever known," Alan continued. "The person who captures Phantom, will get instant recognition all the way at the top in Washington DC. If I can solve this case, it will show everyone that I could do something that no one else had been able to do in decades. This could be the crown jewel of my DEA career. So as you can see, Chet. I can't share this with anyone."

Chet thought about it grimly, but understood. He too didn't want to share the story with anyone else, but felt very uneasy about being unprotected. He searched for other possibilities.

"What about the local sheriffs department?" Chet asked after a moment of thought. "Have you contacted them?"

"I don't want to bring them into it until I have to. This Henderson seems like a pretty slick fellow. There's no telling who he's got in his pocket."

"How can you tell?"

"I had a tough time tracking him down. He doesn't have an address just a PO Box in Morton where the Army sends his retirement checks. He also doesn't have a bank account. He just cashes his checks and disappears."

"Then how are we going to find him?" Chet questioned. "He could be a million miles from Morton."

"We will go down there and ask a few locals, real quiet like, so as not to tip him off. If that doesn't work we will stakeout the PO Box and wait until he shows up. Then follow him home." Alan looked over at his friend for some kind of sign. "Are you with me?"

"I don't know, Alan. We would be going alone with no idea what to expect. It sounds pretty risky to me," Chet said, worriedly.

Chet had always been a bit of a weenie, Alan thought. "I'll tell you what we'll do then," he said, reassuringly. "We'll go down there, find Henderson, and stake him out. If it looks too big we will call in the troops. Now are you with me?" Alan asked again.

"This story of yours is awful thin, but you are the luckiest guesser I've ever known. Yeah, I'll burn up a couple of days with you to see what happens," Chet replied with a smile.

"Great!" Alan exclaimed. He stood and walked to the grill to check the food.

"But if things get too hairy I'll call Cranston myself if you won't!"

Alan ignored him as he checked the salmon. "Perfect! Let's eat."

12
Issues Unresolved

Jim's eyes wandered from the paper work on his desk to the wall clock, and he was surprised to see that it was almost ten-thirty at night. *Where had the day gone?* It was normal for him to lose track of the time when he was busy.

Jim slowly pushed the chair away from the desk, then leaned back and rubbed his tired eyes. *Maybe Rissley was right,* he thought. For months Joe had been suggesting that he delegate more of the paperwork to her, but he resisted. He had been doing it by himself all these years and didn't feel comfortable letting someone else make these decisions, no matter how minor. He didn't want to feel out of touch, and admittedly liked to be sure everything was under control.

What was he afraid of? It's not like the whole department would fall apart if he let someone else take care of a few details. Especially someone like Rissley. She was smart, creative, and innovative. Within the last few years, he had come to rely on her more and more. He respected her opinion.

She was instrumental in getting the department switched over to computer filing, and a couple of years ago she suggested that they have their own website. He didn't like either idea at the time, but, after stewing on it awhile, he changed his mind. It was a good thing, too. Both ideas saved countless hours of wasted time, freeing everyone up to do more important work.

I suppose you have to take the good with the bad, though, he thought. He liked how helpful she was, but she also constantly analyzed his methods and tactics for doing business. Like the way he handled short falls in the monthly operating budget. For years, whenever they operated in the red, he had sent all the deputies out to Interstate Five to set up speed traps. The added revenue, from extra speeding tickets, filled the gaps in the budget nicely.

He'd been doing it so long he had it down to a science. It was one of his favorite moneymakers because it targeted people from outside the county. Interstate Five connected Seattle and Portland. Thousands of people traveled between the two large cities every month, and they all had to drive through Lewis County to do it.

Big city money was like new blood to his community. The more they needed, the longer the deputies stayed out on the Intestate until they were in the black again. Occasionally, a deputy would ask why they all had to be out on the Interstate so much. Each deputy had other, more important, duties that were being neglected. He would answer the question by saying it was for the safety of the motorist. All the speeding tickets made the drivers slow down and be more careful.

That argument always worked until Joe disputed it. Now that all the data was easily accessible on the computer, Joe was able to create a statistical report. Her report showed that the additional deputies and extended hours on speed trap duty did not decrease the accident rate. It did, however, increase the county coffers by a significant amount.

Jim hated to be proven wrong. For years, he had suspected that was the case, but the safety argument was always easy justification. Confronted with the facts, she expected him to reduce the amount of speed trap duty, but he refused.

"Okay, so I can no longer tell the deputies to get out there and keep the roads safe for the tax payer," he remembered saying. "I'll call it what it is. From now on I'll say, 'Get out there and keep this county from going bankrupt.'"

She didn't like that answer, and argued against it, saying it was unethical for a law enforcement officer to write tickets strictly for the purpose of generating revenue- it was like creating a toll road through the county.

"You're artificially creating a tax that the citizens have to pay," she had stated. "It's not the duty of law enforcement to create taxes."

He had countered by saying, "Year after year, the Federal and State governments remove money from the county by either increasing taxes or reduce the amount of subsidies they provide for necessary programs. Either way, this county is forced to survive on a continually shrinking annual budget. When that happens, sometimes you have to fight fire with fire."

"For years I've heard your speech about the evils of big government and big cities," she had said. "Your fire with fire policy is stooping to their level. It's *hypocritical!*"

That hit Jim like a punch in the gut. He'd been called a lot of things, but never a hypocrite, and it made him reexamine his policies. Later, after he was able to think about it, he came to the conclusion that Joe was right. His fire with fire policy was hypocritical, but he still felt justified in using it. Technically, the speeders were breaking the law. Since it was Jim's duty to enforce the law, he could ticket them all he wanted.

Jim had other tactics as well, that he used either to raise or save money. He made deals, trades, or found unnamed donors for whatever was needed. Was it wrong? He didn't think so. Everyone got what they wanted and nobody got hurt—he saw to that.

Jim looked out his glass door to the front office. Everyone except the dispatcher was gone. The deputies had either gone home or were on patrol. *Perhaps I'll assign Joe some of the paper work,* he thought to himself. Maybe if she realized how difficult the job was, she wouldn't be so critical of his tactics. And maybe with her help, they could come up with better methods of doing business.

He had been independent for too long, and was uneasy with the idea of anyone helping him. Well, at least he would think about it. He looked down at the paperwork on his desk then rubbed his eyes, again. He'd spent too much time on the stuff already, and it never seemed to end or change.

Another accident at the four way stop at Pine and Kesler— that made the second one this year. He'd have to go see the County Council again about putting in a stoplight. He stood up. What's the use? They'd give him that same dry speech about there not being enough money in the budget and he was tired of hearing that every year.

He considered sending Rissley to talk to them. It would be good experience for her and give him a rest as well. That's what he'd do, he decided. Starting tomorrow, Joe's in charge of getting a new streetlight.

Jim walked around the desk, picked up a small backpack lying on the floor, and walked out of the office. After closing the door behind him, he walked down the hall and into the men's room. A few minutes later, he emerged in sweats, wearing the backpack and carrying a bike helmet and goggles.

"Good night, Sullivan. Have a good one," Jim said, walking past the night radio dispatcher.

"Goodnight, Sheriff," replied the heavy set man as he looked up from the thick novel he was reading.

Jim walked out the front door of the building and over to the rack where he unlocked his mountain bike. It had been another late night with no time for a decent meal. That meant a plate of hotdogs again. He cringed at the thought, then he gazed at the sky. It looked like rain and he hoped it would hold off until he got home.

He put on his helmet and goggles. He hated wearing them and thought they kind of took some of the fun out of it. As a kid, he never used either, but now things were different. He was Sheriff and he had to set an example for the young kids in the community. Jim mounted the bike and peddled down the street.

He rolled he eyes thinking of all the angry phone calls he got from parents when their children didn't wear their helmets because they saw the Sheriff without one. That was one of the hassles of being a small town Sheriff. Everybody knew him, so he had to pay close attention to what he said or did and who was watching.

As Jim rounded a corner, he waved to the house without really looking. She was in the window, as always. That went especially for Mrs. Miller, he thought distastefully. There wasn't anything that happened in this town without her knowing about it. Yes sirree-Bob, she was the original information super highway.

He smiled. That was all right, people around here have treated him real well over the years. He knew everyone by name. He watched the kids grow up, get jobs, and move away. Twice a year, he'd go to the grade school to talk to kids about safety and respecting the law. Then, when they got there driver's license, he would have to pull them over for one thing or another, and he worried about each of them as if they were his own.

That had made up for Jim not having a family of his own, and he wouldn't change a thing for the world. At least he never had to change diapers. He smiled at that added benefit. This was a quiet little town, and he liked it that way. Heck, the majority of the headaches he got were from parents yelling at him from the stands when he umpired the summer little league games, and he could live with that.

Whew! He was half way home. Looking at his watch, he realized that if he picked up the pace he could make a new record. But then again, the last few months were full of new records. He'd put some extra pounds on over the years and, a short time ago, decided to get back into shape. He tried running, but that reminded him too much of the Army, and weights made his joints ache. He wasn't sure why the bike was different—it just was. Anyway, he felt more relaxed and slept better since he took it up. That's a good enough reason to exercise, he thought as the road changed from pavement to gravel. One more mile and he would be home free.

Still a long way off, he could see his home. It was a small log house with a covered porch in the front and a shop in back. Lights were on in the house and smoke was coming from the chimney. But then there were other reasons to get in shape, too, he knew as he smiled to himself. That wonderful woman was always full of surprises. Without realizing it, Jim picked up the pace as he got close to the house.

Most all his life he'd never been influenced by a single woman. Within the past few years, however, he found himself pulled in different directions by two of them. *Perhaps fate was trying to make up for lost time*, he thought. Jim wasn't someone who cared for change, and he didn't feel comfortable having people try to rattle him out of his structured existence.

But Joe and Nikki were good, positive influences. The kind he hadn't known since his Grandfather. Surely their persuasion could only be good for him. Still, he felt comfortable in his rut of a life and was uneasy about deviating from it. He trusted that they would be there to support him if he did.

Joe and Nikki had become friends. Some days he felt like he was on the wrong end of a tag team wresting match. Joe would work him over against the ropes during the day, then send him home to be worked over by Nikki.

There was never a moment's rest. Often, he'd find them having lunch at the Main Street Diner and accused them of exchanging notes and plotting the demise of his independence. They assured him, in a not so innocent manner, that they wouldn't dream of it. He didn't believe them. Still, they had been like a ray of sunshine on his normally boring life. He wasn't sure how he had managed in the past, and couldn't imagine another day without them.

There she was, sitting on the front porch. She stood up, when he rolled to a stop and got off the bike, then she walked to the edge of the porch. She looked down at him with a smile. The white cotton summer dress she wore moved gently in the soft breeze. She looked good in white because it contrasted against her tan skin.

But she was no sun worshipper, he knew. He remembered seeing a picture of her and her mother once. They had the same deep dark eyes and long shiny black curly hair that came from a gene pool originating somewhere in the middle-east.

"It's good to see you," she greeted him.

"*Nikki!* What a wonderful surprise," Jim said as he walked up the steps and tried to embrace her.

"Not on your life!" she exclaimed as she took a step back and held her hand out in protest. "Not until you've taken a shower." She pointed towards the door. "I laid some clean cloths out for you in the bathroom."

"Yes ma'am," he replied teasingly, then marched past her.

"And don't call me ma'am," Nikki giggled and slapping him on the butt as he went by. Jim walked in the house and through the living room. When he had left that morning, the place was a mess, but it was now spotless.

"Thank you for cleaning up," he said, and hesitated. "I see you've rearranged some things."

"I like to think of them as improvements." She followed him to the kitchen.

"Mmm! What smells so good?" he asked as he passed through the kitchen and into the bathroom.

"Just a little something I whipped up." She smiled, happy that he'd noticed. "It's a recipe my grandmother taught me."

"Oh! Not one of *those* again," he said as he turned on the shower and adjusted the temperature.

"I thought you said you liked the last one?"

"I did, I'm just not used to *exotic* food."

"Well you've got to get weaned off meat and potatoes someday," she said, and peered into the bathroom.

"I like things just the way they are, thank you." He was about to take his shirt off when he noticed she was watching.

"Excuse me," he said, then started to close the door.

"What's the matter? Are you shy?" she asked, playfully.

His face immediately turned beat red, and Nikki laughed when she saw it. *I hate it when that happens*, Jim didn't say as he closed the door. Finally alone, he took off his clothes, opened the shower door and stepped in.

What was it about her that made him feel this way? he wondered. He felt so young and alive when she was around. Of course, it wasn't hard to figure it out—all he had to do was look at her. She was the most beautiful woman he had ever seen. And smart, too. She was only in her mid-thirties and she was the head nurse at the county hospital.

He simply had a high school diploma and liked the way she spoke without talking down to him. He guessed that there were a lot of things about her life that were different from his. She came from

168

a rich family, got the best education available, and traveled the world! Jim hadn't left the county in almost three decades.

One thing was the same though, he thought as he finished his shower and shut off the water. They were both stubborn as mules. That was something that took getting use to.

They say a man picks a woman like his mother. He wished he could've known his mother long enough to find out if that were true, he thought sadly as he dried himself off. But then he really hadn't picked her—he hadn't even said that word to her. Was he really in love? Yes, of course he was, but he was too afraid to say anything. What if she didn't feel the same? It would crush him. Jim wiped the condensation off the mirror.

"How could she love you?" he asked the reflection that starred back at him. Jim looked at himself. Five foot ten inches tall, and one hundred seventy five pounds. There was nothing about him that would set Jim apart from any other man in town. Except for the slightly gray hair, he thought as he lathered his face with shaving cream. It made him look distinguished, she had told him. "Old" was more like it. *Lord!, I am so much older than she is*, he thought, then hung his head in despair. *There's no way she could love you*, he told himself as the blade of the razor slid down his face. *No, if there's one word that describes you, Jim Harper, it's "average".*

Nikki was lighting the candles on the dinning table when Jim emerged from the bathroom in the faded jeans, sweat shirt, and tennis shoes she had left for him.

"Now that's more like it," she said as she walked over to him in the kitchen, wrapped her arms around him, and kissed him. "Mmm, I knew there was a man somewhere under all that sweat." Jim had a worried, distant look on his face that made her curious. "What's wrong?"

"Nothing. I'm just glad you're here," he replied, looking into her eyes.

"Good." She smiled, then let go of him. "Why don't you open the wine while I serve dinner?"

"All right." He turned and disappeared into the dinning room. Nikki carefully placed food on each plate precisely and evenly. Then she added a mint leaf as garnish, even though she knew Jim wouldn't notice the extra touch. He scarcely noticed anything else when food was involved.

Perfect, she thought. It was just the right amount of color. Nikki lifted the two plates and walked into the dinning room. After placing one in front of Jim, she sat down on the other side of the table.

"Mmm!" Jim exclaimed, as he stuffed a fork full of food into his mouth.

"Slow down, Jim! That's a fork, not a shovel," Nikki scolded in an irritated voice.

"Sorry," Jim said, looking over to her. "It sure is good."

"I'm glad you like it." She was happy that he appreciated her efforts. "I'll get some culture in you yet." Nikki tried to make small talk, but saw that Jim had something on his mind. He looked worried, so she let him finish his meal in silence. When Jim was finished he sat back in his chair and smiled.

"Why don't you go in the living room and sit down while I clear the dishes," Nikki suggested. Without saying anything Jim got up, took his glass and the wine bottle, and walked into the living room.

He placed his glass and the bottle on the floor, moved the coffee table out of the way, then took four large pillows off of the couch and placed them on the floor to be closer to the fire. Seeing that the flames were dying, he knelt in front of it and placed another log on top. When Jim stood up he was surprised to see a black and white picture of his parents staring back at him from the mantle. He slowly reached for it, picked it up, and stared at it.

"I hope you don't mind," came a voice behind him. "I found it in a drawer. They looked so young and in love I thought it should be on the mantle." Jim didn't answer. He just stood there staring at it. Nikki placed her hand on his shoulder. "Jim?"

"What? Oh, yes, it's all right. I just haven't seen it in so long," he replied, snapping out of the trance. He returned it to the mantle. Sitting down on the floor in front of the fire, Jim leaned on the pillows. Nikki sat next to him and poured herself a glass of wine, then filled his glass as well.

"Why haven't you told me about them?" she asked.

"I don't know. It's such a long story," Jim replied before taking a drink from his glass.

"I've got the time," Nikki assured him, as she eased in under his arm and rested her head on his chest. After a long moment Jim began to speak.

"It was such a long time ago," he repeated. "I barely remember them. They were childhood sweethearts-small town kids in too much of a hurry to go no where. That's what my grandfather used to say. They got married young. My mother wasn't even eighteen.

My father drove a logging truck until he got drafted. I was too young to remember when he left. All I can recall is that one day my mother was holding a piece of paper from the war department and crying on grandpa's shoulder. I tried to ask what was wrong but they both where crying too much to know I was there."

"Was that Korea?" Nikki asked.

"Yeah. Anyway, my mom didn't seem to notice me most of the time after that. Although, sometimes, she would grab me and hold me tight and cry. One day, not long afterwards, there was an ambulance at my house when I came home from school. Grandpa met me at the door and tried to explain to me that my mother had left and went to be with my father. I didn't understand then, but I figured it out when I was older."

Jim took a long drink as he stared into the fire. "My grandfather raised me. We only had each other, and that made every moment important, especially for him. We did everything together-hunting and fishing mostly. Heck, we lived for the steelhead run on the Cowlitz!"

"What about your grandmother, what happened to her?"

"I don't know exactly… she died before I was born, before grandpa got back from the war. He was a paratrooper in World War II. I would hate to think what would've happened to him if I wouldn't have been around. He always called me son, and sometimes he would slip and call me by my father's name. I didn't mind, for all practical purposes he was my father."

Jim hesitated before continuing. "I still remember the pain in his eyes when I got my notice. I was so mad I ran down to the draft office and swore at them. I felt that my family had suffered enough and that they had gone too far. But grandpa went down there and got me, took me home, and gave me the speech about duty, honor and country. Then he walked into his room and cried his eyes out.

Grandpa had a bad heart, and stress and lack of sleep was taking its toll. I filed for a hardship case in order to take care of him, but it was denied. They said that if my grandfather's condition got worse, they would reconsider and send me home. Grandpa had too much pride, though. He helped me get ready for boot camp when he should have been in the hospital."

"So what branch of service were you in?" Nikki asked.

"Army Airborne, like my grandfather," Jim said with a smile, then finished his glass and refilled it. They laid there, staring at the fire for a few moments in silence.

"So what happened?" Nikki finally asked.

Again, a sad distant look appeared on Jim's face. "Several months later, my grandfather collapsed and was hospitalized."

"Did they send you home?" Nikki asked, sitting up to look at him.

"My Airborne unit was a special squad," he explained. "We were dropped behind the lines to cut the enemy off as they retreated. By the time the hospital notified the Army, it was too late to notify me. I was deep in the jungle. When my unit got back to base, my grandfather had already died and was buried," Jim said with a tear in his eye.

"Oh, I'm sorry, honey," Nikki tried to console him.

"I was very angry at what I felt my country had done to my family. But out of respect for my grandfather, I buried those feelings deep inside."

"So what did you do?"

"I did the only thing I could do—my job. I just wasn't ready to deal with all the emotions, so I concentrated on my Army duties to keep my mind occupied." He took a moment before continuing.

"My unit was assigned to cut off the retreat of the enemy. Do you know what that's like? It's like cornering a wild animal, and the only way for it to escape is straight through you. Only, the North Vietnamese Army was like no animal I've ever seen. They came from all directions, screaming like mad men as they attacked. That's what war is—*madness.* It didn't take long before you were as crazy as they were. When the bullets ran out, it was hand to hand combat."

We turned into animals as well, he didn't say, for fear of how she might think of him. Once he had hunted the NVA for a whole night with only a rock in his hand. He had no idea how he had found them in the dark, but back then, he swore he could smell the bastards.

Jim's hand shook as he drank his wine. "War changes people," he said, after a moment. "I think I resented the government more for what they turned me into than for destroying my family. But those were the feelings of a foolish young kid," he said, almost as if he believed it and was slightly embarrassed for saying so.

Jim's body language told Nikki that these experiences still disturbed him and she tried to move the conversation in a less painful direction. "So what rank were you?"

"Rank doesn't mean much when you're in the bush," he frowned. "All us grunts started as privates. I got promoted to Corporal, then to Sergeant because I seemed to have a natural talent for out maneuvering the enemy. Besides, promotions come quickly in the jungle when people are dying around you. Several times I found myself in command of the whole platoon, or what was left of it."

Jim didn't know why he continued. It just seemed to feel better telling someone about it after all these years. "My last mission was the worst. We were to be dropped deep behind enemy lines at a location the Intelligence had told us was clear. Reconnaissance photos had shown a large, heavily damaged NVA unit trying to escape north. In order to do so, they had to go through the deserted valley we were being dropped into. But we didn't know that their destination *was* that valley."

As Nikki listened, Jim remembered the events still vivid in his mind as if they had happened yesterday. A slight chill of anxiety went up his spine as his trembling lips spoke of the images that still occasionally wake him from deep sleep.

"I recall the jumpmaster saying, it was a bomber's moon, with a smile and a thumbs up. That meant good luck, especially to night bombers who needed the full moon to see their target clearly, and to paratroopers whose lives depended on their hitting the mark. That relieved some of the tension in the jump plane that had been building since take off.

"What we didn't anticipate, however, was that the same advantage could be used by soldiers on the ground to track the fall of jumpers. What Intelligence didn't know, and what couldn't be revealed by any aerial reconnaissance photos, was that this supposedly deserted jungle valley was, in fact, an underground NVA base linked together by countless tunnels.

"Our luck had just run out," Jim continued. "Moments after I and the others had jumped, I looked down and saw what appeared to be thousands of ants coming out of holes. To my horror, I realized they were NVA troops preparing to lay in wait for us. We were falling into a trap. As soon as the jumpers were in range, tracer fire lit up the night, picking off the paratroopers one by one. We were like lambs to the slaughter, as each in turn came into range of the guns.

He continued to recount the event. Jim cut away his chute just as a streak of bullets sliced past him. He fell towards the darkened earth at an alarming rate then pulled his back up chute just above the tree tops. The enemy failed to target him accurately and he slid into the trees before they could draw a bead.

The branches hit him hard, ripping into cloth and flesh. Then he crashed into the ground with a jolt that knocked the wind out of him. Bruised and bloody, he struggled to his feet in time to see the first of the enemy come down upon him.

"My squad fought for several hours," he said, looking into the fire. "When it was all over, there were only five of us left. We were cut off from the main troop with just a little food and no radio. Our moods were grim- none of us thought we'd make it out alive." Jim hesitated, as if stuck in some distant place in his mind.

Nikki looked at him. His facial expression was frozen and pale, but she could feel his heart pound rapidly through shallow breathing. She could tell that he was reliving the experience in his mind. She thought that maybe they should stop talking about it, but then she decided she must help him continue.

"So, what did you do?" she finally asked.

"I decided to be as unpredictable as possible, so instead of heading south back to base, we retreated north." The moment he started talking again, Nikki felt his heart rate slow, returning to normal. "The further north we got the fewer NVA we ran into. We came upon a NVA outpost about the same time we ran out of food. We had to do something, so that night I took all the claymores and flares we had and climbed to the opposite hill above the camp. I fired off the flares and started throwing grenades everywhere to make it seem like there were a whole lot of us."

"What were the other guys doing?"

"They were on the edge of camp, on the other side, hiding in the bushes and protecting their eyes from the flares. By the time the NVA came up the hill after me I had booby-traps set. When the flares burnt out, my men came out of the bushes and into camp. The few NVA left behind were night blinded by the flares and were easy targets. We stole as much food and weapons as we could carry, then booby-trapped the camp. When what was left of the NVA troop got back to camp, they got a big surprise."

"That sounds pretty risky."

"Well, they were young and not well trained, so it wasn't too difficult," he assured her. "Anyway, we continued to head north. Climbing over the mountains, we then headed south down a different drainage. We only fought when we had to, especially when we were out of food or ammo. Then we would retreat north again until things cooled off.

It became more difficult and movement was slowed as we went further south. The NVA had their best and most experienced troops on the front lines. They didn't fall for many of our tricks, and it became bloody. We all got beat up pretty bad, but we made it back alive and a month overdue. That's when I met Buck. He was a Major in command of Special Operations and he came to debrief me. He seemed amazed at what we had done. He wrote it all down to use it in an officers training course on surprise tactics. I was surprised as well when Buck told me my tour had ended when I was in the jungle."

Nikki looked at him questioningly. She had talked to Buck only a few times and never would have pictured him as an officer… especially one in Special Operations! "Buck doesn't give me the impression of the type of person I would think of in that kind of position."

"You're right. He really wasn't cut out for that type of work. Buck was a good soldier and an excellent drill instructor, but when it came to planning strategies for covert military operations he was in way over his head," Jim stated.

"Then how did he get assigned such an important job?" Nikki asked, intently.

"Well, to understand that you have to know a little more about Buck." Jim paused a long moment wondering how to begin. "Buck is basically just an old trader and story teller," Jim began by saying. Nikki listened as Jim explained everything he had come to know about his friend.

"Buck was raised on a small farm in the Midwest. It was the depression era mentality. Nobody had much money so most everything you needed had to be bartered for. Buck learned from his father how to get the best deals. Chickens and pigs were not valued in dollars, but by how many meals they represented. That, in turn, was balanced by the number of acres that could be planted or harvested by the fuel or spare parts you had for trade.

So, Buck became an expert trader. It helped that he liked people, and, no matter where he was, he always made it a point of meeting everyone. Through regular visits, he would always remember what people needed or had and he would arrange trades between different groups and families.

Trades would become all day events, and sometimes stretch into the night. They would have bon fires, cookouts, and dances. When it got late people huddled around the fire to listen to the old men compete by exchanging stories of their adventures. Buck learned fast and was soon spinning his own tales. He was a natural at reading an audience, and could change the direction of a story depending on the mood of each.

"Then how did he become a soldier?" she asked.

"Buck never liked farming. He wanted to travel the world and have the type of adventures he talked about in his stories." Jim continued after a moment.

"Buck finally left home and joined the Army. Sent to Europe, he fought in the final months of World War II, where it was discovered he had another valuable skill—*tracking*. The farm where Buck grew up was next to an Indian Reservation, and he had learned from his Native American friends how to hunt and track animals. The things he knew about birds using camouflage or animals building hiding places were valuable skills when looking for the enemy.

"Buck quickly became popular. Not only could he find the enemy better than anyone else, but he usually returned from patrol with a mountain grouse or wild boar. These were valuable commodities among soldiers tired of Army rations. His troop would have a barbecue, then Buck would provide entertainment with a few stories. The only part Buck couldn't stand was the killing. It made him feel sick and he was glad when the war ended.

"Post-war life was good to Buck. Staying in Europe as part of the Occupational Forces, he got a chance to travel and let his trading skill flourish. Inflation was rampant in post-war Europe making currency almost useless. Bartering on the black market became a way of life, and, although it was technically illegal, you could never convince Buck of that.

Buck facilitated trades and made sure everyone got what they wanted in a fair manner. Just like back at the farm, anything could be traded. The locals had chickens, pigs, fresh baked breads, pies, and such while a post-war Army had an over abundance of fuel, lubricants, and spare parts.

Officers looked the other way, knowing that they could expect a good meal and a portion of Buck's trading fee. Buck quickly made a lot of money for an Army Private. Banks were insecure and currency rates were volatile, so he learned from other black marketers to convert paper money into diamonds. This method came in handy for a soldier who was routinely moved from base to base on a moments notice. A few diamonds could easily be carried in his pocket or footlocker.

A few years later, the Korean War started and Buck was transferred from Europe to the Asian continent. Again he was put on the front lines where killing the enemy became a daily event. The guilty feelings were too much for him, and that's when he began drinking. So Buck devised a plan to get as far away from the fighting as possible. A discrete inquiry, a couple of diamonds here or there, and Buck found himself moving up the chain of command and into an officers training program. He managed to stay out of combat, and by the end of the war he was a Lieutenant.

Post-war Korea had the same problems Europe had-insolvent banks, rampant inflation, volatile currency and a population with needs that had to be met. It was the perfect environment for a trader like Buck. Being an officer had an added bonus. He now had access to even more capital, and soon his personal wealth increased dramatically.

Again, a few donations to the right people and a couple years before the start of the hostilities in Vietnam, Buck had Captain's bars added to his uniform. He was getting older now, it wouldn't be long before he would have to retire, so his focus changed to securing the best retirement possible. He already had a sack of diamonds, but wanted the added security of the large monthly retirement checks received by higher ranking officers, so Buck searched for a choice position to sit back and retire in.

A few inquires turned up an answer that surprised him. It seemed that a Police Action was being declared in Vietnam and the US was taking an advisory roll. Rumors throughout the ranks stated that these hostilities would be governed by new rules of engagement handed down by politicians. The Armed Forces could not go across the 49th Parallel or cross boarders. The enemy was not to be destroyed, but contained and the use of Special Forces would be strictly prohibited.

After lining the right pockets, Buck was promoted to Major and given command of Special Operations. There he hoped to sit back for a few years taking it easy while his unit conducted drills from the safety of a base far away from enemy lines. However, these hostilities were not controlled by a General who commanded forces from the battle field with the intention of destroying the enemy. Instead, orders came directly from Washington DC, and Buck started receiving top secret instructions to conduct surgical strikes behind enemy lines.

As the hostilities progressed the situation changed, and a full-fledged war was declared. For the first few years things had gone as the politicians in DC had planned it. The NVA were young, inexperienced troops who were easily pushed back and controlled. As time went by, however, they became battle tested. Rumors of help from Soviet military advisors were going around, and US tactics were analyzed and countered.

US troops started dying. Instead of changing strategies, the politicians left their so called rules of engagement in place. Although his men were well trained, they were now going against battle hardened NVA– trained and advised by Soviet military specialist. Buck was suddenly out of his league. He sent men out into the jungle and they returned in body bags. The few people he had helping him plan strategies were taught in the same classes and out of the same book that he had, but each new move seemed to be anticipated by the enemy.

Buck felt guilty and responsible for the deaths of his men and started drinking heavily. He asked for a transfer, but it was refused. It seemed that only a few people in DC knew of his secret orders. They didn't want any reassignment drawing attention to the project. Buck was ordered to keep his mouth shut and do a better job. He was stuck between a rock and a hard place.

That was about the time Buck met Jim. Buck was intrigued by a story about a small group of soldiers who had survived more than a month behind enemy lines. They conducted surprise attacks and out maneuvered Charley while trying to make their way back to base. Buck rushed down to the Army hospital, where the soldiers were recovering, to meet the man who had out witted the NVA.

After listening to Jim's story, Buck asked a hypothetical question. If you were planning missions based on tactics learned from books you suspected the enemy has also read, what would you do? Jim's answer was simple- throw away the book. Or better yet, use what you believed the enemy knew about the book to out maneuver him. Jim was like a breath of fresh air. Here was someone with a natural instinct for tactics, and it wasn't taught to him by any military school.

Jim's tour of duty was over, but he needed a few weeks in the hospital to fully recover from his injures. This gave him time to help Buck plan the next mission. By the time they were through, Jim was healthy and ready to go home. After saying goodbye to Buck, he boarded a transport and flew back to the States.

Jim was only home a few days when he received a message from Buck. Jim's plan had worked perfectly. Not only did they strike a serious blow to the enemy, but every member of the assault team came back without a scratch. Buck begged Jim to come back to Vietnam to help him, but Jim insisted that he was through with the Army for good. He hadn't wanted to join in the first place, and had no intention of re-enlisting. However, he was happy that his plan had such positive results.

Jim's feelings were mixed. Coming home had not given him the peace he was looking for—he was still too angry and confused. Jim didn't like the war, nor did he understand it. He made it very clear to Buck he had no intention of supporting it. However, he felt he had an obligation to the people involved, many of whom were there involuntarily as he was. He figured they probably felt the way he did- angry, confused, and just wanted to make it home alive. He couldn't help with the first two problems, but if he could help with the third, then he knew he *had* to.

Jim boarded the next transport back to Asia. In his usual way, Buck arranged a special job assignment. Jim was given a civilian job as a paper pusher in the American Embassy in Saigon. The situation worked out well for everyone. Jim helped Buck plan missions, and having a project to dive into helped him take his mind off some of the emotional issues he had been dealing with.

Neither one of them cared much for the mission's actual purpose, but agreed that the safety of the men was a must and their plans reflected those intentions. Successful missions were carried out and men came home alive. Buck's conscience was clearing up, his drinking decreased significantly, and the two men quickly became close friends. Buck was promoted to Colonel, for which he was very proud because it was the first promotion he didn't have to buy.

Feeling better, Buck again went back to planning for retirement. All the pockets he had to line to get his promotions and Jim's embassy job had dwindled his nest egg in half. In between missions, Buck introduced Jim to the black market and taught him how to trade. Jim learned quickly and soon he and Buck were in a friendly competition against each other to see who could make the best deals.

Jim discovered that products for women were scarce in a war zone. He started making routine trips to Japan to pick up perfume, silk stockings and makeup. When he returned, he sold them for ten fold.

Buck had only a couple of months left until retirement and his nest egg was still lower than he had wanted. So he got involved with trades that were more risky but had higher profit margins and was doing quite well. After getting a tip from an unscrupulous black marketer, Buck went to a local bank inquiring about a shipping company which needed investors. The banker explained that he needed money to finance the startup of a company to bring goods into this war torn region. This company would quickly have a monopoly controlling all goods coming in and going out of the country.

Buck saw it as a way to get rich quickly and put up every cent he had. After a few weeks of not being able to reach his new partner, he went back to the bank. He met with the bank's president, who explained that a former employee had run a con game on some of the bank's customers. He had taken a lot of peoples money, including Buck's, then left the country.

"Buck must have been devastated," Nikki spoke up.

"Oh, he was," Jim continued. "He was so angry that he went on an all night drinking binge and the next morning he stole a tank and drove it right through the front of the bank."

"So how did Buck end up here?"

"Well, neither one of us had much of a family so we kind of adopted each other. I remembered Buck talked about starting an outfitting service so I convinced him to move here. After the loss of his nest egg, Buck suffered somewhat of a breakdown. We came back from Asia, and we were both surprised at the changes we saw.

Buck hadn't been back to the States since he was a teenager. The big city was like a different world to him, and he didn't like it. He wanted to return to the old days, like the ones he knew on the farm. I told him I knew a place where the small town culture was still alive and well," Jim continued telling his story.

When they arrived in Lewis County, they didn't like what they saw—it wasn't the way Jim had left it. Big city influences had moved in. Hippies from out of town were having "love-ins" and protests. Buck didn't like it either, and was ready to leave but Jim changed his mind.

They had a new mission and set out to clean up the town and restore the small town culture to its former glory. It was an election year and Jim got on the ballot for Sheriff. Buck went door to door meeting everyone convincing people to vote for Jim. With the support of the community, Jim and his small town culture platform won the election by a land slide.

Jim went to work immediately. He pushed the riff raff out and back to the cities. As drifters came in, Jim would screen them to determine their motives. If they were seeking a quiet life and could be a valued member of the community, Jim allowed them to stay. If not, they were quickly given a bus ticket to the city and run out of town.

"And that's the way it's been for almost three decades," Jim finished. "It's been a constant battle, but it's been worth it." Jim had

180

never talked this much in his life. He was comfortable talking to Nikki, and felt as if a weight had been lifted from him.

His story had gone so long, he hadn't noticed that the fire was almost down to embers.

"It's getting cold. Let me put some more wood on the fire." They both slowly moved out of their embrace. Jim went to the fire, tossed another log on it then stoked it back to life. Nikki stood up, then walked around the room stretching her legs, glad that Jim had shared so much.

"So is that why Buck drinks so much?" Nikki asked. "Does he still feel guilty about the war?"

Jim stood up, picked up his wine glass, and pondered the question. "I don't think so. I know his drinking has increased in the past few years, but for a long time he had always kept it in check. Although, every few years or so, something would happen to set it off and Buck would go on a week long binge. Then, I go spend a few days with him. He calms down, dries out, and everything is fine again."

"It sounds like you've spent a lot of time helping him," Nikki observed. "I've been told you spend a lot of your time helping others with problems, as well."

"The job of a Sheriff is kind of like that of a shepherd," Jim replied after a moment. "Sometimes the flock needs to be tended to."

"I know, Jim, but they don't seem to get any better. You don't have to do it alone, you know." She rubbed his back gently. "Buck seems to have some unresolved issues he's dealing with. Has he ever considered seeking professional help?"

"You mean like a *shrink*?" Jim cocked his head and frowned at the idea. He and Buck both knew the problems their friend Rick had with the Army doctors and didn't think it would help. "The only therapy Buck has ever gotten he found on the end of his fishing pole or at the bottom of a bottle."

"Maybe you both should consider talking to a professional about your problems."

"*Both!*" Jim looked up with surprise at the suggestion. "What do you mean both?"

"Both of you obviously have emotional issues you haven't been able to work through. Buck looks for relief by drinking and you hide in your work. You said it yourself. You needed a project to dive into to get your mind off of it," Nikki replied. "Maybe that's why you're such a work-a-holic."

"There's nothing wrong with *me*," Jim defended.

181

"That's just denial," she returned. "Much of what you said makes it clear. Shock, anger, denial, guilt—they're all symptoms of an emotional trauma." Nikki looked at Jim, thoughtfully. "It's a normal process, Jim. Anytime someone gets emotionally hurt they have to go through these steps to get to forgiveness and healing. You both seem to be stuck in some stage or another and just need a little help to get through it and move on."

"You sound like an expert," Jim noted.

She put her arms around him and held him. "I'm not," she said softly. "I'm just passing on some of the things I've learned from Josephine. She says that some times people can't recognize they have a problem because they're too personally involved to see it. It sounds as if there's something in both your lives that's holding you back from reaching healing. Like not seeing the forest through the trees, you may be too close to the situation to be able to identify what the problem is."

She pulled away slightly and looked into his eyes. "I'm reminded of some words my favorite poet, Emily Dickinson, once wrote, 'The mind is so near itself it can not see distinctly'.

Psychologists are trained professionals, Jim. They can help you identify what's wrong and help you come to grips with it and eliminate it." Then a thought occurred to Nikki. "If you won't see a doctor, maybe you should do like I do and talk to Joe. I bet she could help quite a bit. She's working on her doctorate in psychology, you know."

Jim listened to Nikki's words. She always had a way of explaining things in a straight forward, nonjudgmental manner and he wondered if perhaps she was right. He had never considered that he may have a problem, at least not one that could be fixed by a doctor. He then considered her suggestion about talking to Joe and that troubled him.

"I don't know... maybe." Jim said, thinking about it as he held her. He wasn't ready to share *that* much with Rissley, he decided. "If it's all right, I'd rather start with you and work my way up."

"That's just fine," she replied with a squeeze.

They held each other for a long while, and Jim was glad to have Nikki there. For years he had to be the strong one taking care of everyone else's needs, protecting them from harm, and picking up the pieces if something went wrong. He had never been able to consider his own needs.

Jim took a deep breath and smelled Nikki's perfume. It was nice having someone as wonderful as Nikki looking out for him and taking care of him. He knew he never wanted it to end. Then a thought occurred to him. "Have you been talking to Rissley about me?"

"No, I would never do that," She assured him as she looked into his eyes. Then she slowly looked away sadly. "Joe has been helping me resolve some issues I haven't been able to work through. Some problems I've had with my parents."

"Is that why you've never mentioned them?" he asked.

"Yeah, I guess so. It's just been too hard to deal with alone."

"Would you like to talk about it?"

It only took a second for her to know that she did want to tell him about it. She had wanted to for some time, and thought it would be helpful to get a male perspective of the situation.

"We had a falling out a several years back," she started by saying. She slowly turned away from him and stared distantly into the fire. "It all started about the time I graduated from college. I had finished my finals two days before commencement. Mom was back east visiting my grandparents, so I thought I would drive home to surprise my father and maybe make him a decent meal. I arrived in Seattle as the sun came up and walked into the house. I caught my father in the kitchen kissing another woman. They stood right in front of me!" she exclaimed. "That little tramp was wearing nothing but one of my fathers dress shirts!"

"What happened?" Jim asked.

"I was *furious!* My father took me in the other room and tried to calm me down. We argued for awhile then I ran out of the house and drove back to school. The next day my father and mother showed up for my graduation looking like the perfect couple. They held hands and even kissed each other."

"What did you do? Did you tell your mother?"

"Of course. I had to tell her," Nikki said. "When I was able to get her alone I told her the whole story."

"Was she angry?" Jim asked as he watched her pace nervously.

"No! Not in the least! She said that she had hoped that I would never find out." Nikki exclaimed. "My mother told me that she had first caught him with another woman when she was pregnant with me and that, although she was angry then, she had come to accept his affairs as long as he was discrete."

"So what did you say to her?"

"I was dumb founded. I didn't know what to say," Nikki replied. "My mother explained to me that women have come and

183

gone over the years and that my father loved us both very much and would never leave."

"Why didn't she divorce him?"

"My mother's side of the family has always been concerned about outward appearances. My grandmother is from Saudi Arabia. She met my grandfather, who was a rich American oil man, when he was there on business. They fell in love, which was taboo to her side of the family so they kept it a secret. Finally, they ran away, flew to America, and got married. My mother grew up being taught that women were subservient to their husbands. Mother fell in love with my father, who is a brilliant surgeon, and she spends most of her time alone at home while he practically lives at the hospital. No, she won't leave him because somehow she thinks it would disgrace her in her family's eyes."

"So you haven't talked to them since?" Jim asked.

"I still call mother from time to time, especially on holidays. I haven't talked to him, though. He's always at the hospital anyway. That's the way it's been my whole life. I rarely saw my father," she said sadly. "And when I did we were always arguing."

"What about?"

"You name it, we argued about it. Especially about my career. I was an only child, so he naturally expected that I would follow in his footsteps and become a doctor."

"And you didn't want that?"

"No I didn't. I wanted to *really* help people. Don't get me wrong, doctors' work very hard and save a lot of lives, but it's not the same as a nurse. Doctors are usually too busy to get to know their patients or even care. They run out of one operating room and into the next. When they do talk to their patients, it's just long enough to look at their charts and prescribe medication. Then it's out the door again."

"A nurse is different." She assured him. "We sit and talk to the patients and make sure that they have everything they need. A hospital is not a fun place to be, especially if you're a patient or a member of the family. Nurses take care of the whole family. We comfort them and make them feel at ease. Doctors aren't very good at that sort of thing," she said as she again stared into the fire. "So as you can see, I've gone through some of the stages of trauma, as well-shock at finding my father with another woman, anger at realizing what the situation was. Joe says that moving here from Seattle is a form of denial as I tried to forget my feelings. I know it sounds silly, but I've even felt guilty. Wondering if I had been a better daughter, would things be different?" She looked over to him. "I'm stuck. I can't seem to resolve these feelings and get to forgiveness and healing." She looked back to the fire and stared at it for a long time in silence.

"If you never saw your father, how is it that you became such a tom-boy?" Jim asked, trying to break the tension.

Nikki looked at him and smiled, happy to change the subject. I mainly started hiking and camping when I was in college. Most of the students there were into nature. 'Granolas', I called them. Do you remember when we first met?" she said with a big smile on her face. "You pulled me over for going through a stop sign, or something stupid like that, then you couldn't bring yourself to give me a ticket."

"I let you off with a warning because you were from out of town and didn't know where you were going," he protested.

"Yeah, sure," she said smiling, not believing him. "I suppose that's why, when I asked you directions to the camp ground on Riffe lake, you personally escorted me there."

"That was because I didn't want a big city driver causing any accidents in my county. I've got a responsibility to the community, you know," Jim argued.

Nikki laughed at this. "Is that why you showed up at my camp everyday to see me?"

Jim didn't answer. He just sat there fuming.

"You were so cute! Everyday your face would get bright red as you tried to come up with another lame excuse for just being in the neighborhood. Jim you can't lie to save your life!"

"I can too! You don't know anything." Jim tried defending himself as he felt his face turned red again. *Damn! I wish I could control that*, he thought to himself as Nikki let out a huge laugh at the sight of him.

"Oh yeah," he countered. "Well, you're the one who decided to move here after only knowing me for a few days."

"What!" she exclaimed. "I didn't move here to be with you, I moved here to work at the county hospital."

"You already had a job. Why did you need another one?"

"I've told you this before," she defended herself. "When I saw the hospital here I just fell in love with it. It wasn't like the hustle and bustle of a big city hospital. The nurses have time to get to know their patients. It feels more like a family taking care of its own than a hospital." Nikki's face turned sad, then she put her hands to her face and started to cry.

Jim rushed to her and held her. "I can't believe it, Jim. My whole life I grew up believing that certain things were good, decent,

185

and sacred. Every week my parents and I would walk into church looking like the model family, and it was all just a show for the public!" She cried on his shirt.

After a few moments she stopped and looked at him, then kissed him. "You would never do that would you, Jim? Of course not, you could *never* lie to me," she said as their eyes met. "I guess that's why I love you so much."

Jim was too surprised to speak. He just froze.

Seeing his expression, Nikki nervously looked past him and out the window. "Look at it outside, it's really coming down," she said as she stepped away from him, changing the subject.

Jim then walked over to her at the window and wrapped his arms around her trembling body. "It's a bad storm," he agreed. He hadn't noticed, until then, that it was even raining. "Maybe you should stay here tonight." He didn't want her out in the weather trying to get home.

She turned around and looked at him. "I don't know, Jim," she said with a skeptical tone. "I know that's against your *rules.*"

Ring!

The phone rang in the kitchen, but they didn't even notice it, they just stared at each other.

Ring!

"I'm sure of it," he replied, then kissed her gently. "You can have the bed and I'll take the couch."

Ring!

She rolled her eyes. *Of course,* she thought. She'd never known Jim to do anything improper—even when no one was looking. "Oh, Jim," she said with a hint of frustration. "You're always so…"

"Boring?" he finished for her.

Ring!

"No," she replied with a slight giggle. Jim wasn't like any man she'd ever known. He was always reliable. He would *never* lie to her or fool around behind her back like her father had. And that's what she desperately needed in her life. Even if they did nothing wrong, she knew he'd still feel guilty for even the *appearance* of impropriety.

Ring!

"No, Jim," she said with complete sincerity. "You're always so…*perfect.*"

Ring!

He blushed with embarrassment.

Ring!

The phone distracted her. "I think you had better get that, it might be important," she said softly as she smiled at him.

Ring!

"It'll go away," he replied, and hoped that it would, as he tried to kiss her again.

Ring!

She stopped him and gave him a stern look. Growing up in a home with a doctor, she knew calls this late at night were usually important.

"All right," he said, then stepped away from her and walked towards the kitchen.

Ring!

He lifted the receiver. "Jim, here."

"Jim! I'm glad I got a hold of you," said the voice on the line.

"Buck, is that you?"

"Yeah, it's me. I'm sorry to call you so late but I need you to do me a favor."

"Lord! Buck its three o'clock in the morning!" Jim said impatiently as he glanced at the clock, then looked at Nikki in the living room.

"I know, I'm sorry but I need you to take the trail garbage to the land fill."

"Why can't this wait until tomorrow?"

"Marcellous called and told me that he's taking a couple of days off, but that he would open the land fill for this load this morning."

"Why can't *you* take it in?"

"It's a long story, Jim. Will you come out and get it?" Buck pleaded.

"Yeah, all right," Jim said reluctantly. "I'll head out right away."

"Thanks! See you in a little while."

Jim hung up the phone and rubbed his tired eyes.

"What's wrong?" Nikki asked as she walked into the kitchen.

"That was Buck. He needs me to dump all the garbage he picked up on the trail," Jim replied.

"*What!*" she exclaimed. "Why can't it wait until tomorrow?"

"The land fill will be closed for a couple of days." Jim answered.

"Then why can't it wait a couple of days?"

187

"Buck picks the garbage up so that it won't attract the bears closer to town. He doesn't like to keep it at his place because he doesn't want bears messing with his mules."

"Do you have to go?" she asked as she put her arms around him. She already knew what her *reliable* man would say.

"Yeah, I'd better. That way I can get home and get some sleep. Looks like I'll be going into work a little late tomorrow," he said, again looking at the clock. "You should get some sleep, too. What time do you have to work tomorrow?"

"Not until the afternoon. I'll get plenty of sleep," she assured him.

"All right then, why don't you crawl into bed and I'll see you in the morning."

"I'll be waiting," she replied, then kissed him.

Jim turned around and headed for the back door where he put on his rubber boots, raincoat, and hat. He then opened the door and walked outside. It was really coming down, he noticed. The rain beat hard against him as he waded through the puddles around Nikki's car to his 4x4. He got in the Blazer, started it up, and turned the wipers to full, and then decided to lock in the hubs.

The road to Buck's place was bound to be a mud pit, and he didn't want to get stuck in the ditch. Jim jumped out of the Blazer, made the adjustments at the wheels, then got back in. He pulled the vehicle around behind the shop, then ran over to a small homemade trailer. Pulling it to the back of the Blazer, he attached it to the hitch. He jumped back into the driver's seat, drove the truck down the driveway and onto the gravel road.

His tired mind thought about the trip. It was fifty miles to Buck's place so he'd better get comfortable. Jim turned on his dispatch radio and listened to the calls being sent out. He heard nothing unusual as the Blazer rolled through town, then turned onto the ramp to I-5 South. A short time later, he turned onto Highway 12 and headed east.

Jim turned off the dispatch radio and just listened to the sound of the hard rain as it tried to hammer its way through the roof. An hour later, the Blazer pulled into Morton. Jim made the turn north and knew that Buck's place wasn't far away now. He was glad that the road had lots of turns to keep his weary mind's attention. He slowed down to make sure he made the slippery turns. There was nobody else on the road, and Jim wished he was like everyone else- snuggled warm and safe in a bed as the storm raged on outside, unnoticed.

13
Spin

Friday morning.

A few minutes later, corvette headlights cut through the stormy darkness. "Entering Morton" was on the sign as Alan sped past. Alan slowed down as he looked around, then pulled into the poorly lit motel parking lot. A few moments later, Chet pulled in and parked next to him. Both men got out and ran through the rain to the door. In red neon, "vacancy" was displayed in the dark window. Wiping off their feet they went in.

The small lobby was dark, with just a single light on over the counter. A small sign next to a bell read, "Ring for service". Alan hit the bell several times, but nothing happened. He rang it again, this time louder. Finally, a light went on in the back. The sound of tired, sleepy feet being drug slowly across the floor came from the back room. The door behind the counter creaked open and out walked a skinny old man in a striped robe and slippers.

"Good morning," Mr. Brunner, the elderly owner of the small motel, said as he stepped up to the counter. "How can I help you?"

"We'd like a room," Alan replied.

"Oh, of course you would," Brunner said, rubbing the sleep out of his eyes. Picking up a sign-in book, he placed it in front of his customers and turned around and thumbed through some keys in a drawer. Alan pointed to Chet then the sign-in book. Chet stepped up and did as indicated.

"I'll put you in number four," he said as he placed the key on the desk.

"Perhaps you can help us find a friend of ours," Alan said.

"Who's that?"

"We're looking for a man named Henderson. Do you know him?"

The old man looked the two up and down suspiciously, and rubbed his chin. "I know why you're here," he said after a moment with a slight grin on his face.

"You do?" Alan questioned as he and Chet exchanged worried glances.

"Uh-huh, it's no secret. You're from the city, aren't you?" Brunner looked back and forth between them. "Buck gets a lot of visitors from the city. Although, he usually calls me if his people coming in need rooms."

"Buck?" Alan thought fast. "Yeah, old Buck. He's expecting us and I lost the directions he gave me. Can you tell me how to get to his place?"

"Do you have a map?"

Alan pulled a map from his pocket and laid it on the counter. Chet watched over Alan's shoulder as the man gave instructions. "Alright, got it. Thanks." Alan said, then folded the map and put it in his pocket. Chet grabbed the key and the two walked towards the door.

"Good luck fishing," the old man said. "Oh, and how long are you planning on staying?"

"Fishing?" Alan questioned as he opened the door then turned around. "We don't know. It all depends on how good the fishing is." He winked at Chet, then the two walked out the door closing it behind them. "Did you hear that? It looks like Henderson brings a lot of strangers around."

"Why did you have me sign-in and not you?" Chet questioned.

"Don't underestimate this operation," Alan replied. "That clerk may not look so bright, but if he works for Henderson he could be checking up on you right now. It's no big deal if you're a reporter, but if he found out I'm DEA this whole raid could be shot."

"So what do we do now?"

"Lets unpack what we don't need, then we'll take your Chief. The roads on this map were not made for sports cars. We'll have to hurry if we want to get there before it gets light."

"Right," Chet replied as both men hurried to their vehicles.

190

There it was. Jim's high beams lit up the sign– "Mineral Lake Exit". Jim slowed down and pulled onto the muddy road. He was glad he thought about locking in the hubs, he wouldn't want to get stuck out here. Jim drove around the lake to Buck's house. As he pulled up in front, Buck stepped out onto the porch. Jim got out of the Blazer and ran through the mud towards the porch. Most of the rain had stopped by now, there was just a mist left in the air.

"Thanks for coming, Jim." Buck said.

"Are you all right? You look *terrible*," Jim replied. "Have you been drinking again? You know we've talked about this before, Buck—"

"—I know Jim, tone it down a little will ya? My heads *killing* me." Buck cut him off.

"All right," Jim nodded. They were both tired, and Jim wanted to take care of business now that the rain had stopped. "Where's the garbage?"

"In the barn, next to the straw pile. Here, I'll help you."

"That's all right, there's no use in both of us getting muddy."

"Then I'll put some coffee on. You look like you could use some," Buck said as Jim ran back to the Blazer. Jim drove it around in a circle and stopped in front of the barn. He jumped out, opened the barn door, and walked in. Pulling a flashlight out of his raincoat, Jim turned it on and looked around until he found the bags of garbage. The mules moved restlessly in their stables as Jim walked to the straw pile.

"It's all right girls, it's just old Jim," he reassured the mules as he picked up a couple bags. The animals calmed down upon hearing the familiar voice. Jim made two more trips into the barn for the rest of the bags, then closed the doors and ran to the house. He stopped on the porch, took off his muddy boots then entered the house. Inside he took off his raincoat and hat, and hung them on a peg next to the door. A fire was ragging in the fireplace and Jim moved over to it and warmed himself. Buck emerged from the kitchen with two mugs of hot coffee and handed one to him.

"Thanks," Jim said, accepting it.

"I'm sorry you had to come all the way out here, but Clifford left and took the Suburban," Buck explained.

"*What?* Do you want me to put out an APB out on it?"

"No, he's just an antsy kid. His mother called just before I called you. Apparently Clifford went to Seattle to party, but ended up at home when he ran out of money. His mother said she'll send him back in a week or so."

"Well, alright if that's the way you want it," Jim replied then moved to a chair and sat down. Jim looked at Buck. Buck had a beard that was several days old and his clothes looked like they had been slept in. "What's wrong, Buck?" Jim asked, worriedly. "You promised me you'd quit drinking."

"I know Jim, I'm sorry," Buck apologized. "I was doing well for awhile, then I just needed a drink."

"Well you had better get a grip on it. You know it's bad for business," Jim scolded. "*Especially* with Clifford around."

"I know Jim, settle down."

Jim didn't feel like arguing, so he changed the subject. "Have you got any charters yet?" he asked after a long moment.

"No, but the seasons still early. When are you going to come fishing with me?" he replied, happy for the change in topics.

"I don't know. Soon I hope," Harper answered, slumping low in his seat and warming his hands with his coffee cup.

"Tell you what. Why don't you dump the garbage and come back. I'll have the gear in the boat and waiting. We'll have a great time, just like we use to," Buck said with a smile.

Jim's eyes wanted to close, but he fought it. "Not today Buck, I'm just too tired," he replied, then took a long drink from his cup knowing that Nikki was waiting back at the house.

"It's that *dang blasted* woman of yours isn't it?" Buck scowled. "I *warned* you about her."

"No, I'm just tired," Jim defended himself.

"Being tired never stopped you from fishing before. Listen to it out there, the rain has stopped. In a few hours the clouds will break and the fish will be biting. We'll have the lake to ourselves." Buck pleaded.

"It sounds tempting, but not today. I'll come next week, I promise," Jim assured him. "I'd better get going if I'm to catch Marcellous at the landfill." Jim set the cup on the coffee table then stood up, and Buck followed him through the door and onto the porch. As he sat on a chair putting his boots on, the water clock chimed.

Ding!

Jim looked at it, then to his watch. "Looks like you're an hour slow, Buck."

Buck frowned, slightly embarrassed. "Yeah, I'm still working on it."

192

"I'll call you in a couple of days. We'll talk about fishing then," Jim told him as he stood up.

"Okay, Jim. I'll be waiting," Buck said with a smile. Jim walked off the porch and into the darkness to the Blazer, carrying his hat and coat. He hopped in. Waving to Buck as he drove past, Jim rolled back up the muddy road with his high beams on, to the paved highway and turned north. The Blazer slowly accelerated, kicking mud clods from its tires, as it went down the road and around the bend.

A few seconds later, headlights came around the bend from the south. "Slow down, there it is," Alan said as he pointed a small flashlight at a map on his lap.

"Mineral lake," Chet confirmed, pulling onto the muddy road. He reached down and pulled the lever on the floor putting the Chief in four-wheel drive.

"According to the directions we got from the hotel manager, it should be coming up in about a mile," Alan said. "When we get half way there, we can pull off the road and walk the rest of the way." Chet drove down the road then pulled off, into a stand of trees. With flashlights on, they stepped out of the Chief and moved around to the back.

"Damn it, Alan! Look at this mud! You'd better be right about this place, the cleaning bill will cost me a fortune," Chet complained as his dress shoes slipped around in the mud.

"Yeah, I know. I didn't think about mud, I was in too big of a hurry."

Chet opened the back of the Chief, grabbed a large case, and opened it. He reached in and pulled out a video camera.

While he fiddled with it, Alan opened a duffel bag and pulled out his binoculars. Shining the flash light on his watch, he saw that it was just past five in the morning. "We'd better hurry. It'll be light soon, and I want to be at a good observation point by then."

"I'm ready," Chet replied as he closed up the back of the vehicle. They both walked onto the road and moved quickly down it, using their flashlights to guide them towards the lake. Although dark, the sky was just starting to get a hint of dawn. Light from the sun, still below the horizon, filtered dully through the low laying clouds. A few minutes later, they could see their destination.

"Shut off your light, there it is," Alan said in a low tone.

"What do we do now?" whispered Chet.

"Follow me." Alan stepped off the road and worked his way through the brush above and behind the barn. "Now we wait and watch." There was just enough light now so that Alan could see the whole place.

"What's down there?" Chet asked from his crouched position.

"Lets see now." Alan carefully pushed the vine maple and sticker bushes apart so that he could see through. "We're directly above and behind an empty corral which is attached to a barn. Just beyond that is the lake with a dock reaching into it. Attached to the dock is a small boat. To the right of the barn about fifty feet away is a small cabin. There are lights on in the cabin and one on the porch. Smoke is coming out of the chimney. The whole area is surrounded by pine trees and bushes."

"Early risers," Chet noted as he looked into the sky. "The clouds are slowly starting to break up, so it'll get light quickly."

"Hold it," Alan ordered. "I've got one man. He just came out of the house and is moving around. Now he's walking towards the barn."

After a long pause Chet asked. "What's he doing?"

"I don't know. He disappeared in front of the barn. He probably went inside."

Buck opened the two big double doors at the front of the barn letting some light in. *Maybe I'll light up a lantern*, he thought then looked across the lake at the sun slowly creeping above the horizon, but still obscured by clouds. *No, those clouds will break shortly and fill this place with sunshine*, he decided. Buck stepped inside, grabbed a pitchfork, and started throwing straw onto some of the wet spots on the ground. He would have to fix this roof this summer, he knew. The holes in the roof were getting bigger.

"I wonder what he's doing down there?" Chet asked as he peered over Alan's shoulder.

"I don't know, but I'm going to find out."

"*What?* You said we'd stay here for a while and scope it out!" Chet objected.

"I know, but this could be my only opportunity to get one of them alone."

"What are you going to do?"

"*We* are going down to that barn and surprise him. After I have the cuffs on him, I'll make him tell us how many others there are."

"I don't like it, Alan," Chet said worriedly. "What if there are other people in the barn?"

"Well, we won't know that until we go down there, will we?" Before Chet could object, Alan quickly turned and slipped past the brush and started moving down the hill.

"Damn it, Alan." Chet nervously checked his camera then followed Alan down the hill.

Buck picked up a metal bucket and opened the large feed bin next to the straw pile. He dipped the bucket in and filed it with a mixture of oats and barley. At that moment, the clouds started breaking from around the morning sun and filled the barn with light. The rays were like long needles, piercing Buck's eyes and into his hangover.

Oh lord! My head! Buck thought as the brightness made every artery in his brain pound. *I'd better get some aspirin.* Buck set the bucket down in the middle of the barn's walkway, then grabbed the pitchfork to steady himself. Shielding his eyes from the light with his hand, he walked out of the barn and towards the house carrying the pitchfork.

Crouching down low, Alan and Chet moved quickly down the side of the corral. "Hold it," Alan whispered as he caught a glimpse of the old man rushing into the house.

"Maybe he saw us and went for help," Chet whispered, worriedly.

"No, he couldn't have seen us. Keep moving," Alan replied unconvincingly. He ducked under and stepped through the railings of the corral fence. Chet was right behind him when he got to the back door of the barn. "Is your camera ready to go?"

"Yes," Chet confirmed as he lifted it to his shoulder and turned it on.

"Follow me in and find a vantage point with some cover. We don't know what we're up against in there." Alan pulled the Desert Eagle from his shoulder holster, then pulled the slide back loading a round in the chamber. Opening the door, he slowly peered in. On either side of the door were stables with mules in them, and down the center was a walkway. Alan quickly moved in, and crouched next to one of the stables, with Chet following closely behind.

Alan lifted his hand in order to block the light coming from the opposite door. The sun was shining directly into the barn and its reflection off the lake made it impossible to see into the shadows. The mules in the stables moved around nervously knowing instantly two strangers were present.

As Buck threw a handful of pain relievers in his mouth, and chased them down his throat with water, he heard one of the mules whinny. "Don't get your panties in a bunch, Molly. You'll get your oats," he said out loud, walking towards the front door of the cabin.

The mule's uneasy movements worried Alan. "You stay here while I go forward and try to get a better look at the house," he whispered. Chet nodded, with camera rolling, as Alan started moving towards the front of the barn.

Buck grabbed the pitchfork that he had left leaning on the porch, and moved as quickly as his hangover would allow toward the barn.

Alan heard foot steps as he moved through the middle of the barn. *Someone was coming!* He couldn't get caught out in the open, he thought nervously to himself. So he rushed towards the straw pile for protection while squinting hard against the glare from the door, trying to see. Suddenly, a silhouette of a man moved into the light of the doorway. Alan didn't see the oat bucket as his foot squarely hit it and, kicking it across the walkway.

196

Clang!

The bucket crashed against one of the supports, then bounced across the ground. Alan stumbled to one side then dropped to one knee, lifting his .44 magnum towards the silhouette.

"Federal Agent! Don't move!" he yelled.

Startled by the noise, Buck turned quickly holding the pitchfork in both hands.

It was like slow motion to Alan, as he saw the silhouette turn towards him in the glare of the light. Alan saw what looked like a long barrel pointing at him. *"Gun!"* His finger instantly squeezed the trigger.

Boom! Boom!

Thrown backward, the silhouette then fell and lay motionless in the mud as the shots echoed throughout the barn. Each of the mules simultaneously filled the once empty air with complaining grunts and whinnies. Alan ran to the door with his gun ready and peered around the corner as the echo of the shots faded.

With all senses fully alert, Alan paused watching for a long moment, but nothing happened. No sound or movement came from the cabin. Alan turned and ran to the back of the barn. "Stay here," he told Chet as he ran past him and out the back door. Chet watched Alan through his camera as he made his way around the corral, then across the road to the side of the cabin. Alan moved to the back of the house and disappeared behind it.

Chet turned his attention to the body. With the camera rolling, he walked over toward it. Chet panned the scene with the camera then stopped when the body filled his viewfinder. "Oh my gosh," Chet said softly to himself. He slowly lowered the camera and looked around in shock. At that moment, Alan walked out the front door of the cabin and onto the porch, looking around. When he saw Chet standing next to the body, Alan holstered his pistol and started walking over to him.

"There's nobody else here," Alan said as he approached. With a pale expression, Chet looked at Alan and didn't say anything. "What's wrong? Haven't you seen a dead body before?" Alan said to his friend.

"Alan," Chet replied. "There's no gun."

"*What?*" Alan replied in disbelief as he looked down at the body. "But I saw…" His words trailed off as he frantically looked around. As the shocking realization of what just happened hit him, Alan slowly stepped back and leaned against the barn.

"Oh no!" Alan was horrified as he crouched next to the barn and put his hands over his face. A few moments later, his hands slowly came away from his face and he stared at the body lying in the mud. Instantly, his whole career flashed before his eyes.

Alan had no sympathy for drug smugglers, so he felt no remorse for killing Henderson. He was, however, gravely concerned about his career. In each of his other controversial stunts, his actions had been excused because of technicalities. He had claimed that during the normal course of doing his job, he had come across suspicious circumstances, investigated, and found himself in a situation where he had to take immediate action without backup. It ended up being a case of his word against someone else's.

This time it was different. He clearly came down here on his own without notifying his superiors even though he had plenty of time to do so. In other cases, his actions were justified because there were always a huge amount of drugs to prove guilt and the dead men had guns. He was able to claim "just cause".

Alan looked down at Henderson's body lying in the mud. No gun and no drugs. He had to find the drugs, that would justify being here. As far as Henderson's death was concerned, he could then excuse it as being an accident. At the time he pulled the trigger, he truly believed he was in danger and acted in self defense.

But he needed the drugs. Alan, again, looked down at Henderson and shook his head in despair as thoughts raced though his mind. If only the light wasn't in his eyes. If only he had recognized the pitchfork for what it was. *If only…* That thought trailed off in his mind.

He saw his plan of solving this case quickly and easily fade. He had counted on interrogating Henderson. Having him lead Alan to the drugs and anyone else involved. Alan wanted it clean and neat, but that was now *impossible.*

He'd now have to do it the hard way—find a clue and let one clue lead him to another then another until he found the drugs. *Find the drugs and you've found your case*, he told himself. *Find the drugs, and you can spin the killing anyway you want.*

They both stood there in silence for what seemed like forever, Alan thinking while Chet was just in shock. Chet finally spoke out and stated the obvious. "Alan, you just killed an unarmed man carrying a pitchfork."

"I couldn't see. The sun was in my eyes." Alan defended himself. "You saw what happened. I thought it was a rifle." Chet didn't say anything. He just stared at the body with a distant look on his face. "I'll tell you one thing," Alan said. "I'm not going to let the death of a drug smuggler ruin my career."

"*What?*!" Chet said angrily. "You just killed a man in cold blood and all you can worry about is your *career.*"

"It was an *accident*! It could've happened to anyone."

"This wouldn't have happened if you would've come down here with proper back up like you are supposed to," Chet said angrily. "But no! You've got to be the Lone Ranger!"

"Oh yeah! My operating style doesn't bothered you when you get a big story from it!" Alan shot back angrily. "If this ruins my career, you can forget about any more *exclusives!*" Chet didn't answer. He slowly walked past the body and stared out at the lake in a daze.

After a few moments, Alan realized that arguing was unconstructive and stepped over to him. "Listen," he said in a calm voice trying to smooth the waters. "This isn't that bad. If we can prove he was a drug smuggler nobody will care how he died." Chet just stared out at the water as if he wasn't listening. "I'm going to need your help, Chet, if I'm going to be able to prove that."

Alan was right. He always was, Chet decided. No one would care and the impact this situation would have on his career could be devastating. He had to do everything possible to help, he knew. He could do this. With Alan's help, they had been able to manipulate other situations successfully. Granted, nothing as severe as this, but he was confident they could pull it off.

It would be the ultimate test of his journalistic, spin-doctor talents, and he was looking forward to the challenge. After a moment Chet slowly turned around. "What do you want me to do?"

Alan was relieved. "We have to search this place for the drugs," he stated decisively.

"Where should we start?"

Alan looked around. "Let's start with the barn. Maybe we can figure out what he was doing in there." Alan stepped past the body and back into the doorway of the barn before turning back towards Henderson questioningly. "Where did you hide the opium?" he asked, almost as if interrogating the dead.

Standing in the same spot that Henderson was when he was shot, Alan noticed what the impact of the two bullets had done to him. The impact threw Henderson's body nearly ten yards away, to where it now lay in the mud. He was dead before he hit the ground.

199

Standing back from this prospective, Alan could see clearly the entire area surrounding the body.

"I thought we were going in the barn?" Chet asked.

Alan wasn't listening. He just stared out at the body as if waiting for an answer to his question. Without consciously being aware of it, Alan's eyes followed a set of lines in the mud that Henderson's body was laying across. He followed them from the body, out and around in front of the house, then up the road.

Chet was about to say something, then saw the new look on his friends face and instantly froze. He had been with Alan for many years and knew this look all too well. Gears were turning in Alan's mind, and this look was always followed by something brilliant.

Perhaps that's the first clue leading to the answer to my question, Alan thought as he slowly stepped forward to take a closer look at the body. Henderson's body lay directly in the center of a set of tire tracks. One of Henderson's arms laid outstretched with a hand and finger in position pointing at the tracks, almost as if trying to tell Alan something. The tracks were crisp and clear. *Perhaps dead men can talk*, Alan thought with a smile. "Someone was here this morning, before we arrived."

"What? How do you know that?" Chet asked curiously as he looked around for the answer.

Chet still didn't get it and the blank stare told Alan so. "I thought reporters were supposed to be observant. Can't you see those tire tracks?"

Chet stepped forward and looked. "Well, yes I can, but I guess I didn't pay any attention to them."

"Look at them," Alan said as he stepped out of the way so Chet could see clearly. "They come down the road, circle in front of the house, and stop right here in front of the barn. It looks like our friend had an early morning visitor."

"How can you tell when it was?"

"Because of the rainstorm last night. Look at how distinct the tracts are. They *had* to be made after the rain stopped, otherwise they would be…"

"—washed out." Chet finished it for him.

"And look here," Alan said as he pointed at the ground. "There appears to be some large tracts and some smaller ones. Probably a truck with a trailer attached. I'll bet you ten to one…" Alan said as he pulled out a pen from his inside jacket pocket, and knelt by the smaller track.

"Bet me what?" Chet asked.

Alan stuck the end of the pen into the track and marked the depth. He then walked over to the same tire track, before it had stopped in front of the barn. "The trailer track is almost a half inch deeper when it left than when it came in."

"So whoever came here loaded up the trailer with something."

"Exactly," Alan said as he stood up. "And what would be so important to move that it had to be done before the sun came up in a rainstorm."

"Drugs!" Chet exclaimed.

"And where did the drugs come from?"

"The barn!"

"Now you're catching on." Alan smiled. "I'll make an investigative reporter out of you yet."

"You're better than Dick Tracy!" Chet exclaimed with a smile, and then corrected his friend. "That's journalist— *investigative journalist.*"

"Whatever. Let's check the barn, I want to know what he was doing in there."

The two men walked away from the body and into the barn. Even though the barn was lit up by the morning sun, they used their flashlights in order to see into the shadows. Chet walked the entire length of the barn waving his flashlight at the rafters and looking into the stalls. The mules again moved nervously as he did so.

"I think it's obvious what he was doing," Chet said as he stared at the bucket of oats spilled on the ground. "He was feeding the animals."

"That may be true, but there was something else going on as well," Alan said as he crouched by the straw pile.

Chet walked over to him. "What did you find?"

Alan didn't answer. He stood up, walked to the door, and looked outside. "Uh-huh, that's it," he said. After a moment, he turned around and walked back to Chet.

"What's it?"

Alan knelt down and pointed his flashlight at the corner. "See how the straw is crushed down here. There was something here, and now it's gone. It looks like we just missed the shipment." Alan shook his head in disappointment. "I *knew* we had to get down here quickly, but I didn't anticipate them closing up shop so soon." He couldn't do anything about that now, and decided not to dwell on it.

"Let's check the house." Alan stood, walked out of the barn, and towards the cabin. The two men walked over to the cabin and onto the porch. "Take off your shoes." Alan ordered as he kicked off his slip-on loafers. "I don't want to dirty things up anymore than we have to." Chet did as he was told, then entered the front door behind Alan.

"This place is a real pit," Chet said. Alan didn't answer as his eyes gazed around the room. "What are we looking for?" Chet asked as he, too, looked around.

"Well..." Alan replied, walking to the coffee table. "For starters, something like this."

"Two coffee cups– someone else was here." Chet confirmed.

"It looks like Henderson knew him well enough to invite him in for coffee," Alan commented.

"By the way the handles are turned, it looks like one man was right handed and the other left handed."

"Is that important?" Chet asked.

"Probably not, but you never know. Ah, crap!" Alan exclaimed as he stepped on a glob of mud that had fallen on the floor from his shoes the first time he came through from the back way. Alan pulled a handkerchief from his pocket and wiped the mud from his stocking foot. "I'd better clean this stuff up before we have it all over the house. Whatever you do, don't touch those cups. We may be able to get some finger prints off them," Alan ordered, then walked into the kitchen.

Chet looked around the living room and stopped in front of the bookcase where something caught his attention. *"That's it!"* he exclaimed as he reached for and removed a book from the shelf.

"What's it?" Alan asked excitedly, as he returned from the kitchen with a broom and dustpan.

"Where I remember the name Morton from! This is one of the places where the Feds looked for D.B. Cooper," Chet answered.

"Oh," Alan said, disappointedly as he returned to what he was doing.

"Who's D.B. Copper?"

"Don't you remember the hijacking that everyone was talking about when we were kids?"

"Oh yeah, that guy." Alan recalled as he bent over to sweep some mud into the pan.

"This book, called *Sky Pirate*, discusses the whole case. It was written by Special Agent Richard Blake of the FBI. He was the man who headed up the search for Cooper. I read it in college and it totally fascinated me. When I was senior class president, I arranged for Blake to give a talk on the subject at the college."

"What is it all about, anyway?" Alan asked.

"Well, back in the early seventies, a man purchased a ticket under the name of Dan Cooper and boarded a plane in Portland bound for Seattle."

"I thought you said his name was '*D.B.* Cooper'?" Alan interrupted.

"It was really Dan, but the press reported it wrong and the name D.B. just stuck." replied Chet.

"The press screwed something up? Imagine that," Alan said, sarcastically.

Chet ignored his friend and continued. "When the plane was in the air, Cooper told the stewardess he had a bomb in the small case he was carrying, and that he would detonate it if his demands weren't met. When the plane landed in Seattle, Cooper let all of the passengers go in exchange for two hundred thousand dollars and a parachute. He than ordered the plane to take off in the dark and fly to Reno with only himself, the flight crew and the stewardess on board.

Blake already had a score of Agents in planes and helicopters in the air along the flight route. Cooper ordered the pilot to fly low and slow and told the stewardess to stay in the cockpit. He then lowered the rear steps of the plane and waited."

"Waited for what?"

"Apparently for when they got to where he wanted to jump. From time to time, the stewardess slipped back to see if he was still there, and when she saw that he was gone the pilot radioed the tower and Blake and his men moved in quick."

"So did they catch him?" Alan asked as he finished cleaning up the mud.

"No they didn't. First of all there was a terrible storm in the area making it impossible to see the ground, and, secondly they couldn't be certain of the exact jump site, since nobody actually saw him jump."

"So what did they do?"

"Well they narrowed it down to three counties– Lewis, Cowlitz and Clark. Blake immediately notified the Sheriff's departments of each County, and had them set up road blocks. He then landed in Portland and within hours had bases set up in each of the Sheriff's offices. The road blocks didn't turn up anything, so Blake brought three hundred soldiers from Fort Lewis to comb the hills."

"Did they find him?" Alan asked as he walked back into the living room.

"No, not a trace," Chet answered. "That is, until a fisherman found some of the hijacked money washed up on the shore of the Cowlitz River down stream from here."

"So what did Blake do?"

"Well, since there was no evidence found, Blake concluded that Cooper must have accidentally landed in the river, or one of the many lakes around here, and drowned taking the parachute and money with him to the bottom. Case closed."

"That can't be right," Alan argued. "How can a man who is smart enough to pull off what would seem to be the perfect hijacking, cover his escape with a storm, but not plan exactly where he wanted to land? It just doesn't make sense."

"That's exactly what I thought," Chet replied. "So after Blake finished his talk I took him out to dinner and started feeding him drinks."

"You got him drunk?"

"Mumble'n, stumble'n, bumble'n," Chet laughed.

"So did he talk?"

"Of course he talked. Blake was a real tough nut to crack, but you know how persistent I get when I think someone's holding out on a story."

"Yeah, your inquiring mind wants to know." Alan said jokingly. "So what did he say?"

"Well the drowning was the official report, but Blake doesn't believe it. Apparently the investigation started off well, but quickly turned sour. Blake said that, with the road blocks and Army troops, they should have had Cooper trapped."

"So what happened?" Alan asked, curiously.

"The case got such huge publicity that by the middle of the first day of the investigation, tourists, sightseers, and would be D.B. Cooper hunters started showing up. The local Sheriff's departments were under staffed and not very well trained for the situation. They couldn't keep the hordes of people out of the mountains.

Blake's initial report stated that any evidence left behind by Cooper was probably either washed away by the many rainstorms or carried off by people looking for souvenirs. Blake thinks Cooper planted the money on the banks of the river, so that someone would find it, then just lost himself in the crowd and disappeared."

"So why did he change the report?"

"It was politics. Blake said his superiors forced him to," Chet replied. "Can you imagine what the FBI would look like if the public found out that a hijacker escaped right out from under their noses?"

"Yeah, heads would roll on all levels."

"Exactly," Chet confirmed. "They had no evidence to prove Copper lived or died, no witnesses, and an operating budget already ten times the amount hijacked."

"So Blake botches the investigation, comes up with a story that covers everyone's butts, then makes a mint selling books and talking to college students?"

"Basically, yes."

"What a sweet set up," Alan acknowledged. "Did you ever publish your story?"

"No, Blake would've denied everything. Not even the tabloids would've touched it then," Chet said. "Do you mind if I put some more wood on the fire? It's a little cool in here."

"Go ahead," Alan agreed.

Chet walked over to the wood pile, picked up a couple of small logs, then knelt in front of the fire place and stacked them on the top the hot coals. As flames rose from the once smoldering ashes, Chet waved his hands over it warming them. Chet turned to see Alan opening the doors of the gun cabinet.

"What did you find?" Chet asked as he stepped over to Alan.

"It looks like Henderson had his own *arsenal*," Alan replied. "He has shot guns, right handed bolt action rifles—that means Henderson is right handed so his friend must be the south paw. Wait a minute, look at this beauty." Alan reached in and pulled out the M-16.

"A military assault rifle!" Chet exclaimed. "What kind is it?"

"It's an M-16. It can fire semi-automatically or with a flip of a switch fully automatically," Alan said as he handed it to Chet then turned back to the cabinet. "Hello! What do we have here?" Alan reached back into the cabinet.

Chet watched as Alan removed the machine gun. "What is *that?*"

"I'm not sure, exactly, but it's definitely a machine gun," Alan replied.

"*Holy crap*, Alan!" Chet exclaimed. "If Henderson would've had company here when we arrived, we wouldn't have had a chance!"

"I suppose we should feel lucky that *he's* laying in the mud and not us." Alan could see the worried look on Chet's face. "Relax. We're not in any danger and we never were, so lets try to stay focused on what we're here for." Alan returned the rifles to the cabinet, and closed the door.

"All right, what do you want me to do?" Chet asked in a nervous, but controlled voice.

"We'll have to split up. Otherwise this will take too long." Alan then looked around. "You stay here and see what you can find. I'll start with the rooms in back."

"Sounds good." Chet watched his friend walk past him and around the corner towards the bedrooms.

Jim was still along way off, but he could see the proprietor clearly. Anthony Marcellous had run the land fill for years. Covered from head to toe in rain gear, Jim thought he looked like a giant neon yellow warning sign. He would've thought Marcellous looked comical as he finished his chores, but Jim was just too tired to smile. Jim pulled up to a gate with a large sign, *Lewis County Municipal Landfill*, and honked the horn.

Jim watched as Marcellous moved quickly through the muddy slop towards the gate. Except for his face, not an inch was exposed. Boots, pants, coat, and gloves. Even his hat was pulled snug and tight down close to his eyes.

Jim didn't blame him. Working with garbage in the rain had to be a messy job. The man unlatched the gate and slid it out of the way. Jim saw the concerned look on his face as he pulled forward a few feet and rolled down the window.

"What's wrong with Buck?" Was the first thing out of the man's mouth.

Jim didn't feel like telling a long story so he kept it short. "Suburban problems. So Buck called me and, well, here's your garbage."

Anthony nodded then asked. "Did Buck have any problems with the bears?"

"None that he mentioned."

Then Marcellous took a closer look at Jim. "You look *terrible*."

"I *feel* terrible." Jim was unusually grumpy this morning. No sleep and coffee on an empty stomach made him especially irritable. "Listen, I'm exhausted and have been up all night. Do you think we can take care of this so I can get some sleep?"

Marcellous looked at him with a sympathetic smile. "Tell you what, Jim. Why don't you drive in and turn around? Leave the trailer here with me, then go home and get some rest. I'll empty it out and you can pick it up next week when I get back."

"Thanks, that's awfully considerate of you." Jim drove forward and pulled around in a large loop, then stopped.

Marcellous moved behind the Blazer, unlatched the trailer, then walked up to the driver's side window. "Okay, you're unhooked. Maybe next week we can get together with Buck and do some fishing. You know, like we used to."

"Sure thing," came the reply. Jim rolled up the window then slowly pressed down on the accelerator and drove out the gate. Marcellous waved goodbye, but Jim was too tired to notice.

Jim turned south onto highway seven then looked at the clock on the dashboard. It was seven-thirty, another hour and he would be back in Centralia. Jim pushed on the gas peddle to increase his velocity. He knew he shouldn't drive so fast while tired, but he really wanted to get home. Jim turned on the radio for company as he drove.

Nikki flipped the eggs over in the pan then glanced out the window. Jim's Blazer had just turned the corner and she could see it coming up the road. *Finally*, she thought, then returned to the frying pan. A few minutes later, the back door opened and Jim walked in.

"Ah!" Nikki said as she pointed at his muddy boots. "I just mopped this floor."

Jim sat down and removed his boots as he watched her. She was wearing one of his oversized flannel shirts, a pair of his thick cotton socks, and her hair was out of place from laying on his pillow. She was just taking the eggs from the pan and putting them on the plate next to the toast when he walked up behind her and wrapped his arms around her.

"Here, I made myself some breakfast, but you can have it," she said as she turned around and saw the strange look on his face. "What are you looking at?"

"You are the most beautiful woman I have ever seen."

"Oh, Jim, stop it," she said with an embarrassed smile. "I'm a *total* mess."

"No you're not, you look wonderful."

"Do you want the eggs or don't you?" she said, changing the subject.

"No, you go ahead and eat it. I just want to get some sleep."

"Then go. You must be exhausted."

"All right, but don't let me sleep too long, I need to get some paperwork done at the station."

"All right," she said, then she walked him to the bedroom. "If the station calls, get me up right away."

"I will, don't worry." He began to say something else, but she covered his mouth with her hand. "And if the sky starts to fall, I'll wake you up."

He smiled then leaned down and kissed her. "I'll see you in a few hours."

"I'll be here," she assured him, then watched him step into the bedroom and close the door behind him. Nikki turned around and walked into the dinning room. She placed the plate on the table. As an after thought, she looked towards the bedroom for a moment and bit her thumb, then she looked toward the phone.

Jim needed his sleep more than he needed to get paperwork done, and she knew that nothing ever happened in this sleepy little town. Nikki made up her mind. She walked to the phone and disconnected its cord from the wall. Satisfied, she returned to the table, sat down, and started to eat her breakfast.

14

Deception

Almost an hour later, Alan emerged from Henderson's bedroom carrying three large coffee cans. "Check this out," he said to his friend. Chet was sitting on the floor in front of the bookcase. He had a small book open on his lap and a large one lying next to him on the floor with newspaper clippings hanging out of it.

"What did you find?" Chet asked as he looked up from the books.

"Money." Alan sat down on the couch and pulled the plastic lid off one of the coffee cans. "They're stuffed *full* of it."

"How much?" Chet asked, curiously.

"I'm not sure yet. I'll count it now." Alan started pulling wads of money from the can and sorted it on the coffee table. He glanced at his friend who seemed to be mesmerized as he looked into the book in his lap. "What is that?"

"What? ...Oh," Chet replied, as if awaken from deep concentration. "It's Henderson's journal. It's really tough to read. All of the words are like chicken scratch and some of the sentences are incomplete. It's really strange. It appears that Henderson was a D.B. Cooper *fanatic.*"

"Why do you say that?" Alan counted the money and laid it in stacks side by side on the table.

Chet opened the book on the floor next to him. "See this scrapbook? It's crammed full of newspaper and magazine articles

209

about Cooper. That's not all, this journal makes reference to Cooper as if they knew each other. Listen to this." Chet lifted the book and began to read. "I felt terrible this morning. I haven't seen or talked to anyone in a couple of weeks, until today when Cooper showed up to see how I was doing. We broke open a bottle of the good stuff and went fishing. We had a great time as always. I caught four and Cooper caught two. Good old Coop."

"It sounds like he was a real *loony*," Alan remarked as he finished stacking the money. "It looks like about twenty-seven thousand and change."

"It's a lot, but not exactly a pirate's bounty."

"No it's not, but it's something," Alan replied, optimistically.

"Did you find any drugs?"

"No, not yet. This place is going to take more than two people to search it effectively."

"So it's time to call in the troops?"

"I sure don't want to," Alan said as he sank low into the couch. "The minute Cranston finds out about Henderson, I'll be suspended for sure. Then O'Leary will take over and claim all the credit."

"Do you think you'll go to jail for this?"

"No, my father has too many political friends for that to happen," Alan replied as he stood up, walked to the door, and looked out at Henderson's body laying in the mud. "But I'll probably lose my badge." The last part saddened him tremendously.

"I'm sorry to hear that, Alan. If you could've only found some drugs you would have a case." Chet commented, sympathetically. "But without it, all you have is an eccentric old man who sleeps with his money."

"Henderson is dirty as sin." Alan defended. "You can *count* on it. If I just had more time I could prove it. But the trail leading to the guy with the trailer is getting colder by the minute. I'm going to have to bring in help soon, or I may never find him. If I could've just been here a couple of hours earlier I would've *nailed* the guy."

"That's funny," Chet commented offhandedly. "That's exactly what Blake said."

"What?" Alan asked curiously as he looked over towards his friend.

"When I interviewed Agent Blake he said that he was right on Cooper's butt until he jumped into that storm. Blake said that he's *sure* he would've caught Cooper red handed if he could've just been here a couple of hours sooner."

210

Alan rested his forehead on the door jam. "Now it looks like I might be chasing a ghost as well," he said softly.

"If you think about it, you and Blake have a lot in common. It's just too bad that you can't turn you problems into a gold mine like he did," Chet remarked then returned to reading the journal.

"Yeah, no kidding," Alan said softly then closed his eyes and rested his forehead back on the door jam. He began drumming his fingers against it.

Chet was right. There were similarities between Alan's drug case and Blake's Cooper case– neither one of them could find evidence to lead them to the guilty party, and time was both critical and running out.

But it was the *differences* that mattered. Blake had an Army of investigators to support him and he always remained in control of the investigation. Alan was alone and when he did bring in help, he would lose control of the case.

It was for those reasons Blake was able to close the Cooper case so successfully. He had investigated the case thoroughly and found no evidence to prove whether Cooper survived the jump or ended up in a watery grave. The *lack* of evidence made it work— Blake could deny that Cooper survived the jump. That claim had held up because there was no evidence to the contrary and the authority of Blake's position as an FBI Agent gave it weight. Nobody questioned it.

Alan's drug case was different. There *was* evidence and, other than the brick of opium, it all incriminated Alan. Henderson's death was like a huge anchor around Alan's neck keeping him from proceeding. *What would my father do?* he wondered.

At times when Alan didn't know what to do, he always asked himself to consider what his father would do in this situation. Alan's father's experiences are what helped him develop many of the tactics he used to get things done, and Alan learned quickly what those tactics were. Bribery, intimidation, discreditation, blackmail and *denial.*

Alan recalled the long discussions he and his father had about the Watergate scandal. When allegations were raised, Alan's father denied everything and it would've worked if he could've destroyed the evidence in time. Denial worked for Blake because there was no evidence and it was evidence that kept Alan's father, and now Alan from using denial effectively.

He remembered what his father had told him. "If only he could've stopped time, or turned the hands of the clock backwards just a few hours," his father had said. "I could've destroyed all the evidence and denied everything successfully." It was too bad he couldn't turn the hands of time back a few hours to before he killed Henderson and before the drugs had left the premises…too bad.

A moment later Alan's head snapped up. "It just might work," he said then turned toward his friend.

Chet looked up at him. "What might work?" he asked curiously. Chet then saw the look on Alan's face. "I hate it when you get that look, Alan. It always means trouble," he said scornfully. "What are you thinking?"

"A plan that will allow me to remain in control of the investigation and still get the help I need."

"What are you talking about?" Chet asked as he put the journal down, then stood up.

Alan ignored him as he, again, looked out the window. *The tire tracks, the crushed straw and the coffee cup*, he thought to himself. He then looked around the room. *One clue leading to another*, he reminded himself as he looked at the gun cabinet, to the money, then next to the journal.

Chet's eyes looked at Alan suspiciously as if he could see the gears turning in his friends head. "What plan?" he begged Alan to speak.

"Just a minute." Alan walked hurriedly past Chet to the door, where he slipped on his shoes and ran out to the body.

Chet watched from the doorway as Alan rolled the body to one side and examined its back. Alan then put the body in its original position and stared out towards the lake. He then walked back to the house, slipped off his shoes, and looked at Chet in an excited yet serious fashion.

"I think I have a solution to my problem," Alan said as he stepped past his friend and into the living room. "But in order to do it, I'm going to have to lie."

"That's it, count me out!" Chet protested, shaking his head. "I don't even want to hear it."

Alan turned around and looked at his friend. "I wish I could, Chet, but I'm going to need your help in order to generate the publicity required to make it work," Alan pleaded.

Chet turned around and stared out the window. "I can't report lies, Alan, its unethical," he said firmly.

"Don't act so pious. The news is full of misinformation, of which you've added your share. What's wrong with a little more," Alan pleaded again.

That was true, Chet admitted to himself. In the past, he had bent things just enough when necessary, but he always believed that he never actually crossed the line into lying—no matter how thin that line really was. Still, he shouldn't judge Alan's plan until he heard it through. What was the harm in that? "What's your plan?" Chet asked after a moment.

"We're a little pressed for time, right now. I'll explain it to you on the way back to town."

"At least tell me *why* you have to lie!" Chet demanded.

"Nobody can find out that I shot Henderson. There's no way that I can conduct an effective investigation if I'm under suspicion." Chet didn't say anything. He just stared out the window in silence. "Look, if it makes you feel any better, when this is all over you can print a retraction on page forty but right now I need *headlines*," Alan said in a calm voice.

After a moment of silence, Chet turned around. "All right," he said quietly. "What do you want me to do?"

Alan stepped toward him, placed both hands on each of Chet's shoulders, and looked him squarely in the eye. "You have to burn the video tape."

Chet's eyes widened. "*No!* That's going too far," he said, decisively. "You didn't say anything about destroying evidence!" Chet pulled away and walked toward the book case.

"Listen, Chet. You and I are the only two people who know what really happened. The video tape is a loose end. It doesn't matter how well we pull this off. If it accidentally falls into the wrong hands we're sunk!"

Again Chet didn't answer as if the words had fallen on deaf ears. He just stared down at his video camera which lay on the floor next to the bookshelf.

"You're going to have to trust me on this one, Chet," Alan said calmly as he looked for a reaction.

Chet wanted desperately to trust his friend. But lying to the public with the intent to misleading and destroying evidence went beyond ethics, it was downright criminal. He then thought about his career, and the effect losing Alan would have on it. That thought concerned him more than the first.

To save his career, he had to protect Alan, and that meant complete solidarity. The idea scared him to death, but Alan was right. For it to work, there could be no loose ends. "I guess you're right," he said after a moment.

Alan quickly walked to the fireplace and tossed some more kindling on the fire. As the flames rose he looked over at his friend. Chet leaned over and removed the video tape from the camera and walked it over to Alan. Alan stood as Chet lifted the cassette in order to hand it to his friend, but Alan didn't take it.

"You're going to have to do it, Chet. That way we'll both know you're dedicated enough to make this work."

Chet looked at the fire, then slowly knelt on one knee in front of it. He didn't know if he could do it. He didn't know if his loyalty to Alan went that far. From that moment on, he would be forever locked into whatever Alan wanted to do.

Alan saw that last questioning look and tried again to be reassuring. "What I have planned, Chet, could be the biggest story of your life. Don't let a little question of ethics screw it up for you." Still, Chet didn't move. "Don't worry, everything will work out fine. I promise."

A second later, Chet tossed the cassette on the fire then stood up. Both men watched as black smoke went up the chimney. The cassette warped and buckled, and within moments it was reduced to an unrecognizable bubbling black blob. Alan leaned over and tossed a log on top of it. "By the time we get back, it should be long gone."

"What's next?" Chet asked.

Alan walked to the front porch and started slipping his shoes on. "Put everything back the way you found it. I'll be right back."

Chet watched as Alan hurried up the road. Chet turned and walked across the room. He picked up each book that lay on the floor and replaced it back into the bookcase, exactly where he had found it. He then placed the rifles in the gun cabinet, and closed it up. After that, he stuffed the money back into the coffee cans. Chet paced nervously as he waited.

Alan stepped onto the porch, slipped off his shoes, and walked into the cabin carrying a small package wrapped in plastic. "What's that?" Chet asked as he watched his friend place it into one of the coffee cans and close it up.

"Its some of the opium from the brick I got yesterday."

"Damn it, Alan! I *knew* you would pull something like this," Chet said angrily. "Why do you need to plant drugs?"

"I'm not *planting* anything. This opium came from here and belongs here. I'm just turning back the clock to a time when it was in this room. I'm just making it as if it had never left," Alan explained. "And besides, think about it, Chet. As a Drug Enforcement Agent, I can't exactly control an investigation if there aren't any drugs now can I?"

Chet didn't answer. He just stood there, fuming nervously, hoping his friend knew what he was doing. Chet watched Alan pick up the cans and disappear into the bedroom. A few moments later, he returned. "All right, we can go now."

Chet picked up his camera and followed Alan to the door where they both began to put on their shoes.

Ding!

Both men looked over at the water clock. "Nine o'clock!" Chet exclaimed, surprised at the time lost.

"It can't be that late," Alan looked at his watch questioningly. "No, its only seven. That thing is two hours fast."

"Good." Chet was relieved to hear it.

"Let's go." The two men walked off the porch, hurried up the road, and disappeared over the hill.

An hour later, in the Sheriff's Station, Milhouse picked up the coffee pot and filled his cup. "So I pulled this Lexus with California plates over for doing eighty-seven in a fifty-five," he said as he turned around and walked back towards his desk. Conley was sitting at the desk next to Milhouse. With a coffee cup in one hand and a foot up on the desk, he fiddled through the newspaper on his lap. "When I walked up to the car, I noticed a shot gun laying on the back seat," Milhouse said as he glanced at the paper over Conley's shoulder. "Are you through with the sports page?"

"Yeah," came the reply as Conley separated the paper, then handed a section over.

"So with one hand on my revolver, I asked the driver to step out of the car." Milhouse continued his story as he sat down in his chair and looked at the paper. "The guy gets out, wearing a brand new Eddie Bauer hunting suit, and has a huge smile on his face. He said that he'd been pheasant hunting in Yakama all morning and had shot three of them as they sat on a barbed wire fence next to the road."

The front door of the station opened, and Alan walked in and up to the front counter. "I want to talk to the Sheriff."

Conley lowered his paper slightly to look at the other deputy. "It ain't hunt'n season," he said curiously, as the two men ignored Alan.

"I *know*, so I asked if I could see the birds."

"Where's the Sheriff?" Alan interrupted impatiently.

"So this *city boy*," Milhouse said with a distasteful look on his face as he glanced at Alan and lifted his index finger towards him, as if to indicate that he should wait a moment. "Looking all

215

proud of himself, opens the trunk and inside were three magpies all shot to pieces."

"Those are a fifty dollar fine each. Did you write him up?"

"No, I didn't have the heart. I told him that the birds would be good eating and sent him on his way." The two men exchanged a glance, then burst into laughter.

"That'll teach him," Conley said in between laughs. "He probably ain't ever come'n back."

"What do you need?" Milhouse finally said to Alan as he finished laughing.

"I want you to get me the Sheriff," Alan replied firmly.

Milhouse got up from the desk and walked towards the counter. "The Sheriff isn't here right now. Maybe there's something I can do for you."

"Whose in charge when the Sheriffs not in?"

Milhouse and Conley exchanged confused looks then Milhouse said. "Well, I guess that would be me."

"In that case, Deputy...Milhouse," Alan said looking at the nameplate while reaching into his coat to pull out his badge. "I'm Special Agent Alan Bradley, of the Drug Enforcement Agency, and I'm here to report a homicide."

Conley nearly choked as he spilled coffee on himself and Milhouse's eyes widened. "I'd better get the Sheriff!" he exclaimed as he rushed toward the dispatcher's booth and picked up the microphone. "Dispatch to Sheriff Harper," he said into it. There was no reply. "Milhouse to Sheriff Harper," he said more loudly. "Jim are you out there?" Again there was no reply. "Try his house," Milhouse ordered Conley. Conley picked up the phone and dialed a number. The three men waited in silence and stared at the phone.

"Every minute you waste, deputy, a murderer is getting away," Alan said sternly.

"Right! Ah...," Milhouse paced as he tried to think. "What should we do?" He finally asked Alan.

"How many deputies are there?"

"There are two on patrol, then there's Conley and me. Ten in all, if you count second and third shifts."

"Call them all in. We're going to need all the help we can get. You and I had better get up there now and get started."

"Right!" Milhouse replied. "Conley, call in all the guys and keep trying Harper's house. We've got to get going!"

"Where do I send them?" Conley asked as he watched Milhouse and Alan walk towards the front door.

"Mineral Lake!" Alan replied, before disappearing out the door.

Alan watched from the cabin's porch as two men in white uniforms loaded the body into the back of an ambulance. Milhouse was by the barn pouring a white mixture into the tire tracks. Alan turned towards the female deputy sitting on a chair. "Deputy..." he started to say as he tried to see the name tag.

"Rissley." She informed him.

"How are things going?"

"Fine, sir," came the reply. "As the evidence is brought out, I'm tagging it, then recording it in this book."

"Good. Keep up the good work," Alan said encouragingly as he looked at his watch, it was ten forty-five. Alan looked up the road. Chet's vehicle came over the hill and was stopped at the barricade by a deputy. Right on time, he thought as he stepped off the porch and walked up the road. Alan could hear the two men arguing as he approached.

"Haven't you heard of the first amendment?" Chet said, angrily.

"Yes sir, but I've got my orders," the deputy replied.

"It's all right, deputy. Let him through," Alan ordered.

"Yes sir." The deputy moved out of the way.

Chet picked up his tripod and camera cases, then followed Alan down the road.

"Where do you want to set up?" Alan asked.

"Let's do it right over here," Chet replied. "I want to get a shot of the lake." Chet set up the tripod and fixed his video camera to it. Alan removed his jacket and threw it over his shoulder. "No! Not this time. Leave the jacket on. We don't want to give the audience the impression that you're some sort of gun slinger." Alan put his jacket back on and Chet stepped over to him. "Give me your badge." Alan removed it from his pocket and handed it over. "There." He hooked the badge to Alan's lapel. "We want the audience to see a public protector behind his shield with the authority of the Federal government."

"Do you have it all straight?" Alan asked quietly.

"Don't worry. I've got it memorized," Chet answered confidently. He then returned to his camera and looked through the viewfinder. Something was missing, he thought about it for a moment. "Why don't we bring a couple of deputies in? They can

217

stand behind you during the interview. It will show the audience that you've got the support of the local authorities."

"Good idea," Alan agreed. "A little publicity may also motivate them to work harder. Milhouse! Conley! Come here!"

The two deputies hurried over.

"Yes sir?" Milhouse said.

"How would you like to be on the news?"

The two deputies smiled at each other. "You bet!" Milhouse said, excitedly. "I can't wait for my wife to see me."

"Great," Chet said. "Now stand behind Agent Bradley and look official." They all got into position. "All right here we go."

Chet looked at the camera and lifted his microphone. "I'm standing on the shores of Mineral Lake, in southwest Washington. In the past twenty-four hours, at this pristine location, some of the most unpure events have occurred. With me now is Special Agent Alan Bradley of the United States Drug Enforcement Agency. Agent Bradley, can you tell us what happened?" Chet asked, then moved the microphone in front of Alan.

"Yes I can, Chet." Alan looked seriously into the camera. "After a long and growling investigation, I finally got the break I was looking for when late last night an informant told me that a large amount of opium was being moved through this location. I got here as soon as I could, but, unfortunately, I was too late."

"Why do you say that?" Chet moved the microphone between them.

"Well, Chet, when I got here most of the drugs were gone and the only person left behind was brutally murdered."

"What do you mean by most?"

"I found some opium which was left behind. It was probably used by the victim himself."

"That's very interesting. What else did you find?"

"We found some drug money and an arsenal of weapons, including military assault rifles."

"*Amazing!*" Chet exclaimed. "Tell us about the victim. Do you have any suspects into his murder?"

"Actually, Chet, we know *exactly* who he is. It's locating him that's the problem. You see, he's been eluding authorities for years."

"Can you tell us who he is?"

"The murderer is none other than D.B. Cooper," Alan said confidently.

"Are you talking about the man who hijacked a plane and parachuted out of it into these mountains almost thirty years ago?" Chet asked in amazement.

"The very same." Alan confirmed.

"How do you know this?"

"Most of the evidence to support this has been provided by the victim himself. The victim kept a journal in which he claims to know Cooper personally and in fact that they were close friends. It states in the journal that Cooper often came to visit the victim."

"*Amazing!*" Chet exclaimed. "But I thought Cooper died when he jumped from the plane?"

"That's not the case, Chet," Alan explained. "According to my informant, Cooper parachuted into this area because he knew these mountains very well. He then hid out somewhere until the investigation was closed. Cooper then used the hijacked money to start a drug smuggling operation."

"That's *incredible!* Can you tell us more?"

"Not at this time, Chet. But as my investigation progresses, I'll keep you informed."

Chet turned back to the camera. "Thank you Agent Bradley. I'll be here to bring you the latest news as it unfolds. But for now, this is Chester Green coming to you from the shores of Mineral Lake, Washington." A moment later the camera lights went out. "That's it," he said after a short pause.

"Thanks guys, you can go back to work now," Alan told the deputies. Milhouse and Conley walked away in silence. Chet walked over to the camera with Alan close behind. "How do you think it went?"

"I don't like it, Alan," Chet said nervously. "You're really reaching this time."

"Just relax," Alan reassured him.

"How can I?" Chet replied. "Did you see the look on Beavis and Butthead's faces when you said D.B. Cooper? They think you're *nuts!* If you can't convince those two idiots, no one will believe you."

Alan looked over at Milhouse and Conley. They were standing together near the porch, with Rissley, whispering and occasionally looked towards Alan. "You're right. They aren't very bright. I practically had to spoon-feed them all the evidence. Don't worry though, I can keep them under control."

"It's not them I'm worried about." Chet lifted his equipment. "If you don't find some real evidence soon, this will

219

blow up in our faces. Why did you have to pick Cooper anyway? Why not just make someone up?"

"I told you that earlier," Alan replied. "I need a target that's captivating– one so intriguing that people can't help but focus on it. Cooper will generate excitement and headlines. If I can keep them focused on a target as big as Cooper, they won't get around to looking at me."

"I'd better get moving if I'm going to make the noon news." Chet looked at his watch. "I'll see you in a couple of hours."

Alan could see that he hadn't convinced him as he watched his friend walk up the road towards his vehicle. *Chet is right*, Alan thought to himself as he turned around and stared at the lake. *I've got to find something fast.* "Milhouse!" Alan yelled without taking his eyes off the lake. A second later, Alan heard footsteps approaching.

Milhouse turned and ran towards Alan when he was called. He was anxious to make a good impression. This morning, at the station, Tom hadn't recognized Agent Bradley and felt stupid for it. It only took a few minutes for Tom to realize who Bradley was and he immediately got excited.

Tom had seen Agent Bradley on TV many times. He recalled the TV show *The Worlds Most Dangerous Car Chases*, which had featured one of Agent Bradley's arrests. It was the most exciting thing Milhouse had ever witnessed!

Agent Bradley was in hot pursuit of a drug dealer on a high performance motorcycle. As the news helicopter recorded everything from the air, Tom watched the motorcycle weave through traffic on I-5 at speeds exceeding a hundred miles an hour with Bradley's black corvette on his tail.

Realizing he couldn't get away on the highway, the dealer took an exit to try and lose Bradley in the residential areas. They came to a corner, where each slammed on the brakes then the gas. The tires screeched, creating long black skid marks. Then they squealed and smoked as the two vehicles sped off to the next intersection to do it all again. The dealer tried everything he could to shake Bradley, but Alan didn't falter. Up one street, then down another. The duel continued until finally a mistake was made.

Dodging a car, the motorcycle fishtailed then launched its rider into the air. Both the cycle and driver spun across the pavement into the middle of an intersection. Instantly, the black vette squealed to a halt, just inches from the dealer. Jumping out with gun in hand, Agent Bradley raced to the man, threw him on the vette's hood, and cuffed him.

Special Agent Alan Bradley turned, looked up at the camera in the helicopter, then waved and smiled. It was the coolest thing Milhouse had ever seen! Agent Bradley was *exactly* what Tom hoped to become and he was determined to learn everything he could. In real life, Tom towered over Alan, maybe that was why he didn't recognize him earlier. Because on TV, Special Agent Alan Bradley was larger than life.

"Yes sir," Milhouse said when he finally reached Alan.

"When will those other deputies get here?" Alan said impatiently. "We're *wasting* time."

"They should be here any minute." Milhouse assured him as a low flying plane buzzed overhead at treetop level and flew out over the lake. "Do you want me to call them on the radio?"

Alan didn't answer. He watched as the small plane with pontoons circle the lake. "Sir?" Milhouse asked after a moment, waiting for an answer.

"What's that plane doing?" Alan asked curiously.

Milhouse looked at the plane as it leveled off, then landed in the center of the lake. "It's probably bringing in fishermen."

Alan took the small pair of binoculars from his pocket and trained them on the plane. "They come in by plane?"

"Not all of them. Most drive," Milhouse answered. "That looks like Steve Grey's plane. He's an outfitter like Henderson."

Alan watched the plane as a man stood on the pontoon and inflated a large yellow rubber raft. "Do any of the planes come to Henderson's dock?"

"I suppose so." Milhouse shrugged. "Buck gets a lot of business. Like I said, most people drive here, then Buck packs them up into the higher lakes. Some of the higher rollers, from the city, fly in and Buck has a camp waiting for them."

"Do pilots make enough money transporting people back and forth from Portland?"

"During the season people come from all over– Portland, Seattle, LA. Some even come from back east. I would imagine that they make a pretty good living."

Alan watched as the raft, filled with men and fishing poles, rowed away from the plane. "What do they do in the off-season?"

"I don't know." Milhouse again shrugged, sorry he didn't have an answer.

Both men stood in silence as the plane started its engine and began to move towards them. As the plane gained speed, it slowly lifted off the water and flew right over their heads. Alan turned and watched as it flew down the valley.

"That could be it," Alan said softly.

"What's that, sir?" Milhouse asked.

"Oh, nothing," Alan said as he thought to himself. "Let's get back to work." Alan then walked back to the cabin with Milhouse close behind. Walking up the porch, they disappeared through the front door.

Nikki lay on the couch reading a novel and drinking coffee. As she took a sip from her cup, she glanced at the clock. It was noon, and she wanted to see what was happening in the world.

Nikki reached for the remote on the coffee table, and with a push of a button the TV lit up. She adjusted the volume so as not to disturb Jim in the next room. She continued to read her book while she listened inattentively to the newscaster.

"We now take you to southwest Washington State, where a very interesting story has developed." She heard the newscaster say. Nikki slowly lowered her book as the broadcast continued. Her eyes widened, then she quickly got up and rushed into the bedroom.

O'Leary burst into Cranston's office. "Sir! You'd better come see this!" Seeing the urgency on his best agent's face, Cranston rushed out of the office and followed him into the conference room. The room was filled with other agents who were staring at the wall-mounted television. Cranston's jaw dropped open as he watched the report.

Nikki rushed out of the bedroom followed by Jim who was wearing a robe and rubbing his eyes. Jim grabbed the clicker and turned up the volume. As the report continued he slowly sat down on the couch.

"That's Buck's place."

222

"How can you tell?" Nikki asked as she looked at his shocked pale face.

"That's his dock in the background."

"Oh my gosh," Nikki said a moment later, in an uneasy voice. "Does that mean that Buck is the victim?"

Jim didn't hear her. His entire attention was focused on the screen. They watched the remainder of the broadcast in silence. When it was over, Jim pushed a button on the remote and the TV went black.

"What's going on, Jim?" Nikki asked worriedly.

"I'm not sure," he replied with a shocked look on his face. "Buck was fine when I left him." After a moment of silence Jim looked at Nikki. "Why didn't anyone call me?"

Her face became red. "I'm sorry, Jim. I disconnected the phone so that you could get some rest," she bit her lip, hoping he wouldn't be mad.

Jim gave her a stern look. "I'd better get out there." He stood and rushed into the bedroom.

"Rodriguez, find Mineral Lake on that map," O'Leary ordered as the broadcast came to an end. "Then call the garage and tell them to have five vehicles waiting." Angela stood and looked at the wall map. "Anderson, you and Peterson get the gear together."

"Hold it!" Cranston ordered. Everyone in the room stopped and looked at him. "Did Bradley say anything to anyone about this?" Everyone looked at each other.

"Yesterday, he asked me to run a plate for him," Angela spoke up. "The owner of the vehicle lives right here in Morton." She found it on the map. "That's real close to Mineral Lake."

"So *that's* his growling investigation," Cranston said with a smirk. "Everyone resume your normal duties." All of the agents hesitated, looked at each other, then back to Cranston questioningly.

"You heard the Director!" O'Leary barked, taking charge. "Now move!" All of the agents filed out of the conference room leaving O'Leary and Cranston alone.

"What gives, sir?" O'Leary finally asked. "Aren't we going down there to help him?"

"He went down there alone. He can stay there alone," Cranston replied. "We'll help him as much as possible, but only if he asks for it."

"What's your plan?"

"D.B. Cooper my butt!" Cranston chuckled. "I'm going to give him all the rope he wants on this one. When he hangs himself with it, not even the Governor will be able to save him." They stood and began to walk towards the door. "Why not let him be someone else's problem for awhile." Both men got a laugh out of that.

Before they could get to the door, Agent Rodriguez met them with a report in her hand. "You'd better look at this, sir." As Cranston looked over the report, Agent Rodriguez explained. "I ran this profile yesterday for Bradley. Henderson, the man in question, is retired military. His last assignment was as head of Special Operations in Vietnam."

"Bradley did say opium, didn't he?" Cranston asked as the connection clicked in both his and O'Leary's mind.

"Do you think Bradley is on to Phantom?" O'Leary asked. They all exchanged excited glances.

This could change everything, Cranston thought. *Or did it?* His training and years of experience instantly took hold and made him consider the hard facts. The few items in Bradley's case certainly resembled the Phantom file, but the Phantom file was filled with speculations and guesswork. It couldn't even be called a theory because there were absolutely no facts to support it.

Throughout the history of the Phantom file, some of the finest investigative minds had worked on it and failed to turn up anything. Was he now to believe that Bradley, with his mediocre and rushed methods, had found Phantom? Not likely. Was he to pull resources off Kingpin to chase a ghost?

The Kingpin case, on the other hand, was solid, and the last two busts hurt the operation severely. The street price of cocaine had more than doubled because of the short supply. Kingpin had to bring in a large shipment soon, and in order to do that he would have to take some risks.

Cranston had every available agent out on the street trying to find out when and where that would be. Was he to turn his attention away from Kingpin when they were so close to shutting him down for good? All because of a hunch?

Nobody wanted to nail Phantom more than he did, but he had to go with the hard facts and the odds of success. If Bradley had stumbled onto Phantom, then Phantom would be long gone by now. Cranston was *sure* of it. To go down there now would be useless. The few clues they could get would still be there in a week or so. Bradley was on the case and, for now, that was plenty.

Because of Bradley, he reminded himself, the fate of his hard earned career was teetering on the edge. He needed to solve a big, high visibility case. Without Bradley around to screw it up, Kingpin looked like a sure thing. He couldn't allow emotion to overrule what his experience was telling him.

"No," Cranston answered the unasked question in O'Leary and Rodriguez's eyes. "All our agents are to stay on Kingpin. Now let's get back to work." As the three of them started out of the room, O'Leary's experience made him decide that it couldn't hurt to be prepared. When he got to his desk, he made some phone calls to make sure he'd have equipment and other resources ready to move at a moments notice. Just in case Bradley *did* turn something up...

Jim walked out of the bedroom buttoning the shirt of his sheriff's uniform. Nikki just finished pouring fresh coffee into a travel mug and handed it to him when he walked into the kitchen. Jim took a drink as Nikki finished buttoning his shirt.

"I'm really sorry about the phone, Jim."

"That's all right. I'd just better get out there and straighten this out."

"I've got to go, too," Nikki said. "I have to report to work in a couple of hours."

"Maybe I'll see you tonight, then." Jim stepped past her and walked hurriedly out the door.

15

Playing Catch Up

By the time Jim reached the barricade he was wide-awake and determined to get some answers. The long ride had given his tired brain a chance to sift through the information provided by the news report, but he couldn't shake the worried feeling deep in his gut. He desperately needed more information. He jumped out of the Blazer and rushed past the deputy standing there.

"Hello, Sheriff," the deputy said.

Jim didn't answer. He just hurried down the hill towards Milhouse who was standing in the middle of the courtyard with a camera taking pictures. "*Damn it!* Milhouse!" Jim said, angrily. "Why didn't you come out to my house and get me."

"Sorry, Sheriff," Milhouse answered as he turned around. "I guess I got caught up in all the excitement."

"*Excitement!*" Jim snapped.

"Yeah, did you see me on the news?" Milhouse said with a smile. "We're going after D.B. Cooper."

"You don't actually believe that crap, do you?" Jim's voice was noticeably irritated.

Milhouse began to speak. "Well, Agent Bradley said—

"Agent Bradley!" Jim cut him off. "That reminds me, where is he anyway?"

"He's in the house."

"I guess he can wait a minute." Jim decided after looking towards the house, then his demeanor became more concerned. "Where's Buck?"

227

Milhouse hesitated for a second before replying sadly. "He's dead. I'm sorry, Jim, I know you guys were close." Jim didn't answer. He just stood there and started to feel sick. "Sheriff, are you all right?"

Jim again didn't answer. The acids in his stomach burned from too much coffee and no food. It definitely wasn't being helped by the news of his friend. *Come on, Jim,* he thought to himself. *Clear you mind and get in the game.*

He felt uneasy. It had been a long time since he had handled a major case and the fact that he was playing catch up wasn't to his advantage. He had to pull himself together. After a moment, Jim's face changed to a more determined look. "Tell me what happened."

As Milhouse described the scene, Jim listened intently then asked. "Where was Buck found?"

"It was over here," Milhouse replied, then walked over to the impression in the now dry mud.

"I hope you got good photos of him before he was moved."

"I did Sheriff," replied Milhouse. "I took a whole roll of the body from all different angles."

It, the body. Hearing Milhouse describe Buck in those terms filled Jim with pain. He couldn't think of Buck that way—not yet. He tried to ignore the cold, detached descriptions so that he could get the facts he needed without breaking down. "Good, I want to see the photos as soon as possible. Where's Buck now?"

"It was taken to County General."

Jim nodded. "Where was he shot from?"

"It looks like the shots came from this direction." Milhouse pointed then both men stepped towards the barn.

Jim turned around in front of the door and looked at the scene trying to imagine what might have happened. "What about bullets?"

"Buck was shot twice. Both bullets traveled through the body then landed in the lake."

"How do you know where they landed?" Harper asked as he looked towards the lake. "From this direction, you can see the shoreline, some trees and part of the house on the right there. Since we don't know exactly where the shooter was standing, a foot or so in either direction could put those bullets anywhere."

"Well, Agent Bradley said—" Milhouse started to say but was cut off.

"Agent Bradley, again!" Jim snapped. "Damn it! Milhouse, don't you know how to run an investigation?"

He wanted facts. Speculation on top of frustration and despair only made him angry. Milhouse just looked at the ground and said nothing. "Where's everyone else?"

Milhouse pointed towards the house. "Rissley, Conley, Johnson, and Simms are in the house. Brown, Thomson, and Kruger are in the crawl space under it looking for drugs."

"Drugs?" Jim said as he rolled his eyes. "Really, and exactly what have you been doing all this time?"

Milhouse could see that Jim was angry. "Well, mostly taking pictures and plaster castings of tire tracks."

"*What?*" Jim was confused.

"Yeah, look over here," Milhouse said as he stepped forward and pointed at the ground. "These are the suspect's tire tracks."

Jim stepped forward and immediately recognized the tracks as his own. "And how exactly do you know that?" Jim glared at Milhouse. Milhouse began to speak but Jim already knew the answer. "Don't tell me. Agent Bradley, again." Milhouse again just looked at the ground. "This has gone far enough," Jim scolded. "Let's get everyone together at the porch. I want to talk to them."

"Yes sir," Milhouse said softly, then turned and rushed toward the entrance of the house and disappeared in it.

Deputy Rissley had been watching Sheriff Harper and Deputy Milhouse talking in the courtyard. She was glad Jim was finally here and instantly felt sad for him because of the loss of his friend. *He must feel horrible*, she thought.

As she watched him, she could tell he was upset. Showing up late didn't help matters, which clearly added to his frustration. She too had shown up late and was also frustrated with the direction this investigation had taken.

She was in her backyard working on her fastball, when the call came in. The message on the answering machine had been almost an hour old before she had gone in the house. She immediately changed her clothes and rushed out to Mineral Lake fully expecting Jim to be here and have everything under control.

When she found out that wasn't the case, she tried to call him but there was no answer. So, she joined the investigation already in progress hoping Jim would get there soon. When Joe arrived, Deputy Milhouse had taken charge of the others and was handing out work assignments, while clearly under the direction of Agent Bradley.

When Tom explained who Bradley was and told the stories of his exceptional exploits, she was very impressed—they all were. She gladly accepted her job assignment, to log in evidence, so that she could examine it and quickly catch up on the case.

It didn't take long before she started questioning the validity of some of the evidence. Her questions were swiftly rebuked by Agent Bradley, however, and she backed down. After all, he was a Special Agent of the DEA, an expert criminal investigator while she had never investigated anything more complicated than a fender bender.

She continued to log in the evidence, quietly scrutinizing it and eventually became more skeptical. She had watched the interview from the porch and by the end of it she was *flabbergasted.* There was something not right about Agent Bradley and his investigation—she was sure of it.

The only intriguing item in the evidence box was Buck's journal. She hadn't the time to look at it yet, but wanted to in depth. Physiologists often have patients write stories as a part of treatment. Reading the stories helped the doctor get to know the patient better and helped in diagnosis.

Although she had known Buck for years, she always wanted to get to know him better. But now, sadly, that would be impossible. She hoped by reading his journal, she might get a glimpse of who Buck was on the inside and not just what she knew about him on the surface.

Jim walked to the house and stepped onto the porch towards Rissley.

"Hello Sheriff," she said with a thoughtful smile. "I'm sorry about Buck."

Jim nodded his appreciation, but he wasn't ready to deal with that yet. He looked at the collection of goods on the porch. "What are you doing?"

"Logging in the…uh…*evidence.*"

By her tone and facial expression, Jim knew she was as skeptical as he was. "How do you know this is evidence?" Harper asked, even though he knew what the answer would be. "Agent Bradley," they both said in unison.

"Where is this Agent Bradley, anyway?" Jim wanted to know.

230

"I'm right here, Sheriff," Alan said as he stepped through the doorway and onto the porch behind Jim.

Jim turned to look at Alan. "Then I suppose you have some identification."

"Right here," came the reply as Alan reached into his jacket and brought out the ID and handed it to Jim.

"Where do you get off starting an investigation in my County without notifying me first?" Jim examined the picture ID and badge.

"I didn't have time, Sheriff. As you can see, I was too late as it was."

Jim handed the ID back to Alan. "I find it hard to believe that you couldn't find time to make a phone call before you got here." Jim scolded then turned towards the cabin door and peered in. "What have you done?" he exclaimed.

The place was in shambles. All of the books were off of the shelves and scattered on the floor. The elk's head was lying on the floor in front of the fireplace with its back broken open. The deer mount was lying next to it in the same condition. The steelhead was cut open and its contents were spewed over the floor. The couch was tipped over. Each side of it and its cushions were cut open and its stuffing was pulled out. Jim saw one of his deputies behind the chair. "Conley!"

The deputy stood up with a handful of stuffing and a knife. "Yes, sir?"

"Get everyone out here, now!" Jim replied, turning around to see Milhouse walking up to the porch accompanied by a few other deputies. Then the rest of them filed past Jim through the doorway. One of the deputies had his sleeves rolled up wearing latex gloves and carrying a mayonnaise jar. "You're going through his fridge, too!" He scowled at Alan.

"In a drug investigation you have to go through everything," Alan defended.

Jim turned his attention back to his deputies. "Now that you're all here, I have something to tell you. As of this moment, on behalf of the Sheriff's department, I'm taking over this investigation."

Alan spoke up. "*You can't do that!* On what grounds—"

"On the grounds that you have no evidence," Jim cut Alan off. "This is a *homicide* case."

"What do you call this?" Alan said as he stepped around Rissley, picked up a plastic bag with a yellow marker and handed it to Jim. Jim opened it up and looked at it closely.

"Its opium." Alan told him.

"I *know* what it is," Jim scowled. "But it takes more than a handful of drugs for the Feds to get involved."

"This was a drug smuggling operation!"

"So *you* say!" Jim snapped. "But I don't see anything here that leads me to that conclusion."

"What about this store house of weapons?" Alan asked as he pointed towards the dozen or so fire arms leaning against the porch rail.

"Buck was an outfitter. He always kept extra rifles around for those of his customers who didn't own one."

"These aren't used for hunting!" Alan protested as he lifted the assault rifles.

"They're war souvenirs," Jim stated. "Buck doesn't even have ammunition for them."

"What about all this money? I've asked some of your deputies. Henderson always paid for things in cash. That's a sure sign that he was involved in something illegal."

Jim looked at Rissley. "How much is there?"

"Twenty-seven thousand dollars and thirty two cents," came the reply.

"So what if Bucks a little strange when it comes to money. He's never trusted banks and has always kept it with him." Jim explained calmly.

"If you knew him so well, how do you explain this?" Alan said as he lifted a book and handed it to Jim. "Why does his journal have several references to D.B. Cooper?"

"This is probably the worst of your so called evidence," Jim snarled. "There are also references to bigfoot sightings in it as well. Are you going to believe that too?" Alan didn't answer. "This is a story book. You would've known that if you had spent more than a few minutes looking through it. Buck wrote these for his pack trips. He liked to tell them in the evenings while his customers were huddled around the campfire. *Hell!* You all should know that!" Jim looked at each of his deputies in turn. "You've all been fishing and hunting with him. Now look at you," he said with disgust. "Selling him as a criminal, to the media, so that you can get your picture on the news."

Milhouse felt ashamed of himself and looked at the ground as Jim spoke. "Now let's turn this investigation around and find ourselves a murderer. We *owe* Buck that much."

Alan saw that he was losing control of the deputies so he spoke up. "Well isn't this cozy," he growled as he stepped in front of Jim and looked accusingly around. "A man pals around with the Sheriff, takes the deputies out fishing, and they look the other way while he runs an illegal smuggling operation!" All of the deputies looked around at each other nervously.

"That's not true—" Jim started to say but Alan cut him off.

"You can't deny the facts, Sheriff!" Alan lifted two plastic bags of evidence. "I've got drugs and I've got the finger prints on this coffee cup of the man who drove that truck and killed Henderson!"

"You've got it all wrong! That's not what happened at all!" Jim barked.

"If you have all the answers, Sheriff, maybe you can tell us who drove that truck because the instant I find him I'm arresting him for murder!" Alan yelled loudly into Jim's face as he lifted the evidence.

Jim froze, looked at the coffee cup and opium and wasn't sure what to say. "Well, Sheriff, we're waiting. Do you know who was here this morning or not?" Alan scowled after a moment of awkward silence. Jim could feel the questioning eyes of his deputies on him waiting for an answer.

Click-chikeeg, click-chikeeg, click-chikeeg.

Jim turned as Chet's camera recorded the face-off just a few feet away. "What's that reporter doing here? *Milhouse!* Get him out of here!" Milhouse grabbed Chet by the arm and started to pull him away from the porch.

"You can't suppress the news, Sheriff!" Chet yelled as he was dragged away.

Jim ignored him but was relieved by the break it gave him. Thinking quickly, he immediately barked out orders. "All right. I want Simms, Brown and Kruger to comb the dock, the beach, and the tree line for any signs of bullets." Three men started to move. Alan slipped off the porch while Jim was turned the other way and moved quickly to where Chet and Milhouse were standing.

"I'll take care of him, deputy," Alan said.

"Yes, sir." Milhouse turned and walked back towards the cabin.

"Let's go," Alan said as he walked up the road.

"That jerk of a Sheriff, really ripped into you, didn't he?" Chet commented.

"It wasn't that bad, I recovered nicely."

"Well, it was a good thing I was there to distract him, otherwise he would've finished you off." They reached the Chief and Chet put his camera in its case.

233

"Nothing happened that wasn't planned for," Alan defended.

"Really!" Chet said sharply. "Look at him down there. He just took over."

"Let him. I got everything I wanted before he arrived. His intervention was anticipated. When the time is right, I'll pull in the reins a little and ride him and his department until he falls on his face," Alan said, smugly.

"I hope you're right," Chet said nervously as he closed the back of the Chief and walked around to the driver's seat and got in. Alan got into the passenger seat. "Aren't you going back down there?"

"No, there isn't anything left to find. Let them waste their time."

"What if they find the bullets?"

"They won't. I know exactly which direction I fired. They can't be anywhere other than the bottom of the lake." Alan assured him.

"What about the spent cartridges?"

"I picked them up earlier," Alan replied. "Now relax."

Chet tried to calm himself but it was hard. Earlier, he was uneasy about Alan's plan, and now he felt a whole lot worse. He was upset with himself for going along with it and even more upset that he allowed Alan to manipulate him yet again.

But there was no way out for him now—he was locked in. Still, a part of him couldn't help but feel excited about what this story could do for his career. If he had to be in this situation with anyone, he was glad it was Alan. "What do we do now?"

"Let's go back to the motel." Alan pulled Blake's book, Sky Pirate, from his pocket. "I have some reading to do. Maybe there's some other information in here that I can use."

"That's it?" Chet objected. *"That's* your great plan?"

"Not all of it. I also have a lead to follow up on. It's just going to take a little time to figure out how to use it."

"It's a real lead, right?" Chet asked, hopefully. "I mean, this isn't just another one of your hunches is it?"

"You just concentrate on doing your job and let me do mine," Alan said firmly. Chet started the Chief, turned it around, and drove back up the road.

Jim and Milhouse walked out of the barn. "It's hard to say what went on here," Jim said, discouragingly. "Everything's all trampled down."

"I'm sorry about that, Sheriff," Milhouse replied. "But Agent Bradley had us search the barn, then the ambulance drivers had to walk around. You'll be able to see the area more clearly in the photos."

"I hope you're right," Jim said, then turned his attention to the animals. "Listen, I want you to make arrangements for Buck's mules. Call some of the ranchers and see if they can hold on to them for a while. Then help the others look for those bullets."

"Yes, sir."

"I'm going over to the hospital and see if Doc Gresham has the autopsy done. Maybe that'll tell us something." Jim started to turn to walk away, then stopped and looked at Milhouse. "I want to see you and those photos in my office by five sharp. Do you understand?"

"Yes, sir." Milhouse nodded.

Jim walked up the hill, got into his blazer, and stared down at the cabin. He was baffled. *What happened? What could've possibly gone wrong?* he wondered. Questions poured through his mind as he wished that his lost friend could give him the answers. Maybe he still could, he thought optimistically. After a few moments he started the Blazer, turned it around and drove back up the road.

An hour later, Jim walked through the front door of the County Hospital and up to the receptionist's desk. "I'd like to see Doctor Gresham, please."

Before the receptionist could answer him, an elderly gray haired man in a white lab coat emerged from the open door behind her. "Hello, Jim," he said with a smile. "It's been a long time." The two men shook hands.

"Hello, Doc, how are you?"

"I'm fine, but you don't look so good," Gresham said with painful concern in his voice.

"I haven't been getting much sleep. Have you finished with Buck's autopsy?" Harper asked, changing the subject.

"Yes, my report is complete, however, the photos will be a few more minutes," came the answer. "Why don't you have a cup of coffee and relax. I'll call you when they're ready."

"Thanks, Doc." Jim then turned and walked over to the coffee pot where he pulled a paper cup off the stack.

"Jim," a familiar voice said from behind him. He turned to see Nikki standing there in her nurse's uniform. "Are you all right?" she asked with concern. "Doctor Gresham told me about Buck—I'm sorry."

"I think so, but the shock hasn't hit me," and he knew he couldn't allow it to—not yet. He had to keep it buried, for now, so that he could continue his investigation. Nikki reached for the coffee pot, and filled his cup.

"Well I don't envy your job. After what I've been told, by some of the other nurses, this D.B. Cooper guy is going to be hard to catch."

"Oh Nikki, not you too!" Jim said in frustration. "Cooper is dead. He drowned in the Cowlitz River when he jumped from that plane."

"How can you be so sure? No one found any trace of him."

"Look, Nikki. I was a part of that investigation. It was my first year as Sheriff. If he had survived, I'm certain we would've found him." His voice was calm and confident.

"Okay, Jim. If you say so." Nikki was not so convinced. Everyone she'd talked to had a story about Cooper and the Feds failure to catch him, and she couldn't help but wonder if her small town Sheriff wasn't a little out of his league. "But everyone in town is talking about it."

"*Great!*" That's all I need is for *that* ghost to come back and haunt me at a time like this," he thought in frustration.

"Did you tell that DEA guy it wasn't Cooper?" Nikki asked.

"I tried to straighten him out earlier, but he's convinced Buck was hiding some sort of drug ring." Jim shook his head. "Oh, that reminds me." He took Nikki's hand and walked her a few paces away from anyone that could possible over hear them. "Have you told anyone that I was out at Buck's place this morning?" he asked, quietly.

"No, it hasn't come up. Why?" She answered curiously.

"Agent Bradley found a coffee cup with my finger prints on it. He thinks they belongs to the murderer and said he'll arrest whoever they belong too." Jim kept his voice down as he looked around slowly.

"Arrest *you?*" she said with surprise. "Can he do that?"

"Well, no, he doesn't have any real evidence. But he could slow me down for a while and I can't afford that right now."

"Do you mean you haven't told them?" she asked sternly.

"No I haven't, and I don't want you to say anything either."

Nikki looked at him in a strange manner. Her lower lip began to quiver and her eyes water. "You can't ask me to do that, Jim, you know how I feel about lies."

"It's not lying. I just need to postpone the truth for a while."

"It's the *same* thing," she insisted firmly as she pulled her hand out of his, then folded her arms in front of her.

"When this is all over the truth will come out, but I don't want you to volunteer the information until I'm ready for it." Jim could see that his words were less than persuasive. "Nikki, you've *got* to believe me."

"I don't know what to believe, Jim," she said as she wiped the tears from her eyes. "All I know is that you were out there about the same time Buck was killed, and now you're asking me to lie for you."

"Honey, you're just going to have to trust me." Jim pleaded, trying to convince her.

Jim's words reminded her of the conversation she had with her father. The one where he tried to convince her that he hadn't been with another woman, and it made her feel insecure and betrayed. She didn't want to feel that way towards Jim and needed something tangible to grasp onto. "Why can't you tell them the truth? You're the Sheriff, they'll believe you."

"Nikki, I can't conduct an effective homicide investigation if I'm under suspicion," he replied after a moment of awkward silence.

At that moment, Gresham emerged from his office. "Jim, I'm ready."

"All right, Doc, I'll be right with you," Jim replied, then turned his attention back to Nikki. "Listen, why don't you come by tonight and I'll explain everything." He put a hand on her arm to reassure her, but she began to cry.

"I don't know if I ever want to go to your place again, Jim. I'm not sure if I know you as well as I thought I did." Nikki pulled away and ran down the hall.

"Nikki!" Jim called after her as he watched her disappear into the lady's room. After a moment, Jim let out a heavy sigh then slowly turned and walked towards the Doctor.

"Is Miss Taylor all right?" Gresham asked with concern.

"She will be. She's just upset about Buck." Jim lied as he walked past Gresham and into the office. The office was different from the sanitized white hallways of the rest of the hospital. The wood paneling on the walls was covered with professional licenses and certificates while the wall behind the desk was a series of shelves filled with medical textbooks.

"Have a seat." Gresham offered and pointed to the chair in front of the desk. Gresham walked behind the desk and sat down in his chair. He pulled a pair of reading glasses from his shirt pocket, put them on, then opened a folder which was lying on the desk.

Jim pulled the chair up close to the desk and sat off the edge of it. He didn't like the question but he had to ask. "Doc, did Buck have any traces of drugs in his system?"

"I did a full blood analysis and it came up negative," Gresham replied. "That is except for some alcohol, but that wasn't unusual for Buck. I also took a sample of his liver and ran tests on it." He handed a stack of papers to Jim. "If he had been using drugs, even in small amounts, it would've been detected there, but it was negative as well."

"So that means the drugs weren't his," Jim said as he sat back in the chair and examined the report. Somehow he felt guilty for asking that question in the first place, but he knew it was necessary and was relieved by the answer. "What about the time of death?"

"I put it at about 6 AM."

Jim nodded. "What about bullets?"

Gresham opened a large envelope on his desk and pulled out a stack of photos. "Buck was killed by two large caliber bullets. Each struck the center of the chest, passed through the heart, then exited through the back."

"What about bullet fragments?"

Gresham pulled an enlargement of the exit wound from the stack. "Look here. This bullet just passed clean through to the left of the vertebra. This other one, however, crushed the vertebra before exiting the body. If there were bullet fragments, they would be here. I thoroughly searched this area, but found none."

Jim examined the photos more closely. "Look Doc," he said as he pointed to the photo. "This one that hit the vertebra, it looks like it was deflected slightly more to the right due to the impact."

Gresham looked at the photo through his reading glasses and nodded. "Not much, but maybe a little. Is that important?"

"Well it might help me find it if I know which direction it traveled," Jim replied hopefully, then continued with his questions. "What about the caliber of the bullets?"

"Anywhere from a forty-one to a forty-five," the doctor answered.

"Can't you be more specific from the entry wound?" Jim questioned.

"Usually, but not in this case." Gresham fingered through a stack of photographs then pulled out an enlargement of the chest. "As you can see, the two bullets crushed the sternum moving the bone and tissue around. That makes it impossible to be completely accurate."

Jim took the photo, sat back in his chair, and examined it closely. It felt strange looking at his friend this way, and he struggled to block out his feelings. He had to keep his mind clear in order to stay objective.

After a few moments Gresham spoke up. "You know, Jim, I've known Buck for a long time, but even I think it's highly suspicious that he would have drugs and be killed by a shooter as accurate as this one. Exactly what was going on out there?" Jim didn't seem to hear him. "Jim?" Gresham finally said in a loud voice after a moment.

"Huh?" Jim was pulled from deep concentration.

"Do you think this was a professional killing?"

"No, not at all," Jim said matter of factly. He recalled some of the facts about bullets and killing that he had learned during the war. "A professional wouldn't have used this type of bullet. You said that there were no fragments—that means the killer used fully jacketed bullets, similar to the type used by the military and law enforcement. They make fairly clean wounds, consistent with what we see here. On impact, they may flatten or mushroom slightly but only a little.

A pro would've used a hollow point bullet, which peals back and tends to come apart. It would rip a big hole to ensure a kill. With a hollow point bullet, we would've found metal fragments in the wound. Besides, anyone with enough practice can be this accurate at point blank range."

"He wasn't standing that close, Jim. In fact, he was quite a ways away." Gresham replied.

"*What?*" Jim found that hard to believe.

Gresham pulled another photo from the stack. "Here's a photo of Buck's shirt. At point blank range there would've been powder burns here." Gresham indicated an area with the tip of a pencil. "As you can see, there are none."

Jim stood, picked up the photo and examined it closely. "What about residue?"

"Anywhere out to about six feet I would've found powder residue. Even at ten feet I should've found something, but all tests came up negative."

Jim didn't say anything, but continued to stare at the photo in amazement. Then he picked up the written report from the desk. Gresham knew what he was looking for so he spoke up.

"The center to center distance of the bullets at entry is 2.5 mm or about one inch." Jim glanced at Gresham with a surprised look, then stared back at the photo without saying anything.

After a long moment, Jim looked at his watch. "Is there anything else, Doc? I told Milhouse I would meet him at five and it looks like I'm late."

"No, that's all I've got for you." Gresham collected the photos and began stuffing the stack back into the envelope.

"Can I get copies of those?"

"You can have these," Gresham replied as he handed the envelope over. "I can make duplicates for my file."

"Thanks, Doc." Jim said as he took it.

The two men walked to the office door and out into the hallway. "Good luck, Jim. I hope you find this guy," Gresham said as they shook hands.

"Thanks again, Doc," Jim replied, then turned and walked down the hallway. *And thank you, Buck*, he thought to himself. It wasn't much, but it was more than he had earlier.

As he got closer to the door he noticed a group of patients and hospital personnel standing around a wall mounted television. The national evening news was on and Jim could hear the commentator speaking.

"We go now live to Morton Washington, where the hunt for D.B. Cooper continues." Jim stopped and stared at the screen. He immediately recognized the reporter and his guest.

"I'm standing here at the city limits of Morton, Washington, where events which occurred almost three decades ago are being replayed as we speak. I'm talking, of course, about D.B Cooper, the slippery assailant that continues to elude authorities. With me tonight is Special Agent Alan Bradley of the Drug Enforcement Agency to give us an update. Agent Bradley, how close are you to capturing this clever felon." Chet placed the microphone in front of Alan.

"Unfortunately, Chet, the investigation is moving slower than expected." Alan's face was grim as he spoke.

"How so?"

"Well, although the Sheriff's department is trying very hard, it appears that they are under staffed and aren't well trained for this type of investigation. The investigation continues to progress, but not at the rate necessary to ensure success."

Jim looked slowly around the room as the report continued. His eyes stopped when he saw Nikki at the back of the room staring at the screen and biting her thumb. She was standing with a group of older nurses who appeared to be watching the screen and whispering to each other.

Nikki occasionally looked at the women and appeared to be listening to their every word. Then Jim and Nikki's eyes met. Nikki stared at him with a strangely sad and questioning look, then turned and walked hurriedly down the hall.

Jim wanted to run after her and reassure her, but he knew there was no time for that now. He noticed other people glancing at him with similar questioning looks, but he tried to ignore them as he turned his attention back to the screen. The report was just concluding. He listened as Chet finished.

"D.B. Cooper—the man hunt continues. Back to you, Dan."

Jim turned and walked hurriedly out the front door, disappearing into the parking lot.

"All right! That's a wrap!" The producer, Ms. Stapleton, a ten-year veteran of network news coverage yelled from behind the camera.

Chet turned to Alan. "Why don't you wait for me at the Chief? I'll only be a minute." Alan nodded then walked to the edge of the two-lane highway and looked both ways before darting across through traffic. On the other side he walked to his corvette, opened the trunk, and pulled two bottles of water from the cooler. He opened one, took a long drink, and then walked in front of the car to where Chet's vehicle was parked.

Alan stood there and watched Chet. He was talking to the producer and technicians huddled next to their large van with its network emblem and a satellite dish on the roof. When Chet was done, Alan watched as he too darted through traffic to the Chief. "What was that all about?" Alan asked after handing Chet the other bottle of water.

"After this morning's interview, all the major networks sent crews out here to cover the story. When they found out I have the exclusive to your interviews, they each tried to outbid the other for the scoop. These guys had the best offer. Isn't that great! I get to work with Dan Rather!" Chet hadn't been this excited about a story in years.

"What about the other networks? Where are they?"

"They're trying to cover the story as best they can, but I just found out from the producer that the others just purchased the rights to this interview in order to run it on their programs," Chet said, excitedly. "Of course, I'll get a large chunk of that payment as well. This story is bigger than the O.J. trial and it's all mine!"

"Well good for you!" Alan congratulated him.

"Everything's working just as you said it would," Chet said quietly. His earlier apprehension about Alan's plan had faded and been replaced with child like wonderment. "Look at them pour in." Chet pointed at the highway. Vehicles of all sorts filed by- small cars pulling tent trailers, trucks with campers, Winnebagos, and fifth wheelers.

"Look." Alan pointed to a license plate. "That one's from California."

"The TV crew has to stay in Centralia because the motel we're in is booked solid," Chet informed him.

Even Alan had to admit that the public's reaction to the story was more than he had expected. "This seems to be working better then I thought." He smiled as they leaned against the side of the Chief enjoying their water and watching the traffic go by.

After a few moments, Chet turned to Alan. "Explain to me again how we have the best of both worlds. I don't think I understood it very well this morning."

"Well, Chet, it's like this," Alan began to explain. "If the lead I got this morning pans out and I get a line on this smuggling operation, then we'll nail Phantom and walk away with all the glory on national television."

"But what if the guy in the truck comes forward and says he didn't shoot Henderson?"

"He won't," Alan replied. "I bet he's holed up somewhere trying to figure out who in the organization is trying to pull a double cross and wondering if he's next. Then when we capture him, who is going to believe a drug smuggler? Definitely not a court of law."

Chet started to worry again. "But then it will look like I reported lies about it being Cooper. I'll be *ruined!*"

"Relax," Alan assured him. "When it's all over I'll do another interview. I'll explain that I concocted the Cooper story in order to make the smugglers think that I was off their track and lull them into a false sense of security while I continued to search for them. I'll also explain that you knew nothing of the lies and that you reported the facts as you knew them. That way you keep your integrity, and I look like a clever cop."

Chet nodded with relief. "But what if you don't find them? What happens then?"

"That part is developing as we speak," Alan answered with a smug smile on his face. "It's important that I don't get blamed for a botched case. That's why it was essential that the Sheriff take charge. You heard him in front of all of his deputies, he officially took over the investigation." Alan laughed.

"Then these hordes of people will comb the forest looking for Cooper, and you can claim that they destroyed any evidence that may have led you to him." Chet added.

"Exactly."

"How did you know the Sheriff would take over?" Chet asked after a moment.

"Actually I didn't think a small town Sheriff would have enough brains let alone balls to do it, but he was right. There isn't enough evidence to bring in the Feds. Actually, I was expecting Cranston to show up and take over. That's why I worked those deputies so hard this morning. I wanted to have at least one lead to follow up on my own when Cranston showed up."

"Yeah, where is that guy? I would've expected him here by now." Chet asked curiously.

"I don't know. The old geezer must be slipping more than I thought," Alan remarked.

"After today's press, you should easily slip into his position," Chet said with a smile on his face.

"Forget Cranston, you've got to think bigger than that."

"What are you talking about?" Chet cocked his head with the question.

243

Alan looked at his friend and decided it was time to let him in on a small portion of his master plan. "How would you like to be my press secretary when I'm elected Mayor of Seattle?"

Chet's eyes lit up. "*Wow!* With a job like that I'll be able to control which stories go out to the media and how they get developed. I'll *really* be able to change things then!"

"That's right," Alan told his friend in a firm voice. "If you keep your cool and do everything I tell you, I'll be able to lay the whole Emerald City at our feet."

Chet stared out at the mountains for a while thinking about the possibilities, then another question hit him. "But what if the public doesn't believe you? I mean, after all, there's no way you can give them Cooper. What if they see that as a chink in your armor and don't elect you?"

Alan slowly swept his arm out in front of him, pointing to the wave of vehicles passing by. "Look at them, Chet. They'll believe because they desperately want to believe. They see Cooper as some sort of Robin Hood hero who put one over on the government and got away with it. Each of them probably has their own idea about who Cooper was and what he did with the money. Heck, the beauty of it is that they don't really want me to find him."

"They *don't?*" Chet asked, questioningly.

"No! Right now, the hunt for Cooper is a shining spot in their otherwise pathetic lives. They don't want to know the truth about Cooper because that would ruin their image of him. They don't want him found so that they can go back to their family and friends and say they went searching for D.B. Cooper. They want to believe that Cooper is clever enough to outsmart the authorities one more time then disappear. Finding him would only ruin the adventure for them."

"Yeah, I guess you're right. It *is* the perfect setup." Chet was amazed at its simplicity. "What do we do now?"

Alan looked at his watch. "I'm going to the Sheriff's Station. I need to pull in the reins a little and get some help working on this lead. I want you to start hitting the campgrounds. Get lots of photos of the chaos and confusion for the morning papers."

"Good idea, lets get going," Chet replied starting to turn away, then stopped. "Hey, Alan." Alan stopped and turned back towards his friend. "What do you think *really* happened to Cooper?"

"I don't know," Alan shrugged, after he thought for a moment. "One thing is for certain though."

"What's that?" Chet asked, curiously.

"If he did survive—he won't be showing up here to call me a liar." Alan laughed then turned around, walked to his car, and got in. Chet did the same and started up the Chief. After watching his friend merge into traffic, Chet waited for the traffic to clear, then spun a U-turn and headed up the highway in the opposite direction.

16
Revelations

Centralia Sheriff's Station. 6:00 PM.

"Hi, Sheriff, I have the photos you've asked for," Tom said when he saw Jim come in the front door of the station. He'd been pacing nervously for almost an hour waiting for Jim to arrive. The excitement from this morning's events had worn off and hindsight told him he screwed up.

The last thing he wanted to do was disappoint Jim. But now, on the day when Jim needed him most, Tom had failed. He promised himself he wouldn't make that mistake again.

"Good, bring the pictures in here," Jim replied, then walked past Tom and into his office. Milhouse grabbed the large folder from his desk and followed Jim in, closing the door behind him. Jim sat down behind his desk and pointed toward one of the chairs in front of it. "Have a seat." Milhouse placed the photo package on the desk, then sat down.

"Have you found anything out there, yet?" Harper asked as he leaned forward, putting both elbows on the desk.

"No... not yet, but we're still looking," came the nervous reply. Jim leaned back in his chair and looked at the wall. After a few moments of silence, Milhouse spoke up. "Do you have any idea what might've happened?"

Jim didn't take his eyes off the wall, he'd been running that question over in his head for hours, and, as of yet, he'd come up empty. "Have you seen any strangers in town?" he finally asked.

"Well…no," Milhouse said as he tried to think. "Not any more than usual. Why?"

"I don't know," Jim glanced at Milhouse, then back at the wall. "Maybe someone from out of town saw Buck flashing his money around at one of the local taverns. You know how Buck was when he drank. He was always buying people drinks, especially strangers who haven't heard his stories a million times." Jim managed a slight smile as he thought of his friend.

Milhouse didn't say anything. He just sat waiting for Jim to continue. "Maybe one of these strangers found out where Buck lived, then snuck out there early this morning and tried to rob him."

Milhouse thought for a moment. "If it was a robbery, why didn't he take the money? We found Buck's wallet on his dresser and the cans of cash in his closet."

"I don't know," Jim leaned forward against his desk and racked his brain. "Maybe he didn't mean to kill him. Buck may have surprised him while he was searching for the money and the guy accidentally shot him. He then got scared and ran out of there, abandoning the search."

Milhouse pondered that for a moment then replied. "But what about the drugs, where do they fit in?"

Jim shrugged. "Maybe this guy was some sort of junky. He may have brought it with him, then in the heat of the moment when he was scared, accidentally dropped it at the scene and took off without it."

"That wouldn't work," Milhouse replied. "The drugs were found in the coffee can with the money. If he had dropped it, it wouldn't have been until after he found the money. Then he probably wouldn't have been so scared that he would leave without everything he came for."

"Yeah, I guess you're right," Jim said in frustration. As of yet, he had too few facts to go on. He'd hoped the autopsy report would tell more, but instead it only confused him further. He was glad Tom was there with his report and photos. It would be his first opportunity to examine the evidence as it was collected that morning.

"What about the kid who was staying with Buck?" Milhouse asked. "Could he have done it?"

"No, Clifford went back to Seattle yesterday. There's no way he could have anything to do with it." Jim reached for the package on the desk. "Is your report in here?"

"Yes, it's on top of the photos."

Jim opened the envelope and emptied its contents onto the desk. He picked up the written report and began to examine it.

Alan parked his Corvette on the side of the station, then walked around the corner to the entrance. He went through the front door and stopped when he saw Jim and Milhouse in the office. The two men hadn't noticed him, so he stepped out of sight in the hallway and tried to listen in, but all he heard was garble.

He didn't want to have another confrontation with Sheriff Harper unless they were alone. If it didn't go well, he didn't want any deputies seeing it. If they saw them argue, they might decide loyalty to Harper was more important than helping him. He stood back and tried to listen while he waited.

At that moment, Deputy Rissley pulled into the station's lot and parked her Blazer next to Milhouse and Harper's. While back at Buck's place her job was to tag and catalog evidence—she never left the porch. After Jim had arrived, she was assigned to look for bullets. That was the first chance she had gotten to examine the crime scene for herself.

Earlier, Milhouse had arranged for Mr. Miller, a local rancher, to pick up Buck's animals. By the time Miller arrived, Milhouse had already left to meet with Harper, so it was up to Joe to assist in the loading of the animals into the trailer.

On her way, she left the cabin. Heading over to the barn, she glanced at the tire tracks as she stepped over them when something caught her eye. She stopped for a moment to get a closer look. Earlier, she had tagged and cataloged a plaster impression of the track but didn't notice anything out of the ordinary.

But now, she could see the wheel and axle spacing. There was something strangely familiar about them, but she couldn't put her finger on it. There were animals to move so she shook off the feeling, knowing she would come back to it later.

In order to preserve the crime scene, she decided to take the mules out the back way. Joe took each mule one by one out of the stable, through the back doors of the barn, and into the corral. Then she closed the barn's back door and opened the corral gate letting each mule though individually into the trailer.

During this process, Joe had to walk to the back of the corral several times and in doing so noticed something unusual. The ground was disturbed along the side of the corral and up the hill. After she finished loading the mules, she went back for a closer look.

Two sets of footprints came down the hill through the brush and along the corral. She probably wouldn't have noticed them at all except that they had been made more pronounced by all the slipping their owners had done while coming down the hill. After a closer examination, Joe saw that the prints were from shoes with little to no tread, like a street shoe or loafer. Except for her own, there were no other prints around.

They weren't made by any of the deputies, she knew. The Sheriff's department provided its personnel with different uniform options depending on the situation. For patrol and office work they wore light street shoes, but today in these conditions, all the deputies were wearing boots with a waffle style tread.

She didn't know if they were important and wondered if anyone else had seen them, but decided to get some pictures of them anyway. Joe got the camera and tape measure from her Blazer. After photographing and measuring the prints, she followed them up the hill. Joe came upon a small opening in the brush where the tracks were all jumbled up as if someone had been standing there for awhile.

A little further investigation led her to a conclusion that surprised her. It was obvious that two people stood up there and watched the property below. Looking through the brush, she could see everything. These were the footprints of the shooter, she was *sure* of it. She had to tell Jim. They were looking for *two* people not one.

After quickly taking some pictures with her 35mm camera, Joe rushed to Centralia to get them developed. That had taken a long time and she wished the department had bought the digital camera she had wanted last month. She kicked herself for not pushing the issue further with Jim who insisted it was too expensive.

But in this situation, time was even more expensive. With a digital camera she could've taken the pictures, loaded them onto her laptop, then e-mailed them to the station over the internet. She wouldn't have wasted all that time on the road or waiting for development.

Joe got out of the Blazer and hurried to the rear to get the box of evidence from the back. She reached for the tailgate handle and froze. On the ground in front of her were her tire tracks. Before entering the lot, she had driven through a puddle wetting the tires. She then made a slow arching turn into the parking space.

What she saw now reminded her of the tracks at Buck's house. She shook off the surprise knowing she had to check this out. The evidence box in her Blazer held the plaster tire mold and she knew she had a tape measure somewhere. *Where was it?* She went to the cab to look.

Jim finished reading the report and glanced at a few photos.

"This is going to be a real tough one, isn't it Sheriff?" Milhouse said.

"Yes it is," Jim replied softly, after a long moment. "It's going to require a lot of thought." Jim reached down and opened the lower drawer of his desk, pulling out his gun belt and a box of shells. Then both men stood up and walked towards the door.

When Alan saw this, he quietly slipped into the men's room and listened at the door.

Jim opened the office door, then followed Milhouse out of it. "I set up the conference room so that we could follow the flow of evidence better," Milhouse said.

"Good idea. Lets have a look."

They both went into the conference room where Jim saw what Tom had done. Pinned to the wall were blown up pictures of the evidence and crime scene. From left to right, in chronological order, were pictures of the arching tire tracks, drugs, and money.

The middle was a piece of paper with the word "body" on it. He was glad to see that Tom was sensitive enough to Buck's death not to include a photo. On the black board was a list of evidence as well as a list titled "Things We Know". On the list was…

1.) D.B. Cooper, with pick up truck and trailer, loaded drugs from the barn.

2.) Cooper shoots victim.

3.) Cooper drives away.

4.) Fingerprints on cup.

Jim was instantly annoyed, but tried not to show it. "These aren't things you *know*, they're speculations."

"I understand that now, Sheriff," Tom replied with embarrassment. "These are from the notes I took while with Agent Bradley. I wrote them on the chalkboard when the excitement of the case was still flowing. I haven't had a chance to revise it."

"Well, let's do that now," Jim said, thoughtfully. He picked up an eraser and chalk, and went to the board. He erased any reference to Cooper or drugs, then filled in the blanks.

1.) *Someone,* with a pickup and trailer, loaded *something* from the barn.
2.) *Someone* shoots victim.
3.) *Shooter* escapes.
4.) Fingerprints on cup.

Jim pointed to the list. "You're clear on the fact that this is not a drug case or a search for D.B. Cooper, correct?"

Tom nodded, still ashamed of his earlier exuberance. Hearing Jim say it now, it seemed so ridiculous and he felt foolish for even believing it.

"Good." Jim looked around the room. He didn't like the first item on the list or the picture of the tire tracks, but they were things they knew and he wasn't ready to come clean about them. He decided to leave them for now. He'd have to justify the removal otherwise. "It's not much now, but as the investigation progresses, this room will come in handy." Jim said, then turned and walked back out of the conference room with Tom following.

"I'm sorry I yelled at you this morning, it was uncalled for." Jim apologized. He'd been angry and after settling down, realized it was only natural for them to follow Bradley's lead. None of his deputies were trained for this type of investigation.

"That's all right, Sheriff," Milhouse replied. "I had it coming. I guess I got excited about how a high profile case like D.B. Cooper would look on my resume."

"I don't know why you want to work in the city, but if that's what you want I'm sure you'll get there," Jim said as they stopped in the hallway. "It won't be a big case people notice. It'll be work like that report of yours." Jim patted Milhouse on the back. "You did a real good job, and the photos are excellent."

"Thanks, I've been practicing with the camera on my days off," Milhouse said with a smile.

"Well it shows," Jim said, then turned more serious. "I hope the other deputies are straightened out about this Cooper thing."

"I think so," Milhouse nodded. "They seem to have accepted the fact it's a bunch of bunk."

"Good. But just to be on the safe side, tell everyone if I hear anymore crap about it from anyone I'll have them removed from the case," Jim said sternly.

"Yes sir."

Jim looked at his watch then back to Milhouse. "I want you to relieve Simms on patrol on highway seven, then have him relieve Kruger on watch at Mineral Lake. Tell Rissley, Conley, and Johnson to go home and get some rest, but they have to be back in eight hours so that you and the others can get some rest as well. Then I want you to be back here at six tomorrow morning. That doesn't give you much sleep. Do you think you can handle it?" Jim looked sternly at Milhouse.

"Yes, sir. You can count on me," he replied assuredly.

"Good. Now why don't you call Peggy and tell her you're going to be working late. You don't want her to worry do you?"

"No, I don't, and thanks for reminding me." Milhouse then turned and walked towards his desk.

"One more thing." Jim began to say. Milhouse turned to look at him. "Pass this along to the rest of the guys. If that DEA agent comes back and starts to give orders tell him he has to see me. We'll be too busy with our own investigation, so no one is to help him unless it's okayed by me first. You got that?"

"Yes, sir. I'll tell them."

"Good," Jim said, then walked towards the back door. With his gun belt and shells in hand, he disappeared through it.

Alan heard everything. He slightly pulled open the restroom door and peered through it. Milhouse was sitting on the corner of his desk with his back to the hallway talking on the phone. Alan slipped out of the restroom and walked to the front of the counter. He could hear Milhouse talking.

"Honey, you know I can't discuss the case. If Harper found out he'd chew my butt." Milhouse said into the receiver.

"Excuse me, Deputy," Alan interrupted.

Milhouse turned and saw Alan. "Oh, I'm sorry Agent Bradley, I didn't hear you come in," he said then spoke back into the receiver. "Listen, Peg, I've got to go. Don't hold dinner for me, I'll be working late. And please stop listening to all the gossip from Mrs. Nelson. You *know* she makes that stuff up…All right, I'll talk to you later." Milhouse hung up the phone, then looked at Alan. "What can I do for you?"

"Did the fingerprints from the coffee cup come back from the lab yet?" Alan asked.

"Yes they have. Most of them were smudged but we got a good thumb print and a good partial of the index finger."

"Great! I need a copy to fax to Seattle and have my people run it through the Federal computer banks. If our man has been fingerprinted before, for any reason, we'll find him."

"Good idea, why didn't I think of that," Milhouse said then walked to a cabinet, pulled open a drawer, and retrieved a file. "This could lead to the first real break in the case."

"One more thing. Remember that float plane we saw this morning."

"Yeah, what about it?" Milhouse replied.

"Do they have to file flight plans with the FAA?"

"I don't think something that small has to. I think they're required to keep flight logbooks though. Why?"

"This smuggling operation has to get its drugs in and out of here quickly and unnoticed. They may be using float planes."

"Oh, that again," Milhouse said as his expression turned sour. Milhouse walked to the copy machine with the file.

Alan walked around the counter and over to him. "Listen, my source has never lied to me. If he says that D.B. Cooper is running a drug operation out here then I believe him." Milhouse ignored him as he prepared the items from the file. "It doesn't matter if you don't believe it, but we're both still looking for the same man. The man who drove that truck."

Alan saw that he had lost the deputy's confidence. Remembering what he had just heard from behind the restroom door, he attempted a different approach. "I hear you're looking for a job in the city."

"Where did you hear that?" Milhouse asked in a short-tempered tone.

"Oh, one of the other deputies told me," Alan lied.

"So what of it?" Milhouse asked, pushing the copy button.

"Well, I know a lot of important people. I could make some phone calls. Who knows, by this time next week you could be packing your family up and moving them out of this awful town."

Milhouse's eyes lit up with excitement. "You'd do that for *me*?"

"Of course I would…that is, if you showed me a little interdepartmental cooperation."

Agent Bradley was right, Milhouse thought. They were both looking for the same person. He pondered it for a moment, then handed Alan a copy of the prints. "Well I guess we are both on the same side. What do you want me to do?"

"That's the spirit!" Alan said, encouragingly. "Now, if I'm going to get these flight records, I'll need a warrant. Who's the closest judge that can issue one?"

"That would be Judge Lundeberg," Milhouse replied.

"Do you know him very well?"

"I should, he's my father-in-law."

"Well it looks like I came to the right person," Alan said. "Now, where would these records be kept?"

"At Morton field, out on highway seven."

"Excellent! Since you'll be on patrol near there this evening, it won't take you long. You can drop by Lundeberg's, pick up the warrant, then stop by the field and get the records. When you're finished with patrol duty you can drop everything off at my motel."

"Listen." Milhouse shook his head. "I don't think I'll have time—" Milhouse tried to say but Alan cut him off.

"When you get to my motel, we can talk more about your career ambitions. You know, there aren't many jobs out there, but there's always room for a good cop. One who's a team player. That's why you need someone with my connections."

Milhouse thought about that for a moment. Perhaps, if he hurried, it wouldn't take so long. "Do you want just the outfitters?"

"What else is there?"

"Well, there are a few private helicopters with pontoons and then there's the Forest Service. They have a plane they use for fighting fires."

"I want to see anything that lands on water and has enough range to make it to Portland or Seattle."

"All right, that shouldn't take long." Milhouse decided with a smile. "All I have to do is clear it with Sheriff Harper and I'll be on my way," he said as he took a step towards the back door.

Alan put a hand on Milhouse's arm and stopped him. "Deputy Milhouse—Ah—listen, I know you're in a hurry and I have to talk with Harper anyway. I'll tell him what we've planned and if he doesn't like it he can call you on the radio."

Milhouse hesitated for a moment uneasily and was about to refuse when Alan cut him off.

"Just think, Tom," Alan said with a friendly smile. "We may soon be calling you *Special Agent* Milhouse instead of deputy. It has a nice ring to it, don't you think?"

Milhouse smiled hopefully at the suggestive remark. "Yeah, I suppose you're right," he said, then changed directions and walked to the coat hook for his jacket.

"What's he doing out there, anyway?" Alan pointed to the back door.

"He's out at the pistol range," Milhouse replied as he slipped on his jacket. "He says it helps him think." Tom started walking towards the front door then stopped. "Don't forget to tell him about what I'm doing," he reminded Alan.

"I won't," he assured him. "I'll be waiting for you at the motel."

Milhouse turned and disappeared through the front door.

Alan folded the copy Milhouse had given him and put it in his pocket as he walked out the back door. He stopped and looked at the pistol range. It was a small section of land crudely cut out of the dense trees and brush. Mounds of dirt were piled up at different distances from the firing line. Atop each mound was a large log to which targets were attached. Alan watched Harper as he walked back to the firing line from hanging the last of his targets.

Joe finished measuring the length and distance between the axles of her Blazer and compared the plaster cast to her tires. They were identical. Everyone in the department drove Blazers, and last fall each one was outfitted with brand new tires. Her tracks would be identical to everyone else's from her department and they matched the ones from the crime scene.

The revelation stunned her. Someone from the Sheriff's department was the drive from the crime scene! But *who...*? The answer popped into her head before she could finish the question. *Jim! Of course!* she thought to herself as she heard the front door of the station swing shut.

She looked over to see Milhouse walking hurriedly towards the parking lot. She quickly looked at the tracks then back to Milhouse. She wasn't ready to reveal what she'd discovered until she could talk to Jim. Grabbing the box of evidence, she slammed the tailgate shut, then hurried to the sidewalk to meet Milhouse.

"I thought you'd be at Buck's?" Tom said.

"I was, but there's something I need to discuss with Jim."

Boom!...Boom!...Boom!

The gunshots startled her at first, but the recognizable sound calmed her. "Jim must be *thinking.*"

256

"Uh-huh," Milhouse confirmed, then sighed. "He seems to be holding up all right, but I can't help worrying about him."

"How do you mean?"

"He seems distant. I mean, who could blame him with his best friend getting killed and all, but I hope it's not affecting his judgment," Milhouse replied.

"You don't think Harper is up to this case?" Joe asked.

"No, it's not that, its just…well…" Milhouse was trying to find the right words.

Joe saw the questions on his face. "You have mixed feelings," she helped him start.

Tom nodded. "On one hand, we've known Buck forever and wouldn't think of him as a criminal, but that doesn't mean we shouldn't investigate that possibility. I'm worried that because of his close ties to the case, Sheriff Harper may not be as impartial as he needs to be. And besides, there can only be one explanation for what happened out there, right?"

"Right," Joe confirmed.

"Then why is it that Harper and Agent Bradley are so far apart on their views? I mean, Agent Bradley's story sounds crazy and all, but he *is* an expert at this type of work. There's got to be something to his story, right?" He looked at her for an answer.

Joe looked at him thoughtfully. "I understand where you're coming from. In fact, I've asked myself similar questions."

"You have?" Tom was relieved that he wasn't alone in his concern.

"Sure, everyone probably is, it's only natural," she assured him. "But I know Jim. I don't know Bradley. Jim will come up to speed quickly, and when he does, we'll find our killer."

"I hope you're right."

"I'm sure of it," she insisted. "As his deputies, we need to— no— we're obligated to do everything we can to help him catch up. That's what I plan on doing. That's our *job*." Joe tried to emphasis that last point.

"Yeah, you're right," he finally agreed.

"We can talk about this more later," she told him. "As for now, this box is getting heavy." She laughed, trying to end on a lighter note.

"All right," he smiled. "I have to be going anyway."

They both turned and walked their separate ways. When she got to the front door she turned to watch Tom drive away. His words disturbed her. In order to solve this case, they all had to work as a team—as one united force.

Questions like that needed to be satisfied quickly. Getting Jim up to speed was now more urgent than ever. If the other deputies lost confidence, they may shift their support to Agent Bradley. She couldn't let that happen.

Boom!...Boom!...Boom!

Joe turned as she heard three more shots from the firing range. *Don't worry, Jim, you'll always have me,* she thought to herself then opened the door and walked through it.

Jim stepped in front of a target thirty feet away, then lifted his revolver.

Boom!...Boom!...Boom!

Jim lowered the gun and saw that his shots were wild. The bullets hit the outer edges of the target. Everything raced through his head at a thousand miles an hour. He told his mind to relax, be quiet... and he tried to wipe it free of distractions.

It was hard. The look Nikki gave him at the hospital was burned into his mind. She looked so crushed, as if she didn't recognize him anymore. *She's a good woman,* he told himself. She would keep quiet for now, he knew, but if he didn't find something soon, her conscious wouldn't be able to handle it and she'd have tell someone.

It was a race against time, and he was losing. It didn't matter much to him if people found out he was with Buck before he died or even if they thought he'd killed him. But he couldn't let Nikki's confidence be destroyed. He couldn't lose her love. *No!* he told himself. He wouldn't allow that!

Jim's face turned to stone and his eyes narrowed. *Concentrate and think,* he told himself as he raised his gun.

Boom!...Boom!...Boom!

He lowered the revolver and looked at the target— a two and a half inch grouping around dead center. *Much better,* he thought to himself.

"Nice weapon," came a voice beside him.

Jim looked over to see Alan standing there, but he said nothing.

"Ruger 357 model GP100 isn't it?"

Again Jim didn't answer. He was still upset by the way Bradley had started an investigation in *his* county and manipulated *his* staff to do so. He especially didn't like the awkward position he was in because of the news reports.

He lifted the revolver, pulled the stem up, and swung the cylinder open allowing the spent shells to fall to the ground. Jim heard the impact of the shells tinkle on the gravel at his feet, then lowered the gun. He turned and walked down the firing line to the next target forty feet away. Jim pulled a speed loader from his belt, dropped it into position, then turned the locking knob. The bullets fell into the cylinder and Jim swung it back into position.

"Sheriff, you *have* to allow me to conduct my drug investigation," Alan said, calmly. "I can help you. You're undermanned as it is, you can use my experience and expertise."

Jim lifted his gun.

Boom!...Boom!...Boom!

He lowered it again then looked at Alan. "All right," Jim said hesitantly. He didn't like it, but he *could* use the help. "But only if you agree to a few conditions."

"Conditions?" Alan said loudly, then put his ego in check and composed himself. Then speaking in a calm voice. "Anything, just name it."

"First of all, you're not the press spokesman for this department. If there's anything to tell the media I will do it. Is that clear?" Jim said sternly.

Alan could feel his face getting red, but he fought to control his temper. "Got it. What else?"

Jim was pleased to see that this upset Bradley. He turned back towards the target, so as not to let Bradley see the smirk on his face, and lifted the pistol again.

Boom!...Boom!...Boom!

Jim turned the gun and lifted the cylinder stem allowing the spent shells to fall out. "I don't want to hear anymore bull about D.B. Cooper. Is that clear?" Jim spoke in a loud yet controlled manner.

Orders from a two-bit sheriff was just a little too much for Alan to take and he stepped forward, close to Jim, and speaking angrily. "Are you calling me a liar?"

"What I'm saying is that you're following some bad information. Its time for you to drop it, and move on with your investigation," Jim said, tactfully.

Although he liked irritating Bradley, he didn't want to completely alienate him. Alan tried to reply, but Jim quickly turned his back on him and walked down the firing line towards the next target. Jim pulled another speed loader from his belt, placed it in position and dropped the bullets into place.

Alan composed himself before following. "What else?"

"My deputies are off limits," Jim said calmly as he locked the cylinder in place and looked at the target fifty feet away. "If you need help, you'll have to bring in your own staff. Is that clear?" There was no answer.

After a moment, Jim looked over at Alan and saw that he was fuming mad. Jim had to find out how cooperative Alan would be. If Alan couldn't work under these conditions, it would slow down Jim's murder investigation, and that kind of help he didn't need. "If you can't handle that, Agent Bradley, maybe I should call your superiors and have you removed from this case." Jim spoke in a firm voice trying to push one more button.

That's the last straw, Alan thought. His anger couldn't be held back any longer and he stepped quickly in front of Jim. "Are you *threatening* me?" He snapped into Jim's face.

"You take it anyway you like!" Jim barked back seeing that negotiations had just broken down.

"There's something you should know about people who get in my way, Sheriff!" Alan yelled angrily.

"What's that?"

Alan spun towards the target and dropped to one knee quickly pulling the Desert Eagle from his shoulder holster.

Boom! Boom!

It was all over in little more than a second and Jim was amazed at Alan's quickness and speed. Alan stood, and both men looked at the target.

"They always lose," Alan replied smugly as he returned his weapon to its holster. "Keep that in mind, Sheriff." Alan turned and walked back towards the station.

Jim didn't hear him as he stared in amazement at the target. The bullets hit almost dead center and about one inch apart. Then it hit him like a ton of bricks. *No, it couldn't be that simple*, he told himself.

Jim looked over at Alan and watched him walk towards the side of the station. Bradley was at Buck's place after Jim left. He had found Buck's body, Jim remembered. He stepped forward, picked up the two spent shells ejected from Alan's gun and looked at the bottom of them. 44 mag. *But why would he want to kill Buck?* he asked himself.

"Deputy Kruger to Sheriff Harper. Come in, Sheriff." The radio on Jim's belt interrupted his thought.

Jim lifted the radio to his mouth. "Go ahead, Kruger."

"Sir, I've got a lot of people out here. They started showing up an hour ago. I've been turning them away, but now there are just too many of them," the radio squawked.

"Get Simms and Conley to help you. I'll be there as soon as I can," Jim said, then holstered his weapon and hurried towards the station.

Joe was in the conference room, updating the board, when she heard the last two shots. She had been around guns long enough to recognize that they were different from the ones she had heard previously. That made her curious enough to look out the back window.

Agent Bradley was walking toward the side of the building, and on the range she saw Jim frozen like a statue. The look on his face told her something significant had just happened, and she was dying to know what it was. Seeing Jim hurry towards the station, she left the conference room and met him at the back door.

"What's wrong, Sheriff?" she asked.

Jim didn't hear her. He was stone faced as he walked past her back, then into his office where he collected the report and photos, then stuffed them into the envelope. Looking out the window, he saw Alan's black Corvette merge into the now heavy traffic. *It is a* crazy *thought*, he said to himself. Even if it were true, no one would believe it. Jim turned and rushed out the office and towards the front door.

"Sheriff! I *need* to talk to you!" Joe exclaimed as Jim rushed past her for the second time.

"There's no time for a meeting," Jim said, sarcastically. "I'm in a hurry."

"*Sheriff!*" Joe said as she threw her arms up in frustration.

Jim thought better of it and stopped at the door. "I have to get out to Buck's place," he said thoughtfully. "Meet me out there and we can talk all you want." He then pushed the door open and left.

"*Men!*" Joe exclaimed as she was left in the hallway with her hands on her hips glaring at the front door. "Always running off like the cavalry!" After a moment, she calmed down and decided to finish updating the conference room. But first, she wanted to know what had happened on the range and she headed for the back door at a trot.

At the range, she walked around slowly looking for anything unusual. Jim had left a pile of brass at each target. Jim was a pretty good shot but out of practice, she could see from his results.

The targets at twenty, thirty, and forty feet each had some loose, lazy shots as well as a few nice ones near the center. There were only two brass casings in front of the target at fifty feet. This was where Jim froze.

She bent down to examine the casings. .44 magnum. Jim owned a 357. These had to be from Agent Bradley's gun. She looked at the target but didn't see anything. Dropping the casings, she walked out towards the target. As she approached it, she saw the bullets plain as day in the bull's eye.

Wow, she thought. Her jaw dropped open as she ran her fingers over the holes. Now *that* was good shooting. Looking around some more, she saw nothing else out of the ordinary. *Hmmm,* she thought. *Jim must've just been impressed by Bradley's shooting skills.* She shrugged her shoulders and didn't give it another thought as she walked to the station.

Back in the conference room, she pulled evidence from the box and laid it on the table. Taking down the photo of the tire tracks, she replaced it with the ones of the shoe prints. She then turned her attention to the chalkboard list and stared at item one.

Someone, with a pick up truck and trailer, loaded something from the barn. She knew that person was Jim and she was *sure* he didn't kill Buck. It didn't matter why he was out there, she knew there was a perfectly reasonable explanation for it and the timing of his trip with that of the murder had to be purely coincidental.

She picked up the eraser and with one decisive stroke, swept item one clean. Since her revelation in the parking lot, she had time for calm reflection and had come up with the reason why Jim hadn't told anyone the truth. By nature, Jim was a controlling person, she knew. He wouldn't be able to control the investigation or influence its direction if he was in any way under suspicion. That's why she had to keep it a secret and help him cover his tracks.

She recalled what a professor had once told her. *The human mind tends to ignore the obvious, if the obvious is one they wouldn't generally consider to be an option.* Like the car theft case she had studied some years back.

Everyone blamed a young, homeless, high school drop out because he was found carrying a crowbar. Nobody suspected the nice old lady next door who baked fresh apple pies, even if she was seen driving a different car every week. But in that case as she was

262

sure it would be in this one, the criminal's time would eventually run out.

After a while someone always figures it out. Once all the other options have dried up, people will revisit the obvious. The other deputies must have noticed something familiar about the tracks, but hadn't yet put it together as she had. She had to buy Jim some time. She had to refocus everyone's attention on the true target.

She looked again at the board. Item four, *Finger prints on cup.* She gasped. *Oh my gosh,* she thought. *They must be Jim's, too!* She hurried out of the conference room to Milhouse's file cabinet. She knew where he kept everything. Opening it, she removed the folder labeled *D.B. COOPER CASE.* *That's got to go,* she thought, then got a new label from the drawer, put it over the old one and wrote– HENDERSON MURDER CASE. She then opened the file, removed the pages pertaining to the fingerprints, then put the file back in the cabinet.

She had no idea Milhouse had already given the prints to Bradley. Rushing back to the conference room, she stuffed the prints and tire track casting and photo into the bottom of her evidence box. After placing other items on top, she placed the box in the corner of the room where she stacked other evidence boxes on top of it. *There, it's buried,* she thought. Back at the board, she grabbed the chalk and eraser and made revisions.

1.) Two people staked out victim's home.
2.) They came down the hill to the barn.
3.) Shooter kills victim.
4.) The two escape.

She looked at the list and nodded in agreement, then gazed around the room for anything else out of place. Her eyes rested on the now buried evidence box, and she wondered if by hiding the truth she was doing something unethical. *No,* she finally decided. She was just ensuring that the pertinent facts came to the forefront and the irrelevant ones were left behind. She checked her watch, it was almost eight o'clock. Time to get out to Buck's and talk to Jim. She quickly turned, walked out of the room, then out the front door.

17
Puzzle Pieces

Mineral Lake. 8:45 PM.

As Jim drove around the bend in the road, he came upon an assortment of vehicles stopped ahead of him. He turned on the switch and the red and blue-flashing lights on the roof came alive. Jim turned into the oncoming traffic lane. At first, he expected to have to dodge traffic coming from the other direction, but everyone appeared to be going his way. A quick examination of the vehicles showed that many were on the side of the road and empty. Some had people inside, waiting patiently while the occupants of still other vehicles were walking about, wondering what the hold up was.

When he reached the turnoff, he saw that Deputy Kruger had the road blocked. Jim pulled off the road, got out of the vehicle, and walked up to him.

"Where did all these people come from?" he asked with astonishment. Kruger handed him a piece of paper and Jim examined it. It was a map of the area with an "X" at Buck's house. The map was titled "D.B. Cooper's Secret Hideout".

Before Jim could ask, Kruger spoke up. "Mr. Brunner's been selling these, at his motel, for twenty dollars per copy."

"What the *heck* does he think he's doing?" Jim said angrily. "It's going to take *hours* to get these people out of here!"

"Do you want me to go down and talk with him?" Kruger asked.

Harper thought about it for a moment. "No, we've lost too much time as it is. I'll deal with him personally. What have you got going here?"

"Crowd control mostly," Kruger replied. "I've got the road blocked off. There're a few stuck in the mud by Henderson's and Townsend is helping them. Some of the people parked on the road and are in the woods. Conley is watching from the house. When they show up, he sends them up the road to Townsend who then sends them packing."

"Where's Simms?" Harper asked looking around. "He was supposed to relieve you by now."

"I don't know," Kruger shrugged. "He must be as busy as we are."

"All right, you seem to have things under control here. I'm going down to the house." Jim turned and walked back to his Blazer. As he drove up the gravel road he noticed several cars stuck in the ditch. From their appearance, Jim concluded that, although the road was now dry, the ditch was still quite muddy. He came up upon Townsend's Blazer sitting in the road. Townsend was hooking the cable of his winch to the frame of a Volkswagen rabbit.

Jim maneuvered slowly around the scene so as not to go in the ditch himself, and then gave a quick hello wave to Townsend. He continued down the hill and parked in front of the porch of Buck's home. When he got out he noticed Deputy Conley standing on the porch with binoculars staring out at the lake. As Jim walked up the porch he glanced towards the lake, but it was dusk and too dark for his old and tired eyes to see anything very far away.

"What are you looking at, Conley?"

Conley pointed out into the distance. "About two hundred yards out is a small aluminum boat. A man has been out there with a camera and huge telephoto lens snapping pictures. He's been there for almost two hours."

Jim squinted and could barely make it out in the low light.

"Here, use these." Conley suggested as he handed over the binoculars. "They'll bring in more light."

Jim lifted and adjusted them to his eyes. "Oh yeah, I see him now."

"Do you think I should run him off?" Conley asked.

"No, he doesn't seem to be bothering anything. He probably came from the camp on the other side of the lake. He'll have to head back soon anyway or get caught out there in the dark." Jim trained the binoculars on the opposite shore. He could make out almost a dozen small campfires and a large bonfire on the beach. "It looks like the campground is busting at the seams."

"Yeah, it's *way* over capacity. I drove through there earlier and had to break up a few arguments about who was there first, but everyone seems to have settled down now."

Jim lowered the glasses and looked around, then trained them back on the boat. The man was rowing away from them. "See, there he goes now."

It was a full moon, which helped him make out the tree line. Just inside the trees, Jim saw the beam of a flashlight. "I hope that's one of ours."

"It is," Conley nodded. "That's Thomson. He's been walking the trails behind the house and along the beach in order to get everyone out of here before it gets too dark."

"Good idea. We don't want these city folks getting lost. Have many sightseers made it to the house? Harper asked.

"Quite a few," Conley confirmed. "Most went peacefully, but others wouldn't leave until I took a picture of them in front of the house."

"They got all the way up here?" Jim said, surprisingly. "I hope none walked off with any souvenirs."

"Don't worry, Sheriff. Most of the evidence has been taken back to the station. All that's left is this box which I've been guarding like a hawk," Conley replied.

Jim turned around to see the box. In it were Buck's scrapbook, storybook and the two coffee cups. "Why don't you give Thompson a hand? I'll look after things here."

"Right," Conley replied, then picked up his flashlight and both men walked towards the steps. "I'll see you in a little while, Sheriff." He turned and walked towards the corner of the building.

"I'll be here," Jim assured him, then walked to his Blazer. Opening the door, he reached over and pulled the envelope with the photos over to him. Jim looked up and watched Conley disappear into the trees. He then glanced back at the box on the porch and frowned. Taking a long, slow look around, he saw no one, so he left the envelope where it was and walked back towards the porch where he picked up the box and returned to the Blazer with it.

He sat it on the seat and examined the contents. Lifting the storybook, he paged through it slowly. *I wouldn't want this stuff to fall into the wrong hands*, he thought. After a few moments, Jim looked around again, then placed the book back where he found it and placed the box behind the front seat. Pulling an old, raggedy blanket off the backseat, he placed it over the box. After closing and locking the door, Jim, with envelope in hand, walked toward the barn.

Pushing open both big doors, the darkness inside was impenetrable even for the full moon. Jim turned on his penlight and used it to find the two Coleman lanterns. Firing both up, he hung them from their hooks. They hissed and hummed as they lit up the inside of the barn.

That's better, he thought as he walked to the feed bin, pulled the photos and report from the envelope, and scattered them on top. Jim looked around and was relieved to see that the animals were removed as he had asked. That was one more thing he didn't have to worry about.

"Let's see now," Jim thought as he picked up the report, then fumbled through the photos and pulled a few out. He only needed three, each was of Buck lying in the mud and taken from different locations. Jim walked outside the barn and placed one on the ground where Buck had last rested. It was taken from directly above.

The light from the barn cast long shadows that streamed off into the distant lake. Jim could hear frogs croaking in the marshy shadows, as he watched the bonfires on the opposite shore flicker and reflect off the water.

He looked down at the picture of Buck. Haunting eyes stared back at him, and a half opened mouth seemed to say, *"Figure it out, Jim. I know you can do it."* But Jim didn't know if he could.

Harper let out a heavy sigh as he lifted his head in the air. Looking out at the millions of twinkling stars and the edge of the Milky Way Galaxy, he said out loud. "What happened, Buck? What in the *hell* went wrong?"

He was half hoping for an answer as he stared off into space wondering where Buck was now. Was Buck looking down on him, watching? He hoped so. He could use some guidance, and in a silent prayer, he asked for it.

Joe drove down the hill and came to a stop behind Jim's Blazer. It had taken a lot longer to get here than she expected. She never liked city traffic, but that's exactly what she just experienced. Normally, on this stretch of lazy highway, she felt comfortable enough to do her nails or put on makeup, but not tonight. It was both hands on the wheel, gas, break, stop. Gas, break, stop. Gas, break, stop.

She finally got frustrated, put on her lights and siren, and sped past everyone in a huff. She didn't realize she was still gripping the wheel so tight. She pried her fingers off it, then took a deep breath of relief, releasing it slowly. Grabbing the two brown paper bags on the opposite seat, she got out. As she walked towards Jim, she wondered what he was thinking as he stared into the sky.

After a long moment, Jim finished his thought, shook off the feeling of helplessness and got back to work. He walked out a few paces then looked back and compared the scene to the photo in his hand, which was taken from where he stood.

No, something wasn't right, he thought as he flipped through the pages of the report.

"Hello, Sheriff," came a voice from behind him. Jim turned to see Deputy Rissley standing there. He'd been thinking too hard to notice her drive up.

"Hello, Joe. I'm glad you're here. Right now I could use some help."

"Sure thing, Sheriff. What do you want me to do?"

"First of all, stand over here and hold this." Jim handed her the report and positioned her where Buck must've been standing when he was shot. "Read to me the last paragraph of the first page." Jim stepped back between the two double doors of the barn and looked towards her.

Rissley pulled a penlight from her pocket and trained it on the report. "The victim's shoulders were parallel to those of the assailant and to the front of the barn when he was shot at point blank range."

"Hold it," Jim stopped her. "Buck wasn't shot from point blank range. Milhouse didn't know that until he read the autopsy report in my office this afternoon, and I can see that Buck's shoulder must've been parallel to those of the shooter, because of the direct path the bullets took through the body. But how does he come up with the idea that they were square with the front of the barn?" Jim examined the photos intently looking for the answer.

"What do you mean," Rissley asked, curiously.

"Hold on here a second." Jim walked over and adjusted her shoulder so that it was slightly closer to the barn. "Now straighten out your feet...good." Jim then repositioned the picture of Buck on the ground behind her to reflect the slight change. He then pulled a pencil from his pocket and stuck it into the ground marking her feet.

"Now come here," he said stepping off ten feet into the barn from where Rissley was standing and turned around. "Do you have a pencil?" Harper asked as his deputy approached. Rissley pulled one from her shirt pocket and handed it over. Jim stuck it into the ground marking his feet as Rissley stepped closer to him.

"Now look at these photos. Buck was obviously facing the shooter when he was killed, but look how he landed. He's slightly angled to the right. Buck didn't fall that way by accident. A bullet from a large caliber pistol would've pushed him in the same direction it was traveling."

Rissley looked over Jim's shoulder at the picture. "Yeah, you're right, but not that much. I'd say Buck was turned about twenty-five degrees. What's the big deal?"

"Well, it's no big deal if he was shot at point blank range because you're only talking a couple of inches. But if you're trying to find out where the shooter stood, from a range of ten feet or farther, you're talking at least a foot or more to the left." Jim took a step to his left. "Yeah, right about like this. That *completely* changes where the bullets had to have landed."

She adjusted her line of sight. "Not exactly, Sheriff. They still land in the lake. Looks like at least twenty yards from the right shoreline."

"Only one of them did — look at this." Jim turned and walked towards the feed bin for more photos with Rissley following him. As Jim fingered through the stack, Joe set the two bags on the bin next to him.

"What are those?"

"I figured you hadn't taken the time to eat, so I stopped by the deli and got us some sandwiches."

He looked at her thoughtfully. "Thanks Joe. You're right, I haven't had anything all day. I'm starving!" Truth was his stomach burned from a mixture of stress and too much coffee. He could use a good meal.

Joe grabbed a bag and opened it up. "Well, you can have either beef and cheddar or turkey and Swiss."

"Beef," he said with a mouth-watering smile.

She handed it over and watched as he peeled back the wrapper and wolfed down half of it in three bites. She rolled her eyes as she opened a carton of skim milk for him. "Here, wash it down with this," she said as she handed it over. He took it and started gulping it down.

Men, she thought. Watching Jim eat reminded her of sitting around the dinner table with her brothers. It was always one big pig fest. She had just barely opened her own milk when she noticed Jim had finished his sandwich and was now eyeing her turkey and Swiss.

It was only for a second. Just a fleeting moment of selfishness quickly considered then just as quickly squashed. She was nice enough to bring him dinner, he couldn't ask for hers, too. Then he noticed that she had caught him looking, and a guilty blush went over his face.

"Oh, go ahead," she finally said. *It's a good thing I brought some fruit along for later*, she thought watching Jim first hesitate, then reach for the other sandwich.

"Thanks," was all he was able to get out before stuffing it into his mouth.

At least he was slowing down and chewing a little, she thought. For a second, he reminded her of a shark in a feeding frenzy. She half expected his eyes to roll back in their sockets as he took a bite. Maybe she could at least get a word in edgewise while his mouth was full.

"Sheriff, I found something earlier that I thought might interest you."

Jim looked up from his sandwich between bites. "What's that?"

"I found footprints. It appears that two people watched this place from a spot on the hill above the corral. They then came down the hill and probably through the corral and into the barn."

Jim stopped chewing and looked at her seriously. "I didn't see anything like that in the report."

"I know, that's what I was trying to tell you at the station. I didn't hear one word about them all day from anyone."

"Well that explains a lot," he said as he finished his sandwich and milk and put the trash in the bag. "Now, if we can put a few more puzzle pieces together we just might figure out what happened here." Jim fumbled with some pictures. "Now where was I?"

"The angle of the body," Joe reminded him.

"Oh, yeah, here it is. Look at this picture." Jim handed it over. "These are the exit wounds made by each bullet. The one on the left traveled straight through and is probably in the drink, but the other one hit the back bone, ricocheting to the right."

"Yeah, I see what you're saying," Rissley replied as she examined it closely.

"There's a close up in here somewhere," Jim said as he fumbled through the pile then pulled it out. "Ah, here it is." He handed it to his deputy and they both examined it.

"It's hard to tell from all the damage, but it looks like the bullet was deflected about twenty degrees." Rissley confirmed.

"Add that to the twenty-five degree turn of the body, and you're looking for the bullet in a completely different area." Rissley followed Jim out of the barn to where the photo was laying in the dirt.

"Lets see now. Twenty-five degree turn for Buck," Jim rotated his body as he spoke, then lifted his arm in the direction of the line of fire. "Now another twenty degrees for the deflection." Jim slowly rotated his body. They both stared down Jim's outstretched arm.

"The porch!" Rissley exclaimed.

""Has anyone searched it yet?" Harper asked.

"No, we concentrated on the dock and shoreline like you wanted."

"Then lets get after it," Jim said, encouragingly. They both turned and walked towards the porch.

Jim was more determined then ever. The food and the fact that puzzle pieces were starting to fall into place revitalized him. He was feeling more in control and started to get his confidence back.

Joe walked beside Harper, matching his stride and pace. Tom's words back at the station had worried her, but no longer. She had watched Jim closely and listened to how he spoke. He was uninhibited and thinking clearly.

Her sheriff was on the case and in charge, for which she felt both happy and relieved. Sure, Jim seemed to view the photos with a sort of impersonal distance and she hadn't yet heard him refer to Buck as dead, but that was all right. It was an avoidance reaction. It was perfectly normal when the human mind is affected by a trauma such as this.

He would eventually have to get through it and get on to grieving and healing, but not right now. Avoidance would be fine until this case was solved, at which point, she hoped to have the opportunity to help him through it. But for now, she planned on helping and supporting her sheriff anyway necessary to solve this case. She considered telling him she knew he was the driver, but then thought better of it. If Jim wanted his little secret, he could have it. It didn't matter anyway.

When they reached the porch the dim lights cast large shadows. "Why don't you start down here, I'll work on the porch," Jim said.

Joe pulled her flashlight out and trained it on the front beam and railing next to the steps, then slowly started working her way towards the corner feeling with her hands as she went. Headlights approached from the road, and Townsend pulled up to the front of the house and got out.

"I'm glad you're back," Jim said to him. "Why don't you help Rissley with the front of the porch?"

"What are we looking for?" he asked.

"A bullet," Joe replied.

"But I thought…" Townsend started to say.

"I'll explain later, just look," Jim ordered. As he said this the beams from two flashlights came out of the darkness and Thomson and Conley walked into the porch light. "You two can pick a spot on the porch and start looking for anything that looks like a bullet hit it."

Before either one could ask, Townsend and Rissley spoke up in unison. "He'll explain later, just look." The two men took up positions and did as they were told.

Jim reached the water clock. As he looked and felt around it he could here the water flowing through it and the gears turning inside. He examined it closely. The round sides were smooth and undamaged, and the front was clear of any marks. He then moved to the porch rail to examine it.

They all worked in silence as they slowly checked every nook and cranny. As each finished their search, they all reported the same result.

"Nothing," Jim said, discouragingly. "Let's check it again. I'll go get the rest of the photos. Maybe there's something we've missed." As the deputies did what they were told, Jim headed towards the barn.

A few minutes later he returned with a jumbled up mess of papers and photos under his arm. Jim laid them out on the porch bench and began looking at them one by one.

Rissley saw the questioning look on his face as he examined them. "What's wrong, Sheriff?"

"I was just thinking about the angle of the body again. I'm surprised Milhouse missed that. He's usually quite thorough."

"I'm not surprised," Conley spoke up. "He followed that DEA agent around, like a puppy dog, this morning taking notes. I'd be surprised if he had time to do anything else."

"No kidding! Milhouse was so far up that Feds butt, I couldn't tell where Bradley ended and Milhouse started," Townsend added.

That brought a hearty laugh from the two deputies. They quickly quieted down when they saw Jim wasn't laughing. Jim and Rissley exchanged concerned looks.

"It looks like I'm going to have to have a talk with Milhouse. I thought that was one of the first things I taught you guys about a crime scene. Never let someone else tell you what you're looking at. Examine the evidence at the scene and allow *it* to tell you what happened," Harper said.

"I'm surprised that DEA agent missed it. I thought they were suppose to be experts at this sort of stuff," Thomson commented.

"Maybe Agent Bradley isn't as smart as you think. Anyone who comes up with a story like this can't be playing with a full deck," Jim replied as he continued to look at the photos, then stopped at one of them. It was a picture of the front of the barn. There was a small dark shape lying on the ground next to one of the support beams of the first stall. He couldn't quite tell what it was.

"What do you make of this?" he asked as he stood and handed the picture to Rissley.

"I don't know. I didn't see anything there when I was in the barn," came the reply.

"Why don't the rest of you come here and look at it," Jim suggested. Each deputy stopped their search and walked over to him.

"It's too far away to tell what it is," Thomson said, looking over Harper's shoulder.

"Wait a minute," Conley spoke up. "That's the feed pail. It was laying there when I started searching the barn for drugs this morning."

"Why isn't it there now?" Harper asked.

"I saw Agent Bradley pick it up and put it in the feed bin," Conley reported.

"Why didn't you stop him? He's not supposed to disturb anything at the crime scene," Jim scolded.

"I'm sorry, Sheriff. I figured he knew what he was doing," Conley replied.

"Come on. Show me where it was," Jim ordered.

The two men walked off the porch and into the darkness towards the barn with Rissley right behind them. Jim followed Conley towards the doors.

"Watch out for the markers on the ground," Jim instructed, following Conley around them and to the feed bin. Conley lifted the lid and pulled out the metal pale. He carried it to where he had seen it laying and placed it on the ground.

"There, it was like that."

Jim stood back and looked at it. "What's this?" he pointed to the scattering of grain on the ground.

Rissley bent over to look. "It looks like oats."

Jim knelt down and examined it.

"Yeah, there were oats scattered around, but they must've been trampled down with all the foot traffic in and out of here." Conley confirmed.

Jim stood back up and looked at the ground. "It looks like there's a small path of oats originating from back here, in the center of the isle. The path angles forward, and to the left, towards this support. Then the oats just flew all over the place as if...wait a minute." Jim hesitated, then picked up the pail and pointed to a sharp crease in its side. "Look, it's been dented."

"Yeah, almost as if it hit the support and bounced forward to where it was found," Rissley agreed.

"Exactly. It must've been sitting on the ground here. Then someone, who's facing the front doors and moving right to left, kicked the pail causing it to spill all over."

"Maybe, but that person would've had to kick it pretty hard to put that big of a dent into it." Rissley noted.

"Stand back. Let's give it a try." Jim moved to the center of the aisle and positioned the pail.

Conley and Rissley moved behind the feed bin as Jim stepped behind the pail and lined it up with the support. Jim stepped forward quickly and kicked it. He couldn't help, but fall forward a few steps after doing so and regained his balance near the support. The pail did what he thought it would.

Clang!

It bounced off the support, rolled down the aisle way and came to rest close to where it showed in the picture.

"All right, so that solves the oats in the pail mystery, but how does that fit into this case?" Conley asked.

Jim shrugged. "It probably doesn't, but at least we've eliminated one more question from the photos. Let's get back to looking for that bullet."

"All right," replied Conley. They all took a step towards the door when Jim froze.

Joe saw the look on his face. It was the same one from the shooting range. She instantly looked around to see what she'd missed and it hit her a second later.

275

"Hold everything." Jim looked at the pencils in the ground. "What's wrong?" Conley asked, curiously.

Jim stepped back to where he was and Joe moved in behind him in order to see what he did and confirm her suspicion. "I'm in almost the exact line of fire as the shooter. This *has* to be where the killer fired from."

Joe's eyes widened with amazement. "Wow! That's good shooting."

Conley hurried over to look for himself, but was skeptical. "I don't know, Sheriff. I saw the bullet wounds in Henderson's chest. This is over forty feet away. That would've had to been quite a shot—not once, but *twice*. And the shooter was off balance from kicking the pail."

Jim didn't answer. His mind took him back to earlier that evening when Bradley fired his weapon on the target range. *It could've been him after all,* he thought to himself.

Rissley saw the strange look on Jim's face, and could almost see the gears turning in his head, but hadn't yet put it together. "What is it, Sheriff?" she asked intently.

"Come on." Jim hurried out of the barn and to the house with his deputies close behind. Jim reached the bench on the porch and rummaged through the photos.

"Where's the report?" he said loudly. He finally found it and quickly flipped through it looking for the time that Bradley arrived on the scene. There it was. Agent Bradley found Buck at 07:00. Jim's heart sank. Buck had been shot at 06:00. *I guess it wasn't him after all,* he thought.

Joe didn't like not knowing what was going on and was starting to get impatient. "Sheriff! What are you looking for?" she pleaded.

All the deputies looked at him for an answer. Jim was about to tell then his suspicions but decided to keep it to himself for the time being. After all, he had no proof and it sounded far-fetched.

"Oh, I don't know. I guess it's nothing. Let's get back to looking for that bullet." Jim took the report and sat down next to the photos as the deputies, one by one, slowly went back to work.

Rissley was the last. She knew he wasn't telling her the truth, but decided not to press him on it right now. She reluctantly turned and went back to work.

Jim rubbed his eyes as he paged through the report slowly. He was *exhausted*. *How long had it been since I've slept?* he thought as he looked at his watch. It was 1:00 AM, later than he had thought. He then looked at his deputies. He hadn't realized until then how beat they looked. "Hold on everyone."

The deputies stopped and looked at him. "There's not much more we can do in the dark. I want you all to stay here tonight. Buck has plenty of room and there's food in the pantry. I would let you go home, but I'm afraid the traffic might be rough tomorrow and I want to get an early start. Joe, set up a look out on the porch and at the road's entrance, and set up a schedule for relief.

"Those sightseers will probably be coming around early. I want you all fresh and lively. As for me, I've got a motel clerk to talk to. If you need me, I'll be at the station later."

Tired acknowledgement was returned from the group. "Good, now hop to it," Jim said, then collected his photos and walked off the porch to his Blazer.

Joe followed him to his vehicle. "I'll go with you, Sheriff. I want to see how you handle Mr. Brunner."

"No!" Jim insisted. He was tired and in no mood to have his methods witnessed or critiqued. "If you want to help me, Joe, I need you here. I need to be sure the search for that bullet progresses smoothly. First thing in the morning, I want as many people as possible here to search the porch and that stand of trees to the left of it."

"All right," she replied. She was disappointed, but knew he was right. "At least let me borrow both Milhouse's and the autopsy reports. I haven't read them yet and can't help but feel like I'm missing something." Then she changed her mind. "Better yet, why don't you fax them to me."

"Fax?" he said, dumbfounded.

"Yeah, I've got it all set up at the station," she replied. "Put the reports through the scanner and they'll pop up on the computer screen at my desk. Then, with the mouse, drag them to the icon labeled Joe's e-mail. I'll pull them up on my lap-top later."

Jim chuckled. "Okay. I suppose not even *I* could screw that up."

She smiled. "Thanks, Sheriff." Then she remembered something. "Hold on, don't go anywhere." She hurried to her Blazer where she retrieved another brown paper bag.

"What's this?" Harper asked.

"It's a few apples and oranges. I thought you might like to keep them in your Blazer in case you get hungry again."

Jim looked at her thoughtfully and smiled. "You're a lifesaver. Thanks again." He took the bag and got into his Blazer.

Joe watched the Blazer turn around and head up the road. She then turned her attention back to the porch. Taking a deep breath, she let it out slowly as her eyes moved from the porch to the large dark shadow of trees next to it.

That stand of trees is going to take every man we've got tomorrow, she thought. We'd better give the porch another going over before we turn in, but this time with more light. Joe got in her Blazer, pulled it around facing the porch, then turned on her headlights and floodlights. She then rounded up the other deputies and began methodically combing the front of the house.

After a few minutes, Conley commented as he worked his way along. "You know, I just don't get it." He was confused. "Agent Bradley overlooked the angle of the body, the feed pail, and never once had us look for a bullet. How does a professional investigator miss all that?" He reached the water clock and could hear the water flowing inside it. He examined its smooth, clean surface then moved on.

"That's not all," Joe added. "He missed the footprints coming down the hill behind the barn."

Ding!

The water clock chimed as another number rotated into place.

Conley ignored it and looked at Rissley strangely. "No, he didn't. I found them first thing this morning."

Joe stopped what she was doing and looked at him. "Then why weren't they in the report?"

Conley shrugged. Because they're Agent Bradley's tracks."

"They are?" she questioned.

"Yeah, he said that when he and that reporter showed up this morning, they came down the hill through the trees in order to get the drop on the drug smugglers, but all they found was a cleaned out barn and Buck lying in the mud. Because they were Bradley's, we didn't give them a second thought," Conley reported.

Joe shrugged then went back to work. After a moment, she stopped as a crazy thought went through her head. She was reminded of what she'd recalled earlier. *The human mind tends to ignore the obvious, if the obvious is one they wouldn't generally consider to be an option.* She thought of Agent Bradley, then after a moment shrugged it off. *No,* she decided. *That idea was just too crazy.* They all continued to work in silence.

18
Poker Face

Morton. Saturday 2:00 AM.

As Jim approached the town of Morton, he saw the lit up motel sign. SLEEPY HOLLOW INN—NO VACANCIES. The parking lot was full, so he parked behind some cars in front of the office. Jim noticed the homemade sign on the office door. In florescent orange it read.

We're booked solid.   There's no more room.
DON'T EVEN ASK!

Jim opened the door, walked up to the front desk and pounded hard on the service bell.
Ding! Ding! Ding!
Nothing happened so he hit it even harder.
Ding! Ding! Ding! Ding! Ding! Ding!
"All right! All right! I'm coming. You don't have to break it." An elderly man's voice said from the back room. Jim watched the older man moving slowly up the dark hallway behind the counter struggling to get his robe on.
"Can't you read the sign? It says no vacancies!" His voice was filled with disgust as he fumbled with his glasses then turned up the dimmer switch to light up the room. "Oh, I'm sorry, Sheriff," Mr. Brunner forced a tired smile. "I thought you were another one of those tourists. I've been booked solid since three this afternoon and they just keep coming. Heck, I'm renting parking space for three campers too!"

279

Jim pulled out the map and slammed it down on the desk startling the man. "Are you responsible for this, Brunner?" he said with a serious tone.

Mr. Brunner rubbed his tired eyes then glanced at the paper and started to giggle. "Yeah, pretty cleaver, eh? I've made almost five hundred dollars today, and hope to do better tomorrow," he said proudly.

"In that case I'm placing you under arrest for obstructing justice," Jim said in a loud authoritative voice as he pulled out his handcuffs and moved around the counter to the older man.

"*Arrested!*" Brunner's eyes bulged out in surprise, now fully awake and aware of his situation. Jim grabbed his arm. "But it was just a prank! I didn't mean to do any harm! Honest, I didn't." Jim pulled Brunner's arms back and snapped the cuffs on tightly. "Sheriff! You've *got* to believe me! I can't be arrested, I've got a business to run!"

Jim said nothing as he pulled Brunner around the counter, and was pleased to see that the old man was traumatized by his situation. He really wasn't going to arrest him and didn't have much time to waste, but Brunner needed to be taught a lesson.

"Sheriff, *please*! You've *got* to listen to me!" Brunner exclaimed in a voice that was both scared and panicked.

"I don't have a choice, the law is the law," Jim replied as he walked Brunner towards the door.

"But I've *never* done anything wrong! Can't you let me off with a warning or something?" Brunner pleaded.

Jim stopped, turned the man around, and looked at him. "That's true, Mr. Brunner, I would really like to help you out, but my hands are tied. Judge Lundeberg would have my badge if I let you go. Especially someone who doesn't participate in any community services," Jim replied calmly, in a sympathetic manner, then resumed his push towards the door.

"What are you talking about?" Brunner asked, dumbfounded.

Jim stopped again. "You know how big a baseball fan Lundeberg is."

"Yeah, I see him every week at the high school games, so what?"

"That's right, and he sees you there as well. In fact, it was just the other day the Judge commented on how disappointed he was with you. I mean, the way you don't contribute to the baseball collection when it comes around," Jim said scornfully, looking down his nose at Brunner. "Now how do you expect to throw yourself on the mercy of the court with a record like that?"

"I'm just a small time motel manager. I'm not made of money!" Brunner insisted in desperation.

"You just made five hundred dollars and wasted my time in the process! If that's your attitude I'll throw your butt in jail until you rot!" Jim again started pulling the old man towards the door.

"Okay! Okay! I'll make a donation!" Brunner exclaimed in panic.

The fear in the old man's crackling voice told Jim he was about to break so he turned Brunner around to look at him. "I *knew* you had it in you." A smile lit up Jim's face. Turning Brunner around, he started taking off the cuffs. "Exactly how much were you thinking about?"

Brunner thought for a second. "How about a hundred bucks?"

"*What!*" Jim instantly squeezed the cuffs even tighter then spun Brunner around to look at him. The old man's wobbly legs almost gave out. "Do you know how much new uniforms cost? The teams playing in rags!"

"All right! *Two* hundred," Brunner replied in a defeated voice as he leaned against a chair for support.

"Five hundred and you promise not to sell any more maps!" Jim barked into Brunner's face.

"That's *extortion!*" Brunner said angrily.

"I'm just trying to show you a way to influence the court," Jim defended himself.

"I know *exactly* what you're trying to do, Sheriff!" Brunner's eyes narrowed as he stared accusingly at Jim.

"Don't be such an old bucket of crust! Legal bills will cost you three times that."

Brunner realized he was out maneuvered, and he lowered his head in defeat. "All right…you win."

"Good, I'll be umpire at the game on Monday, and expect to see you there." Jim took the cuffs off. "I don't think we have to tell the Judge about this. We'll let him think you did it all on your own." Jim walked towards the door.

"Uh-huh, I bet you don't want him to know," came a disgusted reply.

"Good night, Mr. Brunner. It's been a pleasure seeing you again." Jim smiled then closed the door behind him. He walked to his Blazer. *That should teach the old goat. He won't pull another stunt like that again,* Jim laughed to himself. *Buck would've loved to hear about this one.*

He suddenly grew sad as he thought about his friend, but the sight of the black Corvette on the other side of the lot shook him out of it. He thought for a moment then turned and walked back to the office.

Ding! Ding! Ding!

"I'm coming. Keep your shirt on," the voice from the back room said. When Brunner saw it was Jim, his false teeth almost fell out. "Now what do you want me to do, buy Girl Scout cookies?" A sour expression came across the grumpy man's face.

"I want to see the log," Jim demanded, tapping his finger on the counter.

Brunner just grunted, reached under the counter, then set the logbook on top. Jim paged through it until he found the right date, then his finger slid down the list of names, but it wasn't there. "Isn't that Agent Bradley's car out there?"

"Yes it is. I don't know why these young folks need so much car, it'll only get them killed."

Jim ignored the comment. "So, where's his name on the register?"

Brunner turned the book around and looked at it. "He's in room 4, with that reporter feller. See double occupancy." Brunner's bony finger tapped the line on the page.

"What time did they check in?"

"They were ringing this bell at four a.m.," came the reply.

"*Four* a.m.! Are you sure?" Jim said with surprise.

"I sure as heck am! They drug me out of bed. It's starting to become a bad habit!" Brunner scowled.

Jim didn't say anything. He was in deep thought as he turned slowly then walked towards the door. Brunner gave Jim a nasty look as he watched him walk away.

"Yeah, you're welcome!" He slammed the book shut angrily, then dimmed the lights and walked into the back room.

Jim got back into the Blazer and sat in the seat thinking. He looked at room 4. Its lights were the only ones on in the building. *What's going on in there?* he wondered. Should he go over and confront him? It's *got* to be him. He had plenty of time to kill Buck then cover his tracks. But why would he do it? What's his motive?

Jim wanted answers, but decided not to let Bradley know of his suspicions. No, he had better not say anything to anyone. Bradley screwed up today by losing his temper and letting Jim see him shoot. He must think he's safe. If Jim could keep Bradley off

282

guard and even make him mad a little more, maybe he'll slip again. Then *I'll have you- you arrogant, overconfident jerk*, Jim thought as he stared at the door. After a moment, he started the Blazer. "I'd better get back to the station," he said to himself. "There's still a lot to figure out if I'm going to nail this jerk. Jim drove out of the lot and onto the highway.

Alan closed the book on his lap, got off the bed, and walked to the table where Chet was sitting. Chet was staring at his computer screen, moving the mouse around, and occasionally punching a few keys as he did so. Then he noticed Alan leaning over his shoulder.

"Did you get any more from that book?"

"No. I read it cover to cover. There's nothing in it that hasn't already been put into play." Alan moved closer to get a better view of the screen. "What are you doing?"

"This is one of the shots I took this evening. I'm just lightening some of the dark areas a little. Watch this." Chet moved the cursor around with the mouse then punched some keys. "This is a picture of two men arguing over a camp site. Because of the back lighting, this man's face is too dark and you can't make out his facial features. If you can't see the anger on his face, the whole point of the picture is missed."

"So is it ruined?"

"Not at all. I just zoom in on the man," Chet said as he moved the mouse and clicked the buttons. "Isolate him from the rest of the picture. Play with the contrast and presto!"

Alan looked on in amazement as the face brightened up. "Hey, that's pretty cool. But I thought you took this picture tonight? How did you get it developed so fast?"

Chet pushed the eject button on the computers' disk drive and out popped a 3.5 inch computer disc. "It's all on disc." Chet leaned over and picked up his camera from the other side of the desk. "This camera doesn't use film, it's digital. I just slide the disc in here and I'm ready to go." Chet slid the disc into the back of the camera.

"It has a disc drive just like a computer! I was wondering why it's shaped so funny."

"It stores photos electronically, so there's no developing of film. Also, there are fewer moving parts. I can take a series of photos faster than my other camera with its auto-winder. The shape is a little different in order to accommodate the battery pack." Chet depressed a button and out slid a rechargeable battery. "When it gets low on juice, I just take it out and replace it with the one in the charger over there." Chet pointed to the spare battery pack plugged into the wall socket. Pushing the battery back into position, Chet lifted the camera and took a picture of Alan.

"Hey! What did you do that for?" Alan blinked his eyes after the flash went off in his face.

"Let me demonstrate." Chet pressed the disc eject on the camera, then took the disc and inserted it back into the computer.

Alan watched as Chet punched some keys. "So is the camera what you spent all your money on the other day?"

"Part of it," Chet replied. "I used the rest to upgrade my entire computer system. This baby has the latest in hardware and software. I can now hook my video camera directly to the computer and watch the recording on the screen."

"Wow, that must come in handy."

"It sure does," Chet replied. "I can edit video right from my computer. That's what I did with this morning's interview."

Alan examined how the components were wired. "So the video camera and still camera are both digital, same as the computer. That way you can transfer video or pictures to the computer directly by cable or disc."

"That's correct," Chet confirmed. "The video or picture gets massaged by a sophisticated high resolution graphics program before it's sent to the TV networks or Wire Service by way of the internet." Chet continued to explain.

"That's a pretty handy unit," Alan remarked.

"I'll say. Without it I would've had to hand deliver the tape. It would've taken hours, and I would've missed the midday news." Chet stabbed at some buttons on the keyboard. "Now let's get back to the pictures."

Both men's attention was drawn back to the screen. "The computer displays all the pictures as half inch square, thumbnail images. The photo of you is the last one here, but first let's return to the camper's picture. I've got a deadline to meet." Chet punched some more keys, and the picture of the two men arguing filled the screen. "Now, for the written report." He tapped on the keyboard and the picture on the screen was joined by text.

"Mayhem in Morton. Good title," Alan remarked, approvingly.

"Now I import the picture into the text, like so." Chet moved the items around with the mouse. "Now that it's ready, I just send it to the Seattle Times and PI by way of the internet." With a click of the mouse it was sent. "There, my report is now in the hands of the editors. Now, if you allow me one more minute, I'll update my website." Chet brought his home page up onto the screen.

Alan watched as the page came up. A picture of Chet filled the screen with the slogan. *Chet Green—Investigative Journalist. If you've got the poop—I'll get the scoop!* He still thought it sounded ridiculous. Below it was a long list of article titles and dates. "Wow, it looks like you've added a lot of stories over the past couple of years."

"I sure have," Chet said proudly. "This website acts as my online resume. My business card has the website address for anyone interested in hiring me. Each title is a link to the article on the Wire Service. If you click on one of them, it'll take you right to it. I get a lot of extra business that way. Now, let me add *Mayhem in Morton* to the list." Chet stabbed at the keyboard. "There, it's done. Now let's get back to your picture." Chet moved the mouse, and the web page was replaced by the photo image that Chet took of Alan. "Let's see how you'd look with a scraggly beard," Chet said as he punched some keys.

"Hey, that's all right." Alan smiled as his image changed before his eyes. "What else can you do?"

"Virtually anything I want. I can give you bigger ears, change your eye color, hair style and color... maybe even give you a different nose!" Chet tapped away busily on the keyboard.

"Hey! Stop that! I get the idea," Alan exclaimed as his image became unrecognizable. "You've turned me into some sort of freaked out punk rocker! I didn't know you could do that. Do you change pictures like this often?"

"Sometimes. If I want to make a point I'll change a few subtle things. Like that murder case last month."

"The one where the businessman was shot in the parking lot?" Alan asked as he sat back on the bed.

"Yes. In that case, I took the picture of the suspect—"

"—The disgruntled worker." Alan jumped in.

"On my computer, I stretched his face just a touch to make his lips purse. Then I made his skin look slightly dirty and I brightened the whites of his eyes to make it look like he was staring at you. The changes were slight, but just enough to make him appear evil," Chet said proudly. "That picture sold a lot of newspapers and the paper rewarded me with a big bonus."

"But they found him innocent, Chet. They convicted the murdered man's business partner."

"Hey! How was I supposed to know he didn't do it? I'm no *detective.*" Chet defended himself.

"Isn't there some sort of law against doing that?" Alan questioned. "I thought I heard somewhere that the disgruntled worker sued the paper for slander. What ever happened with that?"

"It went to court, but he lost. The court ruled that, under existing law, there wasn't enough evidence to prove slander." Chet reported. "The Legislature is currently looking into adding 'image deprivation' to the definition of slander, but currently the media is pretty much able to do as it pleases. We don't even have to tell anyone we did it."

"That's interesting," Alan said as he filed the information away in his head. *It might come in handy someday,* he thought curiously as he sat back on the bed. "Does the media use this technology often?"

"Well, to a certain extent, yes. Mostly it's used to remove flaws such as in that swimsuit magazine you were looking at the other day. The photographer will remove a woman's freckles or birthmarks. They can even give a woman a darker tan," Chet replied.

"Do you mean they're not as perfect as they look? Why did you have to tell me that? Now it's going to be impossible to look at those bathing beauties without wondering what's wrong with them," Alan said, with a disappointed look.

"Yeah, it kind of takes the fun out of it. That's why they don't tell you the pictures were altered. They wouldn't sell as many magazines."

Suddenly there was a knock on the door, and Alan got up and walked over to it. "Get that picture off the screen," he ordered. Chet depressed a few keys and it disappeared. Alan opened the door to reveal a man standing there with a box of books.

"Deputy Milhouse, how nice to see you again. Come in and put it down over here." Alan stepped away from the door and pointed to a spot on the floor next to the bed. Milhouse did as instructed. "Did you get all the records?"

"Yes, I did. Sorry I'm late. It's been a busy tonight. I had three fender benders to deal with." Milhouse answered.

"That's alright. I knew you would come through. It's what I was telling my friend here. That Milhouse is a real professional. Isn't that right, Chet?"

"That's right, a real professional," Chet echoed.

Milhouse smiled as Alan grabbed him by the arm and started to direct him back to the door. "I don't want to keep you any longer.

I know how busy you are and you're going to need your rest for tomorrow."

Milhouse stopped at the door. "Agent Bradley, remember what you said. You're going to help me find a job in the city, right?"

"Yes of course I am—just as soon as this case is closed. Consider it a done deal. By the way, you're going to be available tomorrow if I need your help, right?" Alan's question sounded more like an order.

"Yeah, I guess so," Milhouse shrugged.

"Good! That's what I was telling Chet earlier. Milhouse is a real team player." Alan gave his friend a look.

"Team player, that's what he said," Chet echoed again.

Milhouse smiled ear to ear.

"Now you get home and get some sleep. I'll see you tomorrow." Alan gently guided Milhouse out the door then closed it behind him.

"What was that all about? Are you really going to help that duffus get a job?" Chet asked after a few moments.

Alan walked to the bed and started examining the contents of the box. "No, that guy will never leave Hicksville. I just need his help for awhile, that's all. I'm going to play him like a fish, then when it's all over, leave him flopping on the shore." They both laughed at that.

"Well I'm going to get some sleep." Chet yawned then walked to the bed next to Alan's. "Don't stay up too late. You need some rest, too."

"Yeah, I won't be too long," Alan replied. He then turned the overhead light off and sat on his bed in the dark examining the books with the help of a reading light.

"Peterson!" Jim shook the night dispatcher behind the counter.

"Oh, sorry, Sheriff. I must've dosed off. It's been a long day. I've been answering the phone and putting out calls constantly since I've come in." He rubbed his eyes. "Things just started quieting down about an hour ago—I'm exhausted!"

"We all are," Jim said sympathetically. "Listen, I'll be here the rest of the night. Why don't you go home and get a few hours of sleep and a good meal. Just be back here at first light."

"Thanks, Sheriff, I'll do that." Peterson got to his feet and stumbled to the hallway and towards the door. "Oh, a fax came in for you earlier." He gestured towards the machine.

"Thanks." Jim went to the machine and grabbed the printout. It was from Joe, reminding him to send her the reports she wanted. Something else, too…

The footprints behind the barn belong to Agent Bradley and Chet Green. Just thought you'd like to know. —Joe.

That was interesting. An eyebrow went up at that. Before pondering it further, he decided to send the reports he promised. He put the documents in the machine and hit the scan button. Then, going to Joe's computer, he dragged the document down to the icon labeled "Joe's e-mail", and it was gone. *That Joe,* he smiled to himself. *She really is a time saver.*

Jim grabbed a handful of donuts from the plate next to the coffee pot as he filled his cup. He then walked into the conference room and sat down. Taking a bite from a donut, he cringed. It was dry and stale.

Don't they ever throw these things away? he thought, as he took a long drink from his cup to wash it down. He scattered the pictures out on the table, then picked one up and looked at it closely. "There's something else here, I *know* it. But what is it?" he said out loud.

Jim looked up at the sequential photos on the board and the list of things they knew. To his surprise, he saw they had been changed. It had to be Joe, he knew. She was so clever and he thanked his lucky stars for her help. He considered the items on the list and was *sure* he had Buck's killer, but it was all circumstantial evidence.

Bradley arrived early enough. He came down the hill into the barn. He was in position to shoot Buck, his skill with a gun spoke for itself. These were all cards Jim held in his hand, but he needed one more to win the pot. He needed one of the bullets, or an eyewitness statement fingering Bradley—but he wasn't likely to get that.

On the other side of the card table was Agent Bradley and he had cards of his own… he *had* to. Either that, or he was still trying to fill his hand as Jim was. Something had tipped Bradley off to come down here, and Jim was dying to know what it was. But that didn't matter now, Bradley was here and nothing could change that.

What cards was he holding? He couldn't be bluffing, waiting for Jim to give up and throw in… could he? If so, he was one cool customer. Jim wondered how many draws it would take before one of them won—or lost. Not many, he knew.

Now that he was sure of it, he wanted to confront Bradley with what he knew, but he fought the urge. No, he thought to himself. Keep your cards close and your poker face on.

This game is going to go on for a while longer. Jim didn't know that the stakes were going to get higher as well. Spreading the photos out over the desk, he stared questioningly at them, sipping his coffee as he did so.

Chet wasn't the only one staying up late and using his computer to get some work done. Joe sat on the porch at Buck's house. An extra long phone line stretched from the kitchen to the laptop in front of her. They'd finished looking for the bullet a couple hours ago and found nothing. It was too dark to find anything outside and everyone was too tired to know what they had found even if it was in their hands. Then, after placing one guard at the entrance to the road, she told the others to get some sleep. She would take the first watch on the porch.

She had spent the entire day going over every piece of evidence brought to her by the other deputies, and concluded that this case *reeked* with inconsistencies. This house contained Buck's entire life, and she'd gone over everything! If she'd wanted to learn about who Buck was, she felt she had a pretty good idea now.

Something was seriously wrong. Why didn't anyone else see it? she wondered. Except for the drugs, there was nothing else in this house that would point to Buck as a criminal. Sure, he was a little different and slightly eccentric, but everything here said that Buck was pretty much like any other single man in the golden years of his life.

From the information she had in front of her, she put together a profile on Buck. It was quick and crude, not the in-depth professional report that she'd normally do, but she felt it was accurate. When she had more time, she would do a better job for her files.

Buck didn't match the description of the man Agent Bradley had painted him to be. She'd done an in-depth evaluation of Ted Katzinski, the Unabomber, a couple of years ago and tried to compare his profile to that of Buck's. Buck wasn't the loner, antisocial hermit living deep in the woods with a deep seeded resentment for society that Bradley believed him to be. He was quite the opposite actually.

Sure, Buck would spend weeks, even months, by himself, but he loved people. Whenever he could, he'd be down in town seeing everyone and telling tales of valor from behind a fishing pole or the sights of his rifle. He knew and liked everyone, and everyone knew and liked him.

Despite this, she had cautioned herself earlier on jumping to conclusions. After all, the Unabomber was found in a small town where the locals believed him to be just an eccentric man who kept to himself and wouldn't hurt a fly. Why was it so hard to believe that something like that couldn't happen here?

Still, it angered her the way no one had defended him. Buck had been a caring, valued member of the community for as long as she could remember. Had everyone forgotten that as they rushed to sell their story to the tabloids? She hadn't, and she knew Jim hadn't either.

The only problem was that Jim had been late to the party, but he was catching up fast. She wondered if he could pull in the reins quick enough to stop this runaway investigation before it sent this county over the cliff. She was confident that he could, but only with her assistance to help him.

"I won't let you down, Jim," she vowed. "If you'd only confide in me, we could put this case back on track together!" But she knew that it was just not his way to do so. She would have to work the case from her angle, and hopefully, they'd meet somewhere in the middle to solve it.

She'd spent the entire day watching Agent Bradley do his investigation. He was somewhat unconventional and hurried, but everyone including her got caught up in it. This morning, Bradley somehow seemed bigger than life. Especially after Tom explained to everyone what a super-cop he was.

Nobody questioned it when he immediately took charge. He gave orders in such a confident commanding fashion that she could tell he was a natural leader. It wasn't until the news report that morning about D. B. Cooper that she started to question the direction and speed of the investigation. When she suggested they slow down, she got a stern scolding from Bradley in front of the other deputies.

"Time is not a luxury I have, Deputy," Bradley had said, disapprovingly. "The drug dealers aren't slowing down, so we can't either. If you can't keep up with the pace, maybe you should find another line of work."

He had made her feel like she was ten years old. It made her mad that he'd treated her like that, but most of all she was mad at herself for taking it. She remembered wishing that Jim would show up and stop the craziness. She was again angry with herself for thinking that, too.

She didn't need Jim to defend her. Why did she back down to his condescending words? She wouldn't have backed down to anyone else and wasn't going to let Bradley push her around again!

After seeing the autopsy report and the little demonstration at the firing range this evening, she knew that she had to find out as much information as possible on Agent Bradley. She called the Regional office of the DEA in Seattle to ask about him. Other than verifying that he worked for the Agency, they wouldn't tell her anything more.

What did she expect? Of course they wouldn't give information about one of their agents to just anyone claiming to be a law enforcement agent over the phone. Especially anything negative. No matter how bad an agent he may be, all departments have a way of protecting their own.

But then Bradley wasn't a *bad* investigator. In fact, he was quite smart, she decided. Watching him all day and listening to his Cooper story, she naturally jumped to the conclusion that Bradley didn't know what he was doing when in fact it was the exact opposite. He knew *exactly* what he was doing.

It was Conley's comments that finally led her to it. Bradley didn't *miss* a thing. He intentionally steered the investigation in one direction with one hand while he used slight-of-hand to cover his tracks with the other. Very clever.

Since she couldn't find anything on Bradley, she decided to check up on Chet Green. To her surprise, that gave her all the information she needed to know. A quick phone call to the Seattle Press Core got her Green's website and every article he'd ever written.

Seeing that almost everything he'd done related somehow to Bradley made her even more suspicious. She read every article and watched every video. Many people believed that too much personal information about someone was available on the net. For a reporter, this proved to be an occupational hazard.

Everything was here. She had more than enough information to complete a profile on Chet Green. More importantly, since almost everything written was about Bradley, she had everything she needed to do one on him as well.

Chet was weak. He was the follower, the tag along. In every interview, something in his eyes and voice told her that he was unsure of himself. It wasn't until Bradley spoke that Chet gained confidence. Bradley was Chet's backbone. Chet was the weak link. She filed that away in her head. Sooner or later, she may have to exploit that little piece of information.

Special Agent Alan Bradley, on the other hand, was a different story. He was strong, confident, and smart. He was used to having his way and getting what he wanted. He surrounded himself with "yes" men, dated bimbos, and used people like tools. He loved fast cars, high society, and the limelight.

In the videos, Bradley was a natural actor. He used his shiny badge and huge gun as glittery props. Bradley effectively spewed an endless stream of bull while hiding behind lying eyes and a cheesy smile. Few people could do it better, she knew. She was very impressed and was not going to underestimate him.

The articles and videos told her something else, too. They weren't about crime or drugs. Bradley had a hidden agenda. Everything was too well played out. It had too much Hollywood and was too well rehearsed. These weren't news stories, but instead were the infomercials of a propaganda machine. They were advertisements. For whatever reason, Bradley was trying to sell himself to the general public.

"What's wrong, Bradley? Didn't you get enough attention in your childhood?" she asked herself coolly. "Well, you've got my attention now, and I'm not letting go until I find out the truth about what happened here today."

Bradley was going to be a tough nut to crack. He was very guarded, and wasn't going to let much slip. But from what she'd seen in these videos and witnessed today, she knew that he was arrogant and overconfident. She had dealt with his type before.

Also, there was a price to pay for putting yourself in the limelight. He was on stage for all to see. If Bradley had a chink in his armor, she was determined to find it.

At first light, she'd be back out searching for that bullet. She decided to keep what she knew to herself, for now. There's no reason to alert Bradley of her suspicions. Like her father coaching a ball game, she'd sit quietly, while watching and thinking. When the right time came to make a move, she'd be ready.

"You're going to make an interesting case study, Agent Bradley," she said with a smile. "That is, just as soon as I put you behind bars."

Alan laid on the bed examining the logbooks and flight plans. He closed the one he was looking at and tossed it on the floor next to the others he'd discarded earlier. Reaching into the box, he pulled out another logbook. Rubbing his eyes, he opened the cover.

As he paged through it slowly something caught his attention. Alan sat up and flipped some more pages. *There it was again,* he thought to himself, curiously. *What the heck was he doing all the way out there?* Alan kept paging through the log. *I can't believe it! He does this every few months or so, why didn't anyone catch on?* Alan got up, walked to the phone, and dialed a number.

"Drug Enforcement Agency, Special Agent Parker speaking. How can I help you?" said the voice on the other side.

"Parker, this is Bradley. I need you to run a name for me."

"Shoot."

Alan opened the cover of the logbook. "Get me everything you can find on a Richard Schaffer. He's a pilot for the Washington State Forest Service. His pilot's license number is 555-WIG."

"Got it. This may take a while."

"As soon as you get it, fax it straight down." Alan gave him Chet's fax number then hung up the phone. After yawning, he walked to the bed, took off his clothes, and got in. A few minutes later, he was fast asleep.

"Alan." Chet shook his friend. "Alan!"

Alan slowly turned and stretched. "What time is it?"

"6:30 a.m.," came the reply.

Alan rubbed his eyes and saw Chet looking in the mirror tying his tie. "That tie is awfully bright," he commented as he stumbled out of bed.

"It's cloudy outside. I don't want to look too bland on TV," Chet replied.

On his way to the bathroom, Alan pulled the curtain away from the window and looked out. "They're low and thin. They'll burn off before noon."

"Do you think so?"

Alan looked again and nodded his head. "I'm sure of it. This isn't Seattle, you know."

"Thanks for reminding me," Chet said sarcastically as he watched Alan walk into the bathroom and turn on the shower.

Removing the tie, Chet discarded it, then grabbed another from his bag. After putting it on, he walked to the front door. "I'm going to the diner across the street. Do you want anything?"

"Yeah, bring me a tall almond latte with whip," Alan replied as he examined his face in the bathroom mirror. "Better make that a double."

Chet opened the door and walked out.

After showering, Alan walked out of the bathroom. *That feels a lot better,* he thought to himself. Alan heard some commotion outside- a car honking and people yelling. Looking out the window, he saw Chet with his arms full yelling at a car that was slowly pulling away. Alan opened the door for him as he approached. "What was that all about?"

"The traffic is real thick. I waited on the curb for five minutes, but none of those idiots would let me cross. So when I saw an opening, I made a run for it. A few of those jerks got mad because they had to put on their brakes a little," Chet replied in an obviously irritated tone.

"Take it easy, Chet," Alan joked. "All these people have gone out of their way to help us out. You should be a little nicer to them."

"Yeah? Well all I wanted was a decent meal and an espresso, but the diner is packed! It's an hour wait, so this is all I could get." Chet set two large cups and a plate on the table. Pulling the foil off the plate, he touched one of the pastries. "Damn! I had them heated, but now they're ice cold. Here, this one is yours." He handed a tall paper cup to Alan.

"What's this?" Alan asked.

"Coffee. Black. Here's some fake sugar and creamer too." He pulled a handful of small envelopes out of his pocket and tossed them on the table.

"No latte?" Alan asked, with a sour look on his face.

"This isn't Seattle, you know," Chet joked.

"I know," Alan rolled his eyes, then took a drink. "Yuck! This sucks."

"There's nothing wrong with regular coffee. You'll live," Chet remarked.

"Yeah, but it's so unsophisticated."

At that moment the fax machine came alive. An eerie green light glowed inside it as it hummed and beeped. Alan walked over and picked up each page as it was spit out, then the phone rang and Alan picked it up. "Hello...yes, Peterson, I got it. Did the finger prints match?...No go, eh. All right then...thanks," he said, then hung up.

"What's that?" Chet asked.

"It's some information on one Richard Schaffer, pilot for the Forest Service. This guy is supposed to be fighting forest fires, but it appears that he may be doing a little moonlighting on the side." Alan examined the papers.

"What do you mean?" Chet asked.

"Several times a week, Schaffer makes practice dumps in the mountains. At least once every couple of months or so, he flies out over the ocean for awhile before he makes his runs."

"So what? I don't get it."

"Don't you see?" Alan said. "Schaffer flies out there and meets up with an Asian fishing trawler or freighter before it enters U.S. waters and has to go through customs. He then flies into the mountains, lands on Mineral Lake, and delivers the shipment to Henderson for processing."

"It's so simple, it's scary," Chet replied with amazement. "What does the report say?"

"Let's see here." Alan paged through it. "He learned to fly in the military and spent time in Vietnam. He doesn't have an address, just a post office box here in Morton."

"Just like Henderson!" Chet exclaimed. "I wonder if they met in Vietnam."

"It says here, Schaffer moved to Morton in 1970. That's the same year Henderson moved here! There are too many coincidences for it to be wrong." Alan continued turning pages. "Bingo! Look at this! It's a rap sheet. Schaffer was arrested for flying drugs into the U.S. from Mexico."

"Looks like you hit it right on the head, Ol' Buddy!" Chet exclaimed. "Do you think he was the man out there yesterday morning?"

"No, Peterson ran his prints. They don't match so it couldn't be him."

"So, what's the plan?"

"I'm going to the Sheriff's station to get some help finding this guy. If he hasn't already flown the coop, I'm going to grill him until he breaks." Alan pounded a determined fist onto his open palm. "I need you to get your TV crew together and keep your phone handy. When this guy spills his guts, I'll be moving fast, so you'll have to be ready."

"You can count on it!"

"Great! Lets get moving." Alan smiled, then they went to work.

Knocking? What's that knocking? Jim pulled himself slowly into consciousness.

"Sheriff, is everything all right?" a voice called from the doorway. Jim lifted his head from his desk and rubbed his eyes. As his eyes came into focus, he saw Deputy Peterson standing at the conference room door knocking on the jam.

"Yeah, everything's fine, Peterson." Jim grabbed the half-full coffee cup and took a drink. *Yuck! Cold coffee is the worst!* he thought.

"I have a message here from Rissley. She's been calling you on the radio all morning and you haven't answered. She said you wanted to get an early start," Deputy Peterson reported.

Jim hadn't heard it. He'd been too tired and slept through any radio calls. He was on his second day with little sleep, and that wasn't working in his favor. Finally, he realized how bright it was outside. "Damn! What time is it?" He stood up with his cup and walked out of the room towards the pot.

"It's just past eight," Peterson replied.

"Where the heck's Milhouse? He was supposed to be here at six!" Jim said angrily as he filled his cup with coffee.

At that instant, the front door swung open and Milhouse rushed in. "Sorry, Sheriff. I over slept and traffic sucks!"

"Get the metal detectors out of the storage room then come back in here," Jim ordered.

Milhouse quickly rushed towards the basement. Jim grabbed his cup and took a drink as he walked to the men's room. After washing his face, he pulled some paper towels from the dispenser and wiped himself off. He then looked into the mirror and examined himself closely.

You've looked better, he told himself as he noticed the dark circles under his sunken eyes. The stubble on his face felt like sand paper. He could feel the acidic coffee burning in his empty stomach, but knew he couldn't bring himself to eat another stale doughnut. He was glad Joe had packed him some fruit.

Milhouse was waiting for him as he walked out of the bathroom. "Are you all right, Sheriff?" Milhouse asked.

"I'll be all right, once I get moving," he replied. I must've dosed off while studying the photos."

Milhouse looked at him oddly. "If you don't mind me asking, Sheriff, isn't that a waste of time? I mean, we've got the fingerprints of the shooter. It should only take a few days at the most to match them, and then we'll have our killer."

"Fingerprints?" Jim said as he leaned his tired body against the counter. "Oh yeah, that's right. Unfortunately, the State isn't very efficient. It could take weeks, even months, for them to get us an answer." That was something Jim had been counting on.

"Didn't Agent Bradley tell you?" Milhouse asked, curiously.

"Tell me what?"

"Well, when he was here last night, I gave him a copy of the prints. He said the Federal computer banks could match them in a day or so."

Jim's face turned white at the news.

"Sheriff, are you all right?"

"Yeah, it must be the lack of sleep," Jim replied, trying to cover his shock. "Is there anything *else* you forgot to tell me?" he said with a glare.

Milhouse immediately realized that Agent Bradley didn't tell Harper about the help Milhouse had given him. He saw the look on Jim's face and decided to keep his mouth shut. "Ah... no, that's it. That was all right, wasn't it? I mean, we're all on the same side, right?"

"Yeah, it was. But from now on, run it past me first. Now get those things out to Buck's and help Rissley. I'll be right behind you in a few minutes, and I'll brief you on the progress we made yesterday when I get out there. I think we may be able to find one of the bullets that killed Buck."

"Really," Milhouse said surprisingly. "That's great! If the killer hasn't gotten rid of the gun, then it's an airtight case."

"That's right, now get moving."

Milhouse turned and rushed down the hall.

Damn! Those fingerprints! he thought with disgust as he walked into the conference room. The clock was ticking faster than he'd expected. *I had better get moving,* he decided. Otherwise, things could fall apart around him and he wouldn't be able to stop it.

Jim started to pile the photos in a stack, then stopped and looked at one of them closely. *I can't believe I didn't see this earlier!* he thought to himself. Jim looked through the pile and pulled out another picture of Buck.

There's no way I could've killed Buck! Buck was lying on top of one of my tire tracks. If I had been there, I would have had to run him over to drive away. This proves that I had to have left before Buck was killed. Jim allowed himself a quick sigh of relief. Stuffing everything into the envelope, he hurried out of the room.

There was just one more thing he needed to do. Running out the back door, he hurried to the range and to the target that Bradley shot at. With his knife, he dug one of the bullets out and examined it. The soft wood hadn't damaged it at all. It was in perfect shape. He put it in his pocket, then headed for the parking lot, when the radio on his belt squawked. "Sheriff Harper, come in Sheriff."

"Go ahead, Peterson," Jim answered.

Carrying the metal detectors, Milhouse walked towards his Blazer which was parked on the side of the building next to Deputy Kruger's. He opened up the back and put them inside.

"Milhouse!" Kruger yelled from the street. Milhouse stopped and saw him dart through traffic, then hurried over to him with a big smile on his face carrying a large paper bag. "Check this out!" Kruger reached into the bag and pulled out a T-shirt. On the front was an artist's rendition of two men in a boat fishing. "Look, it says, *I saw Elvis and D.B. Cooper fishing at Mineral Lake, Washington.*"

"That's great!" Milhouse's eyes lit up. "Where did you get it?"

"They're selling these, and other really cool stuff, at the gas station. Two college students got the idea yesterday when the story broke and immediately got to work on it. They're selling like hot cakes." Kruger pulled another shirt out. "Here, look at this one."

It was a picture of D.B. Cooper wearing sunglasses and hiding behind a tree. At the bottom it said. "Cooper lives! Catch him if you can!"

"Man! I've got to get me some of these!" Milhouse exclaimed.

"Milhouse!" came Harper's voice from behind the station. "Hold on, I want to talk to you." Both men turned to see Jim hurrying towards them.

"Quick, put those things away," Milhouse ordered. Kruger stuffed the shirts back into the bag as they watched Harper run towards them.

298

Wayne Ellis was a fifteen-year veteran on the big rigs. He'd driven his eighteen-wheeler in every situation and weather condition imaginable. Time on the road had taught him to prepare for the unexpected, for it was the unexpected that was dangerous. Ellis was not expecting what would happen next.

He had just driven all night to bring a load of produce up from California for the local stores and was way behind schedule. The traffic he ran into once he crossed the Lewis County line reminded him of LA—only on a one-lane road. When possible, he'd put the pedal down to make up time. This was one of those times.

For now, the road ahead was open and down the way, a green light. He pushed the pedal down further, increasing speed. He wanted to make that light. *Just one more stop then he could head home to his wife and a warm bed,* he thought as he yawned and rubbed his tired eyes. He didn't see the fifth wheel truck and trailer drive into the intersection until it was too late.

Scott Mathews, an insurance salesman from Portland, had just pulled out of the gas station. As he approached the intersection, his mind was on the steak and eggs breakfast he was going to order at the diner down the street. His two boys were arguing in the back seat of his one-ton king cab. Mathews adjusted his rear view mirror to see them more clearly. They were fighting over which D.B. Cooper T-shirt each was going to wear, and he wished he'd gotten them the same one. With his trailer, he was going to have to swing wide to make the turn, he thought as he looked back to his boys to tell them to stop fighting. He didn't see the red light.

"Mrs. Duncan at the Super Mart called," Jim told Milhouse when he finally reached him. "It seems her parking lot is full of people setting up their campers and trailers. I want you to go clear them out of there."

"Where do we send them?" Milhouse asked. "All the campgrounds are spilling over as it is."

"I don't know, tell them to go home. Tell them there's nothing to see around here. I don't care, just get rid of them," Jim ordered.

299

Milhouse started to complain. "Why can't Kruger do it? Rissleys expecting these metal detectors and I need to get back into this investigation."

"I'm sorry, but you're better at this sort of thing than he is. If you get right on it, you can be out there by—

Hoooooooonnnnnnnnnnkkk!

The horn of the big eighteen wheeler startled everyone. An instant later, the fifth wheel trailer exploded. The three men turned to see trailer parts flying in all directions. The Mack truck, coming through the fifth wheel trailer, had swerved to make a last ditch effort at avoiding it, but it was too late. The momentum of the impact pulled the pickup backwards then flipped it on its side like a toy. The semi ran over the curb and into a streetlight, snapping it off and sending it spinning into the air.

"Look out!" Jim yelled as each man darted for safety.

The eighteen-wheeler bucked and spasmed into the station's lot as its driver lay on the brakes. Ellis maneuvered it skillfully as his tires barked across the pavement. As Jim ran away, he watched over his shoulders as the big rig's load shifted suddenly to one side.

The entire rig rolled onto its right set of tires then hung in the air for what seemed like an eternity, before rolling back the other way. Jim could hear the angry scream of strained metal as the rig's frame twisted. It instantly crashed down on all wheels again, bouncing and giggling like a giant blob of jello as it came to a final stop, just missing Jim's Blazer.

Harper and his deputies quickly came out of hiding. "See if anyone's hurt!" Jim commanded. He ran to the cab of the Mack truck as the others ran into the intersection. Several smaller cars had run into the ditch to avoid collisions. Jim climbed up on the cab and pulled open the door. "Are you hurt?"

Jim examined the driver carefully. Ellis's face was pale and he was shaking. His white knuckled hands still gripped the wheel tightly. Through shallow panicked breaths, he managed to say. "He came out of nowhere. I didn't see him."

"It's all right," Jim assured him. "Everything's going to be fine." Jim slowly helped the man pull his hands off the wheel then got him out of the truck.

In all the confusion, Alan managed to pull out of traffic and stopped on the side of the road just down the street of the station. Traffic was blocked, so he decided to run the last hundred yards. Alan was able to get to the side of the station without being noticed and peered around it. He saw Jim standing with the truck driver, and decided he really didn't want another confrontation, especially with the situation as stressed as it was. He decided to stand back, stay out of sight, and watch for awhile.

Kruger ran up to Jim. "Nobody appears to be hurt. They're all pretty shook up though."

"Good. Get on the radio. I want an ambulance just in case and all the tow trucks you can get a hold of. Now go!" Jim watched Kruger run towards his Blazer, then he turned his attention to the intersection in front of the station. Cars from all directions were stopped for several hundred yards back. Passengers from the vehicles were getting out to see what had happened. "Damn! This thing has gotten *way* out of control!"

Just then, Milhouse ran up to him. "Everyone on this side is alright. Now what do we do?"

Jim looked around. The accident victims didn't appear hurt, but, as Sheriff, he felt responsible for taking care of them anyway. "My Blazer is blocked in, so I'll stay here and get this mess straightened out. Give the equipment to Kruger, then get over to the Super Mart."

"But—" Milhouse tried to protest, but Jim was in no mood to argue.

"Just do it!" Jim barked angrily, then he turned and ran towards the intersection.

Milhouse walked towards his Blazer with is head down, depressed at being reduced to crowd control duty. Kruger had heard the order and was already transferring the gear to his Blazer. Milhouse watched as Kruger jumped into the driver's seat.

"I'll see you when you get out there!" Kruger waved and pulled away.

Milhouse's heart sank further as he watched him leave.

Alan took that opportunity to emerge from hiding. "Hello, Milhouse."

Tom turned to see Agent Bradley and his mood turned even more sour. "What do you want?"

"I was hoping you could give me a hand this morning."

"Forget it!" Milhouse snapped as he walked past Alan and got into his Blazer. "You lied to me! You said you'd clear everything with Harper. Do you realize how much trouble I can get into for that?"

"I couldn't tell him!" Alan tried to defend himself. "He would've said no, then where would we be? At a dead stop, that's where." Alan answered his own question as he pleaded with Milhouse. "I need you, Tom. Are you going to help me or not."

"I couldn't even if I wanted to. I've got to go clear some campers out of a parking lot." Milhouse hung his head, discouragingly.

"Tom, you can't allow Harper to shut down the only productive part of this investigation. If it wasn't for your help, we wouldn't be on the brink of busting this case wide open."

"What are you talking about?" Milhouse looked at him curiously.

"How well do you know Richard Schaffer?"

"About as well as anyone around here. He's kind of a loner. He keeps mostly to himself, but he seems to be a nice enough guy. Why?" Milhouse replied.

"Because he's the one hauling all the drugs in here."

Milhouse looked at Alan skeptically. "Schaffer? No way, he doesn't look like the type that would get messed up with that stuff."

"Did you know Schaffer did hard time in prison for smuggling drugs across the boarder from Mexico?" Alan pulled out the rap sheet and handed it over. "Look for yourself."

As Milhouse paged through the report, his mouth dropped open. "I can't believe it! I would *never* have suspected him for a smuggler!"

"That's how they got away with it so long. They're the people you'd least expect," Alan informed him. "Heck, I once busted a group of grandmothers selling dope during church bingo night. Now, are you going to help me?"

Milhouse started to get excited. "Yeah, what do you want me to do?"

"Take this information to your father-in-law and get a warrant. Where does this Schaffer fellow live anyway?"

"He lives out at Morton Field. I think he stays in a back room of one of the hangers."

"Good, I'll meet you there," Alan said, then started to turn to walk away.

"Wait!" Milhouse stopped him. "I'm going to have to clear this with the Sheriff first."

"No! Can't you see what he's doing? He wants the glory for himself. If you take this to him, I bet he makes *you* direct traffic while he solves the case." Alan argued.

"It's my *duty* to report this to the Sheriff," Milhouse said, shaking his head.

"Fine!" Alan snatched the report from Milhouse's hands. "I'll get the warrant myself. It'll take me longer because the Judge

302

doesn't know me, but I'll get it," Alan snapped, then took a few steps away before turning back to Milhouse. "I guess I was wrong about you, I thought you were ready to take the bull by the horns and control your career. You know you were so close to getting out of this town, and now you're throwing it away! And for what! So you can write tickets and direct traffic?" Alan pointed out at Harper. Jim was frantically directing traffic around the wreckage. "You'll be here until you rot!" Alan turned and started to stomp away.

Milhouse looked over to the intersection and watched as Jim waved his arms around directing the now heavy traffic. Yesterday, while helping Agent Bradley at Buck's house and getting the flight log books, he'd never felt more in control of his destiny. He wanted *desperately* to be a Special Agent like Bradley.

He took a look towards Alan and wasn't sure what to do. With every step Bradley took, Milhouse saw his chance of escaping this town fade. Tom looked again at Harper, imagining himself in that position in the future, and cringed. That wasn't what he wanted at all. As quickly as he could, Milhouse jumped out of the Blazer and sprinted towards Bradley. "Agent Bradley!" he yelled as he finally reached him. "I'll do it!"

"Good," Alan smirked. "I'll meet you at the airfield." Alan handed him the report, then turned and walked out of the parking lot.

19
Set Up

Morton Field. Saturday 11:30 AM.

Alan followed the signs along the gravel road until he came to the small airfield. The traffic had been *terrible* and it slowed him down quite a bit. He hoped that it was also slowing down the bad guys.

The airfield was a single runway cut out of the middle of a fifty-acre hay field. Tall pines surrounded the field on all sides with a gravel road leading up to it that continued on into the mountains. On one side of the runway were three hangers. Each was identical except for a small room made of windows on the top of one of them, acting as the field's tower. Alan lifted the car phone and dialed a number.

"Hello, Chet Green here," the voice from the other side said.

"Chet, get out to Morton field. I'm here now, something should be happening soon."

"We're on our way," came the reply.

Alan hung up the phone.

Alan decided to start his inquiry at the tower and pulled up to it. He got out of his car and walked around the building to the tarmac. There were a dozen or so small planes, sitting in front of the three hangers, arranged in neat rows. The big doors of the first hanger were open. Inside Alan saw a man, in greasy coveralls and baseball cap with a rag sticking out of his back pocket, next to a single engine Piper Cub. Alan approached him.

Twenty-five year old engine mechanic Billy Martin was bent over half buried in the engine compartment of the Piper Cub sitting inside the hanger. Moments ago he'd shut off the engine and detached the last of the diagnostic equipment that encircled him. He'd finished the overhaul to within manufacturer's specifications more than an hour ago, but now he had to go the extra mile. Before this plane could go back to its owner, it had to pass the scrutiny of Rick Schaffer.

For almost ten years now, Billy had been coming out to Morton field to watch and learn about planes. While his friends tinkered with cars, he spent every hour he could around planes and eventually learned to fly. He also became intensely interested in aircraft maintenance.

He had met Rick when he took an after school job in Morton field's maintenance department. Mostly just changing aircraft fluids, charging batteries and making sure that the tire pressure was correct, but it was a start. Rick was the only mechanic at the field, and he was too busy with overhauls and tune-ups to worry about the light work.

Like everyone else, Billy thought Rick was pretty strange and at first, he kept his distance from him whenever possible. Then after talking to all the owners of the planes, Billy found out that no matter how crazy people thought he was, they wouldn't trust their aircraft to anyone *but* Rick. Billy decided then that he wanted to learn what Rick did to deserve such a good reputation.

Billy made it a point of paying attention to Rick and asking him questions. Rick was reserved at first, but found that he enjoyed teaching what he knew. After a few months they became good friends and realized that they were essentially kindred spirits. They shared the same passion– they both lived and breathed airplanes.

Billy quickly learned that no matter what the engine type, piston or gas-turbine, jet or propeller driven, Rick was a master. He had almost a mystic sense about what was going on inside an engine. Every time a plane came in for work, Billy watched as Rick walked around it as it ran.

Rick put his hands all over the engine feeling for temperature differences. He'd take a quarter from his pocket and touch it to different places on the engine feeling for vibration. Taking a screwdriver, he'd placed the end on the piston valves and the handle to his ear in order to listen to the valve opening and closing in its housing. He'd smell the exhaust for proper burn and even taste the used engine oil to detect abnormal wear of the metal.

Billy had heard that the Renaissance painters where known for being slightly eccentric, but people ignored their strange ways because of the quality of work they produced. Was it out of the question to think that in his own way, Rick was an artist as well? Billy chose to ignore the way Rick talked to himself or the times when he would start screaming for no apparent reason. These episodes didn't happen very often and Rick was never violent, so Billy decided it was none of his business.

A while back, in order to satisfy some new Federal regulation, the insurance company required the field to purchase a large number of high tech diagnostic analyzers. Rick refused to participate in the training program.

"You can't teach an old dog new tricks," he said as he thumbed his nose at the technology.

Billy, on the other hand, jumped at the chance to learn how to use the new tools. After all, there *had* to be better ways to test for engine wear than to dab some oil on your tongue. He tried without success to change Rick's mind.

"A new era in engine maintenance is knocking on the door," Billy argued. "If you don't learn the new technology, it'll leave you behind."

His warning fell on deaf ears, so Billy went to the training course alone. In the class the engineers and scientists told him that the human senses were no match for the accuracy of the new computerized electronic sensors. He learned everything he could about thermography, vibration sensors, emissions detectors, and oil analysis. He studied and practiced intently until he passed with flying colors.

A couple of months later he returned to Morton Field with a new level of excitement and energy. Eager to show Rick what he'd learned, Billy immediately set up his precision equipment on the first plane that came in and proceeded to tune up the engine.

"All finished." Billy reported proudly.

"Are you sure?" Rick asked him skeptically.

With a questioning look, Billy watched Rick take his usual slow stroll around the plane. After his normal hands on routine, Rick grabbed a torque wrench from the box. "I found your problem."

Billy didn't realize he had one, but watched Rick do his magic.

"The torque on the heads is too tight." Rick replied as he made a few adjustments. "There, that should do it."

Billy hooked his analyzers back up and sure enough they showed that the engine ran smoother than it had just a few minutes ago. He couldn't help but ask Rick how he'd done it.

"They will never come up with a machine to replace experience." Rick replied with a chuckle.

From that day forward, Billy wanted to be as good as Rick when it came to hands on diagnosis. When a plane came in, Billy would first use the techniques taught to him by Rick. Then he'd hook up the electronic analyzers in order to fine tune his work. After that, Rick would check his work and make additional adjustments.

Billy had gotten better, but he knew he still had a lot to learn. He was now to the point where he almost matched the analyzers. However, Rick constantly out performed every computerized machine they had.

Billy was not only surprised by the tap on the shoulder, but worried as well. He knew that Rick was warned by the manager of Morton Field that he had to learn to use the analyzers, otherwise the field could lose its insurance.

Did someone finally complain? Billy wondered. *Would Rick get fired? Or worse... could he be arrested?* Billy didn't know. Why else would they send a Federal Agent all the way out here?

"I'm looking for Richard Schaffer." Alan repeated what he'd said just a moment earlier.

Just then, Billy heard the familiar drone of a Forest Service's engine purring overhead. "That should be him, now." he said, as he looked at the ceiling of the hanger.

Alan followed Billy to the front of the hanger, but stopped at the large doors as Billy continued on. As always, Billy liked to watch Rick come in for a landing. As the white plane with the red stripe banked in and made its approach, his eyes followed its path.

It was a nice day, so Billy knew Rick wouldn't have a problem finding the mark. A perfectionist, Rick had put a marker on the runway to aim for during landings. Even during the worst of weather, Billy had never seen Rick miss the mark by more than a foot.

This time was no different. As the slight whiff of smoke came up from the tires hitting the runway, Billy could see they'd hit exactly dead center of the mark.

He smiled and shook his head in awe. *Was there anything about planes and flying that this man didn't know?* he wondered.

Rick turned the plane at the end of the runway, taxied up in front of the hanger, and shut off the engines. Billy was ready with a pair of wheel chocks, which he put in place before Rick could step out of the cockpit.

"Great landing!" Billy said with a smile.

"Thanks," came the reply. "Fill her back up for me. The port engine is a little sluggish. I want to get her back up in the air and find out what's causing it."

"All right," Billy said. "I've finished with the Cub. Maybe when you're done you can have a look at it?"

"Sure thing."

Billy was about to run off to get the fuel truck when he remembered Alan. "Oh, I almost forgot," he said as he looked towards the hanger. "There's a Federal Agent here to see you."

"For me?" Rick looked at him questioningly.

Billy shrugged his shoulders, then ran off in the direction of the fuel truck.

Rick curiously looked at the suit standing in front of the hanger doors, and hoped it wouldn't take long. He'd been in the air for four hours and had to pee like a racehorse!

At that instant, Milhouse came around the side of the hanger and walked up to Alan. "Did you get it?" Alan asked.

"Right here." Milhouse waved a piece of paper. "How do you want to proceed?"

Alan thought about that for a moment. He really wasn't expecting to find anything. After examining the logs, Alan saw that Schaffer's pattern for flying out to sea, happened about once every two to three months.

Schaffer had just returned from such a trip a few days ago, and wouldn't make another for quite awhile. Alan was holding to his original deduction. Schaffer had picked up the opium at sea, then delivered it to Henderson's house where it was processed into heroin.

Phantom then picked up the heroin, ready for the street, from Henderson's yesterday morning. By the time Alan had gotten there, Phantom and the heroin were probably already on their way to the city. *Who knows,* he thought, *They probably passed each other on the highway.*

If the opium hadn't already been processed and delivered to Seattle by now, he was *sure* Phantom would've dumped it. Phantom was too smooth of an operator to hold onto anything incriminating while an investigation was going on so close to him. Alan knew it was a long shot, but he hoped that Schaffer would be Phantom.

However, watching Schaffer walk towards them, he could easily see that he didn't match the description of a large Sicilian.

Alan regretted not coming down here the day he'd found the brick of opium. If he had, this investigation would already be over. He didn't intend on making that mistake again. He was going to push on as hard as he could to close this case.

He did, however, need to be cautious. He couldn't allow a dead end here to reflect poorly on him. That's why he needed Milhouse. If they didn't find what he was looking for, he could again point his finger at the Sheriff's department. Alan would direct Milhouse and when the time was right, he'd take over and get the information he needed. He turned back to Milhouse.

"You've been doing such a great job so far. I'll let you serve the warrant and conduct the search. I'll help if we find anything." Alan said with a smile.

Milhouse's face lit up. "All right! I'm ready!" He turned and looked towards Schaffer. He was still several yards away, but closing the distance quickly.

"Rick, I've got a warrant to search this plane and your property." Milhouse said in an official tone as he held up the paper.

"For what?" Rick took a step back, both surprised and shocked.

"Opium!" Alan barked. "Go ahead Deputy, conduct your search. I'll watch the prisoner for you."

"Prisoner?" Rick said with a start.

"That's right, Schaffer," Alan said as he showed his badge. "I'm Special Agent Alan Bradley and you're my prisoner." The two men stood in silence as Milhouse searched the plane. After several minutes Milhouse emerged from the door. "Nothing. It's clean."

With that, Rick was able to shake off the shock and his bladder reminded him that he had something to do. "Then if you two are through screwing around, I've got to take a leak." Rick turned and started to walk away.

"Not so fast, Schaffer," Alan barked. "The Deputy wants to search your room, too."

"Yeah, that's right. Show us your room." Milhouse spoke up with more authority.

"I guess if you want to waste your time, that's fine with me." Rick's bladder was too sore to argue. "This way." Rick walked into the hanger as Milhouse and Alan followed.

Milhouse's conscience had been bothering him all morning so he spoke to Alan softly. "I think I should call the Sheriff and fill him in on what's going on."

"Be patient. If we don't find anything, he doesn't have to know at all. There's no harm done, and you won't get in trouble," Alan assured him. "I'm letting you conduct the search. If he was here do you think he'd do the same? Of course not. Wait until we find something, then you'll be a hero. He can't get mad at you then."

Milhouse thought for a moment. "Yeah, I guess you're right."

The three men walked through the hanger and into the back hallway to Rick's room. Pulling the key from his pocket, Rick unlocked the door.

"That's far enough, Schaffer," Alan said. "Deputy, you should go in alone. That way Schaffer won't be able to destroy any evidence. We'll wait for you out here."

"Can't I at least *pee?*" Rick argued. "I've been in the air for *hours!*"

Alan shot Schaffer an annoyed glare and was about to refuse, but Milhouse spoke up first.

"Alright," Milhouse agreed. "But I'll have to search the john first." Milhouse stepped into Rick's room then into the bathroom before Alan could stop him. Alan thought it would be comical to watch a drug smuggler pee his pants. Rick hurried past him and into the bathroom.

"You'd better stay in there with him, to make sure he doesn't flush anything he's not supposed to." Alan recommended.

"Right," Milhouse agreed.

Rick stepped up to the toilet and unzipped his flight suit. Looking over at Milhouse, he saw a look on his face that Rick hadn't seen since his days as a drifter, traveling from town to town looking for work. It was a look of suspicion and mistrust. That look unnerved him so much he couldn't urinate.

After a long moment, Milhouse began to get impatient. "Well, go ahead—pee!"

"Do you mind not watching?" Rick was noticeably shaken and irritated.

Milhouse rolled his eyes then turned and stared at the door with his arms crossed. Rick was finally able to relax.

In the other room, Alan surveyed the layout. It was small, not much bigger than the walk in closet at his condo. A single bed was against the wall next to the window, a footlocker, dresser, mirror and a chair. That was it.

The walls were bare except for a couple of pictures of an airplane. Alan walked to the mirror on the dresser. Taped to the glass were some photos. Some were black and white. Old family pictures Alan figured, while others were more recent.

Wait a minute, Alan thought as he looked at one closely. It was a picture of two men. Both of which held huge fish in their hands and had smiles a mile long on their faces. One of them was Henderson, and the other was Schaffer. They looked a lot younger but it was them.

Yes! I knew there was a connection. Re-energized, Alan quickly searched the room, but found nothing. *Damn!* he thought to himself. He'd figured Schaffer would be too smart to have anything incriminating with him.

Then an evil grin appeared on Alan's face. It was time to go to plan B. Alan pulled a small package of opium from his pocket, and put it in the top drawer. There. All he needed was an edge. Just a little leverage to help him get Schaffer to talk, he decided. Alan heard the toilet flush in the next room. He moved quickly to the door and stepped out into the hallway just before the bathroom door opened.

"All right, Deputy," Alan said from the hallway. "Schaffer and I will wait here while you conduct your search." Rick stepped into the hall, and he and Alan watched as Milhouse moved through the room. Milhouse moved too slowly for Alan's patience. *Come on, hurry up, get to the dresser,* he thought to himself.

Milhouse searched the bed, footlocker, and closet then he finally moved to the dresser. Pulling out the drawer, Milhouse's eyes opened wide with excitement. He reached in and lifted the bag of opium, then looked at Alan. "It's identical to what Henderson had!" he exclaimed.

Alan grabbed Rick's arm and pulled him into the room. "It looks like you've got some explaining to do, Schaffer!" Alan said as he took the package and put it in front of Rick's face. "Where did you get this opium?"

Rick's jaw dropped open in surprise. "How did that get there?"

"That's what *you're* supposed to tell *us!*" Alan said loudly as he gripped Rick's arm tighter. "When I run this through the lab, do you know what they'll tell me? They'll say it's the same purity as the stuff we found at Henderson's. That means it came from the same shipment."

When Rick heard this, he was too astonished to speak.

"Henderson didn't get a chance to tell us where he got it. Someone killed him to keep him quiet. Was that you? Did you kill him?" Alan said accusingly. "You had better start talking or we'll throw the book at you!" Alan's grip tightened until Rick's arm started to hurt.

"Dead? Bucks *dead?*" Rick gasped as he looked from Alan to Milhouse in disbelief.

"Don't pretend you didn't know! It's been on every channel of the TV and in all the papers!" Alan yelled.

"I don't watch much TV, I *swear* I didn't know!" Rick said nervously.

"Don't try lying to me. You'd better start talking." Alan said as he shook the opium in front of Rick's face. "Do you know what this means? Murder one! You'll be behind bars for the rest of your life if you don't cooperate!"

Rick's face turned white, and he looked like he was about to puke.

"Rick, are you all right?" Milhouse asked as he grabbed Rick's other arm to support him. He didn't answer. His legs started to wobble like jello. Milhouse grabbed him so that he wouldn't fall. "Here sit down over here." He said as he guided Rick to the bed. Rick felt dizzy but after sitting down he started to feel a little better. "Do you want me to get you a glass of water?"

"He doesn't need water!" Alan shouted impatiently. "He's *faking!* He's just looking for a way to stall. It's not going to work, Schaffer! We're not leaving this room until I get the answers I need."

Milhouse started to feel uncomfortable. "Maybe I'd better call the Sheriff."

""No!" Alan barked. "Not until I've got a confession."

"But you said that if we found…" Milhouse tried to say, but was cut off.

"No!" Alan insisted.

Milhouse looked at Rick. His face was white and a bead of sweat appeared on his forehead as he continued to stare at the opium. "I think Rick may need a doctor," he said nervously.

"He'll be all right, Milhouse." Alan tried to say calmly as he took him by the arm and gently guided him to the door. "I've seen this dozens of times. Everything will be fine. I'll take full responsibility."

"I don't know," Milhouse replied. "I think we should call an ambulance, just to be on the safe side."

"Listen, why don't you wait outside and guard the door so that we're not disturbed. If he gets any worse, we'll get help," Alan said. Milhouse tried to say something, but Alan spoke first. "I'm afraid I'm going to have to insist." Alan eased Milhouse out of the room. "Now guard the door." Alan closed the door behind Milhouse.

Milhouse paced in the hall nervously and bit his lip. He had to call the Sheriff. *He'll know what to do,* he decided then walked out the door to the parking lot and over to his Blazer.

Jim maneuvered his Blazer around the vehicles on the two-lane highway. He'd finally cleared the accident outside the station an hour ago, and was now in route to Mineral Lake. He shook his head in disgust. Traffic was thick, and moved at a snails pace. Using the flashing lights on the roof, Jim passed the cars as they pulled over to get out of his way. He passed through Morton, and made the turn onto Highway 7 towards Buck's place.

Harper slumped over the wheel as he drove. He was exhausted. His tired eyelids hung heavy as he watched traffic. Cars past, people smiled. Some waved, but he felt nothing. He was a numb blob of emotionless flesh as he maneuvered the wheel unconsciously. He was on auto-pilot. One purpose compelled him forward. *Find that bullet.*

When the radio call first came in, it didn't phase him—he didn't react. It came in again, nagging at his detached consciousness. Jim finally reached for the microphone slowly.

"Milhouse to Sheriff Harper. Come in, Sheriff." The radio squawked.

Jim picked up the mike, "Go ahead."

"Sheriff, I think you'd better get over to Morton field right away. Over." Milhouse said nervously.

"What seems to be the problem? Over."

"Its Rick Schaffer. He doesn't look well, and Agent Bradley insists on questioning him alone. Over."

"What's he questioning him for?! Over." Jim said loudly into the mike.

"We found opium, Sheriff. Just like the stuff at Buck's. Over." Came the nervous reply.

"Damn!" Jim said then lifted up the mike. "Don't do anything else until I get there! I'm just a couple of minutes away!" he ordered. Turning on his siren, Jim spun a quick U-turn and headed south towards the field. "Get out of my way!" he said under his breath as he swerved in and out of traffic.

Alan looked at Rick from across the room. "Why don't you start by telling me where you were early yesterday morning," he said calmly.

"I was here, asleep in my bed. Why?" Rick said nervously.

"How did you know Henderson?"

"We go fishing together. About once a month." Came the reply.

"Why don't you tell me about the smuggling operation you two had going." Alan asked.

"What?" Rick asked questioningly. "Smuggling? What are you talking about?"

"Don't play me for a fool!" Alan said as he lifted the package of drugs in front of Rick's face. "I know about your trips out to sea. What do you meet up with out there? An Asian freighter or a fishing trawler?" He asked firmly.

"I don't know what you're talking about. I—" Rick tried to say, but was cut off.

"I would cooperate if I were you, Schaffer! One mans dead! You knew him, and you don't have an alibi for the time of the murder!"

"I was asleep!" Rick defended.

"Did anyone see you?"

"Well, no," Rick replied as he stared at the floor.

"There! You had the opportunity and a motive!"

"Mo-motive?" Rick asked as he tried to wipe the sweat from his now shaky palms.

"Drugs!" Alan said as he pointed to the opium. "You wanted to keep him quiet so you killed him!"

"N-n-no!" Rick stuttered as his breathing became erratic. "I liked Buck! I wouldn't hurt him!"

"That's not what a court of law will say! When they see this evidence and your past record, they'll throw you in jail until you rot!" Alan yelled.

"*Jail!*" Rick exclaimed. "I can't go to jail!" He moved nervously and started sweating profusely.

"Listen. I may be able to believe that you didn't kill Henderson, but I bet you know who could have," Alan said calmly.

"I don't know anything!" Rick defended.

Alan went to the mirror and pulled the picture of the two men from it. "Who are the people in your gang?" Alan asked as he lifted the picture in front of Rick. "Who took this picture of you and Henderson? Is he in the gang? How many are there?" He snapped off the questions, but Rick didn't hear him. His attention was immediately drawn inward.

From the deep recesses of his mind, an all too familiar sound started to emerge. The laughter started quietly, but slowly grew louder. Rick started to groan, and rock back and forth. "No! Stop it! Go away!" he said as he grabbed the sides of his head with his hands.

Alan saw how upset Rick was and tried to calm him down. "Listen, I can help you. I believe you weren't out there yesterday. You're the drop off man, just a small part of the operation. If you cooperate, I'll make sure that you don't spend much time behind bars." This seemed to calm Rick slightly.

"I can't go to jail! I just *can't!*" Rick pleaded as he wrapped his arms tightly around himself in an attempt to stop his body from shaking. Suddenly Alan heard a siren in the distance. It wasn't far away and it was closing fast.

Damn it, Milhouse! he thought angrily. Alan suddenly grew impatient. "Do you hear that sound, Schaffer?" Rick could hear the siren getting closer. "They're coming for you! I'll cut you a deal. Turn State's evidence and be a witness against the rest of the gang. I'm your only hope! Save yourself!"

Rick's eyes grew larger, and he started to cry as he looked at the window where the noise was coming from then back at Alan.

"What happens to the drugs once Henderson's done with them? Who is the pick up man? Where does he take it? Who took this picture? *Tell me!*" Alan yelled as he pounded on the dresser.

Rick started to hyperventilate, and couldn't speak as demon laughter filed his mind. Suddenly the siren stopped just outside the building and terror clouded Rick's thoughts. *"I can't go to jail!"* he yelled as he grabbed Alan's arm. "I'll say anything you want just don't take me to jail!" Rick buried his face in his hands and cried.

Alan quickly pulled a small tape recorder out of his pocket, turned it on and put it in front of Rick's face. "You and Henderson had a drug smuggling operation going. You picked up the shipments at sea, and delivered them to his house. Hurry! *Say it!*"

At that instant the door flew open and Jim rushed into the room. "You don't have to say anything, Rick!" he said as he pushed past Alan and squatted down in front of Rick. Putting both hands on his shoulders he assured him. "Calm down, everything's going to be all right."

Rick seemed to settle down a little at Jim's words and he lowered his hands from his face. "I can't go to jail, Sheriff." He said in a weary, defeated voice.

Jim looked at the scared, pale face with blood shot eyes staring back at him and he grew angry. "Don't worry, you won't. This has been a big mistake."

"*Mistake?*" Alan said loudly from behind Jim. "What do you think you're doing? I'm on the verge of breaking this case wide open, and you're screwing it up!"

Jim stood and turned around quickly. "You've gone too far this time, Bradley!" Jim said angrily. "You can't come into *my* county and turn it upside down! I'm calling your superiors and having you removed from this case!"

Alan stepped closer to Jim. "You just go ahead and try! Before you hang up the phone, your career will be finished!" All the commotion made Rick uneasy, and he began to shake and cry.

Seeing this, Jim grabbed Alan by the arm. "Let's go outside." Alan pulled his arm out of Jim's grip and walked out of the room. Jim followed, but stopped at the door and turned around. "Everything's going to be all right, Rick. I promise." He said then stepped out of the room, closing the door behind him. Rick slowly stood up, walked to the door, put his ear up to it, and listened nervously.

"Alright, Bradley, start explaining why you started this fiasco." Jim ordered firmly.

"I didn't start anything, Sheriff! I merely accompanied your Deputy as he conducted a legal search." Alan replied calmly as Jim looked at Milhouse.

"What's he talking about?"

"It's true, Sheriff." Milhouse pulled the report and warrant from his pocket and handed it to Jim. "After learning from Agent Bradley that Schaffer had a previous record for smuggling drugs, I got this warrant."

"That's right. Your own deputy conducted the search and found the same grade of opium that Henderson had. Look, they even knew each other." Alan handed over the picture and the bag of drugs.

Jim gave Milhouse a scolding look then glanced at the picture. "When are you going to figure it out, Bradley? This is a small town, everyone knows everyone else. This proves nothing."

"Just the same, Sheriff. I'm going back in there and continue questioning the prisoner." Alan reached for the door.

"Hold it!" Jim said as he stepped in front of the door blocking Alan. "Let me read this report first." Jim opened the report and examined it. He was stalling and wanted a moment to think.

He'd known about Rick's record for years, but told no one. When Rick had thumbed his way into town all those years ago, Harper checked up on him as he does every drifter. Jim confronted Rick with what he knew and Rick told his story.

Jim had looked on Rick with compassion. Rick had already proven himself to be a productive member of the community by fighting forest fires, so Jim thought that the past was nobody's business but Rick's. They even became friends. In fact, Jim thought as he looked at the photo of Buck and Rick, it was Jim who had taken the picture on one of their first fishing trips. Jim knew all too well about Rick's frail mental condition, and he wasn't about to let Bradley interrogate him. Jim just needed a moment to think.

Rick heard everything that was said in the hallway. *No! Lord no!* he thought as the laughter started to come back. That Fed can't come back in here. Rick started to breath erratically and felt closed in.

Air. He need some air. He felt light headed and confused as he wiped the sweat from his brow. Stumbling over to the window, he opened it and stuck his head out. The fresh air helped only slightly as the laughter continued. "Stop it! Please!" He said to himself. "Why don't you leave me alone?"

Rick started to panic and the laughter got louder. "Got to make it stop. Got to get into the air and make it stop." His eyes widened as the idea popped into his head. He looked at the door then out the window.

Got to run! Got to get away! Yes! Do it! Something inside told him. Rick pulled himself up into the window, then slipped through it. When he hit the ground he looked around, but nobody was there. He turned and ran towards the flight line.

Jim finished looking at the papers then folded them up. "Your interrogation is over, Bradley. I'm taking Schaffer into custody. He's not saying another word to anyone until he's seen his lawyer."

"You can't do this Sheriff!" Alan said angrily. "All I need is ten minutes and this case will be wrapped up."

"I *can* do it!" Jim barked. "This warrant was issued to one of my deputies. That makes Schaffer *my* prisoner." Jim grabbed the handle and opened the door.

All three men looked with surprise at the empty room. Jim stepped quickly to the bathroom and opened the door. Alan ran to the window and looked out.

"He's heading for the tarmac!" Alan yelled. Jim ran out the door and down the hall with Milhouse and Bradley close behind. It only took a few strides and the younger, in shape Bradley outran the others.

Rick made it to his plane as the fuel truck was pulling away. He quickly pulled the wheel chocks from the tires and threw them aside, then jumped into the plane. As he reached his seat, he instantly punched the four buttons to start each engine. The engines were still warm and roared to life without so much as a sputter. Rick took one last look back and saw Agent Bradley closing fast. He pushed the throttle down and the plane rolled onto the runway.

Alan could see that he wasn't going to reach the plane in time, so he stopped and pulled the Desert Eagle from its holster. Before he could take aim he was struck from behind.

"No! You, *idiot!*" Jim yelled as he tackled Alan. Both men tumbled to the ground. The gun was jarred from Alan's hand and it slid several yards down the tarmac. Milhouse quickly helped Jim get to his feet, and all three men watched as the plane sped down the runway then climbed into the sky.

Jim ran back towards the hanger with Milhouse beside him. Alan got up, looked around for his gun, then ran to it. As he holstered it, he looked towards the sky. The clouds had broken up, and Alan could see the sun glistening off the plane's metallic body as it distanced itself from the field. He quickly started to run back towards the hanger.

Rick was high in the air, but the laughter continued. *What are you doing? You're not supposed to follow me up here! I've got to get higher,* he thought then pushed the throttle to full and pulled back on the stick, straining the engines.

Jim and Milhouse reached the steps leading up the side of the hanger to the tower and started up them. They were to the top

319

when Alan reached the hanger. Just past the hanger, in the parking lot, Alan's attention was drawn to the figure of a man waving his arms. It was Chet. Alan changed directions and ran towards him.

Jim opened the door to the tower. A man and a woman were inside. The woman had binoculars trained at the sky, while the man was yelling into a microphone. "Tower to XJ1042, come in, over!"

"I didn't give him clearance to take off! That butthead will lose his license for this!" The woman with the binoculars yelled.

Jim hurried to the man with the microphone. "Hand it over," he ordered. Both controllers stopped what they were doing and looked at Jim. The one with the binoculars nodded to the other, and the mike was given to Jim. "Rick, come in, Rick, over." He said as he stared at the sky. There was no answer. "What's he doing?" He asked the woman with the binoculars.

"He's gaining altitude and circling the field." She replied.

Two men with video cameras were standing behind Chet with their lenses trained at the sky. Next to them was a network van with its side door open. Inside was the producer who sat watching several monitors and operating equipment. Alan stopped next to Chet, and bent over grabbing his knees breathing hard.

"We arrived, just after the Sheriff, and set up," Chet said with a smile. "We got the whole chase videoed."

Just then the producer stepped out of the van. "We've got the satellite link with the network. We're breaking into normal broadcasting in fifteen seconds. Camera two, stay on the plane. Camera one, you're on Green and Bradley," She ordered. One of the cameramen lowered his camera and focused in on the two men.

"Wait, let me catch my breath," Alan pleaded.

"Sorry, there's no time," She replied.

Alan stood up and Chet helped brush him off.

In a large conference room in Seattle, Governor Wilson sat at the head of a large table. Mayor Demsey and the other mayors were sitting around the table listening to him speak, when suddenly the door burst open. "Sorry to interrupt, sir," Wilson's aid said winded. "But you said that you wanted to be kept informed on the D.B. Cooper story."

"Yes, what is it?" Wilson turned away from the stack of papers in front of him and looked over his reading glasses at his aid.

"A special report is being broadcast on the television."

Mayor Demsey got up and stepped quickly to the large TV in the corner of the room. "What channel?"

"It doesn't matter. It's on all of them," came the reply.

Demsey turned on the power and Rick's PBY filled the screen.

Lieutenant Cranston was sitting in his office pouring over a stack of paperwork when O'Leary opened the door. "Sir! Bradley is at it again."

Cranston pulled the reading glasses off his face and rushed out of the office towards the conference room. A large group of agents were huddled around the TV and staring at the circling plane.

"What's happening?" Cranston asked.

"I don't know. It just came on." O'Leary replied.

The producer stepped behind the camera. "In five, four, three, two, one," she pointed at Chet.

"Good morning ladies and gentlemen. We interrupt your regularly scheduled program to bring you this special report. A few minutes ago, important events have unfolded in the story that's captured the attention of the Nation. That's right, folks, the story of D.B. Cooper.

"Flying above me as I speak, a lone man circles the airfield. Moments ago that same man eluded authorities and escaped into the air. With me now is Special Agent Alan Bradley to shed some light on this mystery man. Agent Bradley, is D.B. Cooper in that plane?"

"I'm afraid not, Chet. D.B. Cooper is the mastermind behind this drug smuggling operation. The man in the plane is one of Cooper's operatives." Alan said.

"We have a tape of the events leading to the suspect's escape. We're going to play that tape now and I'd like you, Agent Bradley, to describe to us what's happening." Chet pointed to a large monitor behind the producer, which indicated what the public was now watching on TV.

"As you can see," Alan said as he viewed the screen. "The suspect is running down the flight line with myself, the Sheriff, and one of his deputies in hot pursuit. When it was apparent that he'd get away, I did the only thing I could. I pulled my gun out and attempted to shoot the plane and disable it."

"But it looks like you didn't get a chance. The Sheriff ran into you," Chet said.

"He didn't just run into me. He tackled me on *purpose*," Alan replied.

"Tackled you! Why would he do that?"

"I have no idea, Chet. It's hard to say what goes through the mind of a man as incompetent as this Sheriff is," Alan replied, shaking his head disapprovingly.

"*Incompetent?* Isn't that a pretty harsh charge?" Chet asked with astonishment.

"Yes it is, Chet. But the facts speak for themselves. This Sheriff has been grossly uncooperative and has hampered my investigation from the start. In fact, prior to his escape, I had the suspect in custody and was questioning him. Just before the Sheriff arrived, the suspect was about to give me a full confession." Alan said in a matter of fact tone.

"Confess to what?" Chet questioned.

"The suspect, who has a previous record of drug smuggling and was found with opium in his possession, was about to turn States evidence and become a material witness against the others in the operation. He was in the process of telling me about how he delivered the drugs to Henderson, the man killed yesterday."

"*Amazing!* Did he tell you who Cooper is and where he's hiding?" Chet asked.

"He didn't get a chance," Alan explained. "Before the suspect could tell me anything further, the Sheriff showed up and allowed him to escape."

"That's *unbelievable!*" Chet exclaimed. "The Sheriff's responsible for your witness escaping *twice* in one day!"

"Unfortunately, it's true," Alan replied, shaking his head sadly.

"What about your own department?" Chet continued his questioning. "Haven't they been able to keep the Sheriff's department out of your investigation?"

"Actually, Chet, I haven't heard a thing from my department. Since the investigation started, I've been expecting a DEA task force to arrive and assist me. So far, that hasn't happened."

"Damn it!" Governor Wilson yelled. "The biggest investigation in thirty years is going on and Cranston's flat on his butt! Get him on the phone, right now!" Wilson's aid pulled a cellular phone from his pocket, dialed a number and handed it to Wilson.

"Oh, crap!" Cranston said as he listened to the report. "O'Leary! Where are you?" Everyone looked around for him, but he'd already left the room. Cranston walked quickly out of the room and saw O'Leary on the phone. "You and Anderson, get your gear together. We have to move fast!"

"I'm way ahead of you, Sir," he said as he pointed to two large duffel bags behind the desk. O'Leary hung up the phone. "That was the airport. Since yesterday I've had a helicopter standing by. He'll pick us up on the roof in five minutes."

"Good thinking," Cranston said relieved. "He can fly us down to the Sheriff's office. We'll coordinate efforts from there. Now let's go!" Anderson and O'Leary grabbed the bags, and the three men started to run down the hall. The phone rang and one of the other agents answered it.

"Sir! It's the Governor!" he said.

"Tell him I've already left!" Cranston replied as he hurried out of the room.

"Rick, come in, Rick, over," Jim said into the radio. There was no answer. Jim's voice filled the cockpit of the plane but Rick ignored it. His knuckles turned white as he gripped the yoke tightly. "Why are you still here?" he cried in the empty cockpit as the laughter filled his mind. "You've never followed me into the air before. Leave me alone."

"Rick! Please come down. You're not going to jail. *I promise.* Everything is going to be fine," the radio squawked.

Rick couldn't think. It was too loud, there were too many distractions. The laughter, the engines, the radio. They were all too loud. He needed to calm down. He told himself he needed to get a *grip!*

Rick reached up and turned off the radio. Good, one distraction gone. *"Now what do I do?"* he asked himself. *I can run!*

323

Fly to Canada, I don't know, anywhere, he thought hopefully. *No! That won't work,* he finally decided. Wherever he went, they'd catch him.

Rick started to panic again and he began to talk to himself. "I'm going to jail!" His body shook and as the laughter filled his head he thought it would explode. *"No! Everything is still too loud!"* Rick reached over, pushed some buttons and the engines cut out. All he could hear was the air flowing past him. He let out a sigh of relief. *That's better,* he thought.

"Something's wrong!" The tower controller said as she looked through her binoculars. Everyone looked at her for an explanation. "No wait. It's alright. He cut his engines and put himself into a shallow dive. He has plenty of altitude and should be able to maintain his present condition for a couple of minutes before he has to fire them up again."

"Why would he cut his engines?" Milhouse asked with concern.

"I don't know, maybe he'll land," Jim replied hopefully.

Chet was interrupted by the cameraman who was watching the plane. Suddenly he realized that he couldn't hear the engines. "Something appears to be wrong, ladies and gentlemen," Chet said as he looked into the sky frantically trying to locate the plane. "The plane's engines have stopped. What's he doing?" There was a long silence as everyone watched the plane glide effortlessly through the air.

The producer spoke softly into a microphone attached to the small receiver in Chet's ear. "Start talking. We've got to keep the audience's attention."

Chet pushed the earpiece tightly into place in order to hear her clearly. He looked at her confused, and didn't know what to do.

"Nothings happening. We need some filler. Talk about anything." The producer said into the microphone.

Chet thought for a moment and realized that the camera was on him. "You know, Agent Bradley, it's been refreshing to talk to a law enforcement officer such as yourself. You've always been very cooperative and open to the press. Some government officials would've tried to cover up this story, but you've allowed us to follow its progress every step of the way."

"Well, Chet, I'm a firm believer in the public's right to know what's going on around them," Alan replied as he smiled for the camera.

"Really! Well isn't that wonderful," Chet said. "Have you ever thought about running for public office?"

Alan tried to look surprised at the thought. "Who me? No, Chet, all I've ever wanted to do was to be a damn good cop."

"Well you certainly are that. But we sure could use someone like you in government. Maybe someday you'll change your mind," Chet said.

"I don't know, I've never thought of myself as a politician. But if the public would support an average citizen like myself, I guess I would feel it was my duty to serve them," Alan said as he tried to look sincere.

"That dirty rotten…!" Mayor Demsey fumed as he searched for the right word. "He sure is getting a lot of mileage from just one interview!"

"What's the matter, Bob?" Governor Wilson laughed as he lifted his glass of ice water to his lips. "Are you afraid the boy might take your job?" The whole room broke into laughter at the remark as Wilson took a large gulp of water.

"I wouldn't laugh, Ted. With this kind of press he could run for Governor!" Demsey replied.

Suddenly Wilson coughed and choked on the water as he tried to clear his throat. "That's not funny, Bob!" he exclaimed.

Rick tried to decide what to do, but he couldn't think. The laughter horrified him. Images started to appear in his mind of the Vietnamese officer and the pit with the bamboo bars closing in on him. "Why couldn't you have killed me? Why couldn't you let me die?" He yelled into the cockpit. "I can't go to jail! No, I'm not going! You can't *make* me!"

He *had* to silence the demon once and for all. Suddenly it was all too clear what he had to do. He was surprised at how easy the decision was. There was only one answer. Only one final solution. Rick was surprised at how easily he'd accepted it…

After a moment, he gently released the yoke then leaned slowly back in his seat and closed his eyes. He was calm. At peace. The horrific eyes and laughter faded from his mind. Everything was silent, but for the soothing sound of air washing over the plane as it flew through it. His decent accelerated as the angle of attack dove sharply. The plane began to wobble, slowly at first, then into a gentle roll. With outstretched arms, head back, and eyes closed, Rick's body moved back and forth as the plane lazily rolled towards its fate. The dynamic forces on the control surfaces were so great there was no hope of pulling out. But Rick wasn't about to try. No longer would the voice in his head control him.

"He's in a dive! He's going to auger in!" The woman with the binoculars said loudly. Everyone in the tower rushed to the window and looked out.

Jim's heart was in his throat as he watched the hopeless event. "Rick! Don't do it!" he pleaded over the radio. A moment later, he rushed out the door and down the steps while continuing to watch the plane's descent.

The cameraman waved excitedly and Chet looked into the air. "Oh my Gosh! He's going to crash!" Chet yelled. The cameraman followed the plane as it sped towards the ground.

Two miles away, the hillside exploded. A silent bright white and yellow flash burned into Jim's retinas. A half second later, he felt the impact of the deafening shock wave and he felt the heat of it as it past through him.

The fuel from the high capacity tanks erupted skyward. Flames raced higher turning red then rolling, billowing into a giant mushroom cloud. Jim tilted his head back following its path into the sky. The trees on the hillside were now a blaze of fire. Sirens screamed as the emergency trucks from the field raced past him and towards the crash site.

The explosion rocked the TV crew as they continued to tape. The huge fireball filled the screens of every TV in the nation, and the sirens echoed in every living room.

"Oh my Gosh! Oh my Gosh!" Chet exclaimed. "Agent Bradley! Your witness has just committed suicide! What is this going to do to your investigation?"

"I was so close to solving this whole case!" Alan exclaimed as he shook his head. "If it wasn't for that damn Sheriff, I would've had the whole gang in custody by now!"

The producer lifted her microphone and spoke into Chet's earpiece. "We have to break for a few minutes so that we can get closer to the crash site. Go to a commercial."

Chet turned to the camera. "Ladies and gentlemen, please stay tuned while we attempt to gain a better vantage point of the crash site. Now for a word from our sponsors."

"Okay, we're clear!" The producer yelled. Suddenly the whole crew cheered and slapped high fives, shook hands, and exchanged hugs. "Wow! What a shot!" One cameraman said. "I got every bit of it!"

"All right! Pack it up, let's move!" Ordered the producer.

Nikki stood with the other nurses and watched the events as they took place on the screen. She held her hands to keep them from shaking. *Why, Jim, why are you doing this?* she asked herself. She didn't know what to do. *You have to tell someone what you know,* her mind told her, but her heart kept her from doing so. She finally lost control and started to cry. The other nurses looked at her, wondering what was wrong. Nikki ran down the hall and disappeared into the ladies room.

Jim couldn't breathe. Slowly leaning over, he put his hands on his knees and started to feel sick. He hadn't been able to protect Buck or Rick. Guilty feelings flooded his soul.

Milhouse walked up to him. "Sheriff, are you alright?"

Jim didn't answer as he slowly lifted his head. After a few moments, those feelings turned to rage. *No! He wasn't to blame for this,* he knew. *Someone will pay for this outrage!* He promised himself. *Bradley will pay.* Jim quickly looked around, saw Agent Bradley and started towards him. His determined trot slowly turned

327

into a sprint. Seeing what was going to happen, Milhouse had to hustle to keep up.

Chet and Alan stood out of the way as the crew started to pack up the equipment. "How did you like the part about government office? That should help you in your bid for mayor." Chet said.

"Yes, that was quick thinking, but I think you'd better start planning on a grander scale." Alan replied.

"What do you mean?"

"I mean the governor's office." Alan said quietly.

Chet tried not to show his excitement, but it was impossible. "Do you really think so?"

"Of course. But let's keep this between us for now. No use letting the whole world know until we're ready." Alan looked at the camera crew moving about.

"Oh, yeah right," Chet said with a wink then changed the subject. "So what now?"

"I don't know. I guess it's over. Schaffer was my only lead." Alan said soberly.

"What about the finger prints?"

It could take days, even weeks to get a match. Even for the government computers," Alan replied. "No, if Phantom has seen this report, he's probably on his way out of the country by now."

Jim saw Alan and Chet standing across the parking lot next to the van and ran towards them.

"Come on, Chet, we don't have all day!" The producer yelled as the crew closed up the van.

Chet leaned towards Alan. "At least you're off the hook, case closed, right?" He whispered.

"Yeah, I guess so, but I really wanted to nail these smugglers…" Alan started to say when his body was jolted violently to the side. Jim tackled him at a full sprint. Both men fell forward slammed against the van then to the ground. Jim had Alan pinned below him. Chet raced to the aid of his friend and tried to pull Jim off of him.

"You son of a bitch! Two men are dead because of you! I'm not going to rest until you pay for it!" Jim exclaimed angrily.

Chet tried to pull the two men apart, but his efforts were futile. Running for their cameras, the crew tried to get the fight on video.

Milhouse grabbed Jim and wrenched the two men apart. "Don't do it, Sheriff. Its not worth it." Chet held Alan back from retaliating.

"You're responsible!" Jim yelled.

"No! You are!" Alan barked as Chet held him back. "If you wouldn't have interfered, Schaffer would still be alive!"

"His blood is on your hands!" Jim yelled back.

"Get over it, Sheriff! Nobody cares what happens to drug smugglers!"

"You have no *proof* of that!"

"They had identical packages of opium! That's proof enough for me!" Alan replied.

Milhouse pulled Jim farther away. "Take it easy, Sheriff. Calm down." He said as he walked him over to the Blazer. The camera crew looked disappointed that they didn't get it on tape, then began to load the van again.

Jim tried to gain his composure. Pulling away from Milhouse, he opened the door of the Blazer and got in. Taking one last look at the trail of black smoke leaching into the air from the crash site, he started the vehicle and hit the gas. Chet helped Alan brush himself off as they watched Jim's Blazer race out of the parking lot and down the road. Milhouse's Blazer followed close behind.

Chet pulled Alan to the side so that no one could hear them. "Did you hear what he said? Two men are dead because of *you.* Do you think he knows what happened to Henderson?" He asked worriedly.

"No, he couldn't. Even if he suspected it, he has no proof." Alan replied.

"Let's go, Chet!" The producer yelled impatiently.

Chet turned to leave then stopped and looked back at Alan suspiciously.

"What? Why are you looking at me like that?" Alan asked.

"You said identical packages. You didn't by any chance..." Alan didn't have to answer, Chet saw it on his face. "Awe, *damn it,* Alan!" He tried to control himself.

"I *had* to Chet," Alan defended. "I needed something to make Schaffer talk."

"Chet!" The producer yelled.

"We'll talk about this later," Chet said. "I'll meet you back at the motel when I'm through. In the mean time, I suggest you try to find out what the Sheriff *does* know." Chet turned, ran to the van, and got in. Alan watched the van speed away. *He's right. I'd better go to the station and see what they've got,* he thought. Walking to his car, he took one last look at the ribbon of black smoke in the air, then he got in and drove away.

Deputy Rissley and the rest of the crew were painstakingly searching the area around Buck's house when they heard what sounded like distant thunder. *What was that?* They all wondered as they looked to the sky, but saw no sign of a storm. They all looked at each other and shrugged, then continued working.

"Look!" One of them said as he pointed to the sky a minute later. Joe saw a line of black smoke lifting up from the horizon then slowly trail across the sky. A shiver went up her spine, knowing that something terrible had just happened.

She hurried to her Blazer and turned the radio to the emergency station. It was awash with chaos. All she could get straight was something about a fire and plane crash. Remembering the TV set in one of Buck's back rooms, she rushed into the house. She turned it on and played with the rabbit ears until the picture cleared up.

Joe was stunned as she stood in front of the TV. She stared in disbelief as she watched the news anchor recap the events that had just taken place.

She didn't know Shaffer well. Few people did. He was a skeleton in this county's closet that nobody liked to talk about. She knew he had some mental problems and was misunderstood by almost everyone. Instead of monsters, parents would tell their children that if they weren't good, the airfield boogeyman would come get them.

She felt sorry for Jim. He had lost another friend. She knew that whenever there was a problem at the airfield concerning Rick, Jim would be there to straighten things out. She found that out the hard way.

After her first quarter in school, Joe decided to go out to the field and meet Rick. She had just learned about mental illness and

330

was eager to try and help Rick solve his problems. Her attempt backfired and Rick had gone running out of the hanger in a cold sweat.

When she got back to the station, Jim was noticeably upset and called her into his office. He told her that what she had tried to do was wrong. She was not qualified to treat Rick, and he asked her– no– he ordered her to leave Rick alone and never go out there again.

She tried to argue with him. Rick needed help if he was ever going to fit into normal society. She was sure of it. Jim explained to her that he knew all about Rick's problems. He said that Rick had been treated by some of the finest doctors in the military and they could do nothing for him.

"Rick doesn't want to fit in to what you think of as normal society." Jim had explained calmly. "He has done a lot for this community. He just wants to fly his plane and be left alone. He deserves that much. We owe that to him."

She knew that he was right about her not being qualified, but she didn't agree that he shouldn't get more treatment. In the end, she reluctantly promised that she would not go back out there. But she also secretly vowed to herself that someday when she was more qualified, she would return. She felt that no matter what Jim thought or how good his intentions, Rick deserved proper treatment.

She felt sad that she was never going to get the chance to fulfill her vow. She wondered what happened to cause this reaction. *What did Bradley do that pushed you over the edge.*

She knew that it *had* to be Bradley's fault and she started to feel guilty. Why had she not confronted him? Why didn't she arrest him? Why didn't she do something… *anything*, before Bradley hurt someone else?

She knew that there was nothing she could've done. They had no evidence to arrest him. All they could've done was to watch him closely, but they didn't watch him close enough. She vowed to not let this charade go long enough that someone else got hurt. Bradley had come into her county and done this right under her nose, and she was going to make him pay.

20
Coming Clean

Two of his friends were dead—and *why?* Because he was too late, too slow, too tired? *That's a hell of an excuse, Jim! Try telling that to Buck and Rick! You've failed them!* He'd let himself go over the years. His mind and body weren't as quick or as well tuned as they use to be. He'd lost his edge and let his friends down.

At least, that's how he saw it. He'd let himself be out maneuvered. Sure, maybe not today or yesterday, when circumstances and things were against him, but over the years he'd set himself up for this failure. *This wouldn't have happened thirty years ago!* He reminded himself.

Back then you were sharp, prepared and ready for anything and you wouldn't have let it get this far. When you're prepared, the breaks fall your way and time is your ally. But you've grown complacent!

Sure you may not have been able to save Buck, but after that you knew there was a threat! No one else should've been allowed to get hurt. You took your eye off the ball and it hit you in the gut!

The instant he had suspected Bradley, he should've put someone on him to follow him. He should've been watching the enemy, but he hadn't. He allowed the enemy to flank him and attack yet again. It was a costly mistake and in this case—*deadly.*

Jim drove slowly with the speed of traffic. Visions of the diving plane filled his mind and with every blink of his eyes the explosion replayed on his flash burnt retinas. He knew that every detail would haunt him for the rest of his life.

As the scene replayed in his mind, he felt a helplessness that only comes from not being able to control events. He tried to push the memory from his mind, but couldn't. How could he? He'd watched a friend die and was powerless to prevent it.

A short time earlier he'd been filled with rage and adrenaline. The slow drive had allowed him to calm down. The caffeine and adrenaline had now worn off and his exhausted body sunk low in the driver's seat. Refusing to work, his tired mind was again on autopilot, maneuvering the Blazer and replaying events from that morning.

He thought of Nikki and how he wished that they were together. He wanted her to hold and reassure him that everything would be okay, but he knew that was impossible.

He was still the Sheriff and had a job to do. There was no time for grief, feelings of insecurity, or for being comforted. Again, he'd have to bury his feelings and save them for a later date, which was something he'd grown all too accustomed to.

He didn't know where he was driving, just that he was. It wasn't until the Blazer turned off the highway and into Centralia that he realized he'd be back at the station soon. He had no idea what he'd do when he got there, but he would worry about that later.

As he approached the station, his attention was drawn to a crowd of people around it. Six satellite vans were outside and their crews appeared to be filming reports from different angles. Three of the truck logo's he recognized as domestic, and the other three weren't hard to figure out.

One, he saw from the symbols, had to be from somewhere in Asia. Another was definitely South American, and the last had BBC on its side. *You'd think the Brits would have enough scandal with the Royal family. Why would they want more?* he wondered.

He had no strength left for a confrontation, so Jim drove through the parking lot to the back of the station. He had to move fast, the moment they saw him, reports and cameramen ran to his location.

A tall man with a British accent stuck a microphone in his face. "Sheriff! Have you got any idea where the D.B. Cooper gang is hiding out?"

Jim had barely enough energy to muster the words, "No comment." He slowly pushed through them to the door. Inside the station, Jim saw that it was empty except for the dispatcher who was frantically answering the phones and putting people on hold as he put out radio calls to patrol units.

"Peterson, get Rissley on the phone and patch it though to my office," Jim said. He felt depressed and helpless and wanted to talk to someone he could rely on.

"Yes sir, right away." Peterson nodded.

Jim felt old and as depression caught up to him, he started to doubt his ability to do this job. No, he told himself. It was just that he wasn't used to the pace. He'd be his normal self after a cup of coffee.

Jim found his cup and went to the coffee pot. As he filled it, he heard the dispatcher talking on the radio to Rissley. Not bothering to measure, he dumped a large amount of sugar into the cup and stirred it. By the time he got to his desk, the phone was ringing and he picked up the receiver. "Joe?"

"Hello, Sheriff. I'm sorry about Rick," she said thoughtfully. "If you need someone to talk to or if there is anything else I can do, I'd be happy to help."

The kind words helped him somehow and he didn't quite feel as alone as he did a few moments ago. "Thank you, Joe." He smiled at her through the phone. There is something you can do. You can cheer me up by telling me you've found that bullet."

"I'm sorry, Sheriff," she said discouragingly. "We've made several more sweeps of the porch. We've combed the tree line along the side of the house and used the metal detectors to search the dirt and grass along the projected flight path. We even expanded the search to allow for different variations in flight paths, but found nothing."

Jim's heart sank to a new low after hearing this. He sat back in his chair in frustration, sipped from his cup and tried to think.

"Sheriff? Are you still there?" she asked.

"Oh, yes, Joe, good work. I was just trying to think where we should go from here." Jim wanted to regroup. The only thing he could come up with was to gather up everything they knew and look at it from another angle. Perhaps then he could come up with something that would help him nail Bradley. "Has everyone filled out a shift report for yesterday and today?"

"Yes, sir. I've got them here and could fax them to you if you'd like."

"Yes, do that right away," Jim confirmed. "You've done everything possible out there, Joe. Put a guard at the entrance to the road then send everyone else out on patrol. From what I could gather from listening to Peterson's radio calls, the roads are a mess out there." Jim looked at his watch. It was already three o'clock in the afternoon. "Let's plan on meeting back here at eighteen hundred hours. Perhaps, when we're together, we can put this case back on track."

"Yes, sir." Joe was also at her wit's end and was looking forward to a brainstorming session. "You should have the fax in a few minutes, then you'll know everything we did. I only wish there was something in the shift reports that could help, but I looked them over and have to admit their pretty boring."

"You're probably right, but it doesn't hurt to look. I'll see you in a few hours." With that, Jim hung up the phone.

Jim took a long gulp of his coffee and finished what was in his cup. Then wiping his face with his hands, he stretched and took a deep breath. *I've got to pull myself together. Two men are dead and I can't allow this to go on any farther,* Jim thought to himself.

What now? If the bullet can't be found then I'll have to cut my losses and move on. Rissley's words about the shift reports were discouraging, but that seemed to be the standard for this case. Maybe there is something in the shift reports and maybe there wasn't, but he couldn't give up. He had to press on. Perhaps there was something one deputy noticed that the others missed. It was a long shot, but he had nothing else to go on.

Standing up, he grabbed his now empty cup and walked back to the pot. Milhouse was leaning over the counter talking softly to Peterson when Jim walked out of the office. "Milhouse, come in here," he said sternly, then turned around and walked back in.

Milhouse walked to the office door then stepped reluctantly inside. "Yes, sir?"

"You intentionally disobeyed orders and helped Agent Bradley without notifying me first. Isn't that correct?" Jim scowled.

"Yes, sir. I'm sorry. I was just—"

"Just what!" Jim cut him off loudly. "I drove past the Super Mart on my way back here. You obviously didn't obey my orders to clear the campers out. Isn't that correct?!"

"Yes, sir," Milhouse replied as he fidgeted nervously with the feeling of guilt as he looked at the floor.

"I suggest that you get over there now and do that!" Jim ordered.

"But, Sheriff! What about the investigation?" Milhouse exclaimed.

Jim walked to the front of his desk. "As of this moment, you're officially off this case. I expected more from you, Milhouse. You've disobeyed orders and breached the chain of command. If you would've come to me before you got the warrant, we could've taken Schaffer into custody properly. He'd be locked up instead of dead!" Jim said, angrily.

"Still blaming someone else for your screw ups, Sheriff?" Came a voice from the doorway. Milhouse stepped out of the way to reveal Alan standing at the door.

"Bradley!" Jim said, angrily. "What the hell are you doing here?"

"Since my last lead killed himself, I thought I'd go through the evidence again to see if there is something I missed."

Jim thought for a moment, then turned his attention back to Milhouse. "We'll discuss your conduct later. I suggest you get moving. You've got campers to roust."

"Yes, sir," Milhouse said, disappointed, then turned and walked past Bradley. He stopped just past the door and turned around. "Did Rissley turn up anything on that bullet?"

"Bullet?" Alan said with surprise as he looked from Milhouse to Jim. "What bullet?"

"It's nothing." Jim brushed it off calmly. "Rissley was searching for a bullet and found nothing."

"That's too bad," Milhouse said, quietly, then turned and left.

"Why wasn't I notified that you were still looking for a bullet?" Alan asked in an irritated voice.

"I don't have to notify you on aspects of my investigation. Besides, when I get off the phone with your superiors, you'll be headed back to Seattle with your tail between your legs!" Jim said sharply.

"You've got it all wrong, Sheriff!" Alan snapped as he stepped up to Jim's face. "I'll be making a few phone calls of my own, and when I'm through, you'll be the one packing your bags!"

"That's enough, Bradley!" A voice from behind him said.

Alan turned quickly to see a tall black man filling the doorway. "Cranston! It's about time!"

Cranston didn't answer him. Turning his attention to Jim, he walked up to him, removed his badge from his pocket and handed it over. "Good afternoon, Sheriff. I'm Deputy Director Cranston of the Drug Enforcement Agency," he said with a smile.

Jim watched the other two agents file into the room, then he examined the ID and handed it back. "I suppose you're going to tell me you're here to take over the investigation," Jim said, defensively.

"Relax, Sheriff," Cranston said with a smile. "We're here to help."

337

"*Really*," Jim said, sarcastically. "You can start by sending this hot shot home!"

"That's bull!" Alan said angrily as he stepped back into Jim's face. "You're finished! When I get through with you—" he started to say but was interrupted.

"That's enough, Bradley!" Cranston's temper started to flare.

"No, it's not! Not even close!" Alan turned on Cranston. "You're responsible, too! If you'd been here earlier and kept this incompetent Sheriff out of my way, I'd have the whole operation behind bars!"

"I'm warning you, Bradley, one more word and I'll remove you from this case!" Cranston barked.

"Like hell!" Alan snapped. "Heads are going to roll on this one, I promise you. And you two are first!" With that, Alan turned and rushed out of the office.

"*Bradley!* Come back here. That's an order!" Cranston yelled furiously, but Alan kept walking down the hall and out the door.

Cranston tried to calm himself. He slowly pulled the bottle of Pepto from his pocket and took a large gulp. Jim could see Cranston's hands shaking as he drank. When he lowered the bottle he seemed more composed.

"Sheriff, if you don't mind, I'd like these two agents to look over the evidence. Maybe their expertise can shed some light on this case."

Jim thought about it for a moment then said. "Come with me. I'll show you where it is."

Cranston watched Sheriff Harper walked out of the office with O'Leary and Anderson in tow. After taking another drink from the Pepto, he was able to calm himself further and he glanced around the room. It wasn't too much different from his own in Seattle.

Paperwork was stacked a mile high on the desk. There were a few pictures on the wall, and what was this? Seeing the familiar item, Cranston stepped forward to examine it more closely. In a small frame with a navy blue background were Harper's Purple Heart and Silver Star along with a picture of him in uniform. Cranston read the inscription, and immediately felt guilty.

Yesterday, he'd left Bradley on his own, glad to be rid of him if only for a short while, but he neglected to consider how Bradley might affect someone else's department. Bradley was Cranston's responsibility not Harper's. It was selfish of him to drop Bradley on someone else's shoulders, especially a fellow soldier.

Like Cranston, Harper had seen combat first hand and up close. They'd fought the enemy face-to-face and hand-to-hand, unlike the flyboys or Navy pukes that fought the war from a comfortable distance.

Cranston remembered the dark circles under Harper's sunken eyes and recalled looking that same way himself when Bradley was around. Suddenly, he felt ashamed at being derelict in his duties. He decided he'd make it up to Harper if he could. Cranston then examined his own situation and with a heavy sigh of despair. He looked out the window and off into space.

Jim grabbed the fax that Joe had sent from the machine as he and the agents walked to the conference room. Jim opened the door, turned on the lights, and placed the shift reports on the table. "Help yourselves." Neither agent said a word. They filed past Jim and went to work.

Jim turned and from the hallway watched Cranston in the office. Cranston leaned against the desk and took another drink from the bottle. He had a distant look on his face, almost sad, Jim thought. Even from a distance, Cranston looked like a broken man. This obviously wasn't the first time Cranston and Bradley had locked horns. *There is definitely no love lost between those two,* Jim thought to himself.

He watched as Cranston walked slowly to the window and looked out at the horizon. Walking to the coffee pot, Jim picked up a spare cup and filled it up. He added a hearty dose of cream and sugar, then stopped and looked back into the office. Cranston hadn't moved from the window.

Maybe I should tell him, Jim thought to himself. *No, he's DEA, he'd arrest me for sure.* Jim thought about it from another angle. *Maybe not. Maybe he really is here to help.*

"If I only had more *time,*" he swore under his breath. But it was too late for that, he need an ally. Someone who had almost as much to lose as Jim did. *Could Cranston be that person?* Jim asked himself as he walked to the office door and looked in.

Bradley did say *both* their heads would roll. It didn't matter now, he didn't have a choice. Time had run out. Jim decided to test the water a little, then if he didn't get a favorable response, he'd stop.

Walking up to Cranston, Jim held out the cup. "Coffee?"

Cranston looked startled. "Oh, I'm sorry, Sheriff. I guess I was in my own little world there for a second," he said as he took the cup. "Thank you."

"I took the liberty of adding cream and sugar."

"Thanks again. My stomach can't handle it black anymore." Cranston looked at Jim and saw the questioning look on his face. "What is it, Sheriff? What's on your mind?"

Voices came from the hall as three deputies came walking in the door of the station. Jim walked back to the office door and closed it. The room was suddenly dead silent. Jim turned slowly and again looked at Cranston. "Director Cranston," Jim started to say slowly. "What if I told you I think Agent Bradley is making this whole story up."

"Why do you say that?" Cranston asked, curiously.

"Come on," Jim tried to reason with him. "The D.B. Cooper gang? Give me a break."

That brought a short burst of laughter from Cranston. "I see your point. To tell you the truth, I wouldn't put it past that little jerk."

Jim suddenly relaxed. The ice was broken and he decided to wade in farther. "What if I also told you that I have a theory about what happened yesterday? Would you listen to it without departmental prejudice?"

Cranston thought for a moment. "I don't see why not. Shoot."

Jim studied Cranston's face as he spoke. "I believe that Agent Bradley got a bad tip from an informant. Then, in too big of a hurry to do the job right, he rushed down here without backup and unprepared for what he'd be up against. Something went wrong and Bradley accidentally killed Henderson. Then, he started this fiasco in order to cover his tracks."

At hearing this, Cranston became defensive and his mood suddenly turned sour. "You'd better have proof before you start accusing a Federal officer of murder," he warned as he pointed a finger at Jim.

"I'm not accusing anybody of anything, yet." Jim backed off a bit. "Although, there is evidence to show that Bradley's story about what happened yesterday is far from accurate."

Cranston reminded himself which of his agents they were talking about and immediately felt bad for jumping down Harper's throat. The thought that Harper might have something on Bradley was compelling enough to at least listen to. He looked over at Jim. "What evidence is that?"

"First of all, Bradley claims that he and that reporter, Chet Green, showed up at Henderson's place at seven and found the body. I've got a motel manager who says that Bradley and Green, checked in at four. After getting directions to Henderson's, they unpacked

340

their stuff and left by four-thirty. That puts them at the scene with plenty of time to spare." Jim reported.

"So what? That doesn't mean anything," Cranston argued. "Maybe they did something before going there. Maybe they went out to breakfast or something. Going up there with a reporter doesn't make Bradley a murderer and neither does being late."

"It wouldn't make sense to stop for anything. Bradley wanted to get up there and get the drop on Henderson, then he botched the arrest," Jim said.

Cranston thought for a moment. "What else do you have?"

"Bradley has purposely overlooked evidence in order to influence the investigation." Jim stepped over to the desk, opened the manila envelope, and poured its contents onto it.

"Here look." Jim put several photos in a row on the desk in front of Cranston. "Bradley told my deputies that the bullets landed in the lake and were unrecoverable. So no search was made for them until I noticed the angle of the body." Jim pointed to the pictures.

Cranston pulled his reading glasses from his shirt pocket, and examined the photos. "Yes, I see what you mean. The angle of the body indicates that the bullets had to fly over this short stretch of land and the boat dock in order to land in the water. Bradley should never have missed this."

"That's not all. The coroner's report indicates that one of the bullets grazed the backbone which caused it to change course slightly. It could *never* have reached the water," Jim replied.

"Coroner's report?" Cranston asked, questioningly. "I read the report Bradley faxed in last night. It didn't say anything about a coroner's report. I assumed that it wasn't complete yet. I wonder why he didn't send it."

"I'm not surprised. Bradley didn't seem interested in it. He didn't go talk to the doctor who did the autopsy, and he never asked for the report. Almost as if he already *knew* what it would say," Jim replied.

"What *does* it say?"

"Henderson was shot with two rounds from a large caliber hand gun. No smaller than a forty-one caliber, and no larger than a forty-five. The doctor couldn't be sure because of all the damage that was done. The shooter placed these two bullets in the center of Henderson's chest less than an inch apart, and from a distance— from what I could gather from the scene— of just over forty feet," Jim said.

Cranston's eyes widened. "That's good shooting, but sophisticated drug operations have been known to hire professionals."

"Bradley carries a forty-four magnum," Jim continued. "Yesterday he demonstrated it out at the range. He put two rounds within a one inch spread at fifty feet."

"Yes, I know," Cranston said as his mind took in the information and pondered the possibilities. "I've seen him shoot. He's an expert marksman. The best in my department."

"Since late yesterday, I've put my deputies on an all out effort to locate the ricocheted bullet," Jim said.

Cranston's eyes lit up as he looked excitedly at Jim over the top of his reading glasses. "Did you find it? Do you have the bullet?"

"No, we couldn't locate it," Jim said with a discouraged voice.

Cranston's mood suddenly dropped. "That's too damn bad." The room went silent for a few moments as Cranston thought about the information presented to him. "What about this pilot fellow?"

"Rick Schaffer. What about him?" Jim replied.

"I was listening to the news report on the way down here. Bradley said he confessed to having a drug smuggling operation going on with Henderson."

Jim leaned back in his chair as he explained. "I've known both of these men for years. There's no way that they could be drug smugglers. Besides, no one else heard this so called confession. Even if he *did* confess, it was done under duress.

"Schaffer was a POW in Vietnam and had a history of mental problems. They really screwed with his mind over there, and, periodically, he still has flashbacks. Rick would've confessed to anything if he thought it would keep him out of prison. Hell, he killed himself to keep from being put behind bars."

Cranston gave Jim an understanding nod. He had known people who'd been POWs and knew how screwed up some of them were. He then continued his questioning. "In Bradley's report, it says that someone driving a truck and trailer killed Henderson. Bradley calls him D.B. Cooper. Now we both know that's bull, but for the sake of argument, let's call him Mr. X. What about him?"

Jim reached to the photos on the desk and scattered them out until he found the one he wanted. "Look, the man with the truck and trailer couldn't have killed him. Henderson is lying on top of the vehicle's tracks. The truck and trailer had to have been gone before the murder otherwise the truck would have had to drive over him to get away."

Cranston took the photo and examined it closely. "I see what you're saying. It's unlike Bradley to miss such an obvious clue, but that doesn't prove anything. The driver could've stopped up the road then walked back to Henderson's and killed him."

"But he *didn't!*" Jim exclaimed.

"How do you know? If he didn't do it, why doesn't he come forward and say so?" Cranston asked.

"Maybe he's afraid he'll get arrested," Jim replied as he stood up and began to pace nervously.

"Well, he should turn himself in as soon as possible. The longer he waits, the guiltier he looks, especially to a jury. Besides, it's only a matter of time before we find him. The Federal computer banks are busy on the fingerprints right now. And another thing, if you're right, where did the drugs come from?" Cranston said.

"I don't know," Jim admitted. "Bradley was the first person at each scene. He could've planted it. He *is* a drug agent. He probably has access to all kinds of stuff."

Cranston shrugged his shoulders then continued. "What else do you have?"

"That's it. There's nothing else," Jim replied.

"That's *it?*" Cranston exclaimed. "Everything you've told me so far is pure theory. There's no proof to back it up. You can't find a bullet, and without that you have no case. I admit that Bradley hasn't used proper procedure in conducting his investigation, but that means nothing. Mr. X is still the most likely suspect." Cranston tossed the photos back on the desk. "I would really like to believe you, Sheriff. But I'm afraid my money is on Mr. X."

Jim paced behind his desk nervously. *I've got to tell him, I've got to come clean,* he thought to himself. *I can't continue my investigation without his help.* As he stopped in front of the window and stared out at the parking lot filled with reporters he *knew* he had to put his cards on the table.

Cranston was standing in front of the desk reading the coroner's report when Jim began to speak. "I know that Mr. X didn't kill Henderson," Jim said then slowly turned and looked Cranston in the eye. "Because *I'm* Mr. X."

Cranston's jaw dropped open as he placed a hand on the desk to steady himself. "*You're* Mr. X? Why didn't you *say* something?"

"Because that hot shot agent of yours would've tried to arrest me. I can't exactly conduct my investigation from a jail cell, can I?" Jim replied.

Still slightly stunned, Cranston sat down in the chair across from Jim slowly and thought for a moment. "What exactly were you doing out there, anyway?"

"Henderson had a load of garbage that needed to be taken to the dump. He couldn't do it so he called me," Jim replied.

"That early in the morning and in a rainstorm?" Cranston looked at him cockeyed.

"Anthony Marcellous, the man who runs the landfill, was taking a few days off and going to Portland. He agreed to open the landfill first thing yesterday morning if the trash could be delivered before he left. Otherwise, it would have had to stay at Henderson's until Monday," Jim answered.

Lifting his hand to his face, Cranston rubbed his jaw. "What time did you get to Henderson's?"

"I'm not sure, exactly," Jim replied. "I only stayed a short time and left exactly at five. I remember because I checked my watch."

"What time did you reach the landfill?"

"About five-thirty," Jim replied.

"How long did it take to dump the garbage?"

"Only a couple of minutes. I just had Marcellous disconnect the trailer and I left."

"What did you do then?"

"I went home and got some rest."

"Can anyone verify that?"

"Yes, my girlfriend was there when I got home. That was about seven," Jim replied.

"That's no good, Sheriff. The coroner's report says that Henderson was killed around six. There's no way to prove that you didn't go back to Henderson's and kill him." Cranston folded up the report and tossed it on the desk.

"But I'm telling you I didn't do it!" Jim exclaimed.

"Your word isn't enough. You have no alibi. That makes you a suspect."

"Bradley is the only one who could've done it. I *need* you to help me start an investigation into that possibility." Jim urged.

Cranston took a step back and looked at Jim in a strange manner. "I'm not Internal Affairs. I can't launch an investigation of one of my agents without proof. All you've got is speculation and hear say. If you had a bullet it would be a different story, but you have nothing."

"Bradley has nothing, as well! It's his word against mine," Jim replied.

"That's where you're wrong, Sheriff. Bradley found opium at both scenes. That's hard evidence. It holds his story together. It makes it plausible. While your's folds like a card house." Cranston was starting to feel a little irritated.

Jim didn't know what to say, he was at the end of his rope. Then it came to him. "Wait a minute!" he exclaimed. Cranston looked over to him. "I may not have a bullet, but I have a *witness.*"

Cranston looked at Jim as if he were crazy. "What are you talking about?"

"Chet Green," Jim replied. "He was up there with Bradley. He *has* to know exactly what happened."

"He hasn't said anything so far. What makes you think he'll talk now?"

"He'll *have* to! We'll bring him in for questioning and confront him." Jim again stood up and paced nervously as his mind toyed with the idea.

"Now you're getting desperate! This is the nineties and that only works in the movies." Cranston argued as he looked at Jim. He saw a man that was exhausted and not thinking clearly.

The stress had taken its toll and Jim looked fifteen years older than he was. Cranston had already written this case off as a loss. Sure, he had hopes of resurrecting his career, but he wasn't going to risk his pension by doing something foolish.

"Why won't it work?" Harper asked. "If he knows we're on to him, he may want to swing a deal."

"Green isn't going to talk because he's too smart! He knows what the law says and what his rights are. Heck, he's a reporter! Do you know what that means?" Cranston leaned on the desk and looked at Jim. "He'll crucify us on national television if we so much as shine a light in his face!" Cranston shook his head decisively. "No, Sheriff. There will be no interrogation of the press!"

Jim slowly stepped back from the desk and stared at the floor. Turning towards the window, he gazed aimlessly at the distant mountains. After a few moments, Jim spoke quietly. "Now that you know I'm Mr. X, are you going to turn me in?"

Cranston felt sorry for Jim and decided that this man could use a break. In many ways they were in the same situation—only Jim's was worse. He suddenly remembered that he'd felt bad for neglecting his responsibility with regards to Bradley and he wanted to make it up to Harper.

"No, I'm not, Sheriff," he replied thoughtfully. "I think it would be better for both of us if this discussion never happened. Besides, I believe you. I wish I could help, but without that bullet, my hands are tied."

Jim continued to stare at the mountains. "So what's going to happen now?" he said after a long moment of consideration.

Taking a deep breath, Cranston thought about the question as he let it out slowly. "Well, your investigation has stalled." He walked to the window next to Jim and stared out. "It looks like Bradley's has also come to a dead end. The only lead left is the fingerprints and knowing Bradley, he'll probably lose interest before he finds a match and move onto something else. However, eventually, they'll be matched to you using your military file. At which point, you'll have to explain yourself so you'd better have your story straight." Cranston continued to stare out the window as he spoke. "But in the long run, there's not enough real evidence for a conviction, so it'll go nowhere."

Jim felt depressed. "So it's all over...case closed."

"Not in the least." Cranston glanced at Jim then back at the mountains. "You don't think it could be over without someone taking the blame, do you? Bradley was right, you know, he has powerful friends. We're through."

"Do you think we'll be fired?"

"No, I don't think the Governor could do that, but he can force us to retire," Cranston replied.

Jim let out a heavy sigh. Two of his best friends were dead, and his life was in ruins. He used to feel so confident, sometimes cocky. Now he realized how powerless he was in stopping the events of the last couple of days and his heart sank.

At that moment the lack of sleep and exhaustion caught up with him. His head ached and his eyes were red and soar. He needed a cup of coffee to hold himself together. He turned around slowly. Picking up his cup from the desk, he slowly walked to the door and opened it. As he walked to the pot, Jim could hear his deputies discussing the case, but he really wasn't listening very closely.

Agent O'Leary stepped out of the conference room holding a pile of shift reports. "Which one of you is Simms?"

"That would be me," a man said from the desk behind Jim.

O'Leary stepped over to the desk. "I was just going over your shift report from yesterday and I found a discrepancy. Its nothing really, but I hope you can help me correct it."

"What's wrong?" Simms asked as he leaned over the desk to look at the report.

"Well, it's like this," O'Leary started to explain. "You wrote here that you relieved Rissley from sentry duty on Henderson's porch at 8 a.m. this morning."

"That's right, what's the problem?" Simms replied.

"Rissley's report says you relieved her at 6 a.m... Which is it? Eight or six?" O'Leary asked.

"Come to think of it," Simms said as he sat back in his chair. "It didn't start to get light until two to three hours after I started duty. It must've been six o'clock. Otherwise, I would've noticed it getting lighter when I relieved her."

"Well I suggest you get your watch fixed," O'Leary said.

"I wasn't wearing a watch. I got the time from that weird clock on Henderson's porch. It must be two hours fast."

That can't be right, Jim thought to himself as he poured the coffee. When he'd left Buck's place, the clock was an hour slow. Even if Buck corrected the time after he'd left, he wouldn't have set it two hours fast.

Then it hit him like a ton of bricks. "*Dang!* That's hot!" He exclaimed. The whole office looked at him. In the excitement of the moment, Jim had forgotten what he was doing and poured coffee on himself. Setting the pot down on the counter, he rushed back to his office. Cranston was a still staring out of the window as if *he* was the one who'd lost his best friend.

Jim grabbed Cranston. "I know where the bullet is!"

Cranston's eyes lit up with excitement. "Are you sure?" The news was too good to be true.

"It's *got* to be there. There's no other possibility."

"If you're right, Sheriff, we'll be able to nail that little jerk." Cranston's body filled with a strange and welcome new energy. "Where is it?"

"Come with me. I'll explain on the way."

Cranston followed Jim out of the office and to the back door. As they exited the building, a herd of reporters noticed them and rushed toward them.

"Get in quick!" Jim said loudly as he jumped in the driver's side of the Blazer, slamming it shut just as the reporters closed in on them. Cranston was in the passenger seat a moment later just as a young woman with a microphone started pounding on the side of the truck. Jim pulled out quickly to avoid the crowd.

"Whew! That was close," Cranston said as he caught his breath. "We almost didn't make it out of there."

Jim flipped on his lights and siren as he raced down the street. Barely waiting for vehicles to move, he swerved in and out of traffic as car horns blared in reply.

"My Lord, Sheriff! I didn't know we were in this big of a hurry!" Cranston said as he struggled to stay in his seat. "Exactly what are we doing?"

Jim began to explain. "Remember I told you that I knew I'd left Henderson's *before* the murder at 5 a.m., because I had checked my watch."

"Yeah, so what of it?" Cranston shrugged.

"Well, when I checked my watch I noticed that Henderson's porch clock was one hour slow," Jim said without taking his eyes off the road. "But one of my deputies just stated that the porch clock is now two hours fast. That clock is in the line of flight of the bullet we're looking for."

"So you think that the bullet hit the hour hand and moved it three hours ahead?"

"It's a strange clock, it has no hands," Jim replied. "Each hour of the day is painted on a shingle and placed on the end of a spoke of a wheel. The clock has a cover with a pie shape window cut at the top of it. Whatever time of the day it is, hours one through twelve, that shingle shows up in the window."

So you think that the bullet went through that little window and is lodged somewhere inside the clock." Cranston said.

"If Henderson was killed any time during the six o'clock hour—" Jim started to say but was interrupted.

"Then the five o'clock shingle would've been in the window because the clock was slow."

"How much do you want to bet the five o'clock shingle has a hole in it?" Jim asked.

This brought a huge smile to Cranston's face. "Can't this thing go any faster? We've got a bullet to find!"

Jim didn't answer him. As he turned onto the highway, his foot was heavy on the pedal until the speedometer was out of sight.

Chet parked the Chief in front of the room and got out carrying his camera. Walking to the door, he opened it and saw Alan standing in the middle of the room talking on the phone.

"Yes sir, Governor Wilson, and thank you. I appreciate your swift response to this matter." Chet heard Bradley say as he walked to the computer, turned it on, then sat down in front of it. Chet waited until Bradley hung up the phone.

"What was *that* all about?" he asked as he removed a disk from the camera and inserted it into the computer.

"That was Governor Wilson. After I explained the situation down here, he said he'd call an immediate press conference. He's going to denounce the actions of Cranston and Harper and blame them for the whole affair. At this moment, his aids are drawing up the papers to force both of them into retirement," Bradley said with a smile as he lifted the phone and dialed.

"So then it's over." There was noticeable relief in Chet's voice as he said it.

"Not quite," Bradley said and, as he listened to the phone ring in the earpiece, he looked over Chet's shoulder to the computer. "What are you doing?"

"I got some great shots of the plane wreckage and incinerated body for tomorrow's paper," Chet answered, then changed the subject. "What did you mean by not quite?"

Bradley didn't get a chance to answer as the connection was completed.

"Drug Enforcement Agency. This is Agent Angela Rodriguez. How can I help you?" The voice on the other end said.

"Angela, this is Alan."

"What do you want, Bradley?" she said in an irritated voice.

"I need everything you can get for me on Jim Harper. He's the Sheriff of Lewis County and has been for years, so it shouldn't take you long to get it." Bradley said.

"I'll get on it right away." Came the reply.

"Thank you. I need it pronto!" Bradley said, then hung up the phone and set it down on the nightstand.

"What was that all about?" Chet asked, curiously.

"Just that jerk Sheriff," Bradley replied as he turned and walked over to Chet. "I'm going to dig up as much dirt on him as I can. Maybe then he won't think he's so almighty powerful."

"But it's *over*." Chet stood up to face his friend and tried to reason with him. "You got everything you wanted. Someone else is going to take the heat and you step away with all the publicity."

"*Wrong!*" Bradley said angrily as he stepped past Chet and started to pace. "I wanted to nail this drug smuggling operation and that Sheriff ruined it for me."

"Oh get off it, Alan!" Chet argued. "You don't still believe that there are smugglers here do you?"

"Of *course* I do! That's what this is all about!"

"No, it's not! At least not anymore. You're just angry because someone stepped on your toes. It stops now! You *promised* it would!" Chet yelled.

349

"Well I've changed my mind! I have to teach that jerk not to screw with me anymore!" Bradley said angrily, almost losing control.

Chet had never seen Alan so mad before and he continued to try and reason with him. "But he'll be forced to retire! What more do you want?"

"I want his butt!" Alan barked.

"Haven't you caused enough damage? There are two men who are dead that shouldn't be, and the only evidence against them you planted!" Chet argued. "Now let it lie!"

"Don't start giving me orders, Chet!" Alan warned as he shook a finger at his friend. "You don't run things around here!"

"Oh, yeah! Well what are you going to do if you can't find any dirt? What then? Are you going to plant drugs on him *too*?" Chet asked.

"If I have to," Alan said calmly.

Chet's jaw dropped in surprise. "Then you can count me out! I'm not going to stand by and watch you ruin someone else's life. I'm going to pack up my stuff and—" Chet's words were cut short by the impact of Alan's body against his own.

Alan slammed Chet up against the wall with such force that Chet almost collapsed. Holding Chet by the lapels of his jacket, Alan yelled furiously into his face. *"You're not going anywhere! You destroyed evidence, remember! You're in this up to your eyeballs!"* Alan stared into Chet's frightened wide eyes and shook him. "You wouldn't be anything without me, don't forget that! You're lucky I haven't cut you loose and replaced you with someone with more national exposure. There are plenty of reporters out there that would *love* to be in your position, so don't force me to make changes. Now, you'll do as you're told and keep your mouth shut! Do you *understand?*"

Chet couldn't answer. The wind was knocked out of him. For the first time in his life, Chet was afraid of Alan. Alan released his grip and watched as Chet fell to the floor.

Chet lay gasping for air. A few moments later, he reached up to the desk and slowly pulled himself to his feet. Chet watched as Alan walked calmly to the bathroom. Looking in the mirror, Alan checked his hair then straightened his tie.

Trying to compose himself, Chet caught his breath. He could feel his head pounding from the impact with the wall. Chet put his hand on the wall to steady himself as he moved slowly across the room to the door.

"Where are you going?" Alan asked calmly from the bathroom without taking his eyes off his reflection.

Chet looked at the ground and replied timidly. "I'm going for a drive."

"Good idea. Take your time and pull yourself together. Everything's going to be just fine," Alan said with a confident air. "I promise."

Chet opened the door and slowly stepped outside, closing it quietly behind him.

21
Throwing a Curve

The Blazer sped down the blacktop as the highway wound through the trees and grassy farmland. Jim slowed and turned into the empty oncoming traffic lane as vehicles in his lane slowed to a stop.

"What's going on?" Cranston wanted to know as he looked at the line of stopped vehicles and their impatient drivers.

"I'm not sure. There must be—"

Screech!

Jim slammed on the breaks as he came around the bend. Directly in front of them was a large timber log closing off the road. Several other logs covered the road and the ditch on the left hand side. To the right was the logging truck from which they'd come. Turned over on its side, it covered the highway and filled the ditch on the right side with impassable debris.

"I'd better see if anyone's hurt," Jim said urgently as he opened the door, jumped out, and ran to the truck. The rig's driver was sitting on the roadside with his hands on his head. "Are you all right?" Harper asked, when he reached him.

The man looked up at Jim then lowered the white compress from his forehead, revealing a large bruise and small gash above his right eye. "I think I'll be all right," the man said while trying to smile. Jim looked at the wound. "I hit it on the steering wheel when my rig flipped."

"It doesn't look too bad, but just the same you'd better see a doctor," Jim said with a concerned voice. "Did anyone else get hurt?"

"No, just me," the driver replied as he put the compress back on his head.

That was a lucky break, Jim knew. This could've easily turned into a major catastrophe and Jim was glad to see that at least a few things were going his way.

"What happened?" Harper asked as he looked around at the wreckage.

"I was coming around the bend when, coming from the opposite direction, a sports car pulled out to pass a Winnebago on this blind stretch of road. I swerved to get out of the way and it worked, but my trailer caught the edge of the ditch and it flipped the whole rig. Luckily, no one else got hurt," the driver explained.

"No kidding, these logs could've done some real damage." Jim agreed, astonished as he looked at the huge cedar timbers.

Cranston looked at the mess and shook his head. "It's going to take *hours* to clean this mess up, Sheriff. I guess we'd better make ourselves comfortable."

"Not hardly," Jim replied as he looked up at the northern ridge. He wasn't about to wait around when his objective was so close.

"What?" Cranston asked as he tried to figure out what Jim was looking for.

Jim walked back down the road from which they'd come and looked at the barbed wire fence next to it. His eyes followed it as it paralleled the road, and he knew that it continued for miles. "Yeah, that'll do nicely."

"What will do nicely?" Cranston asked.

"There." Jim pointed. "About a hundred yards back is a gate in the fence. I'm going to call this in and get a crew out here, then we'll use that gate to cut across the field."

They both ran back to the Blazer. As Jim put in the call, Cranston wiped the sweat from his brow. He'd been behind a desk for too long and was out of shape. The short jog was enough to remind him of that.

Still, the excitement he felt at that moment reminded him of the times he'd spent on the streets of Seattle. Back then, he headed up his own investigations, found his own clues, and raced against time to nail the bad guys, just as they were doing now and he missed that. It felt good to be back on point again, and it provided a type of energy and thrill that only comes from knowing that what you're doing could make or break the case.

The Blazer arrived at the gate and Cranston leaped out to open it. After driving through, Jim jumped out, locked the hubs then

354

looked at Cranston. "Are you all right?" Harper asked as he looked at Cranston's sweaty face.

Cranston nodded. He welcomed the feel of adrenaline flowing into his blood stream as his heart pounded in his chest, and he knew it was from more than just the exercise. "What are we doing?"

"You don't live out here as long as I have without learning the back roads." Jim smiled as both men got back in the Blazer.

"But there's no road here," Cranston argued.

Jim put his seat belt on. "You'd better buckle up, it's going to get bumpy." With that, he hit the gas.

Cranston was pushed back into his seat from the acceleration. Struggling to get the belt secured, he watched the sea of tall grass bend over and disappear under the Blazer as they sailed through it. On the opposite side of the field, they came to a stand of alder trees and Jim maneuvered through them to a creek bed.

Pulling the steering wheel sharply, Jim punched the gas then launched the vehicle over the steep bank. The Blazer hung in the air, just clearing a deep water hole, then cannon balled into the far side of stream. A wave of water shot over the cab as the tires bit into the streambed. The Blazer leaped forward into shallower water and made its way upstream.

The passengers felt like corn in a popper as the Blazer's shocks and springs were tortured by the rocky terrain. Water was thrown in all directions as the passenger's side wheels spun deep in the stream.

Cranston lifted his legs as water came through the bottom of his door. "What are you trying to do, Sheriff, drown me?"

"Just hold on, we're almost through it," Jim reassured him.

The Blazer serpentined back and forth across the stream, trying to keep from being swallowed up by one of the many deep holes. A minute later, Jim pulled the wheel hard and the Blazer left the streambed, starting up a steep grassy embankment. Jim buried the gas pedal and large clods of dirt and grass were thrown down the hill as the four by four clawed its way towards the top. Cresting the hill, the Blazer moved down a narrow path with tall pine trees on both sides.

"What kind of a trail is this?" Cranston asked.

"It's an old logging road from the early sixties when they clear cut this hill. As you can see, the trees have grown back, covering most of the road. There aren't very many people who know it's here," Jim replied as the Blazer maneuvered through the trees.

"Where's it taking us?"

"It winds back and forth up the hill to the top of the ridge. On the other side is a gravel access road which leads down to Mineral Lake," Jim answered. Like a thousand tiny fingernails on a black board, the branches from the pines scrapped eerily down the sides of the four by four as it pushed through the trees and up the road.

Alan was pacing back and forth in the motel room waiting for the call from the Seattle DEA office. It had been an hour since Chet left, and Alan was able to cool his temper. No one had ever got in his way or made him as mad as Harper had. Not even Cranston. He was determined to make Harper pay and not just a little bit. Alan was set on making it hurt bad. As he paced, his diabolical mind was busy plotting the demise of his enemy.

Remembering what Chet had showed him on the computer, Alan started up the machine and searched the picture file. An evil smile came over his face as he found it. Chet had taken a picture of Harper on the porch, yesterday, and it had been loaded onto the hard drive.

"Let's see now," Alan said to himself as he tried to remember what Chet had done to the picture of the disgruntled worker. Oh yeah, first I have to isolate the head, he thought as he moved the mouse around and punched some keys. Alan stretched the face horizontally to make his lips purse. He then played with the contrast a little to make his skin look dirty. Then he brightened the whites of Harper's eyes to make it appear as if he was staring at you from the picture.

"There, *perfect!*" Alan said with delight. The changes were slight, but just enough to give the audience the visual impression that Alan wanted to portray. In front of Alan's eyes was the picture of a law enforcement officer gone bad, made complete with a soiled uniform and tarnished badge tainted by his many sins. The picture made Alan laugh with pleasure as he hit the print button.

At that instant, the phone rang and he reached for it. "This is Bradley."

"Bradley, this is Rodriguez," said the voice on the line. "I've got the report on your man, but it's not very exciting."

"What does it say?"

"Let's see here," she said as she paged through it. "He was born and raised there in Lewis County...spent some time in Vietnam...got elected Sheriff in 1970 and has been there ever since."

Bradley felt disappointed as he thought for a moment. "What did he do in Vietnam?" He could hear the sound of paper rustling as Rodriguez paged through the report.

"Here it is...hmm, impressive," she remarked as she read it. "Purple heart and silver star. He was part of an Army Airborne unit for a few years, then did a stretch as a consultant at the US Embassy in Saigon."

"Army Airborne? Aren't those the guys who jump out of airplanes?" Bradley asked.

"Yeah, so?"

Bradley's eyes lit up as he saw the possible connection. "So he knows how to parachute just like D.B. Cooper did."

"That doesn't mean anything," Rodriguez remarked. "Thousands of vets have the same training Harper has. You can't go around accusing—" Bradley could hear that Rodriguez was interrupted on the other side. "Hold it a second, Bradley."

Alan's mind was busy calculating and planning how he'd use this tasty bit of information. *Let's see now. Harper was here during the Cooper hijacking and has parachute experience. I wonder if—*

"*Bradley!* It's *him!*" Rodriguez yelled across the line. "I just received the fingerprint check from Harper's military record. They match the ones from the coffee cup *exactly*. Harper's your man!"

Bradley's jaw dropped open, and he was astonished as it was revealed to him. "Harper was the man with the truck and trailer?"

"But why would the Sheriff kill Henderson?" Rodriguez asked, curiously. "That doesn't make sense."

Bradley's eyes lit up with excitement. "*Of course!* Why didn't I see this before?"

"What? See what?"

"Angela, if you were going to start a sophisticated drug operation in a small community, who is the first person you'd bribe?" Alan asked, calmly.

"I don't know. The judge I suppose."

"No! The judge can only help you *after* you've been caught," Bradley exclaimed. "The Sheriff is the *ideal* person to have in your operation. He's the first person in the County who'd find out if a Federal investigation were going on. He can also move freely within and adversely affect an investigation without being noticed. He's one of the few people in the County who would not be under suspicion. That's why he's been interfering with me all along. He had something to hide!"

"Do you think that somehow he found out you were going down there then he got out to Henderson's to close up shop?"

"Exactly. It's the only viable explanation," Bradley replied. "Now fax me that report, I'm in a hurry." Alan hung up the phone.

Moments later, the fax machine hummed, beeped, and emitted an eerie green glow as it slowly spit out the report.

Bradley couldn't believe his luck as he put on his sports coat then lifted the report from the tray. "This is working out better than I expected," he said to himself. "Not only can I pin the Henderson killing on him, but I'm going to pass him off as D.B. Cooper as well!" Bradley lifted his head in the air and laughed heartily. "Forget the Governor's mansion. They'll elect me president of this whole damn country for this one!"

Alan grabbed the now defiled picture of Harper and was elated. It was exactly the image of a drug smuggling Sheriff gone bad, and now D.B. Cooper felon that he'd wanted to portray Harper as. "It'll be as easy as shooting fish in a barrel," he said out loud.

Harper was a part of the drug smuggling ring, he was *sure* of it. Like Henderson and Schaffer, Harper would be too smart to have anything incriminating around, Bradley knew. That's why Alan had to make sure it was an airtight case.

Bradley looked around the room and located his black tote bag. Inside, he found the last third of the opium brick. All he needed to do was find Harper, plant the opium in his Blazer, then report his story on the evening news. In front of the whole world, Alan would conduct a search and find the drugs.

An evil grin stretched across his face as he stuffed the drugs, report, and picture into the bag then closed it up. He rushed out the door, and saw that Chet wasn't back yet. After examining his watch, he saw that it was only an hour until the prime time evening news started. Figuring that Chet was with his camera crew, Alan decided to call him from the road. With that, he ran to his Corvette and jumped in. A moment later, the Corvette roared to life. The tires smoked and screamed as the car shot onto the highway then down the road.

As the Blazer approached the ridge, Cranston saw the road stop at a large rock pile. The road was a washout. "It's a dead end," he said. "What now?"

"I don't know. This road hasn't been used in decades, but I didn't figure there'd be a washout. But somehow we've *got* to get

358

past it and to the access road. I'll have to make this up as I go." Jim maneuvered slowly off the road and into the trees. Both men pulled in the mirrors as the vehicle eased carefully through the tight fit on its way along the top of the ridge. Breaking into a clearing, Jim pointed to the small access road fifty feet below them. "There."

"Now how do we get down there? It's straight down a cliff," Cranston asked.

Jim looked around as he drove slowly out into the clearing. There were two cliffs on either side of a rockslide saddle that stretched from the clearing to the road. "We'll have to take the rocks."

"The *what?*" Cranston exclaimed. "That's crazy! One wrong move on those unstable rocks and we'll end up in that ravine with a ton of boulders to bury us."

"Its not that far, we can make it," Jim reassured him. It had been along time since Jim had taken any major risk, and like Cranston, he was feeling the exciting adrenaline rush that only comes from being on the edge. His entire body and mind was fully alert and engaged as he slowly inched the Blazer out onto the flat shale rocks.

Both men held their breath and Jim maneuvered slowly. Some loose rocks slid out in front of them down the hill and into the ravine. They were half way there when the vibration from the vehicle started the rocks moving. The Blazer started to slide, slowly at first, but quickly accelerated as the flat rocks slid over the top of each other.

"We're going to roll!" Cranston yelled as he braced himself against the dashboard. Jim tried to stay calm as he maneuvered the Blazer like a surfboard across the moving sea of sliding rocks. The roar of the landslide was deafening as he struggled to stay on top of the rocky wave. He was able to stay in just enough control to get the front wheels clear of the rocks when they hit the road.

The front tires dug in while the sliding rocks carried the rear off the far end of the slope as the rocks tumbled over the edge and crashed into the ravine. Just over the cliff edge, the rear axle scraped angrily against the ground as the back wheels dangled in the air. Instantly, Jim gunned the engine and the front wheels pulled them clear of the rocks and onto the road.

"Huh! That was close!" Cranston exclaimed as he looked back realizing how easily they could've been thrown into the ravine and crushed by tons of stone. He immediately felt light headed and sick at the possibility.

Both men could hear the thunderous sounds of rocks crashing against one another, but Jim didn't look back. As he drove quickly down the road, he pointed to a sparkling blue image below them. "There it is!" Jim exclaimed. "It won't be long now." Jim was true to his word as the Blazer covered the distance quickly. Throwing up a cloud of dust, the 4x4 hurried down the empty road to Henderson's home and came to a stop in front of it. Both men jumped out, rushed onto the porch, and looked at the clock.

The seven shingle was showing in the window. Cranston quickly looked at his watch. "Two hours fast, alright."

Jim reached into the little window and turned the wheel back moving it to the five o'clock position. The shingle was completely shattered. Both men looked at each other with excitement.

"Let's get the cover off," Jim said as he checked the right side of the clock. Cranston checked the left side, and in unison both men released the pins and pulled the cover off. Cranston took it and rolled it out of the way. Jim could see the bullet lodged in the back panel of the clock. Removing the Leatherman's accessory tool from his belt, Jim gently dug the bullet loose. *"I've got it!"* He stood up and lifted the bullet in the air in front of Cranston's face.

"*Yes*! I've finally got that little *jerk!*" Cranston cheered. "Let me see it."

Jim handed it over. "Now all we have to do is match it to this one that I took from the firing range and it's all over—case closed!" Jim pulled a small plastic bag from his pocket and showed Cranston the other bullet.

He was suddenly revitalized. The feelings of despair at losing his two friends had been replaced by the elation knowing that he could now avenge them.

The smile on Cranston's face slowly faded as he examined the bullet from the clock carefully. Jim's heart stopped when he noticed his change of expression and was afraid to ask what was wrong.

"It's badly damaged," Cranston said slowly. "I can't be sure without a microscope, but I don't think there's enough here to get a match."

Jim's mood sank when he heard this. In all the excitement he hadn't examined the bullet. In desperation, he grabbed the bullet from Cranston and looked for himself.

The bullet was squished flat. There were some rifling marks on its side, but they were badly scared. Jim slowly sat down on the bench and let out a heavy sigh knowing that the chance of being able to match the two bullets was slim to *impossible*.

"I'm sorry, Sheriff," Cranston said as the deflated feeling returned. "I guess it wasn't meant to be. This kid is lucky beyond belief."

Jim placed his head in his hands and slowly rubbed his temples. He'd come too far to fail now, he told himself. He *couldn't* give up. If there was any possible chance of proving the charges against Bradley, he *had* to try. After a few moments of silence, Jim stood up. "I guess there's only one thing I can do," he said, soberly.

"What's that?"

Pulling another clear plastic evidence bag from his shirt pocket, Jim put the squished bullet inside it. "For the moment, let's say that the bullet is too badly damaged for a match. That only leaves one possibility—Chet Green." Jim's voice was filled with conviction. "I'm going to bring him in for questioning. If we confront him with what we know, he'll cave. I'm *sure* of it."

"*We?*" Cranston looked at him as if he were crazy. "Like I said before, Sheriff, messing with the press is *suicide!* Green is going to know a run around when he sees it." Cranston shook his head. "If you're determined to carry out this course of action, count me out. I think you're playing with fire if you mess with this reporter."

"That's easy for you to say. You're only facing retirement. I've lost two friends, my career, and I'm possibly facing murder charges when they match my prints. Not to mention the position in the community I've worked so hard to attain. I've protected these people like a father for almost thirty years. What'll they think of me now, if I can't bring Buck and Rick's killer to justice?" Jim immediately thought of Nikki and sadly wondered if she'd stay with him through it all. "When Bradley matches the prints, I'm going to lose everything." Jim shook his head. "No, I don't have anything else to lose. I *have* to try something!" Jim walked off the porch and to the Blazer with Cranston following him.

"Remember, Sheriff. If you do this, I can't help you," Cranston said as he got into the passenger seat and closed the door. "I'll stay around and observe, but if it starts to fall apart, there's no way I can save you."

"I understand," Jim replied as he opened his door and reached for the radio. What he needed to do now required the assistance of his best deputy. "Harper to Rissley, come in, Joe."

Deputy Rissley had just straightened out a fender bender when the call came in. "Go ahead, Sheriff," squawked the radio.

"What's your twenty?"

"Highway twelve, just east of Morton," she replied.

"Go into Morton and find Chet Green. I want you to bring him to the station for questioning," Jim ordered.

"Roger that, Sheriff. I'm on my way."

"By the way, highway twelve just west of Morton is closed. You'll have to find another way back," he said into the radio.

"Don't worry, Sheriff. I know a few back road short cuts," Rissley assured him.

Jim looked closely at the bullet one more time, then pressed the button on the radio. "Joe, listen closely. This is what I want you to do."

As Cranston listened to Jim's instructions, his eyes grew wide with shock and he wished he hadn't heard what was being planned. *Crazy fool*, he thought to himself, wondering if Harper actually believed he could pull it off. When the instructions were complete, they both sat in silence for a minute staring at the lake.

"So, how are we going to get back?" Cranston broke the silence.

Jim thought for a second then smiled. "The same way we came in." With that, he hit the gas.

"Oh my gosh," Cranston cringed. The Blazer kicked up dirt as it turned around and headed back up the road.

Bradley slowed his car as he approached the long line of vehicles stopped on highway twelve. *What was going on now?* he wondered as he stopped behind the last car in line. He didn't have much cushion time before the evening news, so he had to arrive at the station early enough to plant the opium, then arrest Harper on prime time television.

Timing was everything, he reminded himself. He thought it ironic that the traffic congestion he created to slow down the Sheriff's department was now working against him. He decided to call Chet to make sure everything was ready when he arrived.

He smiled to himself as he dialed a number on the car phone, then listened to it ring over and over. "Come on, Chet, answer your cell phone," Bradley said impatiently. Maybe he was with his TV crew, he thought. Hanging up, he dialed another number.

"KJY News, this is Ms. Stapleton," came the voice from the other side.

"This is Agent Bradley. Is Chet there?"

"No, he's not," the irritated voice said. She disliked Chet immensely. Since they met, he'd been trying to run the show his way, and that had caused several arguments. She also resented Chet's relationship with Bradley. If it weren't for Chet's *exclusive*, she would've told Chet to hit the road. Unfortunately, she needed him, so she swallowed her pride and took the abuse. "He was supposed to be here by now. We've got to get together and plan out the evening report."

"Don't worry about that, Chet has everything under control," Bradley reassured her. "Just get your crew to the Sheriff's station, pronto."

"We're really close to there, now. What's going on?"

"I can't be specific now, but I'll say that I'm going to make a major arrest that will blow this case wide open," he replied with a smile.

The voice on the other side suddenly became very excited. "I'll page Chet, then we'll meet you there in thirty minutes."

Alan hung up. Well, that takes care of them. Now if this traffic would just cooperate, he thought. Alan wondered where Chet was and hoped he remained focused on what their objective was. He shook off the feeling. He'd known Chet for a long time and knew that after he had a chance to think, he'd see it Alan's way and do what he was told. *Damn*! This traffic was a *nightmare*. Alan waited in his car and tried to stay calm as precious minutes ticked away.

When Deputy Rissley finally found him, Chet was sitting on a stool hunched over a cup of coffee at the diner. With his elbows on the counter and head in his hands, he sat motionless staring at the cup in front of him. Joe walked over and put her hand on his shoulder.

"Excuse me, sir," she said. Chet didn't move. Rissley shook his shoulder gently. "Excuse me, sir," she said again.

"Huh, what?" Chet replied as if shaken from deep concentration. He hadn't realized how much time had gone by since he'd arrived at the diner. Staring at the same cup of coffee he'd ordered an hour ago, he'd been replaying the argument with Alan over in his head.

Alan had never spoken to him like that before, and he'd never physically harmed him like he did this afternoon. Would Alan cut Chet loose and find another reporter like he said? Chet thought they were friends and wanted to believe that Alan would *never* betray him. But over the past hour, he had the chance to reflect on everything he'd known about Alan.

363

Alan was always dangling carrots in front of people to get their help, then failed to live up to his promises. Chet felt depressed as he seriously doubted his so called friend's integrity. So depressed that he barely noticed Rissley when she'd spoken to him.

"Oh hello, Deputy," he finally said. "What can I do for you?"

Rissley looked at him closely. His face was slightly pale and his eyes were bloodshot. She remembered what she'd decided about him. He was the weak link and was now vulnerable. She wondered if she and the Sheriff could pull this off. "Are you all right, sir?" she asked in a genuinely concerned voice.

"Yes I'm fine," he answered as he ran his fingers through his hair then straightened his tie. "Now, what is it you want?"

"May I have a few minutes of your time, sir."

"Shoot."

"Outside please, sir."

Chet looked at her for a moment then shrugged. Standing slowly, he pulled a couple of dollar bills from his pocket and threw them on the counter. Following Rissley outside, he again asked. "What do you want, Deputy?"

"Sir, I've been asked to bring you into the station for questioning."

This brought a faint smile to Chet's face. "I'm just a reporter, Deputy. What kind of questions would someone need to ask me?"

"I'm not sure, sir. I was just ordered to bring you in."

Chet's eyes narrowed. "I'm afraid that's impossible." He looked at his watch and remembered that he'd told Stapleton he'd meet them in Centralia for a planning session. "I'm already late for a meeting with my producer. Anymore of a delay could ruin my evening report. Now if you'll excuse me, I need to be going to Centralia," he said and started to turn away.

"I'm afraid I'm going to have to insist, sir," she said as she grabbed his arm. He turned back to her and gave her an irate look. She'd dealt with people like him before. Though his face looked confident, his eyes showed something else. She hoped that it was enough of an advantage.

"Haven't you heard of the freedom of the press!" he said angrily. "You can't stop me from doing my job!"

"I've got a job to do, as well," she replied as she tried to be tactful. "Besides, unless you go with me, you'll never make it in time for the evening news."

Chet looked at her questioningly. "What are you talking about?"

"Highway twenty has been closed until further notice. There won't be any traffic either way until late tonight," she said calmly. "If you'll answer a couple quick questions, I'd be happy to take you there by another route."

Chet thought about it for a moment. He *had* to get to Centralia soon or blow his chance of giving the evening report. "I guess I have no other choice."

"This way." Rissley led him to her Blazer. Both of them got in, and Rissley put on her seat belt. "I'd buckle up if I were you." She smiled. "This might get a little bumpy." Chet had barely gotten his seat belt buckled when he was thrown back into his seat as Rissley stepped on the gas pedal. The Blazer tore out of the diner's parking lot and raced down the street.

Bradley was starting to get impatient as he waited in the unmoving line of vehicles. Suddenly in his rear view mirror, he saw a group of people in orange vests and hard hats approaching. It was the road crew coming to clean up the load of timber. *They should know what's going on,* Bradley thought as he got out of the car, walked up to one of them, and showed his badge.

"I'm Special Agent Bradley. What's going on here?"

"Hey! You're that FBI guy from the TV!" the man exclaimed. He turned quickly and waved to his companions. "Hey guys! Look who we have here."

Bradley grabbed the man's arm. "That's *DEA* and I'm in a hurry so why don't you tell me what's going on," he said, firmly.

The man turned back to Bradley. "There's been an accident and the road is closed. We're supposed to turn everyone around and send them back the way they came."

"How do I get through? It's an *emergency!*"

"You don't. Not unless you want to sit in your car until dark," came the reply.

"Damn!" Bradley said as he turned and ran to his car. After parking it on the side of the road, he grabbed his black bag and ran down the road towards the scene of the accident. *It can't be far,* he thought as he checked his watch. His only hope was to get to the other side of the blockage and commandeer a vehicle. If his luck holds, he should be able to make it in time.

Jim's beat up Blazer coughed and sputtered its way into the station's lot and stopped near the back door. Reporters quickly covered the distance to the 4x4 as the two men got out. Jim pushed his way through the crowd towards the door as reporter's yelled questions that went unanswered. Cranston reached the door first and went inside. As he walked towards the counter, he pulled out his bottle of Pepto and took a long drink.

"*Cranston!* I should've known!" Came a voice from the front door. Cranston lowered the bottle to see Chet Green walk in escorted by Deputy Rissley. They had just arrived as well, and the terrifying ride he'd experienced irritated him. Chet walked up to Cranston. "If you're trying to suppress this story, I *swear* I'll rip you apart on tonight's news cast!"

"Take it easy, Green. I didn't bring you in," Cranston pointed behind him as Jim came down the hall. "He did."

"What's the meaning of this, Sheriff? Do you realize that your Deputy almost killed me getting us here?" Chet said, heatedly.

"No kidding," Cranston smirked as he took another drink from the bottle. His legs were still wobbly from his own adventure in back road driving.

"Please relax, Mr. Green," Jim said, calmly. "I'm sorry for the inconvenience. This will only take a few minutes, then you can go. Besides, once you know what this is all about, I'm sure you'll agree that it's in your best interest to participate." Jim then turned his attention to his Deputy. "Deputy Rissley."

"Yes, sir," she replied as she stepped forward.

Jim lifted the evidence bag with the bullet from the clock in front of Chet's face. "I've been able to recover one of the bullets that killed Henderson. Take it down stairs to the lab and match it to this one, which I've taken from Agent Bradley's gun." Jim lifted the second bag with the bullet so that Chet could see it. Chet's face immediately went white and his eyes froze, locked onto the two bullets.

"Yes sir," she replied, then snatched the two bullets from Jim's hand and ran down the steps to the basement.

"You found the bullet that killed Henderson?" Chet asked in disbelief.

"It's one of the bullets," Jim assured him. "We just found it." Jim could see the shock in Chet's expression. "Are you all right, Mr. Green?" Harper asked calmly.

Chet quickly composed himself. "Quite all right, thank you," he replied softly. But in his mind, questions raced. *How much did they know?* he wondered. *Obviously, enough to check for a bullet from Alan's gun. But they may only have suspicions,* he reminded himself. That's a long way from proof. "Why have you brought me here?" Chet demanded to know.

"If you follow me, I'll explain everything," Jim assured him. "Right this way, please." Jim walked to the conference room and went in.

Chet looked down the hall in the direction that Rissley had gone. He wanted to refuse and walk out, but he had to find out what they knew. He slowly turned and followed Harper with Cranston close behind.

Bradley was breathing hard as sweat rolled down his face. Coming around the bend, he saw the over turned truck. Highway workers were all around with equipment trying to right the vehicle. Bradley ran around the workmen to the other side of the accident. A flagman was directing the traffic as each vehicle slowly got turned around. Bradley ran to the next one in line as it was about to leave. It was an old beat up sky blue pickup with caged chickens in the back. Stopping the driver, Bradley showed him his badge. "This is official business! I need you to take me to Centralia!"

The barrel chested, unshaven middle-aged driver in overalls smiled through brown teeth and spit his tobacco on the black top next to Bradley's feet. "Sure thing, agent man. Jump in."

Bradley was slightly bent over catching his breath as he walked around to the passenger side. Opening the door, a large shaggy dog sat in the passenger seat and barked.

"Come on, Beach Nut. Leave the man alone," the driver said to the dog as he pulled him towards the middle of the seat.

Bradley looked at the dog hair covering the seat then looked at the long line of campers, Winnebago, and fifth wheels. It'd be a long wait before something better came along, he knew, so he got in and closed the door. The driver hit the gas and the truck backfired as it started chugging down the road.

Chet followed Harper into the conference room. Jim had instructed Rissley, that before picking up Green, to call ahead and have the conference room prepared. Chet looked around the room. On the wall, opposite him, were a series of photos in sequential order. Several pictures of two sets of footprints coming down the hill and into the barn. Then one of Henderson's dead body. Chet stared at the list of knowns written on the board and froze.

<u>Things We Know</u>

Alan Bradley and Chet Green staked out Henderson's house.
Alan Bradley and Chet Green came down the hill and into the barn.
Alan Bradley shot and killed Buck Henderson.
Alan Bradley and Chet Green proceeded to obstruct justice.

In the middle of the room was a small table with a single chair behind it. Off to one side was another table where Agents O'Leary and Anderson were sitting, still going over shift reports.

"Are you alright, Mr. Green," Harper asked.

Chet looked at him out of the corner of his eye. *They know what happened, but could they prove it?* he wondered. He thought for a moment then decided that they couldn't possibly. If they *could*, Alan would be here instead of him, wouldn't he? "What's this all about, Sheriff? Are you charging me with a crime?"

Pointing to the chair behind the small table. "Have a seat, Mr. Green. I have a few questions for you."

"Let's make this fast. I've got a job to do," Chet said, then stepped over to the chair and sat down. Cranston closed the door and the room went dead silent. Jim leaned against the wall opposite of Chet, next to the list, and looked at him.

Jim spoke in a low monotone voice. "Mr. Green, we know what happened out at Henderson's, yesterday, and would like you to clear a few things up for us. You see, we're not sure exactly what role you played in the killing. We need to know this in order to finalize the charges against you. Would you please tell us what happened, as the events occurred from the time you left the motel yesterday morning until Agent Bradley arrived at the station."

Chet looked slowly from Jim to Cranston then back to Jim. If they *did* have proof, why was a small town Sheriff asking the questions and not Cranston, he wondered. "I don't know what you're talking about," Chet finally said after a moment of thought.

"I've got a witness who says he gave you directions to Henderson's and you and Agent Bradley left at four-thirty in your vehicle. That puts both of you at the scene a full hour before the time of death," Jim stated confidently. "Now why don't you tell us what happened next?"

Chet started to get nervous, but was able to calm himself. "Sure we went up there together, but the directions were bad and we got lost. We didn't get there until it was too late."

Jim hesitated a moment in order to plot his next move. "Deputy Rissley is in the lab matching the bullet found at the crime scene with one from Bradley's gun. When she's done matching them, your story will fall apart. At which point, the charges against you for obstructing justice will be magnified."

"I don't know anything!" Chet insisted.

Jim decided to push harder to try to intimidate Chet so he took a step forward. "You two went up there together, Bradley killed Henderson, then you plotted together to obstruct justice and created this false story about D.B. Cooper to cover your tracks. Now isn't that correct!"

As Chet realized that Harper knew everything, he could feel his face getting red and he wiped the sweat from his palm on his pant legs under the table. He needed to stay calm. *Get a grip,* he told himself. *They couldn't have any real evidence, could they? No, if they did they'd be arresting me instead of asking questions.* "Where is Agent Bradley?" Chet finally asked.

Jim could see the questions rolling around in Chet's head and knew he had to keep him off balance. "I've sent a team of Deputies to pick him up as we speak," he lied. He couldn't let Green take too much time to think before responding, otherwise he may clam up and the interrogation would be over. "I'm waiting for an answer, Mr. Green!"

In the basement, Joe looked at the two bullets under the microscope and her heart sank as her worst fears were realized. The bullet that killed Buck was in too bad of shape to match anything. *Poor Jim,* she thought. *What was he going to do?*

Upstairs, Jim was stalling, trying to make Chet Green believe that they had proof of Bradley's guilt. Over the radio, Jim had explained that he didn't think the bullets could be matched and that he wanted to try a last ditch effort at getting a confession. She'd hoped that he was wrong about the damaged bullet and knew now that his stalling would fail.

Green was weak, but not so much that he could be intimidated into talking without some sort of stimulus. They needed something to push him over the edge. *You have to do something,* she thought to herself as she bit her lip. *Think!* A moment later, her eyes narrowed and a mischievous smile appeared on her face.

"It's time to throw this bum a curve," she said out loud. With that, Rissley grabbed another evidence bag. Leaving the damaged bullet on the table, she grabbed the other one, ran up the stairs, and out the back door to the shooting range.

Chet looked into Jim's eyes trying to measure him up and was *convinced* that he was bluffing. No way could those bullets match, could they? *He's trying to scare a confession out of me,* he thought.

But then a different concept crossed Chet's mind. Alan had lied to him so many times that he couldn't be sure what to believe. Could Alan have kept him in the dark about the course of the Sheriff's investigation and the search for a bullet? Chet knew that Alan was certainly capable of it.

Chet suddenly thought better of it. Harper was stalling, trying to see if he'd crack. He *has* to be. "I don't know what you're talking about," Chet said confidently.

Jim stepped forward and slammed his fist on the table in front of Chet. "I'm talking about you and Bradley being out there before six! Bradley killed Henderson and you watched it happen! I'm talking about you being charged with conspiracy to commit murder, withholding evidence, and obstructing justice! You have a lot to answer for, mister! That's what I'm talking about!" Jim slammed his fist down on the table with each charge.

Chet's eyes narrowed. *"No!* You're the one who has something to answer for! Dragging me in here, accusing me of breaking the law and questioning me without my lawyer present! If there's anyone guilty of a crime, it's you and I'm going to make sure everyone knows about it!" Chet barked as he stood up from his chair. "Unless you plan on arresting me, I've got some *news* to report!"

At that instant, the door burst open and Rissley flew into the room. *"They match!"* she exclaimed as she lifted two evidence bags so that everyone could see them. "These two bullets have *identical* makings on them. *Proving* beyond a shadow of a doubt that they came from the same gun. Alan Bradley's gun!"

There was a dead...flat...silence and everyone in the room was stunned as they looked at the two bullets. "Did you hear what I said, Sheriff? It's a positive match!" she said again.

Jim realized that his mouth was wide open, and he closed it quickly. The eyes of everyone in the room went slowly from the bullets to Chet. Putting his hands on the table to steady himself, Chet's eyes grew wide as he looked around the room at everyone staring at him. His legs started to wobble, and he had to sit down as the blood ran out of his head.

Jim quickly turned and took a step towards Chet, but Cranston grabbed him by the arm, stopping him. "Thank you, Sheriff. I'll take it from here."

Jim looked at him, but said nothing. Looking at Chet, he slowly gave his ground and took a step back. Taking the two evidence bags from Rissley, Cranston tossed them on the table in front of Chet. With them right in front of him, Chet could tell that they were identical.

"You can't save Bradley, it's too late for that," Cranston said calmly. "But you can still save yourself." He let that sink in before continuing. "I'm offering you a deal. Become a material witness for the prosecution. Tell us everything you know, and we'll go easy on you. Otherwise, you and Bradley will rot in jail next to each other."

Chet's nerves were shot. He looked from face to face and saw the accusing looks. Collapsing further into his chair, he covered his face and began to cry. "It was an *accident.*" The words came out without Chet being conscious of it, followed by a heavy sigh.

Cranston pointed to O'Leary and snapped his fingers. O'Leary quickly pulled a small tape recorder from his pocket, turned it on, then placed it in front of Chet. Rissley quickly went to the video camera on the tripod in the corner and turned it on. After bringing it closer, she focused in on Chet and started recording.

Chet slowly lowered his hands from his face. "It was an accident," he said again. Somehow those words relieved some of the guilt he'd been feeling since he'd destroyed the videotape. He forced a few more words out, and he felt the weight of the world slip from his shoulders.

He glanced up at the video camera in a daze and suddenly he turned into a journalist again. It felt natural being in front of the camera, and he started to report everything that had happened from the time he and Bradley had arrived in Morton. Everyone listened in silence to Chet's account of the events.

Joe was only half listening. She had a question nagging at the back of her mind. In order to get Chet talking, she'd decided to

371

throw him a curve and ran out to the range to retrieve the second bullet. When she entered the conference room, she held up both bullets from the range and stated that they were identical and that they were from Bradley's gun.

What she'd said was true, not one thing was inaccurate about it. However, in doing so she *implied* that one of them was the bullet that killed Buck, even though she'd never actually said so. That bullet was still lying in the microscope in the basement.

Had she done something unethical? She hadn't thought about that possibility until that moment. All she wanted to do was get the truth and she was willing to do anything to get it.

She remembered all the times she'd been critical of Jim for some of his tactics and methods of getting things accomplished, and she felt guilty. After this little stunt, she could *never* be critical again. She suddenly felt closer to Jim because she had experienced something that he must have quite often. No matter what the task at hand, you had to find a way to accomplish it.

No, she decided. She hadn't done anything unethical. Suddenly she realized that the sharp line that she'd drawn between black and white had a little gray between it.

Jim leaned back against the wall. The adrenaline and caffeine had fully worn off now and he was exhausted. That was it, it was finally over. He wasn't sure whether he felt happy or sad. In fact, he felt nothing. He was just too tired. Two of his friends were dead because of an *accident.* He couldn't listen anymore and there was nothing left for him to do. The Feds could do the cleaning up.

Jim glanced over at Rissley behind the camera and cocked a knowing eyebrow. When he'd seen the two bullets, he knew *exactly* what she'd done and was stunned by it. That was the last thing he'd ever expected from her! He looked at her closely and no longer saw the young naive schoolgirl that had become his deputy some years ago.

For the first time, Jim saw how mature she'd become and he felt proud of her. Perhaps he'd always seen it, but didn't consciously accept it. After today, he knew, he would never think of her in the same way. Perhaps it was time to give up more of the responsibility of running the county to her. She definitely has proven herself, not just now, but everyday.

For decades he had held the reins of the county tightly, afraid that it might get out of control in someone else's hands. As

Jim looked over at Joe he smiled, realizing that when the time came to retire, he'd be leaving this county in good hands. Suddenly fatigue set in and he felt his age.

Perhaps retirement was closer than he'd thought. Jim turned and slowly worked his way to the door, quietly slipping through it. Walking to the drinking fountain, he bent over and took a long drink.

Cranston opened the conference room door, stepped out, and looked around. Seeing Jim, he closed the door and walked quickly over to him. "Listen, Sheriff," he said in a serious voice as he looked around to make sure no one could over hear them. "I realize I don't have the right to ask you this, but how do you think it's going to make me look if a county sheriff arrests one of my men?"

Jim looked at him through tired eyes. "To tell you the truth, I haven't given much thought to what I was going to do next." He rubbed his chin as he thought about it. All of his efforts he'd focused on proving Bradley's guilt. He hadn't planned on doing anything afterwards. In fact, he had assumed that Cranston was going to take over anyway. "I've got what I want and I'm not looking for publicity. So go ahead, you've got the ball. Make your arrest and take the credit."

Cranston smiled from ear to ear. Grabbing Jim's hand, he shook it enthusiastically. "I can't thank you enough, Sheriff."

"Just one thing," Jim said, seriously.

"Sure, anything you want. Just name it."

"Bradley said a lot of unflattering things about me and my department. I expect you to straighten things out."

"Considerate it done," Cranston said, sincerely.

"Well I guess there's nothing left for me to do now except go home and get some sleep," Jim said with a smile.

At that moment, the conference room door opened and Agents O'Leary and Anderson stepped out and walked over to Cranston. "Did you get it all?" Cranston asked.

"Right here." O'Leary held up both audio and videocassettes.

"Good," Cranston said as he straightened his tie. "Let's *nail* that dirty rotten jerk." He turned and the three agents walked towards the front door.

Jim watched them leave, and his tired mind wondered what to do next. Sleep and a good meal, his body decided for him. Jim turned and walked down the hall the other way. When he came to the back door, he looked outside. There was no one around. They had all gone to the front of the station to do the evening report. He lazily pushed open the door and walked to his Blazer.

22

DEJA VU

The blue pickup hadn't come to a complete stop in front of the Sheriff's station before Bradley jumped out carrying the bag under his arm. He quickly located and ran to the satellite truck. "Where is Chet?"

"I don't know," Stapleton said as she directed her crew to set up the equipment. "We just got here ourselves. Traffic was *terrible!*"

Bradley looked around. "I've *got* to find him and fill him in on what's going on."

"There's no time!" she replied. "We go live in ten seconds." She grabbed a microphone and stood next to Bradley. "What happened to you? You look awful."

Bradley looked at his clothes and cringed. They were covered with dog hair and chicken feathers. "Help me get cleaned up!" He said as he tried to wipe himself off.

"There's no time!"

"Damn!" Bradley suddenly realized that there was no time to plant the drugs, either. He'd have to improvise and do it on the fly.

"In five…four…three…two…one!" The technician pointed to Ms. Stapleton.

"Good evening," Stapleton said into the microphone. "Were coming to you live from the Lewis County Sheriff's Station, where what can only be described as a major break through in the D.B. Cooper drug cartel is about to take place. With me now is Special Agent Alan Bradley to give us the details. Agent Bradley, can you tell us what's happening?" She placed the microphone in front of Alan.

Bradley smiled for the camera. "As you can recall, earlier today I stated that the Sheriff's department has *intentionally* interfered with and slowed my investigation. I now know why. Ladies and gentlemen, tonight on this broadcast, I will show that the Sheriff's department has been protecting this drug smuggling operation all along. I will also reveal who killed Henderson. The killer is known to you as D.B. Cooper, but has walked among the people of this small community under another name. Tonight, I will arrest D.B. Cooper and reveal his true identity."

"That's *incredible!*" Stapleton exclaimed, as she couldn't believer her luck at being the one to break the story. "Please, tell us more!"

At that instant, the three agents approached Bradley from behind. Cranston grabbed the black bag from Bradley's hand and Agents O'Leary and Anderson grabbed both arms and pulled them behind him.

"*What the–?*" Bradley exclaimed with astonishment as he struggled with his fellow agents.

"I suppose this is the rest of the opium?" Cranston said, then opened the bag in front of the camera and pulled out the package of drugs and showed it to everyone.

"*What are you doing?!*" Bradley yelled furiously as the two Agents held Alan's arms behind his back. "You *can't* do this to me!"

"Alan Bradley, you are under arrest for the wrongful death of Buck Henderson and, among other things, obstructing justice." Cranston reached into Bradley's coat and pulled out the Desert Eagle and DEA badge.

"You, *idiot*! You can't do this to me!"

"Cuff'em and stuff'em, boys," Cranston ordered. O'Leary and Anderson slapped cuffs on Alan's wrists then pulled him away as he yelled in protest.

At that instant, Jim drove his battered Blazer to the exit of the station's parking lot then stopped. Rolling down his window, he watched and listened with joy as Bradley was drug kicking and screaming to an unmarked car and put into the back seat. "*City boy,*" Jim said with a smile, then shook his head. He hoped Buck

376

and Rick were watching from somewhere and smiling too. Jim slowly put his foot on the gas pedal and merged into traffic.

"Director Cranston!" Stapleton exclaimed. "I can't believe what I've just witnessed. Why have you arrested Agent Bradley?"

Cranston turned towards the camera. "We have an eye witness who has positively identify Alan Bradley as the person who killed Henderson," he said as he lifted the Desert Eagle in front of the camera. "This witness has also stated that Alan Bradley used this weapon to do so."

"But what about D.B. Cooper?"

"Bradley made up the Cooper story in order to focus attention away from himself," Cranston replied. "I'm surprised any of you reporters fell for such a trick."

Stapleton immediately felt embarrassed that she had and changed the subject quickly. "But Agent Bradley said that the Sheriff's department was involved in the drug gang, and that they intentionally got in his way. What about those claims?"

"Those statements are completely false. There is no drug smuggling operation going on here and never has been. Bradley planted false evidence, such as this opium, in order to substantiate his charges," Cranston replied as he lifted the package of drugs in front of the camera. "As far as the Sheriff's department is concerned, they've cooperated *fully* with my department and have done an *excellent* job of investigating this case. In fact, their help has been essential in solving it.

"From the beginning, Sheriff Harper has been in constant contact with me and together we've brought the wrongful party to justice," Cranston lied to the camera. "Under my direction, Sheriff Harper allowed Bradley to conduct his so called investigation in order to lull him into a false sense of security while we investigated him. Alan Bradley finally slipped up and we caught him, just as I planned. Sheriff Harper and his staff should be commended for their efforts."

"But what about the Governor's office?" Stapleton asked. "Just a couple of hours ago, Governor Wilson publicly denounced you and what he called your unprofessional inaction in this case. What about those charges?"

"Governor Wilson has been involved in this case from the start," Cranston lied. Cranston was now behind the steering wheel of the propaganda bus and was going to give Wilson a chance to jump on. Since Bradley arrived in Seattle, Wilson had been one of Cranston's worst critics and that had threatened his position in the department. If he could swing the pendulum of the Governor's political power in his direction, he felt it would be wise to do so.

Bradley wasn't the only one who could spew bull in front of a camera, and Cranston was determined to get some mileage from this opportunity. Cranston would allow Wilson to save face and in doing so, he knew the Governor would be forced to smooth the waters for him with his superiors in DC.

"Governor Wilson has been well aware that Alan Bradley was one of my suspects and had instructed me on how to proceed with this case. The Governor's crime policy not only is intended to take the criminals off the street, but bad cops as well. This case is a testament to how truly effective this policy has become.

"Governor Wilson is a very intelligent man. His denouncement of me publicly was just another ploy in order to lull Bradley into a false sense of security. Governor Wilson's efforts have been essential in causing Bradley to slip up.

"As you can see, Governors Wilson's plan worked *perfectly*. In fact, Governor Wilson is so confident in my abilities, that before I came down here today he called me and said that as soon as this case was closed he was giving me and my staff a commendation." Cranston grinned ear to ear as he lied to the camera.

In the Mayor's office in Seattle, Mayor Demsey and Governor Wilson sat with their aids and watched in astonishment to the newscast. Governor Wilson sat silently in his chair and quickly calculated the ramifications of what just happened. He recalled his earlier fears that his friend Alan Bradley Sr. would propel his son into the Governor's mansion, forcing Wilson out.

His face was like stone as he smiled inside himself. Like father like son, Wilson thought comically. Agent Bradley just stepped in it big time. His political future was doomed. The relief of it quickly faded, though, as his recognized the threat to his *own* future.

After Bradley's harsh criticism of Cranston and Harper on the afternoon news, Wilson adjourned his meeting with the State's Mayors so that he could attend to the situation personally. He'd called every Washington Representative and the two Senators in DC and asked them to help him force Cranston and Harper to retire.

After what had just occurred, he'd now look like a *fool*. Sure, members from his own party would probably be willing to forget it ever happened, but some of those members of Congress were from the other party. There was nothing they'd like more than to help there own parties chances in the next election by crucifying him now.

He had to beat them to the punch and make a statement to the press. A few hours ago he was riding high, but the political tide just changed and he'd have to scramble to avoid being left on the rocks. Cranston had just extended the olive branch, and Wilson had to quickly determine how best to use it.

Mayor Demsey also listened to the broadcast in silence. Occasionally glancing over at Wilson, Demsey knew what had to be going through his mind and he did some political calculating of his own. He could see that Wilson's balloon was sinking fast and in order to save himself, he'd have to throw the dead weight over the side. Bradley was now ballast and he needed to be gotten rid of.

Mayor Demsey had been the only one to witness Wilson's calls to DC on Bradley's behalf, and he tried to figure out how best to use that information. First of all, Wilson would need Demsey to not only remain quiet himself, but also to make things right with his party's Congressman. Demsey and Wilson were from opposite parties and were constantly at odds.

This was Demsey's opportunity to do some back scratching and get something for himself. Wilson would have to move fast and, in order to do so, would be willing to wheel and deal. Mayor Demsey also thought quickly on how to best take advantage of the situation.

Governor Wilson was in deep thought, and knew he had a major problem. It was then that he first considered Demsey and noticed the occasional glances from his counterpart. Wilson turned slowly to face Demsey and leaned forward to address him. For a few moments, they both stared into each other's eyes coldly and knew what the other was thinking.

"All right, Demsey," Governor Wilson finally said. "What's it going to take?"

Mayor Demsey's low-income, inner-city housing project had run into delays and cost overruns. For the last six months, Demsey had been lobbying Wilson for State assistance to finish the project, but was constantly refused. "I want the funds necessary to complete my housing project," Demsey stated firmly.

Wilson's eyes narrowed. He'd purposely withheld funds so that his party could use the situation against Demsey in the next election. But that was now impossible. Through clenched teeth he forced the word from his mouth.

"Agreed." Wilson then turned to his aide. "Gather the press corp. I'm going to make an announcement." The aide quickly turned and rushed out of the room.

It was then that Demsey let the other shoe drop. "There's more," he said coolly.

Wilson looked back at him with surprise. "Don't you think you've taken advantage of me enough for one day?"

"I want to get re-elected too, you know," Demsey stated as he calculated his next move. Both he and Wilson had been on the front cover of the paper last week with Agent Bradley. If Cranston was going to pull Wilson out of the fire, Demsey was going to grab on as well. "I suggest that *we* have a joint press conference, where we'll explain to the public the details of *our* secret project for removing bad cops from the streets."

Again Wilson's eyes narrowed at this suggestion. He didn't want to share the limelight with anyone, especially someone from the opposite party. After a few moments, an eyebrow lifted as he thought of something. "A bipartisan plan to remove bad law enforcement officers from service." He suddenly saw the wisdom in it. "The voters will *love* it!"

Demsey instantly stood and extended his hand with a smile. "Congratulations, Mr. Governor. Our secret bipartisan plan worked!"

Wilson stood and shook Demsey's hand enthusiastically. "And congratulations to you, Mr. Mayor. Our secret plan was a complete success! I couldn't be more pleased!"

At that instant, the aide returned to the room. "Sir, the press corp is waiting."

"Well, let's go make our statement," Wilson said. With that, huge smiles came over their faces and they walked out of the room side by side.

Jim's Blazer made the slow turn onto the gravel road to his house. As he approached it, all he could think of was Nikki. He was *dying* to see, her but knew it best that he get some sleep first, or at least a good shower and shave. Pulling around the back of the house, the vehicle came to a stop in its usual spot.

Jim got out and dragged his tired feet slowly to the backdoor. A few feet away, something about the door caught his eye, and he stopped dead in his tracks. The jam was shattered. A closer examination told Jim that the door had been kicked in. Adrenaline shot through his body, and his mind was fully engaged. Pulling his weapon, he slowly pushed open the door and peered cautiously inside.

He could hear the TV, and the air was filled with cigar smoke. With his gun ready, he slowly and quietly moved through the house towards the living room. As he peered around the corner, he could see that the furniture had been rearranged.

His high backed chair had been turned towards the TV, all he could see was the back of it. The end table was pulled up next to the chair. An ashtray filled with cigar butts sat next to a half empty bottle of whisky and a glass.

On the corner of the table sat a nickel-plated pearl handled nine millimeter Beretta. Beside it with a black band, sat a white fedora. A thin line of cigar smoke rose from the other side of the chair. With his gun ready, Jim moved silently and cautiously until he could see around it.

An older man with black shinny hair and an expensive impeccably tailored, blue pinstriped suit sat in the chair. A huge, flawless diamond tie tack adorned his Italian silk tie and an equally impressive diamond rested in the gold ring on his finger. The man pulled the thick cigar from his teeth and smiled at Jim from ear to ear.

"Marcellous!" Jim relaxed and lowered his gun. "I told you *never* to come here! If someone were to see you, they might make a connection."

The older man ignored the remark, pulled a new cigar from the platinum cigar case in his coat pocket, and extended it towards Jim. "Hello, Cooper. Cuban?" Jim waved it away so Marcellous placed it on the end table. "Maybe later then."

The intruder stood to face Jim. His large body towered over Jim by almost a foot, and his shoulders were almost twice as wide. Anthony Marcellous was known around Lewis County as the man who ran the local landfill and had done so for almost as long as Jim had been Sheriff. Marcellous was also known to the DEA—as *Phantom.*

"Why did you come here?" Harper asked in an irritated voice.

"I felt I had to. When you left the trailer yesterday, I collected the bricks of opium and came up one short. I didn't think much of it until I found out Buck was killed, so I closed up shop. At first, I thought maybe you were trying to double cross me." His eyes narrowed as he looked down his nose at Jim.

Jim felt insulted. "I've been straight with you all these years. How could you think that?"

"Oh, come on, Jim, you saw the news stories. What would *you* have thought?"

Jim thought about it for a few moments, then nodded in agreement. He would've thought the same thing. In fact, one of his initial reactions, when he'd seen the first news cast yesterday morning, was to wonder if Marcellous had done the shooting. It had initially stunned him, but after fully considering it, he knew it was impossible.

"So I came out here last night to get the jump on you, but you never showed."

"I spent the night at the station," Jim said as he turned towards the window.

"Lucky for you. After those news reports, I might've shot you on sight." Marcellous poured whisky into two glasses on the table. Picking them up, he walked the few steps to Jim's side and smiled. "Here, let's drink to the operation."

Jim looked at him with distaste in his eyes. His exhausted mind was still troubled over the loss of his friends, and he wasn't in the mood to be reminded of *why* they had died. "Our relationship has always been purely business. I don't drink with drug dealers." He lashed out coldly.

Marcellous's expression instantly turned nasty. "No, you just smuggle it in for me! *Don't forget.* You came to me, I didn't come to you, so don't get all high and mighty." After a moment, Marcellous's mood slowly changed. He hadn't come here to argue. *That wouldn't benefit anyone,* he thought as he looked out the window with Jim. This was a time for remembering their friends. "Then let's drink to Buck and Rick."

He again extended the glass. Jim hesitated, then taking the glass, they tipped their heads back and swallowed the liquor.

"I still remember the first time I met you." Marcellous changed the subject and a smile came back to his face. "I was a small time black market dealer in a bar in Saigon when Buck introduced us." They both smiled at the recollection. Marcellous had left the States to avoid being arrested for selling drugs.

He ended up in Vietnam and worked the black market selling anything to anyone, but he made most of his money selling drugs to GI's and prostitutes. Like Buck, he had adopted the practice of converting wealth to precious stones and had put together a small fortune. He had traded truck parts, lubricants, and such with Buck for a couple of years and had tried to convince him that the drug trade could be far more lucrative.

Buck refused to have anything to do with drugs. He felt that drugs were evil and would eventually destroy the people that used or dealt with it. He never once traded or used drugs and took pleasure in destroying processing sites in the bush when his troops came across them.

Buck had introduced Jim to Marcellous while showing him the ins and outs of black market trading. Jim was still recovering from the wounds he'd suffered in combat, and he and Marcellous got to know each other well. What Marcellous saw in Jim was an angry young man with a chip on his shoulder for his government and a soft spot in his heart for the little guy.

Jim traded goods and always gave half of his profit to charity. His favorite charities were the local orphanages. Whenever possible, Jim volunteered at the orphanages helping in anyway that he could. Somehow, he felt close to the young children without families of their own. He too had lost his family because of war in one country or another, and he felt obligated to help those like himself. But most situations could only be handled by large sums of money. Food, medicine, clothing– it all came at a high price in the war torn region.

That's when Marcellous explained to Jim about the benefits of dealing in drugs. Marcellous also told him about the vast profits he had once made in the States selling drugs on the streets and expressed a wish that he could establish a smuggling operation. The *real* money was in the States, and anyone that could pull it off would become extremely rich.

He knew that, like Buck, Jim was against drugs, but he explained that those who used drugs were going to do so no matter who supplied it. So, what was the harm in profiting from the inevitable? Jim didn't like the idea and refused to take part in any further discussions about it.

But the idea lingered in Jim's mind as he saw his orphans go without so many things, but he couldn't bring himself to prey on another's weakness as a solution to the problem. Finally, he was healthy and ready to go back to the States. Buck wanted him to stay and help plan missions with him, but Jim wanted to leave the military behind and get on with his life.

That wasn't so easy. When he arrived in the States, Jim and other veterans were protested against. The protesters spoke fowl language, threw garbage, and looked upon him with loathsome eyes.

Jim had never felt so dejected in all his life. What had he done to deserve this? He had been angry with his government and now he was angry with the protesters.

He returned to Lewis County, but could not find peace. Without his grandfather, there was nothing for him there. So he returned to Vietnam and to the adopted family he'd come to know. Only this time, he had *two* missions.

The first, was to help Buck plan strategies for the Special Forces. The other was more personal. On the trip back, Jim had formulated a plan to get the money he needed to help his extended family while also allowing him to strike a blow to the government and protesters he so very much loathed.

Jim went to Marcellous and asked for assurances that the opium would only be sold to the types of people who had protested against him and that they would conduct the operation in such a way that it reduced the chances of being caught. Marcellous quickly agreed and Jim explained his plan in detail.

Marcellous thought fondly about it as he looked out the window with Jim and a smile came back to his face. "I was just a small time dealer until you showed up and told me your plan. It was *brilliant!*" Marcellous tried to recall the details. "Your plan, that is, to get opium out of Asia and into the US... what was it again?" Marcellous answered his own question. "Oh yeah, as a consultant at the Embassy, you found a loop hole in the customs laws. A country's embassy was considered a part of the sovereign land of the occupant. So the American Embassy was considered US soil and therefore packages shipped through it, did not have to go through customs. So, I moved to Portland and you would take small statues of Buddha, stuff them full of pure opium, and ship them to me. *Ha!*" Marcellous laughed heartily.

Jim managed a smile at remembering the set up. "I use to rub Buddha's belly for good luck before shipping each package," he added as he turned from the window to face his long time partner.

"I didn't realize that belly could hold so much. We had an *incredible* opportunity to make a lot of money, all courtesy of the US government. What a wonderful plan." Marcellous patted Jim on the shoulder.

"Yes, it worked perfectly," Jim agreed. Jim handled the delivery of the opium while Marcellous took care of processing, sales, and payments. They never once used any money for their own purposes, except an overseas fund that was established to make donations to the orphanages where Jim volunteered. No money ever went into an account for Jim. Marcellous created a Swiss bank

384

account where they were going to save every penny for retirement when it was all over.

"It worked because neither of us spent any money," Marcellous commented. "That way the authorities were never tipped off."

Jim nodded. "But it ended sooner than we had expected." Buck, who never knew what Jim and Marcellous were doing, ran into his *own* money problems. He was swindled out of his life savings then forced into retirement by an Army trying to sweep Buck's destruction of a bank under the rug. Buck was now angry, humiliated, and penniless. He slipped into depression and started to drink heavily.

Now that the responsibility of helping Buck plan missions was over, Jim saw no reason to continue with it. Besides, he was not as angry as he was before, so Jim took Buck under his wing and they both went back to Lewis County where Jim promised the quiet life Buck had known as a kid. Before he had left, however, Jim had sent enough packages to give Marcellous several months of extra supply.

When Jim returned to Lewis County, he found that it was not the same as when he'd left it. Outside, big city influences had moved in. Protesters came to the small town to have "love ins" and do demonstrations. Big government was bleeding the county's resources and big business was starting to develop every available piece of property they could get a hold of. It was *devastating* to both Jim and Buck, and they decided that they had to put an end to it.

They immediately went to work on Jim's campaign for Sheriff. But campaigns took money, so Jim went to Marcellous for his share of the profits from the operation, but it wasn't as much as he'd hoped. It seems that the start up costs for the operation were more than Marcellous had expected. Hiring and training employees, and setting up contacts and payoffs to people who could make things happen were way beyond what they had figured. Then, pulling the plug early before they had realized a return on those costs left very little to split up.

Jim spent every penny on his campaign and won. Now he was in the thick of it. Every problem that the county had was dropped in Jim's lap, and he was finding it difficult to make things turn out the way he'd hoped. He *knew* that every single problem had to have a solution, but the only universal answer that this young Sheriff could come up with was—*money.* Every one of his problems could be solved with money.

There was only one place where he could get the amount of money he needed, and that was to start the operation back up. Only this time he would need more help. Buck was shocked when Jim came to him for help. At first, Buck had refused to get involved, but after seeing no other solution, Jim was able to talk him into it. It would only be temporary, Jim had promised. Just until they could solve some of these short-term problems, then they would shut down the operation for good.

But Buck gave Jim a stern warning. *Once you start relying on drug money to solve you problems, it will become more and more difficult in the future not to continue doing so.* Jim assured him that would *never* happen.

Jim went to Marcellous with a new plan. One that required more people, but would work just as well. Marcellous refused. He felt that it was too complex and the players were too unreliable. Besides, Jim was broke and Marcellous was nearly so.

He had only enough drugs to keep his customers happy for another couple of weeks or so, then it would be all over. To start a *new* operation, they needed seed money. Without it, they were *doomed* to fail. Jim promised Marcellous that he'd find a way to get the seed money, and tried to convince him that his new plan would work, but Marcellous was skeptical.

"So I came to you for help and what did you do?" Jim recalled the event somewhat distastefully. "You didn't even listen to my proposition seriously. All you could do was worry about your own skin. You rejected *everything* I said and got ready to pack up and high tail it out of the country."

"I *had* to! The drugs had almost run out. When you have drugs to sell, your customers are a lot of fun and it's one endless party. But that all changes if the supply dies out. I was lucky enough to get out with my head. Then you came to the airport and tried to stop me." Marcellous recalled the confrontation they'd had at the Portland airport. "You said you were *sure* that your new plan would work and that you could get the seed money for it quickly. I listened to you, but couldn't believe it. The plan didn't even look good on paper. It just wasn't *practical.*" Marcellous shook his head the same way he had in the Portland airport so many years ago.

"It *was* practical," Jim said in the same manner he did almost thirty years ago. "We learned *so much* and made *too many* contacts from the first operation to let it slip out of our fingers. But you panicked and wanted to run. You said that I wasn't smart enough to hold things together and make it work." It was Jim's turn to shake his finger accusingly.

"You're right. I didn't think you were smart enough. Who could blame me with a plan like that? I mean the idea of it. An

Asian freighter carries the opium across the ocean and rendezvous with a Forest Service float plane just outside US waters. Then the plane, which is flown by a pilot with mental problems, flies into the mountains and conducts a low level-bombing run in a high mountain clearing.

"Of course, nobody sees this happen because the Forest Service has closed the trail claiming that there are too many bears in the area for it to be safe for hikers. Then a Forest Service employee, who talks too much and is drunk half the time, picks up the opium and packs it down on the backs of mules disguised as trail garbage.

Then I work as a garbage man so that I can pick up the drugs. I then process them, make sales and payments— just as I did in the first operation. While all this is going on, as Sheriff, you run interference for us if anyone gets suspicious and starts asking questions." Marcellous remarked with a smile. "We even used a code name for the bricks. We referred to them as "bears" because we didn't want anyone to see or even get close to them. Calling them "bears" also allowed us to talk openly in public about them without anyone getting suspicious."

"It was the *perfect* plan," Jim nodded again with confidence. "As long as I kept Buck and Rick in check everything went like clock work."

"Well who could blame me for not thinking it would? That's why you had to *prove* it to me. You had to demonstrate that you were smart enough and clever enough to keep it all together in a stressful situation. But then you already knew that before you came to the airport to stop me. I remember *exactly* what you said." Marcellous recounted the event as if he were reading it from a book. "You said that you could instantly get the whole nation's attention. Then have the Feds come crashing down right on top of you and you could walk among them, influence their investigation, and point them in all the wrong directions without being under suspicion."

"You said I was crazy. That I had lost it. Then, like a coward, you jumped on the first flight out of town," Jim recalled.

"You obviously knew I would," Marcellous defended. "That's the way you had it planned from the start. I still remember how shocked I was. There I was, sitting in a bar at LAX wondering where to go next when the special report came over the TV. A plane taking off from Portland bound for Seattle was hijacked in mid-flight. They showed a picture of you. You wore make up and sunglasses, but I could tell it was you.

Then they said the name. The newscaster said it as if that's all it was, just a name, but it wasn't. It was a signal to me. One you *knew* would be sent out on the airways and would reach me no matter where I was. A name that only I knew. You bought your ticket under the name that you used on the return address labels on the Buddha packages from Saigon. *Dan Cooper.*" Marcellous again laughed heartily. "Very clever. I nearly fell off the bar stool when I heard it. So, I got on the next flight back, then drove into Centralia. The town was loaded with people coming to hunt for the hijacker. The mountains were filled with Army troops and the Sheriff's station was under the control of the FBI. While the whole time the very man they were looking for was standing right outside the station house, calmly writing parking tickets." Again Marcellous laughed.

It felt good to tell the story, finally after all these years. They had all vowed to keep silent and except for a few drunken slip-ups by Buck, they were successful. But the secret, which was held back for so many years, weighed heavily on all of them and was begging to be told.

Jim felt it, too. Normally he wouldn't have spent this much time alone with the man he had grown to dislike. Over the years, the operation had started to weigh heavily on his conscious and he started to resent Marcellous and the need for the operation as a whole. But he and Marcellous were now the only two people left who knew the truth, and he couldn't help but join in the tale. "I told you I could do it. I told you I had what it took to run this kind of operation."

"And what a beautiful operation it was." Marcellous filled the glasses and handed Jim's to him, then lifted his own. "Lets have a toast to the operation."

"No. I can't drink to that. The operation got Buck and Rick killed."

"*No*, that's not true," Marcellous insisted. "*You're* responsible. Buck and Rick had wanted to stop the operation years ago, but you wouldn't let them. You've never liked me because I've always been in it for the money, but don't forget what they say about birds of a feather," Marcellous pointed a finger at Jim. "You and I are the *same.*"

"*No!* I don't do it for myself, I'm not in this out of greed!" Jim snarled.

"Don't kid yourself, Jim," Marcellous argued. "You don't *really* expect me to believe that you did it for some noble cause, do you? That you were doing it *just* to help the community?" Marcellous's questions momentarily caused Jim to freeze up. "You did it for revenge—to even a score. You wanted to teach your government a lesson."

"*Why not?* They deserved it for what they did to me and my family," Jim admitted as he turned back towards the window. "The things they made me do over there. They turned me into a monster. They *have* to pay for that."

"Your bleeding heart attitude makes me sick, Jim!" Marcellous snapped. "Do you think you're the only one who's had a tough life? *Get over it!*"

These words angered Jim, but he didn't answer.

"You've pulled the wool over the Feds eyes for almost thirty years now. You've proven that you're smarter and better than they are. Now it's time you ended the feud." Marcellous tried to reason with him.

"They *deserved* it!" Jim insisted, again.

"What about the victims? Did *they* deserve it?"

"That's *your* fault, not mine! You were only supposed to sell it to those long haired hippie freaks at their protests and "love ins" or what ever they called it!" He still grew angry at the thought of those people. The same ones that banded together against him and the other soldiers back from the war.

He was stuck in the middle between the government that sent him there and the people he came home to. He wasn't sure who he hated the most, but he *swore* that they all would pay.

"Hate dies hard, doesn't it Jim?" Marcellous observed as he reached for the bottle and poured another round. "It's a funny thing about those hippies, Jim. They grew up, and a lot of them became rich successful people. Heck, ironically they became the very thing they protested against in the first place." He smirked at that, then continued. "They had money to buy, so I sold to them. Now their children have money so I sell to them."

"It was *never* supposed to go this far." Jim lowered his head sadly and closed his eyes.

"You don't have a choice in it, you're strictly delivery! I handle the processing, selling, and payments. If you don't like it, *tough!*" Marcellous barked angrily as he shook a bony finger at his companion. "You should have thought about the consequences *before* you started this, not after."

From the start, Marcellous had always been in it for the money. It was pure greed. He wanted to get rich and he didn't care how he got it. Buck had also wanted the money. Sure, at first he was hesitant, but he was still angry and depressed at the loss of his nest egg. He hadn't been thinking clearly when he decided he was willing to put up with a short-term operation if it meant getting some of it back.

389

Rick was also in it for the money. He wanted desperately to have the freedom to be left alone and fly. He felt that money would allow him to buy his own plane and fly wherever and whenever he wanted.

Jim, on the other hand, was not concerned with what money could do for him, but with what it could do for his extended family. He had adopted the people of the county and he considered their problems to be his own. A couple of years after the operation had started, the warning that Buck had given him finally struck home. Jim had been able to use money to solve the problems he had originally set out to fix. But those problems were soon replaced by new ones, then new ones after that. Jim slowly started relying on one more delivery to solve one more problem.

Marcellous handled everything. An offshore account was created and an anonymous donor would wire in money for whatever needed to be taken care of. It was rumored that someone who had once lived in the county married into royalty in Europe and was now acting as a secret guardian angel to the community. It didn't really matter. No one ever asks too many questions when free money is involved.

But something went wrong along the way. The operation stretched out longer that anyone had expected. They all put down roots and realized that they already had everything they wanted. A secret offshore company purchased the logging rights to millions of acres within the county. That insured that Buck could continue his outfitting for the rest of his life.

The PBY that Rick flew was essentially his and he could fly it anytime he wanted. There was nothing else that the two had needed. Neither Buck nor Rick wanted to leave this place they had come to call home and no longer cared about the money. Their hearts were no longer in it, and they were starting to slip up. Buck was feeling guilty, drinking more than usual, and was starting to talk too much.

Nikki had been right. Jim, Buck, and also Rick were all nursing a secret, personal, and separate pain. And in each case there was one thing holding them back from healing—one common denominator...*the operation.* The operation had prolonged their suffering, caused them to hide further from the truth. Buck hid in his bottle, Rick in his flying, and Jim in his work. As long as the operation continued, there would be no hope for them.

Jim had convinced them to keep the operation going. There was always one last project that needed to be done. Then, he had always promised, they could shut down the operation for good.

Neither one of the three knew how much money they had. The operation was set up so that only Marcellous knew what their one Swiss bank account was worth. In fact, the others never wanted to talk about it because it always made them feel guilty.

Jim only cared that there was enough money to handle the next short fall in county funds. When the operation stopped, that source of money would dry up, then where would he be? Over the years, Jim had come to resent Marcellous more and more because the use of drug money meant that Jim had not been able to control events without it.

He had always wanted to get to a point where he no longer needed it then he could say—*there, I did it.* But, he was never able to. It angered Jim to admit that to himself, now, especially after Marcellous's accusation that the deaths of his friends were his fault.

Marcellous read Jim's mind before he could say anything. "That's right, you could've stopped the operation anytime you wanted, so they are dead because of you."

Jim knew he was telling the truth. He'd been thinking the same thing for hours now, but couldn't quite get himself to admit it. He'd tried to remind himself of all the reasons he had kept the operation going in the first place, but they all seemed so trivial now.

Again, Marcellous seemed to read Jim's mind. "Don't try to give me anymore bull excuses about revenge or one last shipment for one last project," he said before Jim could open his mouth. "I know the *real* reason you've kept the operation going all these years." Marcellous smiled a knowing smile and hesitated for affect before continuing. "You've kept it going because it allows you to be in control. Everyone runs to Jim when there's a problem and you solve it, you're one big hero." Marcellous waved his finger at Jim before continuing. "But that's not all, is it? You're also in it for the *excitement* aren't you?"

Jim's jaw dropped in surprise. *Had I been so transparent?* All these years he'd claimed a need to get even, but that was only in the beginning. After he'd cooled down, he'd then argued that the county needed the money.

It wasn't until years later that he realized he enjoyed the double life he was leading. He never admitted that to anyone. In fact, he felt guilty thinking that his life had been anything but honorable, especially now that his friends were gone. *Had they died because of my selfish desire for excitement?* he wondered. Again he felt guilty, realizing that deep inside he knew it to be true. He had thought that hiding the truth from the other three was so simple.

Turning to look at his companion, he wondered how long he had known. The victorious smile told him the answer.

"I've known since the beginning," Marcellous said as he again read the expression on Jim's face. "I think long before even *you* knew it."

He was right. Marcellous had been perceptive enough to figure out what Jim and the others had really wanted from the operation then *used* what he knew to manipulate them. He controlled the money, and because of that, he was the *true* controller of the operation.

Jim believed that *he* controlled the process because he made the decision each time a shipment was ordered. Marcellous knew this and used it to his own benefit. The operation had supplied more than enough money than they could possibly spend, but he had lied to all of them.

If Jim wanted money for a project, he would have to order another shipment. Although Jim had suspected that his counterpart was holding out on him, he had never been able to prove it and didn't ever push the issue. As he had just admitted, he enjoyed the excitement of it.

But he resented the fact that Marcellous could control enough of the operation to make him have to order shipments. After too many years of feeling the brunt of that resentment, Marcellous enjoyed making Jim feel uncomfortable. He had put up with it because he needed the sometimes arrogant jerk, but no longer. The operation was *over.*

Jim felt off balance and angry at how Marcellous had dissected him so completely. He was tired and unprepared for this type of scrutiny, so he tried to re-enforce his position. "I'm the one in charge here, not you. I stay in control by knowing every detail of what's going on."

"Really?" Marcellous observed. "Did you know that Buck kept a journal?"

Jim had forgotten about that and again felt angry at having it pointed out to him. "No I didn't," he admitted. "But I convinced everyone it was just a story book. I have it in the Blazer and will burn it tonight."

Marcellous decided not to spar with Jim any longer. He had always wanted to take Jim down a few notches, but this was not the time or place. In fact, he admitted to himself, he still needed him. It was time to make up, so he lifted the two glasses. "Let's have another for Buck and Rick?"

Jim hesitated, then nodded and both men tipped their heads back and downed the shots. Marcellous immediately filled both glassed then spoke up. He wanted to end this conversation on a lighter note, and there was a question that had nagged at him for decades. "You know you never told me how you did it."

"Did what?"

Marcellous knew that it always put Jim in a good mood to talk about how smart he was. "When you jumped from that airplane the weather was *horrible.* That whole night it rained cats and dogs. The clouds were so thick that you couldn't have seen the ground. *How did you know when to jump?*"

Jim smiled. It was something that only he and Buck had known. Now that it was all over, Jim thought it fitting to come full circle with an explanation of how this whole adventure had started. "When I met you at the Portland airport, I *knew* you wouldn't listen to me. Weeks in advance, I planned the hijacking. After I watched you take off, I picked up my small suitcase from a locker. Then, while on the plane, I told them it was a bomb. I had everything timed perfectly. I made the airplane take off from Seattle so that by the time it got over the mountains it was dark.

The pilot flew at the speed, altitude, and course that I instructed him to. As you've probably guessed by now, the case was not a bomb. Instead it contained a powerful receiver that I used to pick up the signals from the radio beacons of both the Portland airport and Sea-Tac."

A light went on in Marcellous's brain. "You used the process of *triangelization.* By knowing from which direction the two signals were coming from, you could pin point your exact location."

"That's right, but that was the easy part," Jim continued. "The rest had to be done with timing. I counted in my head and pulled the cord without ever seeing the ground. In fact it was just seconds after the chute opened that I hit the ground."

"Huh! That sounds *dangerous!*" Marcellous exclaimed.

"No, I was in complete control," Jim said, matter-of-factly, and then continued. "Buck was waiting and was able to locate me with a lantern. He also had my Sheriff's uniform and radio. When the Fed's called the station, the station called me. I diverted deputies and roadblocks away from our location while still working our way down on mules. When we got down the mountain, I just *barely* had time to get my own road block set up on highway seven, by Buck's place, before the Feds showed up. I diverted them in a different direction so that Buck could have time to take the parachute, receiver, and other stuff and sink it deep into Mineral Lake."

"So, while the Feds were looking for it, where did you hide the money?"

"That's was the best part," Jim could hardly keep from laughing. "I put it in the cushions of the passenger seat of my Sheriff's vehicle. The whole time I drove that FBI Special Agent in charge around, little did he know that he was sitting on the money and being escorted by the hijacker!"

Both men broke into hysterical laughter. "Oh man! What a sweet set up!" Marcellous said as he patted Jim on the back one more time. "I think that story makes a fitting end to the perfect operation."

"The operation doesn't have to be over," Jim assured him, still trying to believe he could control events. For years Jim had been looking for a way that they could truly make one last shipment so that Buck and Rick could carry on their lives guilt free. He was finally able to come up with a solution when the end of the cold war made it possible. "I've got a line on a Russian submarine. I can get her captain to fill the sub to the brim with opium, then he'll drive it into Puget Sound and in one night, we'll have enough for the rest of our lives."

Marcellous thought about it a second, then nodded. "That's a great plan, really it is, but the operation is *over*," he insisted. "Because after all these years Special Agent Blake is going to figure it all out."

"What do you mean?"

"Oh, come on Jim, the question that ties it all together has been asked," Marcellous replied. "That DEA agent said it on the evening news. He said that the Sheriff's department *intentionally* slowed down the investigation. It *never* occurred to that FBI agent that you were doing it on purpose."

Jim's face turned grim as he realized that Marcellous was right. He'd been too busy the past couple days to think about how the news stories were affecting Special Agent Blake. Jim had often compared himself to Blake in his own mind. He knew that like himself, Blake must pull out his copy of the D.B. Cooper file once each year on the anniversary of the jump. Except that, while Jim was wondering how he could've made the plan work better, Blake was wondering how he'd gone wrong.

Blake was a very intelligent man, but he had one blind spot that Jim manipulated. He never for a moment considered that the Sheriff could be under suspicion. Jim realized just then that Blake must have watched all the news reports and probably had stayed up all night with his file folders open trying to put it all together.

"You know, Blake is running that question over and over in his head right now." Marcellous assured him. "It's only a matter of time before he's knocking on your door wanting answers. In fact, he could be on his way here right now."

The possibility worried Jim. For the first time in his life, he hadn't had time to think or plan. Nikki's face filled his mind, confusing the issue. "What should I do?" The question left his lips without him being conscious of it.

"Let's go to Europe and retire," Marcellous answered.

"I *can't* leave Nikki. What would I tell her?" Jim wondered out loud.

"I don't know, lie to her. You're good at that, remember?" Marcellous again answered. He had to convince Jim to leave. It wasn't a good idea that he stay behind. Jim was a loose end, and loose ends always come back to haunt you. Jim was the only person that could pin anything on Marcellous. He thought briefly about killing him, but he couldn't do that. For all his arrogance, Marcellous liked and admired him. "Tell her you won the lotto, or something. If she won't come with you then leave her. Either way, you can't stay."

Jim instantly felt the other blade of his two-edged life cut into him. Had the excitement of his secret past now destroyed his chances at true happiness with Nikki? He feared the answer. He realized then that all he ever wanted in life was what he had with Nikki. Nothing else mattered. But now, that could all be over.

A few moments later, he thought of something else. "What about the county? How will they get along without me?"

"*Forget* the county!" Marcellous insisted. "If you get arrested, do you think anyone will come to your defense? Do you think it'll matter to any of them that because of you they have a new high school, a new wing on the hospital, or the recreation center and playing fields—just to name a few." Marcellous shook his head decisively. "Not one of them would stick their neck out for you!"

Jim sunk to a new low at this revelation.

A moment later, movement from the window caught his eye, so he turned to look out. Through the dim light of dusk he could see a car coming up the road. It was still far off, but it was moving fast.

"Nikki's coming. You're going to have to leave," Jim ordered.

Marcellous looked out of the window, and then nodded. Moving to the end table, he picked up his pistol, and put it in his coat pocket. He then placed the fedora on his head and pulled it down just above his eyes. Reaching into a pocket, he pulled out several stacks of bound bills and tossed them to Jim.

"Here's fifty thousand dollars. I'm going to Zurich. Meet me there and we'll split the money between us." Marcellous started walking towards the back door when he let out another laugh.

"What is it now?" Harper asked as he watched the car get closer.

"I wonder if that DEA agent realizes how close he came to the truth."

Jim didn't find the irony humorous. He couldn't block the pain at the thought of losing Nikki. "No, he's too stupid," he managed to say.

"Listen, Cooper, I'll wait in Zurich for one week. If you don't show up I'm taking all the money and disappearing," Marcellous said as he reached the back door.

The reference to his past life struck painfully at him. "Marcellous! I don't like it when you call me Cooper!" he lashed out angrily.

Marcellous's expression turned nasty. "One week," he repeated, and then stepped out the door slamming it shut behind him.

Jim immediately stuffed the money in his pockets as he walked out the front door and onto the porch. Nikki's car came to a stop in an instant. Jumping out, she ran to him and threw her arms around him.

"I'm so sorry, Jim!" she cried. "Please forgive me. I should've *never* doubted you! I should've *known* that you would never have lied to me!" She squeezed him tight as she begged him for forgiveness. "Please say something, please!"

With tears in his eyes, Jim was too choked up and couldn't say anything as he squeezed her back. Her words echoed through his mind as he watched the last of the sun disappear behind the distant mountains.

About the Author

James Olszewski is a northwest author who grew up with the legend of D.B. Cooper. Olszewski was a young boy when Cooper had jumped from the 727, and the news coverage captured his attention. As Olszewski grew, the subject of D.B. Cooper continued to spark interest and questions not only about his true physical identify, but also about what drove Cooper to do what he did.

James Olszewski was born and raised in Great Falls, Montana. Graduating with an engineering degree from Montana State University in Bozeman, Montana, Olszewski moved to Seattle to work for the Boeing Company. While in Seattle, Olszewski attended Seattle University, graduating with a masters in business administration. Making the town of Snohomish his home, Olszewski spends much of his time in an effort to bring to light the secrets surrounding Cooper's identity.

Made in the USA
Lexington, KY
28 February 2012